"WHY DO YOU HATE ME SO?"

"I don't hate you, *ma petite*," Alain answered. "Even though you betrayed our love, I don't hate you. I do not feel anything, beyond mild curiosity."

"What do you mean?" She stared up at him.

His face was a cold mask of arrogance. "I wanted to see if you were any truer to Franklin than you were to me."

He pulled her against him, and his mouth touched hers in a fierce, demanding kiss. Simone struggled in his grasp, but her will to resist him began to ebb.

Alain abruptly set her away from him. "Just as I guessed. An unfaithful lover makes an unfaithful wife."

She drew back her hand and slapped him. Then she fled, the sound of his jeering laughter echoing in her ears.

Also by Karen Jones Delk

The Bride Price

Karen Jones Delk

This edition published 1994
by Diamond Books
77–85 Fulham Palace Road
Hammersmith, London W6 8JB

First published by HarperPaperbacks,
A Division of HarperCollins*Publishers*, New York

Cover illustration by Harry Burman

First printing: October 1992

Printed in Great Britain

HarperPaperbacks, HarperMonogram, and colophon are
trademarks of HarperCollins*Publishers*

ISBN 0 261 66500 6

*To Andrea Brown, my agent,
and Carolyn Marino, my editor.
Thanks for your faith in me, not to mention your
patience, guidance, and many kindnesses.*

Prologue

New Orleans, 1831

"*Calas! I got sweet rice cakes.*" The Negro woman selling pastries on the corner noticed the two children bundled against the November chill, marching down the *banquette* toward rue Conti.

"Y'all want a nice warm *cala*?" the *vendeuse* invited.

"*Non, merci,*" the older boy answered with scarcely a glance at her. Clutching the mittened hand of his small companion, he hurried him along the wooden sidewalk toward their destination.

The woman watched them go, laughing when the youngster in tow tugged at his muffler to reveal a charming grin, cheeks pink with cold, and green eyes sparkling merrily. With a shrug of apology, the little one trotted along behind his elder, urging, "Slow down, *cousin*. Your legs are longer than mine."

At the head of Exchange Alley, the adolescent glanced furtively over his shoulder before making a sharp turn into the narrow passageway, jerking the small lad after him.

The child stumbled but followed willingly, his neck

craning as he attempted to take in everything at once. Cafés, shops, and bars crowded together at street level along Exchange Alley as they did on almost any street in the Vieux Carré. But upstairs . . .

The little fellow gazed up excitedly toward *les salles d'armes*. In those mysterious masculine environs, fencing masters gave lessons in swordsmanship and the art of the duel to the young Creoles of New Orleans.

So intent was the child on savoring his adventure, he nearly collided with his guide, who had halted suddenly beside a wall of dusty pink brick.

"Watch where you're going," the older boy commanded. Turning, he groaned, then quickly adjusted the youngster's misshapen wool cap, nervously shoving a brown curl under the knitted brim.

"Why are we stopping here, Fabrice?" his little cousin asked, fairly dancing in anticipation as the clash of swords reached their ears. "Are we not going to see your famous *maître d'armes*?"

"*Oui*, though we should go back instead," Fabrice Chauvin answered impatiently. His face was grim as he glared at his companion. "I don't know why I let you talk me into this."

"Don't make me go home now," the child wailed. "You said that here one could see the finest swordsman in all New Orleans."

"The finest in the world," Fabrice corrected with a scowl. "But how was I to know you were going to come up with this . . . masquerade?"

With an unmistakably feminine pout, ten-year-old Simone Devereaux lifted wide green eyes appealingly to her favorite relative. "How else could I come to the fencing school, *chéri*? You said I could if I were a boy."

Fabrice gave an exasperated sigh. " That is *not* what I meant, and you know it. I said if you *were* a boy, you would be allowed on Exchange Alley. It's an unwritten law that no woman may pass through here."

"How can it be a law if it's not written anywhere?" she demanded reasonably.

"Because that's the way it is. Or *was*, until now," the youth answered glumly.

Smiling cajolingly, Simone laid a hand on his arm. "Allowing only men here is a silly rule, *oui*? And not very fair. After all—"

"I know, I know. 'I can do anything a boy can do,'" Fabrice mimicked. "That is probably true, Simone. You certainly get into as much trouble as any boy I know."

"*Merci*." She dimpled mischievously and clutched her loose trousers, preparing to curtsy.

"Stop that," he snapped. "If you're supposed to be a boy, at least act like one. I don't know why I let you talk me into this," he repeated.

"Because you love me, *chéri*." Placing her hand in his, the little girl looked up with childish candor. "And because we always have such fun together."

"*Oui, ma petite*, because I love you. But your fun always gets me into such trouble." He sighed. "If your *père* hears of this . . ."

"He'll laugh while he scolds me," Simone said with certainty.

"Perhaps, but if *my* father finds out, he will not laugh," Fabrice predicted.

When the pair reached the *salle d'armes* of Serge St. Michel, they found a score of boys were ranged along the staircase up the side of the building, jostling for a spot on the landing at the top. There, sons of aristocratic Creoles and their slaves clustered in the doorway, admiring the fencers within.

Propelling Simone through the crush of bodies, Fabrice positioned his small cousin as close to the front as possible. Drawn by the singing of the swords, she wriggled past elbows and knees to emerge at the doorway. She grimaced with annoyance to discover her view was still blocked by a pair of broad-shouldered dandies who tarried there, unwilling to interrupt the action in the room.

She turned to complain to Fabrice but found he was not beside her, held back, no doubt, by the crowd. Ever resourceful, she ducked and squirmed until she found a niche between the men's bodies, through which she could see a tiny portion of the enormous *salle*. Two windows stretched from the polished wooden floor, to the high ceiling. Between the windows were tiers of benches, upon which young men in various stages of dress lounged, talking among themselves and staring avidly toward the other end of the room. Over their boisterous laughter rang the sound of sword against sword.

Simone yearned to see the swordplay, but she could not. Then one of the men in front of her shifted, giving her a glimpse of a slim, striking mulatto sitting alone at a small table across the room. The moment she saw him, Simone knew that this was the famous Serge St. Michel, *maître d'armes.*

Wintery sun filtering through a huge fanlight washed over the fencing master. Clad in velvet and lace, Fabrice's hero cut an elegant figure indeed. He sipped coffee and smoked a slender black cigar, his amber eyes following the practice duel at the far end of the room.

Simone stood on tiptoe, but she could not better her view. Frustrated, she realized that she would not see the maître—or anyone else—fence. She knew it was time to go; Fabrice was probably anxious.

But her cousin and her good intentions were forgotten when a break in the action prompted the men in front of her to hurry across the room to the students' benches.

Suddenly exposed, Simone poised for flight, but no one seemed to notice her. And when the throng behind her surged forward, she was bumped across the threshold. She was inside a real *salle d'armes*! This was more than she had dared to hope.

Emboldened by her seeming invisibility, the little

girl sidled to stand beside the equipment rack.

At the far end of the room, two young men were preparing to fence with practice foils. Simone recognized the youth facing her. Marcel Baudin, the son of a wealthy Creole family, was almost angelically beautiful with his golden hair, pale blue eyes and flawless, even features.

As he and his opponent donned their masks, assumed the *en garde* position, and began to thrust and parry, Simone decided the men were evenly matched. Darkly handsome Alain de Vallière was tall and lithe, his shoulders muscular under his flowing white shirt, the tense power in his rippling leg muscles the only clue to the effort he expended in holding his position.

"I see you learned a few things in Paris, Alain, *mon ami*," the maître called over the ringing of the swords.

"My money is still on Marcel," announced Charles Greaux, who was related to the Baudins. He surveyed the other spectators. "Does anyone wish to make a small wager?"

"To take your money would be robbery, Charles," another of the idlers teased. "Alain has only toyed with your cousin until now."

Simone imagined she could see Marcel scowl and his pale eyes flash beneath his mask. Doggedly, he parried Alain's thrusts and retired a few steps.

Enthralled, Simone inched forward, but all eyes in the room were on the fencers, and no one noticed.

"Have a care, Marcel," Alain warned mildly as he blocked a balestra by his opponent. "If I had put on a fencing jacket today, I wouldn't mind a slap on the arm. But as it is, it gives you no points and me a bruise."

"Surely you don't bruise so easily. Have you changed so much since we were children?" Marcel's tone was jeering.

Alain countered the other man's advance, and the blades skittered and slid against each other, bringing the fencers almost mask to mask.

"I haven't changed much. I can still beat you," Alain answered dangerously.

With a bellow of anger, Marcel shoved his opponent away and began to advance recklessly. "Let us get it over, de Vallière, and see who is the better swordsman."

Conversation ceased between the combatants, and the only sound was the clash of the swords. Even the spectators fell silent as Marcel advanced ruthlessly. Alain met his assault coolly and slowly yielded ground, allowing his opponent to weary. Gradually, they moved toward the center of the room.

Simone did not notice. Uninterested in the fencers' conversation, she examined the equipment rack beside her, delighted by the polished foils and the leather-lined fencing masks.

A fluttering overhead caught her eye, and she stepped back to look up at the banner bearing the standard of the nobleman under whom Serge St. Michel had trained.

"*Zut*!" the maître exploded, jumping from his seat when he saw the urchin standing in the middle of his salle, gawking upward. "Look out behind you, Alain!"

Simone spun around to discover the fencers bearing down upon her. Glancing over his shoulder, Alain lurched to one side to avoid trampling the child.

Seizing his opportunity in the confusion, Marcel lunged triumphantly, with more force than necessary. The tip of his foil caught the folds of his opponent's linen shirt, and in the sudden silence, the sound of rending fabric was nearly deafening.

Tearing the mask from his head, Alain wheeled on the urchin, his furious brown eyes meeting wide green ones. Without a word, the child bolted for the door, where other youthful spectators were beating a hasty retreat.

"Run, Fabrice, run," Simone shouted. Her heart pounding, she scampered down the stairs with Alain de

Vallière on her heels. Leaping the last few steps, she looked around desperately for a place to hide.

A cramped passageway between the buildings, a storage space for neighboring merchants beckoned. Beyond stacks of boxes and barrels, a tall gate opened onto rue Royal.

Diving through the narrow opening, the child sprinted toward the distant street, praying she had lost her pursuer. But behind her she could hear the man crashing through the cramped space, cursing as he tripped over crates and wooden pallets.

When she reached the gate, she fumbled urgently with the rusty latch, but it would not open. Stepping back, she gauged the height. Too high to scale without help. For an instant, her thin shoulders sagged; then she noticed several packing cases precariously stacked nearby.

With no thought of caution, Simone began to climb the teetering mountain of crates. She was braced to catapult herself over the barrier when her makeshift ladder gave way, the crash nearly obliterating her shout of alarm. She lurched forward and threw her arms over the top of the gate, dangling helplessly in midair, her feet scrabbling in search of a toehold, as she glanced frantically over her shoulder. Her pursuer was almost upon her, his handsome face dark with displeasure, his foil still in hand. Simone tried in vain to heave herself over the gate, but she was seized and dragged backward in one powerful arm.

"Where do you think you're going? I want a word with you, young man!" Alain roared. Clutching his small, squirming captive against his chest, he ducked a windmill of arms and legs as the child fought in his grasp.

"*Mère de Dieu*, I ought to take a switch to you," the Creole announced, setting her on the ground with a jolt. "Oh, no you don't!" He positioned himself so she could not escape.

With a cry of frustration, Simone lowered her head and butted his hard abdomen, but no matter how she shoved, she could not move him. His hand closed on the nape of her neck with a viselike grip.

"A spanking was what I had in mind, boy," Alain grunted, squeezing slightly but painfully, "but if you'd prefer to be throttled, that could be arranged."

All at once, his captive stood very still. Shoulders hunched, the child ducked her head and refused to look up.

Alain placed his foil across the top of a barrel, but he continued to watch the small figure with wary amusement. "You know what you did, don't you?" he asked in a slightly milder tone. "You might have caused a serious accident."

Simone stared stubbornly at the ground and refused to speak.

"What do you have to say for yourself?" de Vallière asked impatiently. "Answer when you're spoken to, lad." He loosened his grip a bit, but the captive did not look at him.

"I ask you again," Alain persisted, "what do you have to say for yourself?" Still no response. He increased the pressure on the child's neck. Finally she lifted her chin and looked him in the face

The urchin's cap was askew, covering one eye, but the one that was visible was green, framed with long, dark lashes, and glaring at him mutinously.

"Still nothing, eh?" Alain sighed. "Come here, my rude young friend, and let me get a better look at you."

Careful to maintain his hold, he knelt beside the child. Immediately, Simone lowered her head and began to twist and turn, trying to escape.

"Be still." He drew her toward him, removing the knit cap with his free hand. To his surprise, silky light brown tresses tumbled down, curling luxuriantly around his fingers.

"Well!" Sitting back on his heels, the Creole exhaled

in a surprised puff. "What are we to make of a girl in boy's clothes?"

"Nothing," Simone mumbled rebelliously.

"An orphan perhaps? An escapee from the Ursuline convent?"

"I am not an orphan," she countered indignantly.

"All right. What is your name then? Where do you live?" His questions met only silence. "Won't say, eh? Well, no matter. I happen to know the good sisters accept girls with no name as well as no home."

"I have a name," she answered with a sullen frown.

"What is it, then? Come on, girl. I have little time and not much tolerance left." He squeezed the back of her neck to demonstrate his impatience.

"Let go. You're hurting me." Grimacing exaggeratedly, she howled, "All right, you big bully, my name is Simone Devereaux."

"*Très bien*, Mademoiselle Devereaux. Now, where do you live?"

"On rue Orleans," she muttered, attempting to shrug off his big hand. Suddenly changing her tack, she smiled winningly. "But I can find my own way, thank you. You really needn't bother."

What a minx this one was going to be in a few years, Alain thought, fighting the urge to smile. But he said gravely, "No bother, mam'selle. This big bully wouldn't think of allowing a young lady to walk through the streets unescorted. Besides," he added, "your parents should know what you've been doing."

"I only wanted to see the fencing master," Simone protested, squirming in his grip.

"You saw Maître St. Michel, and the ruin of my match. Now, come along." Picking up his foil, he steered her down the passage.

When they emerged into Exchange Alley, Serge was standing on the stairs, holding Alain's hat and jacket.

"So you chased the brat through the streets in only your shirtsleeves, *mon ami*," he greeted the young Creole. "For a gentleman, that will never—Oh, ho, what have we here?"

"Another of your female admirers," Alain answered dryly, handing the man his foil. "Do not even think of running," he ordered Simone sternly as he put on his jacket. Eyeing his broad shoulders and remembering his strength, she swiftly reconsidered her plan for escape. She glanced nervously at the fencing master, who flashed her a reassuring smile.

"One of my admirers, eh?" The renowned swordsman bowed extravagantly. "Your servant, mam'selle."

"Save your charm for your *cher amie*, Serge," Alain growled good-naturedly as he jammed his hat onto his head. "I'll see you after I've seen this young lady home."

Simone placed her small hand in the big one Alain extended imperiously. Her head bowed under a cloud of doom, she listened to his lecture on proper feminine behavior all the way to the small, unpretentious house on rue Orleans. There she bobbed in a polite curtsy and smiled prettily. "*Merci*, m'sieur, but you do not have to see me inside. I've caused you enough trouble."

"I agree." Alain opened the wrought-iron gate and gestured for her to lead. "But I insist on speaking to your parents."

"Oh, very well." Glowering, Simone flounced down a passageway and yelled, "Someone to see you, *Papa*."

Alain found himself in the small, shady courtyard at the center of the Devereaux residence. Like most houses in the French Quarter, the compound was built along airy West Indian lines. Sleeping quarters were on the second floor, reached by stairs from the courtyard, the common rooms were downstairs, and the kitchen was set a short distance from the main house.

Hurriedly pulling on his jacket, Nicholas Devereaux met his visitor in the courtyard. He frowned when he saw his daughter's outlandish costume and said severely, "Simone Jeanne-Marie Pauline Devereaux, what kind of trouble have you gotten yourself into now?"

"No great trouble, monsieur," Alain interceded smoothly, "but she seems to think she can wander anywhere in New Orleans."

"Even, I take it, where females are not welcome?" Nicholas asked knowingly.

Alain nodded. "She visited Exchange Alley this afternoon."

Seeing her father's raised eyebrows, Simone said desperately, "I only went to see *les salles d'armes*, *Papa*. I didn't mean to cause any trouble."

"Trouble follows wherever you go, *ma petite*." Nicholas shook his head and sighed. "Go to your room. We'll talk of this escapade later."

"But, *Papa* . . . ," Simone began, but put away her ready defense when she caught sight of the twinkle in her father's eyes. The world knew Nicholas Devereaux as a gambler and a wastrel, but to his daughter, he was the ideal of all manhood: daring, dashing, elegant—and often a partner in her mischief.

Hanging her head, she hid a smile and answered in a small voice, "As you wish, *mon père*."

"Please accept my apology for my daughter's behavior, sir, and my thanks for bringing her home," Nicholas said, turning to his guest. "It's difficult bringing up a child without a mother."

"You're welcome, Monsieur Devereaux, and please don't be too hard on her," Alain requested, watching Simone's dejected-looking little figure trudge up the stairs. "No real harm was done."

"You are gracious, Monsieur . . . ?"

"Alain de Vallière at your service, sir," the young Creole introduced himself.

"I'm happy to meet you, Monsieur de Vallière. I am Nicholas Devereaux, Nicholas to my friends. Please, come into the parlor and sit down. May I offer you some *café* or perhaps a drink?"

"*Café, s'il vous plaît*," Alain responded politely, following his host into the house. "I still have business to which I must attend." The score he wished to settle with the Baudin heir for his crude attack at the *salle d'armes* would wait a short while.

"We know the same people, frequent the same bars, gamble at the same casinos," Nicholas concluded later as they sipped their coffee. "How is it we've never met?"

"I only recently returned to New Orleans," Alain explained. "I've been in Paris."

"In school, I wager."

"Until my father called me home. He felt I spent too much time in the *salles d'armes* and not enough in my studies," the younger man admitted, surprised by his candor with so recent an acquaintance.

"I see." Nicholas chuckled. "My sin was gambling. It makes no difference. I didn't want to be a gentleman planter anyway."

"And I didn't wish to be a lawyer." Alain toasted his host with his cup. Then, setting it down, he said apologetically, "I thank you for your hospitality, Nicholas, but now I must go."

"Ah, yes, your unfinished business. Won't you return for dinner so we may continue our talk?" Simone's father invited. "I promise to keep my daughter under control, and in skirts."

With a hearty laugh, the young Creole accepted. Then he set out to find Marcel.

When he met his opponent under the Dueling Oaks, Alain fought skillfully and quickly drew first blood. No matter that the only casualty was young Monsieur Baudin's pride, the duel was the talk of New Orleans for weeks.

During those weeks, and as the winter days lengthened into sweet-scented spring, Alain visited Nicholas Devereaux frequently. Despite the difference in their ages, the men became fast friends. They drank, gambled, and womanized tirelessly, leading seemingly charmed lives, for the whiskey was always good, the cards, lucky, and the women, plentiful.

Alain was amused that Nicholas insisted on wearing his wedding ring, a slender gold band studded with emeralds.

"Emeralds are lucky—lucky in love!" the gambler explained drunkenly one evening as the men sat in the courtyard, sipping brandy.

"They must be lucky," an equally sodden Alain ruminated, "for you never want for a woman."

"*Non, mon ami.*" Nicholas seemed suddenly sober. "*That* is not love. I have known love. My Marthe gave me this ring."

In her bed upstairs, Simone listened to the voices drifting through her open windows. She, too, knew love, she thought sleepily. She knew, without a doubt, that she loved Alain de Vallière.

She felt as if her ten-year-old heart would break when only days later he announced that he must return to France to conduct some family business.

"Do you have to go?" she asked in a quavering voice.

"I must. My father needs my contacts in court," he explained gently. He had become fond of the child in the past months. "Don't cry, my mischievous little friend."

"I won't." Simone swiped stubbornly at her brimming eyes with the back of her hand. "How long will you be gone, 'Lain?"

"I am not sure, *chérie*. It may be for a very long time—two or three years."

"Then who will bring me candies and teach me to fence?"

Alain laughed. "There will be other admirers. You'll forget all about me in time."

"*Non*," she choked, struggling to control her quivering bottom lip. "I will wait for you."

"A man could ask for nothing more," he murmured with an indulgent smile. "Give me a hug now, *ma petite,* and I must go."

Sniffling a little in spite of herself, Simone held out her arms and was lifted from the ground to be crushed against a muscular chest.

The moment she was released, she fled to the stables to hide so Alain would not see her cry. Hours later, when she emerged, her eyes red, her face tear-stained, her first love, her only love, was gone.

1

Sitting at her father's desk in the parlor, Simone heard the rumble of distant thunder. She looked around apathetically. The corners of the familiar room had fallen into shadow, for she had not yet lit the lamps. The gray afternoon was darkening into night, and the howl of the wind foretold a storm. She had been so engrossed in memories, she had not noticed.

She knew it did no good to brood, but she could not bring herself to stir. She ached at the thought of leaving behind this house she had shared with her father. They had been happy here, even in hard times. Through it all, she had had her *cher papa*—his blithe charm, quick wit, and carefree smile.

Simone's numbed mind tried to comprehend the sudden upheaval in her life. It still did not seem possible her father was dead, killed in a duel by Marcel Baudin. He had fallen on the field of honor—defending the family name, she thought bitterly. But why? She did not even know what Marcel had said or done to cause the older man to challenge him. She knew only that honor had too high a price.

Searching for an answer, her thoughts turned to the

week before, when Marcel had called at their rue Orleans home. She had admitted him herself. She had often seen the arrogant young Creole from a distance, but meeting him face to face had done nothing to dispel the unaccountable dislike she felt for him.

Simone had told herself sensibly that Baudin's reputation for cruelty had reached her through whispered gossip and thus was not to be trusted. Still, she had fought an urge to shudder when his icy blue eyes rested on her. With a polite word, she had hurried to summon her father.

Nicholas Devereaux had greeted his unexpected guest warily and led him to the parlor. They had talked for only a few minutes, their voices growing angrier and louder until Marcel stormed out, slamming the gate behind him.

Simone had found her father composing a note to one of his gambling cronies, asking him to act as his second.

"A duel!" she had cried in exasperation. "Marcel Baudin is one of the finest swordsmen in New Orleans. How could you even think of accepting his challenge?"

"I challenged him," Nicholas revealed calmly. "Don't say it," he commanded before she could speak. "This is an *affaire d'honneur*. Believe me, I wouldn't duel if it weren't necessary."

"Necessary?" She scowled at him.

"Very necessary. I haven't been much of a father, Simone, or even much of a provider, not the way my luck has run recently." With a sigh, the gambler glanced around the shabby room. "It's my fault that we have little now but our pride. I must defend our name." Then he fell silent, refusing to say more.

At dawn, Nicholas had strapped on his sword and gone to the Dueling Oaks, leaving his unhappy daughter at home, helpless worry her only companion.

A flash of lightning and a crack of thunder brought Simone back to the present with a start. Picking up a letter from the desk, she stared at it vacantly, her mind on what remained to be done.

The funeral was past. She had overseen the preparations herself. Honoring the customs surrounding a death among *les bonnes familles*, the Creole aristocracy of New Orleans, she had notified a priest, had black-bordered notices posted throughout the Vieux Carré, and sent invitations to the funeral. When the arrangements were complete, she had sent for her only relative.

Thank *le bon Dieu* for Tante Viviane, Simone thought. Her mother's younger sister had hurried to her side. Married to a man much older than she, the petite Viviane was compassionate, serene, and efficient. She was a good wife to Georges Chauvin, the successful owner of LeFleur plantation, and a loving stepmother to his son, Fabrice. And she had always striven in her quiet way to make sure her niece had some measure of stability in her life.

Viviane had stayed with Simone through her night-long vigil beside Nicholas's body. Gently, she tried to dissuade the girl from attending the graveside ceremony. Creole women simply did not go to funerals, she argued quite correctly. But she had not overcome Simone's determination.

Though she could not defend her niece's decision, Viviane had accepted it. She had waited patiently in the Chauvin coach at the cemetery until Simone returned from seeing Nicholas laid to rest beside his beloved Marthe in a gleaming white tomb. Then Viviane enfolded the numb, dry-eyed girl in a tender embrace.

The traditionally minded Georges was set to berate Simone for her unconventional behavior, but he remained quiet when he saw his wife's warning glance. He said nothing at all, in fact, as they all went to the office of Monsieur Fusilier, Nicholas's attorney, to hear the reading of his will.

In a droning voice, the aged lawyer informed them that, besides Nicholas's emerald wedding band, Simone had inherited a portrait of her mother and a necklace that had belonged to her, a single pearl on a gold chain. Unfortunately, most of the Devereauxs' meager household goods were to be auctioned to pay a portion of her father's debts.

Simone knew they had had no money since the Panic two years before. Many people had lost fortunes overnight. Since Nicholas no longer had a fortune to lose, he had sold off their furnishings piece by piece during those difficult days to buy food and to pay the rent. His daughter had known what he was doing, but she had not known they were deeply in debt.

When it seemed the reading of the will was finished, Simone prepared to rise, saying with a tight smile, "*Merci*, Monsieur Fusilier, and good day."

"There is more, mademoiselle," he squawked. "A handwritten addendum to the will." Adjusting his spectacles, the nearsighted old man picked up a letter from his desk and peered at it owlishly. "Dated Wednesday, May 15, 1839."

"The day before the duel?" She sank back in her seat warily.

"*Oui*. It reads, 'My esteemed Fusilier, should I not return from the field of honor, it is my fervent wish that my dear friend, Alain de Vallière, serve as guardian to my beloved daughter—'"

"*Non*!" she exclaimed in dismayed surprise.

"*Oui*." Monsieur Fusilier blinked at her. "Let me see ... 'fervent wish ... Alain de Vallière ...' Ah, yes, 'guardian to my beloved daughter, Simone, until her twenty-first birthday or her marriage.'"

"How can that be? He said nothing to me of this."

"Perhaps there wasn't time, *chère*. This letter was delivered the morning of the duel. Nicholas must have just made up his mind, but his instructions are quite clear." The lawyer read on. "'I desire him to find a suitable husband for her. Knowing Monsieur de Vallière's loyal character, I trust he will bear her best interests in mind, discharging his responsibilities efficiently and meriting my faith in him.' And it is signed, you see, 'Nicholas Antoine Devereaux.'" He held out the page for Simone's inspection.

Lifting her eyes from her father's familiar scrawl, she stared at the attorney disbelievingly.

"Don't worry, my dear," he reassured her. "It must be frightening to know your guardian is thousands of miles away, but Monsieur de Vallière will be notified of your father's wishes at the earliest opportunity. In fact, I intend to send a letter on the first ship leaving for France."

"Must you?" Simone blurted out.

"Dear child." Monsieur Fusilier smiled gently. "He will wish to be here as quickly as possible. And, indeed, he must come if he is to find a husband for you. Despite the kindness of your aunt and uncle, you don't wish to live at LeFleur forever, *oui*?"

"LeFleur?" she echoed stupidly.

"Well, I assumed . . ." Nonplussed, the man rustled his papers. "I mean, you *are* an unmarried female, and—"

"You assumed correctly," Georges cut in. "Simone's place now is with her family. As her uncle by marriage, I would countenance no other arrangement."

Simone bit her lip and said nothing until she, her aunt, and her uncle had returned to the coach. When they were settled, she said quietly, "I wish to be taken home, *s'il vous plaît*."

"Did you not hear what I said to Fusilier?" Georges demanded. "Your place is with us."

"I want to go home," the girl maintained stubbornly.

Georges blustered, his voice rising as he recounted the embarrassments heaped on his head over the years by his wife's unorthodox relatives, but nothing he said swayed Simone.

Discomfited by the scene they were making on a public street, Viviane interjected, "Georges, Simone must have business to be concluded. Why don't we take her home? Tomorrow or the next day she can move to LeFleur."

"I don't like it, but *très bien*. She may have two days, no longer," he granted grudgingly, unwilling to deny his wife. Bristling with disapproval, he instructed the driver to take them to the Devereaux house. "This is most improper, leaving an unmarried girl on her own," he grumbled. "Perhaps we should send a maid to serve as chaperon."

"*Merci, oncle*," Simone declined graciously, "but that won't be necessary. I just want a little time to decide what I must do."

"What you must do is to come to LeFleur," he retorted. "Though I warn you, Simone, if you are to live under my roof, you will follow my rules. Until your guardian arrives, I feel responsible for you."

"No one need feel responsible for me—not you nor Alain de Vallière," his niece snapped, feeling her patience ebb.

"B-but we're your family, *ma petite*," Viviane stammered, taken aback by Simone's vehemence, "and Monsieur de Vallière is—"

"A cad who will marry me off to the first man who asks for my hand."

"Not a bad idea!" her uncle shouted.

"Georges, please," Viviane protested, peering out the window to see if any pedestrians had witnessed the family quarrel. She turned to her niece reasonably. "Simone, how can you know what your guardian will do? You haven't seen him for years. Alain de Vallière was wild in his youth, but I understand he has settled down to become a most dependable man. Besides, I thought you liked him. He comes from one of the finest families in Louisiana, after all. And you were so fond of him when you were a child."

At the time, Simone had not attempted to counter her aunt's soothing argument, unwilling to explain that she hated Alain, that she had hated him since his visit to New Orleans when she was thirteen.

Even now, sitting alone in the darkened parlor, Simone felt a blush of humiliation. A schoolgirl in braids, she had been thrilled at the handsome young man's return. She had not openly reminded him of her childhood promise to wait for him but had tried in various other ways to convince him that she was a woman, seizing any opportunity to be alone with him.

Evidently annoyed by her inept and none-too-subtle overtures, Alain had swept her into his arms, determined to prove a point to the wayward thirteen-year-old. Simone's alarm at his supposed passion had turned to fury when he released her and she realized he was laughing at her.

"Ever the wildcat, eh, Simone?" he had chuckled when she launched herself at him. He captured her thin wrists easily and held her, spitting and kicking. "I like my women beautiful and spirited. You're feisty enough, if we could just put some meat on those skinny bones of yours."

"I'll show you feisty, 'gator-bait," she had snarled, aiming a kick at his shins.

"Watch that temper when you're truly a woman, *ma petite*," he advised, dancing out of reach, "or you'll scare off potential husbands. Sons of planters like their women sweet and biddable."

"I don't intend to marry some dull planter's son!" she yelled, making contact just above his boot.

"Ow, you little she-devil! You'll change your mind," he taunted. "Every Creole woman I know—well, almost every one—has been happy to settle down to a comfortable life and a houseful of children."

"I'm not like every Creole woman!" Her face crimson with rage and shame, she had wrenched away from him and fled.

He had probably been right to discourage her, Simone thought grimly, but he had been so arrogant. Four years ago, she had been a naive child, certain she loved him. Well, she was no longer a child, and what she felt now was far from love. He would find that out on his return.

She reread the letter she held. It had arrived two weeks ago. Nicholas had known before the duel that Alain was coming home. Why hadn't he told her? And why had he turned her future over to a man she hardly knew anymore?

She would not make Alain's life easy by marrying someone she did not love. Since Tante Viviane had never been able to counter Nicholas's influence enough to teach Simone the niceties a girl needed to "entertain a parlor," she did not know whether or not she could find a husband on her own, or whether she even wanted to. Though she had no desire to be supported by a guardian, she did not want to be a poor relation either, living on charity from her aunt's family. She must make her own way.

However, when she assessed her talents, Simone was forced to admit they were few. She knew how to run a household, but because of her youth, who would hire her as a housekeeper?

Her chances of securing a position as a governess were also slight, for her formal schooling at the Ursuline convent had ceased when her father could no longer afford the tuition. Though the nuns would have allowed her to stay, the Devereaux had their pride, Nicholas had explained. Simone had not minded, preferring to read on her own. Before their library dwindled away, sold off book by book, she had managed a broad, if somewhat irregular, education.

What could she do? she wondered moodily. Neither of the skills Nicholas had taught her—rudimentary swordplay and how to handle cards—was particularly seemly or useful for a seventeen-year-old female.

A rap at the front door jarred Simone from her musing. Ducking to look in the mirror, which leaned against the wainscoting in readiness for the appraiser, she grimaced ruefully. In the ancient glass, her finely chiseled features looked drawn and her green eyes were shaded by sorrow. Although it was nearly evening, her hair was loose, flowing down her back to her waist. She had not had the energy to arrange it this morning.

Self-consciously, she raked her fingers through the thick brown mane and smoothed the skirt of the threadbare green housedress she wore in order to save her black mourning gown for public view. She was hardly dressed for company, she reflected as she went to answer the door, but her caller must take her as she was.

A gust of wind bearing the scent of rain swept over Simone as she turned the corner from the courtyard to the passageway toward the street. She nearly turned back when she saw Marcel Baudin at the other end, waiting outside the gate.

"There you are, Mademoiselle Devereaux," the fair-haired Creole called when he saw her through the murky passage. Doffing his hat, he bowed elegantly. "*Bonsoir.*"

Marcel smiled appreciatively as she approached. One day Simone Devereaux would be among the most beautiful women in New Orleans. She was lovely even now in her worn, outdated frock. He allowed his gaze to skim over her trim body before he looked up—into hate-filled green eyes glittering like emeralds.

"What do you want?" she asked flatly, stopping a distance from the gate.

"To extend my condolences on the death of your father," he answered smoothly.

"How gracious, considering you're the one who murdered him," she retorted.

"It was a fair fight. Ask any of the witnesses."

Simone glared at him. "You knew my father was not up to it. He was a sick man."

"He was a drunkard," Marcel corrected quietly,

bowing to a passing gentleman who was hurrying to reach home before the storm. "And he was a gambler who lost everything—his inheritance, the family home, the bequest your mother left to you, even money he didn't have," he added, his pale eyes holding hers meaningfully.

"What are you talking about?"

The Creole assumed a winsome pout. "Must we discuss our business in the street, mam'selle, or will you invite me in?"

"I don't think we have anything to say to each other," she replied in clipped tones.

"*Au contraire, chère,* we have a great deal to talk about." Marcel reached into his pocket and drew out a sheaf of papers. "I hold all your father's gambling debts, you know. Every one of them."

Simone looked down at the pages riffling in the wind. The writing on them was undeniably her father's. Fighting to maintain her composure, she deliberated before opening the gate. It was not proper to receive the man without a chaperon, but she had to talk to him.

Leading Marcel to the parlor, she gestured to a chair. "Won't you sit down? I must light the lamps. I hadn't realized until you knocked that it was so dark."

"Don't bother," he answered softly. "I don't plan to stay long . . . tonight."

"I assure you, Monsieur Baudin, I intend to pay my father's debts, but it will take time," Simone blurted out anxiously, missing his comment. "I must ask you to be patient."

"Let your other creditors be patient. I demand some payment now," he murmured huskily, stepping nearer.

Simone retreated, straining to see his face in the dimness. "But I have no money."

Smiling down at her, Marcel placed his hands gently on her shoulders. "You have something I desire far more than money."

His meaning was unmistakable. Simone's eyes narrowed in fury, and she tried to jerk from his grasp. "How dare you?" she said.

His hands tightened on her shoulders, and he yanked her toward him. "Because you owe me, *chère* Simone. Though I shall soon demand payment in full, I take this on account."

She tasted blood as his mouth claimed hers roughly, his teeth cutting into her lips. His wet kiss, hot and demanding, smothered her protest, and when she stiffened in resistance, his arms closed around her, pinning her arms and molding her against his body. Through her clothing, she felt, with a shock, the heated evidence of his need, and she knew his intention.

Doubling her knee, she tried to aim a blow at Marcel's groin. Guessing her plan, he loosened his hold and stepped back to avoid the attack. Able to free her hands, Simone placed them against his chest and shoved him away with all her might.

"Get out! Get out and never come back!" she panted, pointing toward the door.

"Why do you resist me?" Marcel asked tauntingly, catching a lock of her flowing hair. Twisting his hand in it, he pulled her toward him and whispered in her ear, "If you continue to fight me, I might have second thoughts about my generosity."

"Generosity?" She tried to jerk away, wincing as he held fast to the silken rope of her hair wrapped around his clenched fist.

"*Oui.* I offer you the same arrangement I offered your father. When you become my mistress, all debts will be cancelled."

She yanked her hair from his grip, unmindful of the burning pain, and retreated to a position behind a chair. "You offered this arrangement to my father? So that's why he challenged you!"

"And why he died." Marcel walked slowly toward her, smiling tolerantly when she edged away, keeping the chair between them. "You have few choices now, Simone. Consider my offer carefully. A rich man won't marry you, and a poor man dare not approach a Devereaux, although the family isn't what it once was. Becoming my mistress is the best you can hope for."

"I'll never become your mistress!"

"Never is a long time to rot in debtors' prison," he said persuasively, continuing to advance.

"A cot in the Cabildo would be better than sharing your bed," she retorted hotly.

"You little bitch," he snarled, his handsome face suddenly transformed into a malevolent mask. He leapt forward and seized the front of Simone's dress. The thin material ripped easily, revealing round white breasts heaving in anger. Simone's startled gaze met his for an instant before she dodged to the side and snatched her father's sword from its resting place on the mantel.

"Stay back! I warn you." She brandished the sword with one hand, clutching the bodice of her dress closed with the other.

Marcel stayed where he was, an indistinct figure in the darkness. "You are *magnifique, ma belle*, and your protests admirable, but why do you delay the inevitable?" he coaxed.

As the storm's heavy threat finally broke over the city, Simone imagined she could see the smirk on the Creole's face while he let her play for time, certain he would soon convince her to drop her guard.

"I will have you," he assured her. "I've wanted you for two months, since I noticed you at the market., the sunlight glistening in your beautiful brown hair. You looked like a dark angel . . . a perfect match for me. Oh, I'd seen Devereaux's waif of a daughter before, but suddenly you were a woman and you were lovely. I knew I had to have you, no matter what it took to get you."

"You must be mad." Simone watched him intently through the gloom.

"Don't say that, *chèrie*." Marcel's tone was almost pleading. "Put down the sword. Let me love you. I swear you'll have all a woman could ever want. I'll take care of you, dress you in silks, shower you with jewels. You would like that, wouldn't you?"

In the silence, the patter of rain on the flagstones of the courtyard was all that could be heard.

"Say something, damn it!" he shouted, lunging without warning. "Don't mock me with silence when I've told you I want you."

Fencing etiquette was forgotten as Simone attempted to defend herself. Panicked, she lifted the heavy sword and swung it wildly, striking a glancing blow to her assailant's forehead.

A jagged bolt of lightning illuminated the night, and by its stark light, Simone glimpsed dark blood streaming down the side of Marcel's face. Muttering dire curses, he clutched at his eye and lurched toward her.

She thrust the sword away from her in horror and ran from the house. As she rounded the corner to the passageway, the wind drove rain into her face and lashed her skirt around her ankles, slowing her. She fought to reach the *banquette*, to find help, but no one was out on the storm-swept street.

In the passageway behind her, Marcel's inarticulate bellow echoed as he staggered after her.

A blinding bolt of lightning split the sky, revealing the ominous clouds roiling overhead. Marcel's horse, hitched outside the house, whinnied shrilly, frightened by the thunderclap that followed. Glancing fearfully over her shoulder, Simone murmured quiet reassurances and hurriedly untied the beast.

Just as she mounted, Marcel burst onto the street, spooking the horse. From the back of the rearing animal, Simone looked down into the man's bloody face as his red-stained hands clawed at the reins.

"You'll pay for this, Simone Devereaux!" he

screamed. "I will have you, and I'll make you pay!"

Struggling to stay in the saddle, she wheeled the horse sharply in the street and galloped away through the pounding rain.

2

Shafts of morning sun angled through glass-paned doors and washed over the foot of the bed. Simone opened her eyes and lay still, uncertain where she was. Propping herself on her elbows, she peered through the mosquito netting around the bed and recognized her guest room at LeFleur. The night's events flooded back, and with a groan she flopped down and closed her eyes again.

She had wounded a man; perhaps he would even die. Then again, the blow had not seemed fatal, Simone told herself optimistically. Marcel had followed her into the street, after all, bellowing as she rode away. She groaned again. *Nom de Dieu,* she had stolen his horse—another crime to add to the list.

Pushing the filmy *baire* away, she sat on the edge of the bed and found herself face to face with the portrait of her mother. It had come to LeFleur with Viviane and Georges last week and was still propped against the wall, not yet hung. She stared at the likeness of the dark-eyed Creole woman she barely remembered. Captured in time as a new bride, Marthe had been about Simone's age when she had posed demurely under a

tree in front of the majestic pillared house at LaVictoire, the lost Devereaux plantation.

Simone contemplated the painting, wondering what
the solemn Marthe would think now if she were alive
to hear what her wayward daughter had done.

"*Bonjour, ma chère.*" Tante Viviane entered, carrying a tray bearing coffee and *beignets*. She paused
beside the bed and regarded her niece appraisingly.
"You look better this morning. How do you feel?"

"Better, *merci*," Simone answered, stepping to the
washstand to cleanse the sleep from her eyes.

"What a fright you gave me, arriving here drenched
and nearly hysterical."

"I'm sorry, *Tante*," the girl apologized as she poured
the tepid contents of the pitcher into the basin, "but I
didn't know where else to go. . . ."

"You did the right thing, coming here, child. After
all, LeFleur is your home now. I'm just relieved Georges
and Fabrice were not here to see your dramatic arrival."

"So am I," Simone agreed wholeheartedly, especially
glad her proud, protective cousin had spent the night in
town. It would have been bad enough to face her uncle,
but Fabrice would have insisted on settling her affairs
himself.

While Simone washed her face, Tante Viviane pulled
a folded newspaper from the pocket of her apron and
perched on the edge of the bed. Spreading the paper
over the disarranged covers, she fanned through the
pages. "I see nothing in the *Gazette* of Marcel Baudin's
death, nor even of an injury," she muttered.

"A *Gazette*? How did you get one so early?" Simone
asked, groping for a towel.

Viviane handed it her. "Barnabas brought it from
town. He returned Monsieur Baudin's horse to the liv-
ery stable at dawn after he, er, found the poor beast
wandering on the River Road."

"I'm sorry you had to lie for me."

"We do what we must to take care of our own," her

aunt said, adding guiltily, "and it was my fault, after all.
I never should have convinced Georges to allow you to
stay in town."

"You didn't know Marcel would try to rape me in
my own home."

"I still find it hard to believe a Creole gentleman
would do such a thing," Viviane sighed with a disturbed frown.

"You didn't see that 'gentleman' when he followed
me into the street last night." Simone shuddered. "He
was like a mad, wounded animal."

"Surely he wouldn't bother you here with . . ." The
woman trailed off when she heard voices from outside.
"That must be Georges. When he hears what happened, he will take care of everything." With a reassuring smile, Viviane hurried from the room.

Simone recognized her uncle's voice, rising from
the *allée* below, but the other one, so strident—could
it be?

She peeped out the window and saw Georges standing beside an open carriage. From the high bench seat,
Marcel Baudin scowled down at him. The young Creole's head was swathed in bandages that covered one
eye, and he was shouting, "I know she is here, Chauvin!
You might as well give her to me."

"I don't know what you're talking about." The
planter stared up at Marcel in puzzlement.

"I am talking about Simone. She attacked me with a
sword," Marcel yelled, the pale eye that was visible
alight with fury.

"Preposterous!" Georges exclaimed. "Simone would
not attack you. She's headstrong and impetuous, yes,
but she is not violent."

"I tell you, she tried to murder me."

"Why would she do such a thing?"

"Because I hold Nicholas Devereaux's IOUs, and I
demanded she work them off."

"How much did my brother-in-law owe you?"

Viviane stepped from the shadowy veranda to stand beside her husband.

Marcel's look was crafty. "That is between Simone and me. She owes me, and I want her as a servant in my house. Give her to me or I will charge her with attempted murder."

"Why didn't you go to the constabulary to begin with?" Simone's uncle asked angrily.

Marcel ignored the question. "Give the girl to me!" he shouted. "I will have justice!"

Georges's ruddy face flushed with anger, but he offered rationally, "If Simone owes you money, if she attacked you—tried to murder you, as you say—we will see justice done. But even if she were here, I wouldn't hand her over to you. We should send for the sheriff at once."

"*Non,* I want her now or I'll take your house apart board by board until I find her."

"You *are* mad," Viviane whispered, truly afraid of the violence the young Creole could turn on her family.

"What!" Marcel stood in his carriage, towering over the couple on the ground. "Mad? I only want what is mine!"

"My niece is not yours," she answered, recovering her voice.

"She will be," he snarled. "And when I get her, I will take every picayune she owes me out of her hide."

"Get off my property, Baudin!" Georges thundered.

"Not until—"

"Get off my property," the planter repeated, holding his ground before Marcel, who was poised as if to leap upon him.

Marcel restrained himself with effort. Sitting down, he gathered the reins, turning slitted eyes on the older man. "I'll be back," he said through clenched teeth, "and I won't be alone."

"Make sure you bring the sheriff with you," Georges responded evenly. Taking Viviane's arm, he led her toward the house.

As she crept downstairs, Simone heard the couple enter the house. "Come into the library, Viviane," her uncle bade his wife brusquely. "I want to talk to you."

Simone waited until he had closed the door behind them before going unabashedly to eavesdrop. She had to know what was afoot.

"Is Simone here?" she heard Georges ask flatly.

"*Oui.*" Her aunt's voice was scarcely audible.

"Do Baudin's accusations have any basis in fact?"

"He tried to force himself on her."

"So Simone did attack him."

"She defended herself."

"None of this would have happened if that girl had conducted herself properly in the first place," Georges erupted. "Of all the outrageous behaviors, attending Nicholas's funeral, insisting on going back to the house instead of coming home with us. This comes at the worst time, just as I am about to affiance Fabrice to Pellarin's youngest daughter. I tell you, Viviane, someone should take Simone in hand."

"Fabrice would like to," she answered coolly. "You know he wants to marry her."

After a moment's silence, Georges asked hoarsely, "How is it we are suddenly discussing a marriage you know I will not permit? Fabrice's infatuation with Simone has been nothing but trouble for years. He knows, and you know, I will never give him permission to marry her. I told you, I am arranging a marriage, a very suitable marriage, for him."

"But, Georges—"

"Just because she is your niece, madame, doesn't mean she is a fit wife for my son," Viviane's husband cut her off. "Fabrice is heir to LeFleur, and Simone is a problem that must be resolved once and for all. *Mon Dieu*, first it was Nicholas with his drinking and gambling, and now his daughter with her scandalous behavior. Sometimes I don't know what kind of family I married into."

In the hallway, Simone clenched her fists and fought the urge to burst in and confront him.

In the study, Viviane drew herself up stiffly. "I'm sorry if you feel tainted by my family, Georges. You won't have to deal with this difficulty, however. I will pay off Marcel Baudin."

"I didn't mean to offend you, *chère*," Georges soothed her quickly. "And I do not want you to pay him off. In fact, I forbid it. We must think of something else."

"I would pay him with money I brought to this marriage—"

"Viviane, you know that under Louisiana law I, as your husband, control your wealth," he interrupted patiently. "That money is set aside to purchase more land. I cannot let you spend it."

After a moment of mutinous silence, the woman said, "Then why don't we send for the sheriff and let him straighten this out?"

"Because if Baudin wants this matter kept quiet, and I believe he does, it is all the better for us. We must make other arrangements for Simone until de Vallière arrives," her husband mused. "Let me see. What about Cousin Henri in the West Indies?" he said excitedly as the idea struck him. "His wife died last year, and he needs a governess for his children. If he hired Simone, she could repay Baudin from her earnings. She'd be safe with family, though distant, and temptation would be removed from Fabrice's path. An excellent solution, I think. What do you say?"

Simone did not remain to hear if her aunt would agree. In matters of importance, Viviane almost always bowed to Georges's will. The girl fled noiselessly to her room. While her uncle was deciding her life downstairs, she sat down to plan.

No matter what he thought, she did not wish to marry Fabrice, nor did she want to go to the West Indies. She would not become Marcel's mistress, and she did not think she could bear to go to prison for debts or for attacking him. And to make matters worse, Alain would be returning soon to be her guardian.

Her dull gaze fell on the newspaper Viviane had left open on her bed. Suddenly an advertisement came into sharp focus: Serge St. Michel needed a boy to assist him at his *salle d'armes*.

Determination replaced hopelessness as Simone developed a scheme. She would disguise herself as a boy, she decided confidently. Maître St. Michel had seemed a kind man. If she could fool him and get the job at his fencing school, even for a few months, she could begin to pay off her father's debts. Perhaps by then, Marcel, a notorious ladies' man, would find someone else to warm his bed, and he would be more interested in cash than in an unwilling mistress. Then she would have only Alain de Vallière to fight.

Her mind made up, the girl stole up to the attic to search the trunks for Fabrice's old clothes.

The bells at St. Louis Cathedral had rung the midday Angelus over the Vieux Carré when a handsome Creole dismounted in front of his tailor's.

"Hold your horse, m'sieur, for only a picayune?" a youngster appeared at his elbow to ask.

"*Oui.*" Fabrice Chauvin tossed the reins to the lad with the merest glance.

But that glance was enough. "Simone!" he gasped in shock.

Clad in a boy's baggy clothing, she looked lanky and underfed. Her beautiful light brown hair had been chopped off and darkened. It was plastered to her head from the heat, her face was caked with dust, and her nose was pink from the sun. But her merry green eyes and broad grin were unmistakable.

Seizing the reins from her with one hand and her elbow tightly with the other, Fabrice tied his horse, then dragged his cousin into the alley beside the building.

"What is the meaning of this?" he demanded.

"You recognized me." Simone pouted as she straightened her jacket. How could he know her when she had hardly recognized herself in the mirror at LeFleur that morning?

"Why shouldn't I? I've known you all your life. Why are you dressed in my old clothes? And what have you done to your beautiful hair?"

"I dyed it with *café* as old Madame Olivier used to do." Simone ran her fingers through her cropped hair with a regretful smile. "Don't you like it?"

"It . . . it's short," her cousin sputtered.

"It must be if I'm to masquerade as a boy."

"What are you thinking to appear in public like this?"

"I must go into hiding, Fabrice, and this disguise is best," she responded patiently.

"What in the name of all the holy saints makes you think that?"

"Because I've passed for a boy before."

"That was years ago, before, er, before . . ." He trailed off, blushing, unwilling to discuss the recent, rather appealing changes in her body. "What is this about hiding?" he asked brusquely.

"If I tell you, do you promise to do as I ask?"

"Absolutely not." Fabrice was well acquainted with Simone's escapades.

"Then I won't say."

"Don't be absurd, Simone. Why are you doing this?"

"Because I'm in trouble."

"You've been in trouble for one thing or another most of your life," he snorted, "and haven't I always gotten you out?"

"I won't let you this time," she answered bluntly. "It's too dangerous."

"You're serious, aren't you?" He regarded her soberly. "At least tell me about it."

"Not unless you promise to do things my way."

Fabrice grudgingly agreed, but his expression became increasingly grim as he heard of Marcel's visit to the house on rue Orleans and his trip to LeFleur, of his father's plan for Simone, and of the return of her guardian.

"There's no need for you to go through all of this alone, *cousine*." He put a comforting arm around her shoulders. "I'll challenge Baudin to a duel, and you'll be free of him."

"I knew you would say that!" she cried in exasperation, shrugging off his companionable embrace. "Don't interfere, Fabrice. Marcel Baudin killed my father. I don't want him to kill you, too."

"Who is to say he would?" he asked stiffly.

"I cannot take the chance."

A spark of hope came into his eyes, and the young Creole urged, "There must be another way. You can stay with me—with us at LeFleur. *Maman* will be worried sick about you."

"I left a note for Tante Viviane, but I can't let your family know where I am. Not only do I wish to keep them safe, but I have no liking for your father's plan to send me to the West Indies."

"Ah, yes, the West Indies," Fabrice muttered gloomily.

"Besides," she said, "if I make some money, I can pay off Marcel. Once that threat is out of the way, I can turn my energy to freeing myself of Alain, as well."

"As I recall de Vallière, you're taking on a formidable foe," he warned.

"Perhaps, but the fight will be worth it if I can marry whom I wish, when I wish. Or choose not to marry at all," she went on.

The young man looked crestfallen. "Couldn't you take a job as a governess or a seamstress?"

"Marcel would find me, as would Oncle Georges and Alain. Please, Fabrice, introduce me to Maître St. Michel," she pleaded. "If you recommend me, perhaps it will be easier for me to get the job."

"Recommend you?" He was taken aback. "What good would that do? He'll never believe you're a boy."

"Yes, he will. You'll see."

"But, Simone, you'd be surrounded by men every day," he argued. "They're sure to see—"

"What they will see is a boy. I'm hardly the belle of the ball in this costume," she pointed out ruefully.

"*Non*," Fabrice agreed, heartsick at her changed appearance.

"Don't worry," she soothed him. "I'll keep to myself. The advertisement said a private room went with the job."

"But look at you," he tried desperately once more. "Even like this, Simone, there's no way—"

"Are you going to help me or not?"

"It's against my better judgment," he said reluctantly after a moment, "but I'll take you to the *salle d'armes*."

"I still say it won't work," he complained as they headed toward the *salle* of Serge St. Michel, their footsteps echoing hollowly on the wooden *banquette*. But when he glanced down at his companion, Fabrice's jaw dropped in surprise.

Walking beside him was a pint-sized lad who looked to be about twelve years old. Every vestige of his lovely, dainty cousin was gone as she added a swagger to her step, tucked her head close to her shoulders, and squinted at the world through skeptical green eyes, whistling tunelessly as she matched her stride with his.

At the head of Exchange Alley, Simone stopped whistling, her breath quickening. She had not been here since her visit as a child, but it looked just as she remembered. She recognized St. Michel's *salle* even before Fabrice halted at the foot of the stairs to ask imploringly, "Are you sure you wish to do this, Simone?"

She nodded nervously and answered in a husky voice, "*Oui*, and the name is Jean-Paul. Jean-Paul Sonnier from Bayou Teche."

"I still don't like it," Fabrice muttered under his breath as he led her up the stairs.

The oddly matched pair found the fencing master at a small table with cup of coffee, a cigar, and a newspaper.

"*Bonjour*, Chauvin," Serge called as they crossed the deserted room toward him. "What brings you here when everyone else is at lunch?"

"I've brought someone who is interested in the job you advertised. His name is J-Jean-Paul." Fabrice nearly choked on the name.

"*Bonjour, Maître.*" Simone extended a small hand in greeting.

"How do you do, Jean-Paul. So you've come about the job." The mulatto's amber eyes looked the youngster over. "I must say, you're small for such work."

"But I need this job, m'sieur. I know I can do it. I'm a hard worker, and I'm strong for my age."

"What age is that?"

"Fourteen," she answered confidently.

"Let us start our friendship with honesty, little one," Serge requested.

"Wh-what do you mean?" Simone starcd at him through startled green eyes.

"Only that you are more likely only twelve years old, *mon ami*, perhaps less. Where are your parents?"

"Both dead," she answered truthfully, meeting his gaze without flinching.

"And have you no family to care for you?"

"None I can stay with." She offered her own version of the truth. "I'm on my own now. I take care of myself."

"I see." Serge rose and began to pace. The lad was a puzzle. The clothes, while ill-fitting and outmoded, were of good quality, and the hand he had offered was smooth and white. This Jean-Paul was obviously from a good family fallen on hard times. There must be a dozen reasons he should not hire this scrawny orphan, but the swordsman's soft heart was touched by the boy's bravado.

"All right, Jean-Paul." He sighed in resignation. "I'll give you a week to prove yourself. If you keep the *salle* clean, tend the equipment with the greatest of care, set up before classes and run errands for me, the job will be yours at . . . let us say, six dollars a month.

The boy's eyes widened at the princely sum. "Before you thank me," he cautioned, "remember that, although there is a room here for you, I do not furnish meals."

"It's still more than I had hoped for," Simone fairly squeaked.

So the lad was not so old. Serge smiled. "You can start first thing tomorrow. Today you may settle into the chamber beside the equipment room." He indicated a pair of doors at the back of the room.

"*Merci, Maître.*" Turning so Serge could not see her dancing eyes, she flashed her cousin a radiant smile and said politely, "*Merci*, M'sieur Chauvin. I won't disappoint you."

Alone that night in her tiny, spartan room, Simone locked the doors. After hiding her mother's necklace in a bedpost, she unpacked a small trunk Fabrice had spirited away from the Chauvin town house. He had not found clothes for her, but he had brought a nightshirt and a broad-brimmed straw hat, giving her strict orders to wear the hat when she went out of doors so she would not ruin her complexion.

Rummaging in the trunk, Simone found a few household items Fabrice thought Viviane would not miss: some linens, soap, candles, and, improbably, a looking glass on a wooden stand. Though she would not keep it where others could see it, she was grateful for Fabrice's thoughtful gift. It would help her maintain her masquerade as Jean-Paul. Deliberately, she schooled her features into a rebellious boy's scornful scowl.

She was glad she was petite, realizing it would be easier to pass for a twelve-year-old than a swaggering adolescent. Even so, acting the part of Jean-Paul was likely to be difficult. Though she must be careful never to challenge, she must make sure those around her knew she was not to be bullied. For the first time, she had doubts about her plan. Resolutely, she pushed them aside and prepared for bed.

Under the boy's shirt, Jean-Paul's scrawny shoulders were shapely and white. Unfastening her baggy trousers, Simone allowed them to slide down over rounded hips. With relief, she unpinned the cloth wrapped tightly around her chest and breathed deeply. Between her firm young breasts was the imprint of her father's emerald wedding band, which she wore on a ribbon around her neck.

As she inspected the mark, her eyes drifted up her unfamiliar reflection. She had never been a beauty, but no one would recognize Simone Devereaux now, she thought sadly. The luxuriant brown tresses that had been her pride were nearly black and chopped haphazardly, making her elfin face look angular and gaunt. Her cheeks were smudged with dust and grime.

She felt tears pricking at her eyelids, but she had made her choice, and she would not cry. Still, as she crawled into bed, it seemed that the emerald ring nestled between her breasts was her sole link to her old life, the only thing that reminded her who she was.

3

Her hat shoved back on her untidy hair,
Simone sprawled on the grass under a tree in the Place
d'Armes, watching churchgoers emerge from the cathedral. She loved Sundays, when the market was packed
with people, when the streets were noisy, and the river-
scented breeze carried music from every corner.

The Kaintocks, the unpolished, industrious Americans who lived on the other side of Canal Street, could
not seem to understand the Creoles' careless Sunday
leisure. But in the sophisticated French section, windows and doors were thrown open, and the inhabitants
greeted friends who passed.

Lying on her stomach, Simone propped herself on her
elbows and plucked juicy strawberries from a basket she
had positioned conveniently close to her mouth. There
were definitely some advantages to being a boy, she
mused, popping another berry past her stained lips. She
had a great sense of well-being today, for she was thriving in her job, and the maître seemed satisfied. Serge's
last assistant had been lax at best. Though the work was
strenuous and she had fallen into bed without supper
several times, Simone had met the challenge with zeal.

During the past week, young men had casually stripped off their shirts in front of her, and she had heard talk that left her face flaming in embarrassment, so that most thought Jean-Paul naive and shy and left him alone.

Now she had money in her pocket, an afternoon to spend as she pleased, and no one bothered with a boy lazing in the shade. No one except Fabrice.

"*Dieu*, what a sight," he hissed when he spied her.

She rolled over and smiled up at him. "*Bonjour, m'sieur*. Just coming from church? Care for a berry?" She offered a handful in sticky fingers.

The immaculately dressed Creole looked down his nose at her. "You have juice all over you. I wish you'd give up this masquerade, Simone."

"Jean-Paul," she corrected, her voice low. "How can I give it up when Marcel is turning the city upside down for me?"

Lounging against the tree trunk, Fabrice confided, "He has offered to reward any of your neighbors who will notify him if Simone Devereaux is seen."

"Then she must not be seen. Sure you won't have a berry?" When he refused, she popped another into her mouth and asked, "Has Marcel bothered Oncle Georges and Tante Viviane anymore?"

"*Non*, but LeFleur is being watched." At her scowl, he added, "Do not worry. I wasn't followed."

"Marcel hasn't troubled you?"

"He sent his bodyguard, Guy la Roche, a big Cajun, to question me. I'm afraid I seemed completely addle-pated. I didn't even realize *ma petite cousine* Simone was missing."

"*Merci*, Fabrice," she sighed in relief. "You're a true gentleman."

"I didn't feel like one," he grumbled.

"But you are." She beamed up at him for one unguarded moment, and he almost forgot he was dealing with Jean-Paul at all.

"Monsieur Chauvin, *bonjour*," a feminine voice

called shrilly. The pair under the tree turned to see a young couple out for a promenade around the square.

"*Bonjour*, mademoiselle, monsieur." Fabrice swept off his hat and bowed politely.

Jumping to her feet, Simone announced, "Think I'll leave you to your fine friends, m'sieur."

The young Creole watched with amazement as his cousin hitched up her baggy pants and sauntered into the crowd on rue St. Ann. Quickly Simone made her way past the Presbytère and over to rue Orleans. She lingered behind the cathedral, wishing she dared to amble down the sunbaked street for a look at her old home. But the house was surely being watched.

Clamping her hat down, almost to her eyebrows, Simone sauntered with boyish nonchalance in the opposite direction. This charade would not go on forever, she reminded herself. Eventually Marcel would forget about her. He had never reported her crime to the police. Perhaps when she had saved enough to repay him, she could return to her own life.

Jingling the coins in her pocket comfortingly, she felt the smooth texture of an envelope. She had forgotten the note she had written to Monsieur Fusilier, informing him that she intended to repay all her father's creditors. She had enclosed two dollars, the first of many payments to be deducted from the amount still owed after the auction. It would take a long time, but she would settle her father's debts as she was honor-bound to do.

Simone hesitated on a street corner, wondering how to get the note to Monsieur Fusilier's office without risking being recognized.

"Hey, Jean-Paul," a youthful voice hailed her.

Obadiah Prejean ambled toward her, a broad smile splitting his black face.

Simone had met the street urchin the week before and already felt he was a friend. Though Obadiah was a couple of years older than "Jean-Paul's" twelve, he had taken a liking to the scrawny boy.

"How come I ain't seen you around here before?" he had asked.

"Haven't been around," had been Simone's laconic answer. "I just came from Bayou Teche."

"Fresh off the farm," the Negro boy had teased. "You prob'ly don't even know your way around yet."

"Know it well enough to get a job with Maître St. Michel," Simone had bragged with just the right amount of boyish pride.

Obadiah had whistled softly, eyeing the stranger with new respect. Eager to know what went on in the *salle*, he had bombarded Jean-Paul with questions. Simone had answered, glad for someone to talk to, and a friendship was begun.

She was happy to see him again today and understanding when he apologized, "Sorry I didn't meet you at the Place d'Armes. I gotta deliver a message backstage at the Opera House. Seems their soprano's got a fit of the vapors."

"You're going backstage?" Simone breathed admiringly.

Gratified that Jean-Paul recognized the significance of his mission, Obadiah said humbly, "Well, it ain't payin' much, but every little bit helps since my daddy died."

"Obie, could you deliver a letter for me when you're done?" she asked impulsively, pulling the envelope from her pocket. "I'll pay you."

With a skeptical snort, the older boy accepted the envelope. "Who'd you be sendin' a letter to, short-stuff?"

"Monsieur Fusilier."

"The lawyer?"

"Family business," she explained vaguely. "You can just slide it under his door."

"I'll do it on my way to the Opera House, but I ain't takin' money from no friend," Obadiah declared. "After I deliver my notes, why don't I meet you on the levee behind the market? We'll watch the ships, and you can tell me 'bout that fencin' school."

"Très bien, but don't eat before you come," she insisted. "I'll find us some lunch."

"Got yourself a deal." Grinning in anticipation, Obadiah trotted off toward Monsieur Fusilier's office.

As Simone walked back toward the River, she heard a voice call out, "You, boy. Yes, you," it repeated when she stopped and looked around. She saw a rotund man beckon from a doorway across the street. She was the boy being summoned.

"I'll give you a quarter to take a note down to Hewlett's," the man said when she approached him.

Simone hesitated. Then, thrilled at the chance to see that male stronghold where women were not allowed, she agreed.

Note and coin in hand, she set off importantly. But on the *banquette* outside Hewlett's Exchange, she faltered. Peeking through the window into the crowded bar, she could see nothing but a knot of broad backs.

Opening the heavy door, she eased into a world scented with sawdust and smoke, bay rum and tobacco. She hovered at the entrance for a moment, half expecting all talk to cease and every eye to turn toward the newcomer. But no one noticed another urchin with a message.

A blue haze of smoke filled the long, narrow room, drifting up to the high pressed-tin ceiling. Men lined the bar, their booted feet propped against the polished rail, the low rumble of their voices broken occasionally by hearty laughter.

When her message was delivered, Simone turned reluctantly to leave. If she dawdled, she was likely to be noticed, and she could not afford to be conspicuous. Near the door, however, a familiar voice made her stop in her tracks, her heart pounding. So many times she had heard that voice in her girlish dreams. And so many times, she had tried to forget it.

Filled with dread, she turned to see Alain de Vallière. His elegantly tailored jacket strained over muscular shoulders as he leaned across a small table to speak to Monsieur Fusilier. Since she had last seen him, his face, bronzed by the sun during his recent voyage from France, had matured. Straight brown hair, lightened by the sun, swept back regally from his brow. Dark, penetrating eyes, so brown they were nearly black, gave his lean, hard visage a watchful intensity. *Ah, non,* the girl thought with something akin to dismay, he was even more handsome than she had remembered. And he looked like a force to be reckoned with.

Engrossed in conversation, neither he nor Monsieur Fusilier noticed the boy lurking nearby. Careful to keep her back to them, Simone edged closer to eavesdrop.

"I appreciate your meeting me on a Sunday, monsieur," Alain was saying.

"My pleasure, Monsieur de Vallière," the attorney responded politely. "Though I do not know where Mademoiselle Devereaux is, I hope I have set your mind at ease by showing you the note that was just slipped under my door."

"Where could she be?" Alain asked, his vexation apparent. "She took nothing with her. No one has seen her for more than a week, not even you. She's not at Lefleur, or she wasn't when I sent word out there yesterday."

"That is worrisome," Monsieur Fusilier murmured with a frown. "But, at least we know she is well."

"Yes, but where?" In a harried gesture, Alain raked his fingers through his hair and frowned. "It's quite trying to come home after four years and find oneself a guardian—then to discover your ward is missing."

Monsieur Fusilier made sympathetic clucking sounds until Alain continued, "What's worse is that Simone's landlady is worried about her. She believes something happened at the house the night she disappeared. She insists Nicholas's sword had blood on it, though by the time I arrived, she had wiped it clean. It may be the prattling of an old woman. The police seem to think so.

They refused even to look for Simone, saying if she doesn't return in a few days, they will question her neighbors."

"Now that we know the young lady is not dead, they certainly will not bother," the attorney said soberly. "You'll continue looking for her then?"

"*Oui*, I'm going out to speak with the Chauvins today."

"Please let me know if you hear anything," Monsieur Fusilier requested. "Simone is such a sweet, helpless child."

The sweet, helpless child and her guardian had nearly identical reactions: They fought back laughter. But Simone forgot her amusement and dodged behind a post when Alain rose and took his leave with a polite bow.

She nearly tripped over her own feet getting out of the big man's way. She smelled the spicy scent of his shaving soap as he passed her, so near she could have touched him, but he did not give the skinny boy so much as a glance.

She waited while he stopped on the *banquette* to don his hat, then she trailed him, lagging a safe distance behind. Running at times to compete with his long-legged stride, she kept his broad-shouldered figure in sight as he strolled toward the river, then veered across the cobblestone street to Exchange Alley.

With sinking heart, she thought she knew where he was going. Alain was already out of sight when she reached the head of the narrow passage. Following at a brisk jog, she managed to arrive at her *salle d'armes* in time to see him disappear within. Why hadn't she remembered he was a friend of Serge's? she wondered despairingly. Now she must be doubly careful not to be recognized.

Creeping silently up the staircase of the building, she slipped into her room and, poised apprehensively at the door to the *salle*, listening to the conversation within.

"I knew you were coming home, 'Lain, but I didn't expect you so soon." Serge sounded pleased.

"I didn't expect to be here so soon," Alain answered soberly. "It became imperative that I leave France at once."

"Trouble with a woman, if I know you," the other man guessed.

"Trouble with her husband," Alain muttered, adding hastily when he saw his friend's lifted brows, "I can explain. Comtesse Marguerite—"

"The king's *cousine*?" the swordsman asked with a chuckle. *"Très jolie."*

"And very determined," Alain added. "She wanted to be more than friends. As you may recall, I do not object to bedding a comely, willing woman, but a man likes to have a say. When I found her in my bed, uninvited, I sent her home."

"And Marguerite did not like that," Serge finished for him.

"She was furious. She told her husband I had seduced her, and the doddering old fool challenged me to a duel to the death."

"Surely he must have known you were the superior swordsman." Serge's expression was incredulous.

"Surely," the big Creole agreed without conceit. "That is why I chose pistols."

"Very honorable," the fencing master approved. "But still you killed him?"

"Not exactly." Alain seemed embarrassed.

"Then why your swift retreat?"

"When the count shot first and missed, I discharged my pistol into the air. I'll be damned if he didn't die of heart failure."

"Zut," Serge swore softly.

"Indeed. The next morning, I was summoned by the king. Louis-Philippe himself advised I flee the comtesse's revenge.

"So here I am." He shrugged sheepishly. "It might be

funny if it were not so tragic. But I tell you this, no more
pistols for me. Give me a good, clean rapier any day."

"Spoken like a true swordsman. Let's have dinner,
'Lain, and talk about old times," Serge said when his
friend rose.

"Not tonight, *mon ami*, but I'll be back soon for a
fencing match," Alain promised.

And I'll avoid you as though you had yellow jack,
Simone promised herself, silently closing the door on
their farewells.

She stayed out of sight as much as possible the next
day, but it was finally necessary to prepare a corner of
the *salle* for a private lesson. She worked with single-
minded energy, paying little attention to the conversations around her until she realized a group of young
blades was talking about Marcel Baudin.

"I heard someone finally bested him," one of them
said confidentially.

"I heard he fell while he was drunk," another hooted.

"I know what happened," a cocky fellow named
Christophe volunteered. "*Ma tante* lives on rue
Orleans, and she saw something very odd. Marcel went
to visit Mademoiselle Simone Devereaux—"

"Nicholas Devereaux's brat?"

"You apparently haven't seen her in ages. She grew
up to be a real beauty," the first young man said wistfully, "petite and dainty, with light brown hair and
green eyes and, *mon Dieu*, such a smile. It could charm
the birds from the trees."

Hunched over the mats she was arranging, Simone
scowled and resolved never to smile again while she
worked at the *salle*.

Christophe continued with gossipy self-importance,
"Apparently the *mam'selle* bested Marcel."

"Mon Dieu! What are you saying? Simone Devereaux is so gentle, so fragile," her admirer protested.

Jean-Paul snorted and wrestled a fencing dummy
into place.

Frowning over his shoulder at the boy, Christophe insisted, "I tell you, my aunt saw, with her own eyes, Marcel stagger from the Devereaux home, bleeding and cursing, while your 'gentle, fragile' beauty made off with his horse. And Marcel has been searching for the girl ever since."

"What do you suppose they quarreled about?"

"Who knows?" The knowledgeable Christophe finally admitted ignorance. "But it certainly causes one to wonder."

"Gossip can be an extremely dangerous activity." Marcel Baudin's voice lashed through the conversation.

Behind the huddle of young men, Simone whirled to see the fair-haired Creole standing nearby. The cut through his eyebrow had not yet healed, leaving a red, raw weal that added to his menace as he stopped in front of Christophe.

"Do you wish to speculate or to confront me directly?" he asked dangerously.

"N-neither." Unwilling to face the notorious swordsman, Christophe retreated, his friends on his heels.

Turning, Marcel saw a skinny lad, standing as if rooted in one spot. "What are you looking at?" he snarled, one hand rising unconsciously to his scar.

"N-nothing," Simone stammered, ducking her head and wishing she could sink into the floor.

"See that you do not stare." Stripping to his shirt-sleeves, Marcel put on his padded fencing jacket and regarded the boy appraisingly. "Who are you anyway?"

"Jean-Paul Sonnier, m'sieur," she mumbled, keeping her head down. "Maître St. Michel's hired boy."

"Do you think you can speak loud enough to tell Serge I wish to see him at once?" Marcel demanded impatiently.

"But sir," she objected, glancing toward the fencing master, who was working with a student, "he's giving a private lesson."

"Then what am I to do for an opponent?"

"Surely there is someone." Simone gestured toward the bleachers, where several young men lounged.

"If I wanted to fence with one of them," Marcel retorted, "I would have challenged that fool, Christophe."

"Then I am afraid you will have to wait for the *maître*, sir," she replied politely.

"I will not wait, you young upstart." Picking up a foil, the Creole tossed it to the stunned youngster. "You will practice with me, and I'll teach you some manners. *En garde.*"

"*Pardon.*" Claude Galvez, Serge's prize student, elbowed Jean-Paul aside. "M'sieur Baudin, I was just looking for a partner. Shall we?"

Marcel's icy glare rested on the young man a long moment, then he shrugged negligently. "Why not? I hear you're becoming quite good, Galvez. At least you'll be more of a challenge than this country bumpkin."

"At the very least," Claude responded smoothly.

Grateful, Simone escaped to stand near the door. Watching the fencers, she wished she were skilled enough to have accepted Marcel's challenge.

"That was close," Fabrice muttered in her ear. "I don't like this."

She glanced over her shoulder. "I didn't see you come in."

"I'm not surprised. Baudin seemed to be holding your attention quite completely," he said grimly. "I need to talk to you, Simone. Meet me tonight at St. Anthony's Garden."

"Are you challenging me, too?" She grinned, for the garden behind the cathedral was a frequent site of duels.

"Just be there." Frowning his annoyance, her cousin hurried across the *salle* to join his friends.

* * *

Simone loped along rue Royal, relishing the cool of the evening. It was the best part of the day in the summer, she decided, when most of the Creoles went to the country to escape the heat and the threat of yellow fever, leaving the Vieux Carré uncrowded.

In the dusk, the city seemed deserted. Those who had not left were at their dinners in the galleried world above the narrow streets. Large families dined al fresco, their voices and the tinkle of silver on china reaching Simone's ears pleasantly as she followed a path into the tiny, serene garden.

"Simone." She heard Fabrice's hushed call.

"Jean-Paul," she muttered stubbornly, locating her cousin behind an azalea bush.

"Did you know your guardian has returned?" he asked without preamble when she joined him. "He rode out to LeFleur yesterday."

"I knew he was going to," she acknowledged airily, dropping down beside him on a bench.

"How did you know?"

"I heard him say so."

"You saw him? Where? When? Did he see you?"

Simone peered at him through the dimness and decided to answer only the last question. "He may have seen me, but he would hardly have noticed me as a boy."

"It's only a matter of time before he recognizes you—even in that outrageous costume," Fabrice fumed.

"I can fool him," she boasted, sounding much like the cocky lad she impersonated.

"I wish I was as sure of that as you seem to be."

"What did Alain say to your parents?" she asked calmly.

Fabrice frowned, remembering how his cousin had adored de Vallière when she was a child—it had been the first time he ever felt jealousy—then suddenly, for some reason, came to hate him. Fabrice decided to keep that animosity alive.

"Alain is not happy to be a guardian, and even more

unhappy to discover your own family does not know where you are. I think he believes you're hiding just to spite him."

"Oh, does he?" Her voice was mild. "And did he say what his plans are?"

"To fulfill his duty, I suppose," he answered carelessly.

"To find a husband for me? Well, he must find me first." Turning to Fabrice, she entreated, "Promise me you will not give me away."

Staring down at her in the moonlight, he would have promised her anything. Even the unbecoming garb she wore could not disguise the Simone he loved. "I would never give you away, *chère*," he vowed huskily.

"I know, *cousin. Merci*." Rising, she planted a delicate kiss on his cheek.

Before he could respond, she was gone. He stepped out onto the *banquette*, straining to see his beloved in the darkness. Her hands shoved into her pockets, she sauntered along the shadowy streets, looking every inch a street urchin.

Sighing deeply, Fabrice turned and trudged away.

4

The heat of the day lingered, and evening promised to become sultry night. Alone in the *salle*, Simone practiced lunges in front of the open door. Not a breath of air stirred in the twilight, and the target affixed to a post in front of her hung limp as she lunged and withdrew. Outfitted in castoffs from Claude Galvez, she sweltered in the heat. Sweat stained her quilted jacket and beaded on her upper lip. It rolled from her short hair onto her forehead, then dripped off the end of her nose.

"This is for Marcel," she muttered under her breath as the buttoned tip of her sword found the center of the target. A regular visitor to the *salle*, the scarred Creole had taken a dislike to Jean-Paul. It seemed no matter how Simone tried to avoid him, he was there to torment her.

"Here is one for Fabrice." She lunged again, remembering her cousin's reaction when she told him that Serge was teaching her to fence. Fabrice had forbidden her to undertake the training.

Straightening slowly, she resumed her original stance and prepared to lunge again. But her mind strayed to the conversation she had overheard that afternoon.

Alain and Serge had sat at the maître's customary table, sipping coffee, when the fencing master asked, "Still no news of your little ward, 'Lain? What is her name?"

"Simone Devereaux." She had been gratified to see Alain's lips tighten at the very thought of her. "No, I've been to every hospital, to the police, even to the morgue. I've kept in touch with Nicholas's attorney and talked to the neighbors. I've put up flyers with her description from here to St. Martinville. No one has seen her."

"You think she may have met with foul play?"

Alain uttered a sharp bark of laughter. "Not likely, since Fusilier mysteriously receives two dollars from her every week. I think she is hiding from me, though God only knows why. She's stubborn and independent, but we always got along well enough. A fine task my old friend set for me, to marry off his prickly daughter. Where will I find a husband strong enough to take Simone in hand? And when I find him, do I offer him a dowry or my sympathy?"

"From what you tell me of your 'little spitfire,' perhaps you should offer both," Serge teased.

"Well, the sooner I find my 'little spitfire,' the sooner I can find a husband for her. And the sooner I'm free of that obligation, the happier I'll be," Alain had said as the men returned to their fencing practice, never noticing Jean-Paul's furious gaze following them balefully from the equipment room.

"Men," Simone said scornfully in the silence of the *salle*. She lunged with deadly accuracy, the tip of her sword snagging the target from its post. "And that is for you, M'sieur de Vallière," she whispered, feeling slightly better.

"Psst, Jean-Paul."

Simone turned to see Obadiah peering through the

open doorway. Though he frequently visited, he never entered the *salle*.

Cutting the air lackadaisically with her sword, she managed to rid herself of the target clinging to its tip. She swooped up the rough piece of canvas and wiped her wet face with it as she joined Obadiah on the landing.

"You finished murderin' that pole, Jean-Paul?" he greeted her with a chuckle.

"It was self-defense," she replied with a cocky grin.

"Uh-huh," Obadiah responded dubiously. Reaching into his pocket, he pulled out a lint-covered praline and broke it, offering her half.

"*Merci*." Simone accepted the candy, removing the worst of the fuzz before she took a bite.

"You wanna go giggin' for frogs tonight?" her friend asked as they chewed the sticky praline.

"I'd like to go," she said regretfully, "but I promised Claude Galvez I would go to a party. It's his eighteenth birthday."

"Where is this party?"

"On rue Dauphine. He said it was a white house with a red door."

Obadiah stared at Jean-Paul goggle-eyed and asked, "You sure you wanna go?"

His skinny young friend scowled at him impatiently. "Are you going to say the same thing as Eugène, that I am too young?"

"I ain't sayin' nothin', 'cept I don't wanna see you get in no trouble," Obadiah replied, unaware of the volcano of feminine ire threatening to erupt from beneath Jean-Paul's scruffy facade.

Men! They were always trying to tell her what to do. Even Obadiah! Frowning, Simone declared, "I won't get into any trouble."

"It's jest you gotta be careful," the Negro boy warned. "That Galvez is pretty wild."

"Claude has looked out for me almost since the day I got here." Simone defended the young blade, unwilling to hear any criticism of him since he had rescued her from Marcel's challenge.

The well-intentioned Claude had taken Serge's assistant under his wing, sometimes to Simone's discomfiture. While he protected her from the persecution of the other students, including his own best friend, Eugène Moreau, he sought to make a man of Jean-Paul, hauling him to cockfights, card games, and duels at Trois Capelines.

"I know he's your friend," Obadiah said soothingly, "but he's a lot older than you, an'—"

"I can take care of myself," she cut in with an intractable glint in her eye.

"Do what you want," Obie sighed, unwilling to argue. "Jest don't say I didn't warn you."

That night, as Jean-Paul and Claude stood with a half dozen other young men in the foyer of the house on rue Dauphine, Simone wished Obadiah had been a bit more specific in his counsel.

"Hello, boys. *Bonsoir*, messieurs." Before the burly doorman had even closed the door, bold voices called down from the top of the stairs. Simone looked up to see two girls leaning over the banister, blowing kisses to the young swains below. She stared up at them in horror, her eyes widening. They wore nothing more than silk kimonos. Deliberately they descended the staircase, each step revealing lengths of creamy leg.

The rhythmic pounding of a piano came from the parlor as another scantily clad woman opened the sliding doors to their right and beckoned invitingly. "Come in, gentlemen."

"*Bonsoir*, Sally," Claude greeted the woman familiarly as she took his hat and handed him a snifter of brandy.

Simone stopped in the doorway beside the worldly young Creole and gawked. Inside were several more young women, wearing kimonos and little else. For the past few months she had often seen men naked from the waist up. She hardly even noticed anymore. But never in her life had she seen women in such advanced stages of undress. And they seemed absolutely at ease, draping themselves over the nearest available male lap.

Her face aflame, Simone tried to back out of the room, but Claude threw a comradely arm around her narrow shoulders and herded her into the room. Before she could think, she blurted out, *"Mon Dieu*, Claude, you've brought me to a—a brothel."

"A house of assignations," he corrected with a smirk. "The nicest in the city. Pay attention, young friend," he instructed, pushing her into a chair. "Maybe you'll learn something."

"Cigar, M'sieur Galvez?" The woman called Sally returned with a brass-hinged humidor.

"Merci," Claude accepted. "Is Mademoiselle Dupré in this evening?"

"She is. She will be out later to wish you a happy birthday."

Simone glanced up at the suave young man and was surprised to see his fair face mottled with red.

"Lisette Dupré is so beautiful. Just wait until you see her," Claude murmured abashedly to Jean-Paul and downed his drink. Pulling the younger lad to his feet, he instructed gruffly, "Come on, let's get something to eat."

He dragged Simone to a table laden with food and insisted she fill her plate. "You're a growing boy, after all," he insisted, already sounding tipsy.

Simone choked down her food as she watched her companions fondling the women they held in their laps. Between lascivious kisses and bold caresses, they all drank heavily. Choked by cigar smoke and the smell of perfume, she couldn't breathe. Rising, she edged toward the door.

"Where are you going, Jean-Paul?" Claude shouted over the noise, catching her when she would have slipped out.

"I was . . . I was going to get some air." She looked

at him guiltily over her shoulder.

"The patio is that way." He pointed his big black cigar toward a pair of French doors on the far side of the room.

Simone's blush deepened when a couple passed, hand in hand, a giggling girl leading one of the young men upstairs. She fled outside and breathed the muggy night air in deep gulps, her breasts straining against the binding she wore beneath her shirt.

Then she explored the tiny well-kept courtyard by the light pouring through the open windows, searching in vain for a way out. The walls were high and she found nothing but a wrought-iron bench that she might use as a ladder. She tried to move the massive bench, but it would not budge. Winded from the exertion, she gave up at last and went back into the house.

In the parlor, she found the smoke thicker and the music louder, though the number of guests had dwindled. She knew without asking where they'd gone: upstairs with *les filles de joie*. The daughters of joy, indeed, she fumed as she strode decisively to her host.

"Claude, thank you for inviting me," she said, shaking his hand, "but I must go."

"What's your hurry?" the young Creole asked merrily. "I have big plans for you. Tonight, my boy, I have arranged for you to become a man." He swayed on his feet and winked with drunken good humor.

"*Non.*" She protested his unmistakable intent, trying to keep the desperation from her voice as she backed away. "*Non, merci.*"

"Can you believe the boy would pass up such an opportunity?" Claude asked the others watching the exchange. Shaking their heads, they bellowed with laughter.

"Consider it a part of your education, Jean-Paul," Claude said magnanimously, refusing to release her hand. "My oldest brother did it for me, and now I do it for you."

"I don't think I'm ready." She nearly danced backward in her attempt to escape, but she could not free herself.

"Jean-Paul has no appreciation for your gift, Claude," Eugène chortled, seizing Simone's other arm. Now even the piano player was watching the scene taking place. "It seems a shame to carry him upstairs kicking and screaming."

"He'll thank us for it later." Claude grinned, passing his drink to one of the women. "Get his feet, someone."

Whooping with laughter, two other young men leapt to obey, each catching one of Jean-Paul's flailing legs.

"Shall we take him to Yolanda's room?" Eugène suggested, enjoying himself immensely.

"She seems to be the woman of the greatest experience," Claude answered judiciously.

"You motherless, misbegotten snakes, put me down, damn you!" Simone howled furiously, drawing upon the vocabulary she had learned in the *salle*. The four young men gathered around Jean-Paul laughed uproariously, as they hauled the lad into the foyer.

Simone arched her back and writhed in an attempt to break free. "Give me a sword, you bastards," she panted fiercely, "and I'll fight any or all of you, but I'm not going up those stairs."

"Don't be afraid, little man," Eugène teased, "we're going with you, as far as Yolanda's door."

"Then you're on your own," guffawed one of the fellows who held her feet.

She continued to twist, straining frenziedly when she felt the bindings around her breasts slipping and her collar button give way. By the time they finished with her, everyone would know she was a girl, she thought, panic-stricken.

She cursed even more loudly and jerked convulsively. "You can't do this!" she yelled. "Claude, make them let me go!"

"Indeed, Monsieur Galvez, make them let him go

before his shrieking drives all my guests away," a female voice commanded lightly, stopping the young men in their tracks. All Simone could see was the skirt of the woman's rich brocade dress.

"Mam'selle Lisette!" Claude breathed, and he immediately loosened his hold. Simone's arm slipped through his lax fingers, and her head and one shoulder hit the floor with a thump.

Twisting to the side, Simone busied herself prying at Eugène's fingers with her free hand, while he too stared, transfixed, at the woman. With a distracted frown at the determined Jean-Paul, Eugène released his grip, so Simone's entire torso now rested on the floor. She propped herself on her elbows and pumped her feet furiously, scooting backward at the same time to slip from the others' grasp.

"And where were you taking this little fish, messieurs? From the looks of him, you should throw him back until he grows," the cultured voice teased.

"W-We were going to give him a night to remember, mam'selle," Claude stammered.

"I'll remember well enough," Simone muttered with a dire glare for him. She scrambled to her feet and looked directly at the madam of the house of assignations, the woman who had just rescued her.

Lisette Dupré was the most beautiful woman she had ever seen, Simone thought at once. Tall and willowy, she carried herself regally, her head held high on a slender white neck. Her hair was so blond it was almost white, but the brows and lashes framing her wideset gray eyes were several shades darker. One eyebrow arched higher than the other, giving her face a droll expressiveness.

The eyebrow was cocked wryly now as the woman jested gently, "We always try to give our gentlemen what they want, M'sieur Galvez, but we never force it on them. Go now and enjoy your birthday. You shouldn't have to worry about your young friend tonight. He can be my guest until you are ready to leave."

Wordlessly, Claude bowed and pressed an ardent kiss on Lisette's hand. Then he led his guests back into the parlor, where the piano playing resumed at once.

"This way, young man," Lisette instructed the lad who stared belligerently after Claude. Sweeping along a hall beside the stairs, she opened the door to an elegant parlor. "Sit down," she invited, gesturing toward a settee.

Nervously, Simone obeyed. Perched on the edge of her seat, she surveyed the madam's airy, feminine suite.

Through an open door, she could see a luxurious bedroom. Against the opposite wall stood a table, its legs adorned with intricate carving. Above it hung a huge mirror, and reflected in it Simone saw, an ornate chiffonier and Lisette's tester bed, awash in soft light from a sconce. In the shadows on the far side of the room, the door to a tiny dressing room stood ajar, revealing the edge of a porcelain bathtub. Simone looked at it longingly.

"I was about to have some *café*," Lisette Dupré said cordially. "Will you join me?"

"*Oui, merci*," Simone murmured. Suddenly the language she had used in her ire, language she had seldom heard and never spoken before a few months ago, flooded back to her, and she blushed. Miserably aware of her rumpled clothes and the way her hair stood up all over her head, she unconsciously smoothed her errant locks and sat up a little straighter.

Lisette watched Jean-Paul closely. "If we are to have *café* together, perhaps you could tell me your name."

"Jean-Paul Sonnier," Simone answered in a low voice, afraid she would give herself away. She had not been around a woman since she had assumed her disguise.

"I am Lisette Dupré. You may call me Lisette if I may call you Jean-Paul." She had a strange expression in her gray eyes.

"Very well . . . Lisette," Simone said shyly.

While Lisette poured the *café*, Simone realized there were already two cups, two saucers—two of everything—on the tray.

"I suspected I was going to have company," the madam explained casually when she saw her curious glance. "I saw you in the garden, trying to escape, but you went back inside before I could show you the way out."

"Thank you for rescuing me," Simone said sincerely.

"You are most welcome." Lisette handed Jean-Paul a cup, then sat back with her own. Stirring it studiedly, she asked, "Will you not tell me what kind of trouble you're in, *ma chère*?"

Simone stared at her, shocked. "Wh-what are you talking about?"

"I'm talking about a girl dressed in boy's clothing."

"You know," Simone whispered apprehensively. "But how?"

"A few unguarded mannerisms. Your face, your hands—they are too fine, too delicate. Your feet are too small for a growing boy."

"Do you think anyone else knows?"

"*Non*, not among your friends."

"Friends," Simone said sharply.

"Not the sort an innocent girl should have, perhaps, but they thought they were doing Jean-Paul a favor," Lisette pointed out, one brow arched in amusement. "What is your name, *ma petite*?"

"Simone."

"Will you tell me the reason for this masquerade?" the woman asked quietly.

Undone by the tumultuous evening, disarmed by Lisette's genuine kindness, and oddly unburdened at being herself for the first time in many weeks, Simone was amazed to find the story—or parts of it, anyway—pouring out of her. She told of her father's death, of Marcel's threats against her, of her uncle's plans for her, of her daring scheme to live in the *salle d'armes*.

"Isn't there anyone to serve as your protector?"

Lisette asked when Simone had finished.

"No one," the girl lied, knowing somehow Lisette would insist she notify her guardian. "I'm doing all right," she maintained stubbornly. "Each week I pay a little more toward my father's debts. I am my own person. And I'm safe as Jean-Paul."

"If you don't go to any more parties with Claude," Lisette amended wryly. She was silent for a moment, then she asked, "What if I paid off Monsieur Baudin, so you could come out of hiding?"

Simone's chin shot up proudly. "Paying my father's debts—all of them—is my duty."

"Be reasonable, *chère.*"

"Even if I allowed it, Marcel wouldn't." Simone's shoulders slumped, and she said sadly, "My aunt wanted to repay him, but he threatened to charge me with attempted murder unless I became a servant in his house."

"Don't you mean his mistress?" Lisette asked.

"*Oui.*" Simone nodded glumly. "So you can see, I'm better off where I am for now. I hope he will find someone else to interest him soon and abandon his search for me. Then I can pay my father's gambling debts and be free of Marcel."

Lisette pondered the matter, but she could see no ready solution to the girl's problem. The Baudin heir was as powerful as he was cruel. He had been banned from her house after he beat one of her girls for accidentally scratching his flawless face. What would he do to Simone if he found her now?

"*Très bien.*" She shuddered delicately. "I'll keep your secret, 'Jean-Paul.' Is there anything I can do to help?"

"There is one thing," Simone answered wistfully.

"Name it, *ma petite.*"

"May I come here one day and take a bath, a real bath?"

"You may come here every day and take a bath." Lisette smiled.

"I don't think that's a good idea, but I'd like to come soon, if you don't mind."

"Come tomorrow. I'll make sure you have privacy, and some time to be Simone."

"*Merci*. You are kind." She smiled in anticipated pleasure.

The very next day, Jean-Paul sauntered into the house on rue Dauphine and, in the seclusion of the madam's suite, was transformed into pretty Simone Devereaux, if only for a few hours.

She lingered in the tub until the water was cold and her skin white and puckered. She lathered herself several times for the sheer, luxurious pleasure of it, and she washed her hair at least five times.

"Oh dear," Lisette fretted when she saw the dingy tinge to the water, "you've been darkening your hair with *café*. We must do something about that." She hastened from the room and returned with a bottle of dye. Simone allowed her to apply it, grateful she would not have to worry about her hair lightening day by day. It was a wonder, she realized, that no one had yet noticed the faint aroma of coffee that clung to Jean-Paul.

Stepping into the bedroom, Simone found the drapes drawn to guard against prying eyes. On the bed was spread a feminine robe. With an excited cry, she put it on and went into the parlor for supper with Lisette.

In the days that followed, Simone's visits became a habit both women enjoyed. During the suppers that followed her baths, they laughed and talked, the difference in their ages forgotten, as if Simone were not seventeen and Lisette, thirty. Simone listened to her new friend's story with the same compassion the madam had shown her.

When her entire family was wiped out by yellow fever, Lisette had found herself, like Simone, at the mercy of an unscrupulous man. She, too, had decided to live life on her own terms. Unwilling to be any man's mistress, she had opened the house of assignations in order to be her own. Her bordello, discreet and elegant, catered to some of New Orleans's finest citizens. While Lisette did not entertain customers herself, she candidly admitted she had no illusions about her profession and no regrets.

"Why should you?" Simone asked. "You are a good person. That is what is important."

And, indeed, as unlikely a pair as they were, Lisette was becoming the mother Simone had never had.

Rapping lightly on the dressing room door, Lisette thrust an arm in. "Here's a lamp so you can see what you're washing," she teased, setting it on a table near the tub. In the flickering light, Nicholas's ring blazed with green fire.

"*Merci*," Simone replied, opening drowsy emerald eyes. "I'll hurry and finish. I did not realize it was so late." The evening sun's last rays angled over the garden wall outside the tiny window and filtered softly through the lace curtains.

"You needed the rest." Lisette frowned in concern at the exhausted girl. "You work too hard at the *salle*. Take your time with your bath. I must check a few things before my guests arrive for the evening. We'll have supper when I return."

"All right." Simone eased even deeper into the water, its lulling warmth making her sleepy. She heard Lisette lighting the sconces in the bedroom, but she hardly knew when the woman slipped out of the suite. She must have dozed for a time, but she awoke when she heard a noise from the other room.

"I'm coming," she cried, rising at once, dripping water as she reached for a towel. Stepping from the tub, she wrapped the towel around herself and gathered it over her breasts as she hurried into the bedroom, where her clothes awaited her on the bed. About to let her scanty covering drop, she called, "I'll be ready in just a moment."

"Don't hurry on my account," a deep, rich voice teased.

Simone whirled with a gasp, clutching the towel more tightly. In the doorway, Alain de Vallière slouched, one broad shoulder braced against the jamb as he watched her.

He had no idea where Lisette had found her, the tall Creole thought appreciatively, but the girl was magnificent. Flickering light from the sconce beside the door gilded her ivory skin, and her short black hair curled in damp tendrils around a delicate, heart-shaped face.

Before she looked away, he saw her blush. Now, there was something you did not see every day, he mused. And the warm color had only enhanced her loveliness. His gaze lowered to where droplets of water from her bath sparkled like diamonds in the hollow of her throat. His eyes dipped to the shadowed cleavage at the top of her towel before drifting down to her shapely legs.

Simone's breath quickened at his leisurely perusal, but when his dark eyes rose to meet hers, he showed no sign of recognition. She was perplexed to find disappointment mingling with her relief that he did not know her.

"What . . . what are you doing here?" Finding her voice at last, she drew herself up to confront the intruder.

"I thought to find my old friend, Lisette." A lazy smile lurked at one corner of his full lips. "But suddenly I find I want more than a friendly chat over a cup of tea."

"Then you've come to the right place, m'sieur," she retorted mockingly, wondering why she should care that Alain visited a brothel.

"I believe I have," the man drawled flirtatiously.

Simone looked away, flustered, her eyes falling upon her clothes folded at the foot of the bed. If she had not wanted him to recognize her as his ward, she wanted him to realize she was Jean-Paul even less. To block his

view of the garments, she stepped around the bed.
"Won't you make yourself comfortable in the parlor,
m'sieur?" she invited Lisette's guest politely.

"I am very comfortable here." Crossing one ankle
over the other, he shifted contentedly in the doorway.
"I think I'll stay, if you don't mind."

"I do mind," Simone snapped, glaring at him. "I
would like to get dressed now."

"Be my guest." He nodded accommodatingly but
made no attempt to move.

The nerve of the man, she seethed inwardly. Perhaps if
she went about the business of laying out her wardrobe
and ignored him, he would go away, she mused. But she
could hardly reveal Jean-Paul's costume. Ever her father's
daughter, Simone decided to bluff. Clutching her towel
around her, she turned a haughty shoulder toward Alain
and sidled between the bed and the chiffonier in the corner. Opening the wardrobe, she chose one of Lisette's day
gowns and laid it on the bed.

"It seems a shame to cover those enticing curves," he
commented.

"It would be a greater shame if I caught my death of
cold because you did not allow me to dress," she
responded tartly.

"I wouldn't mind keeping you undressed," he said
with a mellow laugh, "until I had time to get to know
you . . . very well."

Her face flushed crimson, but she refused to let him
have the upper hand. "I can see you wouldn't mind if I
suffered discomfort at your hands," she accused from
her corner.

"Discomfort is not what you would suffer at my
hands, *chère*." Alain stepped into the room and faced
her. His broad shoulders blocked the light from the
lamp behind him, and she could not see his face, but
his voice, husky with desire, thrilled her. He reached
out and ran his hand down her arm, feeling the goose-
flesh his touch brought.

"Go away," she beseeched, retreating a step, holding her towel tightly in place.

"Why so coy, *ma petite*?" One muscular arm snaked out and caught her by the waist, pulling her against him, trapping her arms against his hard chest.

"You don't understand," she said, panicking. She had felt an odd excitement when he had not recognized her, but now she realized with shock that he thought her one of Lisette's *filles de joie*. She looked around desperately, but she had unwittingly worked herself into a position from which there was no escape. "Please, I have to get dressed."

"A waste of time. I would just have to undress you again," he murmured, his mouth dipping to claim hers.

Her beautiful face pale in the dimness, the girl stiffened in his arms, her hands straining against his chest. But after a moment, Alain felt her resistance slip into tremulous uncertainty. And as her response shifted like a dazzling kaleidoscope into passionate intensity, he felt an explosion of desire such as he had never experienced before.

Her head dropped back into his cradling hand, her short curls feathering over his fingers, as her lips parted beneath his, inviting his tongue to plumb the sweet, warm depths of her mouth.

Alain drew a ragged breath and looked down at her in amazement. Her lips were slack and slightly parted, her eyes closed, the lashes a dark fringe against cheeks now colored a delicate pink. Her arms, no longer trapped, slid up instinctively to wrap around his neck, releasing the towel, which fell to the floor, unnoticed.

"You are lovely, *chère*," he whispered against the pulse that pounded in her throat, matching the beating of his heart. He had intended this kiss as a promise of the things to come when she would take him to her room, but now, as she filled his arms and his senses, he thought only of the here and the now.

Simone shuddered with each new wave of white-hot sensation Alain's touch brought. Though his kisses were demanding, they were strangely gentle, not harsh and cruel like Marcel's. Neither were they shy, chaste kisses like the ones Fabrice had stolen on occasion. She tilted her face unthinkingly toward his, her lips seeking more of what he offered.

With a groan deep in his throat, he cupped her buttocks in his big hands, lifting her from the ground to mold her against his long, hard body as he trailed kisses along her bare shoulders.

Held halfway between heaven and earth, Simone suddenly realized she had lost her towel, and his shirt studs now bit into her naked breasts. Feeling his need jutting so firmly against her very core, she came abruptly to her senses, shocked at her intense response to his kisses. She had to escape the frightening firestorm he ignited in her.

"Let me go, m'sieur," she insisted shakily, pushing at his broad shoulders. Her knees felt weak, from panic and something more, and she hoped she would be able to stand when he released her.

"*Non.*" His voice was muffled as he buried his face between her breasts.

"Please!" she nearly sobbed as his mouth found the peak of one breast, his lips fastening on it with tender purpose. She squirmed wildly at the unfamiliar sensation, trying to escape his grasp. "Put me down."

Her contortions only brought a tortured moan from him. "Enough games, girl," he said hoarsely, his hands tightening as he draped her on the edge of the bed, leaving her legs dangling over the side. Watching her with smoldering intensity, he leaned against her, his powerful thighs bracketing her legs so she could not escape.

"I am not playing games," Simone countered desperately, futilely trying to tug herself free.

"No?" he said, smiling wickedly as he stripped off his jacket.

She stared up at him in fascinated dread, far more frightened of him now than she had been at thirteen.

"Alain de Vallière, what do you think you're doing?"

Lisette snapped from the doorway.

Her eyes wide with horror, the girl froze while Alain swung to look at the woman with a perplexed frown.

The moment she was free, Simone rolled on her shoulder, landing on her feet on the other side of the bed. Snatching up her clothes, she scampered into the dressing room and slammed the door behind her.

Alain frowned toward the noise, but he bowed politely and said, "Lisette, please accept my apologies. This is my fault."

"I have no doubt, you scoundrel," she said coldly.

Her words took him by surprise. "I said I'm sorry, Lise. I'll even say it to her if you like." His eyes rested on the closed door. "I realize I've committed a great breach in etiquette, trying to take one of your girls in your own bed. I don't know what came over me."

"I know what came over you," Lisette exploded. "You saw a pretty girl and had to prove your prowess. You men are all alike."

He winced. "Bitter words from an old friend, but I probably deserve them."

"'Probably'? You try to seduce an innocent guest in my house, and you say 'probably'?"

"A guest," he repeated dumbly. "But I thought—"

"I know what you thought," she cut him off, "if you thought anything at all."

"*Mon Dieu*," Alain said, sitting on the edge of the bed, "what have I done? I must have scared her to death."

"You must have," Lisette answered, slightly mollified by his obvious remorse.

"I must apologize." Striding to the door, he rapped softly. "Mam'selle."

When there was no answer, he knocked again. "Please, open the door. I'm terribly sorry. What's her name, Lisette?"

"I will not say."

Alain glowered at her, but he spoke persuasively through the closed door. "Mam'selle, what I did was inexcusable. I . . . I didn't know you were a guest, and I've seldom seen such a vision of beauty." He waited, but no sound came from within.

"Say you'll forgive me," he coaxed and, again meeting silence. "Say something," he tried with dwindling patience.

"Mam'sclle!" he roared through the door. "I am trying to apologize, and I would prefer to do so face to face."

"That should allay her fears nicely," Lisette said with a withering look. "Let me see if she is all right.

"It's me, *ma chère*," she called softly as she rapped on the closed door. Trying the knob, she found it unlocked.

Alain watched as the woman opened the door slightly and peered inside. Without a word she threw the door open so he could see. The room was empty.

"She's gone. But how?" Suddenly the curtains, waving gently on the night breeze, caught his eye. "She went out the window," he answered his own question wonderingly.

"*Oui*, she went out the window," Lisette echoed flatly. "Come into the parlor, Alain, and I will give you a drink. Though why I should, I don't know."

As she marched from the dressing room, Alain did not notice her hand furtively sweeping the top of the table beside the bathtub and pocketing the ring Simone had left. He lingered to thrust his head out the tiny window and stare at the moonlit garden, but there was no one to be seen. As he pulled back inside, he cracked his head smartly on the sash.

"*Zut*," he swore. The little vixen had gotten away, and he did not know who she was or how to find her. As he rubbed his head, he watched Lisette speculatively through the open door as she settled in the parlor.

"Lisette . . . ," he began.

"No, Alain, and that is that," she replied, implacable.

Knowing she would not tell him what he wanted to know, he followed her, in a foul mood.

5

When Alain appeared at the *salle* the next day with a forbidding frown on his handsome face, Simone waited nervously to see if he would recognize her as the girl from Lisette's bedroom. Even worse to contemplate was the possibility that he would recognize Jean-Paul as his wayward charge. When he did not, her relief gave way to anger at the events of the night past.

Alain had stared at her as if she were a plum ripe for taking, she seethed, conveniently forgetting where he had found her. He had touched her where no man had ever touched her. And he would have bedded her whether she wanted it or not.

She had not wanted it, she told herself firmly. But the memory of his caresses—and her wanton response to them—brought a stain of color to Jean-Paul's cheeks as he went about his tasks. Who knew what might have happened if Lisette had not interrupted them. Thank *le bon Dieu* the woman had shown her the hidden gate in the garden wall so she could come and go without detection.

Throughout the afternoon, Alain engaged in loose play with one opponent after another, leaving them

breathless and exhausted. When he had taken the edge
off his anger and was dripping with sweat, he stripped
to the waist and went to the water bucket. He drank
from the gourd ladle, then sluiced some of the water
over his shoulders and splashed the remainder in his
face. But when he reached for the towel that hung on a
peg nearby, it was gone.

"Jean-Paul!" he grumbled, his irritation not as dull as
he had thought. "Bring a towel, boy, and be quick."

"Get your own damn towel," Jean-Paul grumbled.
"I'm busy."

The man's fury turned into wry amusement as he
observed the boy marking off the *piste* for a match.
What had gotten into the lad? Jean-Paul's face was set
and angry, and he seemed to be muttering under his
breath. Shaking his head, Alain decided to leave him
alone. One day he would teach the Maître's assistant a
lesson, but today was not the day.

That evening, as Simone walked through Exchange
Alley, Claude summoned from a *banquette* café.
Because she could see no way to avoid it, she ambled to
where he, Eugène, and four other young men lounged
at a table, its top cluttered with heavy white cups and
the crumbs of the *beignets* they had consumed.

"*Bonsoir*, Claude, messieurs." Her nod included all
of them.

"Where are you going, *mon ami*?" Claude asked,
taking the lad aside when the others returned to their
conversations.

"To run an errand," she answered vaguely.

"You wouldn't by any chance be delivering a message for Pierre Bordelon to his beloved Fatima?"

"*Oui*," she admitted reluctantly. She was not surprised he had easily guessed her errand. Everyone in the
salle knew of Pierre's involvement with Fatima, a dancer
who performed in one of the seedy taverns of The

Swamp. And everyone knew his family was in town, making it impossible for him to risk going to see her.

"So you're going to The Swamp." Claude frowned disapprovingly. "Do you know what goes on there? It's the reason New Orleans is called The Wickedest City in the World. It is home to rivermen, gamblers, murderers, rapists, thieves—"

"I might have a better chance with them than with some Creole gentlemen I know," she snapped; she had not forgiven the night at the house on rue Dauphine.

Claude looked pained. "I apologized for that. And you were the winner anyway. You're the one who spends time now with Mam'selle Lisette in her private apartment."

"What do you mean by that?" Jean-Paul demanded truculently.

"What I said and nothing more. I wouldn't speak ill of the lady. She is perfect, and I wish . . ." The young Creole sighed. "Never mind. She looks at me as if I were her idiot brother."

"Perhaps you are the idiot brother she never had," Simone retorted.

Claude scowled. "Mind what you say, Jean-Paul. I don't want to end up under the Oaks with you." Rising, he picked up his hat and looked at his young friend expectantly. "Let's go."

"Where are *you* going?" Simone asked hotly.

"With you, to The Swamp."

"The Swamp?" Eugène asked, curious, catching the attention of the others.

"*Oui*. Jean-Paul has an errand to run, and I'm going with him."

Simone considered protesting, but secretly she was glad of Claude's company. She was already beginning to doubt the wisdom of carrying a message to The Swamp.

"You must be taking Bordelon's message to Fatima." Eugène nodded knowingly. "I believe I'll go along and see her for myself."

"We all will," another of them cried.

"*Oui*," the others agreed in unison.

"I don't need you treading on my heels," Simone complained.

"Consider us your bodyguards, Jean-Paul, since Serge won't let you wear a sword yet," Eugène teased.

Eager for excitement, the Creoles set out on foot. Crossing to the American Section, they followed a rutted street to the heart of The Swamp, the road at the river's edge. The stench of raw waste in the gutters was nearly unbearable in the summer heat.

The squalid street, lined on both sides by barrooms, was nearly impassable, teeming with tough, menacing-looking men. Scantily clad, grotesquely painted women seemed to occupy every window, upstairs and down, along the thoroughfare. Their raucous laughter and shrill, suggestive calls to passersby rent the air.

Along the river, tin-roofed shanties seemed to lean against the levee. Behind them, keelboats moored side by side formed almost a solid walkway across the water. Because the level of the Mississippi was higher than New Orleans, the boats seemed to loom over the hovels in the darkness.

When the party reached its destination, the young rakes clambered onto the porch and swaggered into the bar.

"Give me the note, and I'll take it to Fatima," Claude ordered Jean-Paul.

"Pierre told *me* to deliver it," Simone argued, but just then a body flew through the swinging doors, landing facedown in the dirt. The unfortunate lay where he fell, groggily shaking his head. Without a word, she handed the note to Claude.

"I will be right back. Eugène and his cronies think this is a great adventure, but I'll be ready to go as soon as I deliver this," the young Creole muttered as he went inside.

Simone was inclined to agree. She waited on the

porch, trying to shrink into the shadows. Across the street, a brawl spilled out of another tavern, attracting a crowd. She watched in horror as the combatants rose unsteadily and slashed at each other with razors before passing out in a sodden heap.

Even in her guise as a boy she was uneasy. Shrugging her narrow shoulders, she looked around anxiously, wishing her companions would return.

At that very moment Eugène did. He lurched backward through the doorway, powered by a mighty punch. Claude and the others followed, swords drawn, as they retreated from a rabble armed with hefty staffs and wicked-looking knives. The dandies from the *salle* were clearly receiving the worst of it.

Just in front of Simone, a burly Kaintock slammed his stick across Claude's shoulders. Giving a strangled cry, Simone launched herself from the porch and landed on the brute's broad back, kicking and hitting. When he recovered from his surprise, the big men swatted at the youngster who clung to his back. His beefy hand caught her on the side of the head, setting her ears to ringing, but she did not let go.

Bellowing with annoyance, he whirled and bucked, trying to rid himself of the pest. Over his shoulder, Simone caught a glimpse of Claude, watching wide-eyed as Jean-Paul's legs flew out behind him, leveling anyone in the path of his swinging feet. Still she held tight, her arms wrapped tight around the man's grimy neck.

Suddenly Simone was yanked backward, lifted by the scruff of her neck and the seat of her pants. Flailing and hollering, she fought. She folded her body, jack-knifing, then suddenly straightened with all her might to aim a kick at her captor's shins. She was rewarded by a muttered curse before a big hand tightened painfully on the back of her neck, and a voice growled, "You're coming with me, young man."

Her unseen captor maintained his hold on both her

neck and her pants, thrusting her ahead of him like the prow of a ship. As they cut through the fracas, she saw that the Creoles had turned the tables and seemed to be having the time of their lives. At the fringe of the brawl, Simone was set on her feet with a jolt.

"I ought to leave you here, you little barbarian, but I wouldn't do that to them." Alain de Vallière scowled at the disheveled lad.

Alain again! Simone nearly groaned aloud. Then, regaining Jean-Paul's feisty composure, she snapped, "You let me go. I've got to help my friends."

The hand on her neck tensed, reminding her who was in control. "They seem to be doing well enough," Alain observed.

"I won't leave them."

"You'll come, my boy, if I have to carry you."

Afraid he would do just that, Simone allowed him to steer her through dark, deserted streets, the fight having lured everyone to the waterfront.

As they walked, Jean-Paul's hair curled over Alain's fingers, bringing back an indistinct sense of déjà vu. Funny it should be so soft, he thought, glancing down at the sulky boy who walked beside him, his hands in his pockets and his head lowered. Alain ruffled the little fellow's hair amiably and withdrew his hand. Jean-Paul shot him a scathing, sidelong glance but said nothing, and they walked back to the Vieux Carré in silence.

Freed of Alain's touch, Simone could think again, but her thoughts were disturbed. His hand on her had been like fire, and his nearness had an almost physical effect. She could not escape the awareness of him, so tall and strong and masculine, at her side. Just this morning her heart had stood still when she had seen him without his shirt. Now it pounded at the memory.

"What were you doing in The Swamp?" Alain asked as they turned down Exchange Alley. "You had no business there. Even the constabulary stay out. If you had any sense—"

"If you've got so much sense, what were *you* doing there?" she cut in hotly.

"Playing cards—why should I explain to you?" A look of exasperation crossed his face. "A man can go where a boy cannot."

"Whose rule is that?" The belligerent youngster balked. "Yours?"

"Mine and Serge's." Alain dragged the boy to the backstairs of the *salle*. "I happen to know the *Maître* likes to keep his assistants in one piece. So I suggest you get upstairs where you belong." Placing his boot against Jean-Paul's rump, he shoved her in that direction, chuckling at the boy's dire mutterings.

Simone peered into the parlor through the French doors from the garden and called softly, "Lisette."

"Mademoiselle Dupré attends an emergency in the kitchen, m'sieur," an unfamiliar voice answered.

It took a moment for Simone's eyes to adjust to the dim interior after the brilliance of the autumn day. But when they did, she saw a lovely Negro in a chair by the fire, a small wooden case at her feet.

"*Merci.*" Simone prepared to depart with a polite nod.

"Won't you wait with me, *petit*?" the woman invited. As her penetrating black eyes raked Simone, the girl felt as if her disguise were suddenly transparent.

In her best Jean-Paul manner, Simone stepped in and plopped down in a chair.

"My name is Marie LeVeau," the woman introduced herself. "I'm Mademoiselle Dupré's hairdresser. Who might you be?"

Simone surveyed the Negress with interest. She had often heard of Marie LeVeau—the queen of voodoo in New Orleans and confidante to many wealthy Creole women—but she had never seen her. Realizing the woman was regarding her expectantly, she murmured, "I'm Jean-Paul, just a friend."

Marie LeVeau leaned forward, the planes of her handsome face gilded by the fire's glow, and said urgently, "You must hear me. I knew when you came to the door that you were the one the obeah told me of."

Her very tone sent prickles of foreboding up Simone's spine. Suddenly she wished she were anywhere but here, beside the fire with the voodoo queen, but she could not bring herself to stir.

"Yes," the woman hissed, leaning back in her chair with a satisfied smile. "I am not mistaken. You are the one. You have blood on your hands, yet you seek revenge."

"You can't know that," Simone protested, deeply unsettled. "You don't even know me."

"I don't have to. The obeah never lies."

Simone fought back a shudder as the Negress continued, "There is more, a warning that you will bring danger to those you love."

"Wh-what kind of danger?" Simone asked with dread.

For a long moment she thought the voodooienne would not answer. Marie LeVeau sat motionless, her eyes closed and a frown furrowing her brow. "Blood," she whispered at last. "All I see is blood." Then she sagged in her chair, as if exhausted.

Silently, Simone rose and fled. She would not have a bath that day; she would not see Lisette. She wished only to escape the ominous predictions of the voodoo queen.

"I don't like this," Lisette said to her companion as they stepped down from the carriage on rue Chartres.

"I had to come," Simone asserted from behind a heavy black veil.

"I still say it would be better if I went to the shop and bought your father's watch."

"And the clock from LaVictoire, and who knows

what else the shopkeeper bought at the auction?" Simone countered. "You wouldn't know my family's possessions. I have to see them to know what I can buy back. Don't worry so much, Lisette," she soothed. "No one will recognize me—or you—in widow's weeds."

The madam looked around uncomfortably and saw her friend was right. No one appeared to notice them or if they did, they respected the privacy of two women in mourning. But she drew up short when she saw Marcel Baudin in front of them on the *banquette*.

Taking her arm, Simone shyly ducked her head and steered her friend past the handsome young Creole, who did no more than tip his hat in habitual politeness to the ladies.

"This is too dangerous," Lisette muttered when they were past. "What if he had recognized you?"

"He didn't, and no one else will either," Simone replied with growing confidence.

At the shop, the last Devereaux found not only the watch and the clock she had spied in the window, but her mother's carved ivory combs. She was just finishing a round of haggling with the shopkeeper when Lisette announced, "Oh dear, it looks as if it's about to pour."

"Why don't you go on to the carriage?" Simone suggested. "I will be there as soon as I have finished."

His head bowed against the elements, Alain was hurrying along rue Chartres when a veiled woman stepped out of a shop directly in front of him. Trim and petite, her black-clad figure moved with grace, seeming to skim through the mist as if carried by the wind. Alain watched appreciatively as she hurried toward a waiting coach.

As she neared the carriage, she dropped a small parcel. Her skirt billowing around her, she swooped gracefully to pick it up, but with two long strides Alain was there before her.

"Permit me." He bent, his face very close to hers.

Realizing who had come to her aid, Simone stood at once, her petticoats rustling stiffly, and retreated a step to increase the distance between them.

Alain rose slowly, his gaze fixed on her bowed head, trying to see her face through her veil. "Your parcel, mam'selle," he said softly.

His fingers brushed hers as she accepted the package from him and it seemed to Simone she felt his startling heat even through the gloves she wore.

"*Merci,*" she murmured, her voice nearly lost on the whistle of the wind.

"My pleasure." He sprang at once to open the door of the carriage. His eyes on the dainty one beside him, he scarcely noticed the other woman in the cab's dark interior.

Gallantly, Alain offered a hand to assist the girl, and she laid one small gloved hand in his for the merest instant. He closed the door as she settled into the coach on the far side of her companion.

"*Merci,* monsieur." Her voice drifted through the window.

"Your servant, mademoiselle."

She said something he could not hear over the crack of the driver's whip and the rumble of wheels on cobblestone. But as the coach pulled away, he saw a hand lowering the isinglass window covering. And a ring on the slender fingers told Alain the hand belonged to Lisette Dupré.

His brows lowered in displeasure as he stared after the carriage. How blind could he be? He should have recognized her, Alain thought irritably. The veiled woman who had, for some strange reason, set his heart pounding like a green lad with his first love was the black-haired girl he had met at Lisette's!

He had received no answers from the madam to his relentless questions about the mysterious girl. Now he would have them, and from her own lips. Whistling for a cab, he set out for the house on rue Dauphine.

In Lisette's dressing room, Simone rapidly shed her clothes.

"Would it be so bad if he recognized you?" the madam asked again. "Alain wants to meet you. He wants to apologize."

"I don't want his apologies. I want him to leave me alone."

"Alain de Vallière is very handsome, very eligible . . . and very interested in you," Lisette argued.

"Well, I'm not interested in that—that beast." Simone stared at the woman through narrowed eyes while she buttoned her shirt. "I know he's your friend, and you may have forgiven him that night, but I have not." She closed the subject by jamming Jean-Paul's hat over her curls and gathering her parcels.

"Why are you in such a hurry?" Lisette asked. "He didn't seem to recognize you."

"I know, but after the last time I met the roué, I don't want to risk meeting him again." Simone kissed her friend hastily on the cheek, then was gone.

She had barely passed through the garden gate when the door to Lisette's parlor was thrown open with such force it bounced off the wall.

"Where is she?" Alain demanded, striding into the room.

"She's right, you are a beast." Lisette's gray eyes shone in indignation. "What's wrong with you, 'Lain? When did you start bursting into a lady's room without even knocking?"

"When did you join that pretty little trickster in her games? Where is she, Lisette? I want to see her."

"She's gone," the madam told him.

"Where?" Struggling to control his fury, he ground out the question.

"I wish I could tell you," she said. "I wish the two of you could make peace."

"How can we, when she refuses to see me? Why won't she give me a chance to apologize?"

"I think you frightened her."

"I know I did, and I cannot bear the thought of it. I have to see her, to apologize. You must tell me who she is and where I can find her." He towered over the tall woman.

Lisette would not be intimidated. "I gave my word," she declared. "You cannot ask me to break it."

Alain surrendered with a bleak sigh. "I suppose I can't." Raking his fingers through his dark hair, he slumped into a chair beside the fire. "Can't you tell me anything about her? She is well born, is she not?"

Lisette hesitated. The Creole looked unusually disheartened, and she could see no harm in telling him that much. "She comes from a good family."

"Is she truly in mourning?"

"*Oui*, she has had a great deal of sadness in her life. She's completely alone in the world now."

"*Non*," he disagreed softly, "she has you."

"I am her friend."

"A good friend. I would be her friend, as well, if she would give me the chance," he murmured.

"I suspect you would be more than a friend, 'Lain, if she gave you the chance," Lisette countered evenly. "I warn you," she continued when he blinked at her in surprise, "I think of that girl as if she were my own, and I'll protect her however I can. You have loved and left women from here to Paris and back again. Forget this one. She's not for you."

Marcel Baudin attacked his breakfast with zest. After nearly six months, he was close to finding Simone. He had followed false leads up and down the Mississippi, but yesterday he had received a report that she might be in Natchez. Today he would go upriver to search for her.

Even now he could not forget her. How he longed to find her. In time she would accept, even welcome, his attentions. Despite his disfigurement, women still found him attractive.

But they were deceptive bitches, Marcel knew. The truth always came out. Even when he hired them and paid them well, they were afraid of him. Probably they thought him too ugly to love.

Simone had done this to him, he thought, fingering his scar. Things would change when he found her. He would make her love him, or he would have his revenge.

The sun was low, the afternoon sky a dazzling mélange of azure and scarlet, when Alain turned his carriage toward town. The air was crisp, carrying the scent of autumn. In the distance, a fleet-footed swamp deer, no larger than a dog, scurried into the undergrowth. But, absorbed in his thoughts, Alain scarcely noticed the splendor around him.

He had driven to Lake Pontchartrain to escape the Sunday bustle of the Vieux Carré and the problem that plagued him. But he had not been successful. His mind dwelt on Lisette's words. Even after days they rankled, but doubtless she was right. He probably should forget the girl. She was young, not for an experienced man. Still, recollections of the sight and the scent of the black-haired beauty, fresh from her bath, and of her untutored response to his caresses, kept returning. And the memories never failed to bring a stirring to his loins.

As he approached the outskirts of town, Alain remembered a lovely octoroon he had met at a recent Quadroon Ball. She lived with her mother near the cemetery at the edge of town, not far out of his way. It would not hurt to stop at the cottage and inquire as to the mother's terms for her daughter. Many Creole gentlemen kept placees, quadroon mistresses, in small houses along Rampart Street. Why should he be the exception? Alain brooded. He suddenly longed for something more than a different woman every night. Perhaps a placée was what he needed to purge his mind of the green-eyed girl.

As he drove along, looking for the *placée* cottage, he did not notice a black-clad figure sitting beside a white-washed tomb in the cemetery.

Simone paid scant attention to the passing carriage. She sat on a bench in the waning sunlight, savoring her relative freedom. Marcel had left town today. Dressed as Jean-Paul, she had gone to the wharf to watch him board the steamboat that would carry him upriver for a week or more. Then, stealing into Lisette's apartment, she had changed into her mourning costume.

She had not been out in a woman's clothes since she had run into Alain. But there was little danger of meeting him at the cemetery. Simone had not dared to come to her parents' tomb last week on All Saints Day, when Creoles cared for the graves of their dead. Today she would tend it, a duty she preferred to perform in solitude.

Among the newly decorated graves, she wiped the brass nameplates on the Devereaux tomb with her handkerchief and placed fresh flowers in a vase at its door. Then she sat back, relishing the sun's warmth on her shoulders. Feeling a tickle on her hand, she looked down and smiled as she recalled the old saying, "If a lizard runs over your hand in graveyard, you will have good luck."

The best luck to come her way recently was Serge's willingness to teach his assistant to fence. She had decided, as she improved, that if she could not free herself of Marcel's menace, she would prepare to challenge him to a duel. She had learned a great deal so far, but she still had much to learn. Fabrice would be furious, but she didn't care; she wanted the skills Serge was teaching her.

She sighed, for her boyish masquerade, her continual vigilance, was wearing on her. Though being a male carried undeniable freedom, at times she felt trapped, confined to the *salle*, imprisoned in her disguise. Under Jean-Paul's baggy clothes, she was changing from a girl to a woman, but no one knew. She had hardly realized it herself until Alain had stared at her with such passion in his dark eyes.

Still, it was not Simone he had desired, she reminded herself quickly, but a stranger. Longing to be herself again, she wished suddenly he would look at *her* the way he had looked at the black-haired girl.

She stiffened abruptly, disturbed by her reverie. What was she thinking? Why should she care how Alain looked at her? Or even if he looked at her at all? It was too much to hope that she would never have to see him again, but she refused to fall prey to his questionable charms, she thought irritably, shoving away memories of full, sensuous lips and strong, tapering fingers.

All at once Simone realized the hour was late, and she had no wish to be out unaccompanied after dark. A woman alone was apt to attract both attention and trouble. All Fabrice's dire warnings flooded back to her as she hurried toward the iron gate of the cemetery, her heels clacking along the walkway between the tombs and echoing eerily from the white washed walls. Letting herself out, she hastened toward the Vieux Carré through deepening shadows.

Swinging around a corner, she ran headlong into a solid mass, knocking the air out of her and nearly dislocating her hat. A man's arms enfolded her, holding her against a broad chest.

Only moments before, Alain had been irritated to discover that the octoroon's cottage was down an alley, too narrow for his carriage, but now he was glad to be on foot. His arms were full of the girl for whom he had searched so long, and she fit his embrace well. "What do you know?" he breathed. "This is my lucky day."

Righting her bonnet with the one hand free of the

man's embrace, Simone tilted her gaze from the snowy expanse of his shirt past his impeccably tied cravat to a chiseled chin, curved lips, and finally to dark eyes crinkled with amusement.

Uncomfortably aware that her breasts were thrust against him as she strained to see his face, she stared with dread through her veil at none other than Alain de Vallière. Quickly she ducked her head and murmured, "*Pardon*, monsieur." She tried to withdraw from his embrace, but he would not permit it.

"No, no, I beg you to accept *my* apologies, mademoiselle. Are you all right?" he asked, almost tenderly.

"I'm fine, *merci*." Simone's breathing was labored, and, to her vexation, she knew it had little to do with their collision. Determined Alain would not know the effect he had on her, she set her bonnet securely on her head and tried again to step away.

He would not relinquish his hold. "I might have hurt you," he murmured.

She felt his warm breath on her cheek even through her veil, and it sent a wave of unwanted longing through her.

"You didn't hurt me." She twisted her shoulders slightly, trying to free her arm, but succeeded only in pressing one breast more firmly against his starched shirtfront. Closing her eyes, she drew a steadying breath, missing the flicker of pleasure her action brought him. Placing her free hand against his chest, she pushed and said firmly, "Thank you for your concern, m'sieur, but I insist you release me."

The cad stood as unmoving as a boulder and announced, "Not unless you promise not to run away again."

"Please, you must let me go," she said desperately. "It is late, and I have to get back to town."

"Promise you won't run away," he pressed.

She glared up at him and saw that he would stand firm. "I promise," she agreed sullenly.

He released her, but one hand held her elbow as he guided her toward his carriage. "I will take you home."

"You may take me to Mademoiselle Dupré's," she said coldly.

"As you wish." As he lifted her into the carriage, he held her for a moment so his face was close to hers, his eyes seeking hers through the veil. "Do you always wear a veil?" he asked softly, placing her on the seat.

"Do you always make it a practice to waylay women on the road?"

"Only the ones I want to meet."

"We *have* met, M'sieur de Vallière."

"Ah, you know my name." He seemed pleased as he climbed into the carriage. "But I still do not know yours."

When she didn't answer, he asked lightly, "What am I to call you, *ma petite*? Coco Robichaux?" he teased, referring to the imaginary girl Creole children blamed for all manner of mischief.

"You would blame your misdeeds on Coco Robichaux?"

"You mean what happened at Lisette's that night?" he asked.

Her face burned at the memory, and it suddenly seemed she could feel the length of his leg burning through her voluminous skirt.

"What happened between us was not wrong, chère," he said kindly. "It was part of what happens when a man and a woman are attracted to each other. What was wrong was how it happened and when. And for that, I'm truly sorry." He laid a big hand over the ones she had clasped tightly in her lap.

For a moment, Simone thought she would cry. He sounded so like the Alain she remembered. "You couldn't know," she whispered in mortification. "You must have thought—"

"That you looked enticing as you stepped from your bath," he interrupted gently. Then he picked up the reins and turned the rig toward the Vieux Carré.

Uncertain how to respond, she stared down at her hands, wondering that she could not see the mark of his touch.

"What were you doing alone and so far from town?" he asked.

"Visiting the cemetery," she replied guardedly.

"Ah. Lisette told me you are an orphan."

"She did?"

"I was sorry to hear of your losses."

"*Merci*," she muttered uncomfortably. She was silent for a moment, but she had to ask. "What else did Lisette tell you?"

"Very little. She told me she gave her word not to. She said only that you come from a good family and you're alone in the world."

Suddenly even that small amount of information seemed too much and Simone was afraid Alain would recognize her. After the tenderness he had just shown her, she did not think she could bear if he knew *she* was the obligation he chafed under. Huddled on the seat beside him, one eye on his craggy profile, she yearned for escape and refused to be drawn into conversation. At last he gave up, but his gaze shifted toward her frequently. She kept her face carefully averted.

When they stopped in front of the house on rue Dauphine, Simone collected herself rapidly. "Thank you for the ride," she said, ready to bolt. "You don't need to see me to the door."

Alain laid a hand on her arm. "Let me help you."

"*Non, merci.*" She jerked away as if burned and stepped down from the carriage.

"Wait." He slid down from the seat and was beside her in an instant. "When can I see you again?"

"I do not think it would be a good idea for us to see each other again."

"Listen to me," he demanded, catching her arms in

his big hands. "Since the first time I saw you, I have not been able to get you out of my mind. I've stopped women on the street because I thought they were you, but when they turned, they didn't have the green eyes that haunt me. You can't run away again. I must see you."

Simone almost did not hear him for the words echoing in her head, words he had said to Serge. "The sooner I find my little spitfire, the sooner I can find a husband for her." He might be drawn to the woman of his imaginings, but Simone Deveraux was an obligation to him, nothing more.

"I cannot see you again," she answered, near tears. Wrenching herself free, she ran inside before he saw her cry.

Alain lingered on the *banquette*, his pride smarting at having been so flatly dismissed. Slowly he climbed up onto the carriage seat and took the reins in hand, trying to decide whether to drive away and forget he had ever laid eyes on her or to march inside and demand to speak to her.

He was still there, staring unseeingly down the dusky street, when Simone dressed as Jean-Paul, rounded the corner from Lisette's garden gate.

A shapely mulatto girl approached, gracefully, bearing a basket on her head, and it seemed to Simone as she watched that Alain's eyes followed the pretty Negress as she disappeared into an alleyway with a smile and a flirtatious flip of her skirt.

The roué! she fumed. He had pretty words for her— and eyes for the first female who crossed his path. With a determined set to her jaw, she swaggered toward the man's carriage.

"Well, well, look who's loitering in front of the whorehouse," Jean-Paul crowed, his boyish voice cutting annoyingly through Alain's musings. "You going in or waiting to see if they'll come out to you? I always heard you were a ladies' man, but—"

"You heard right," Alain growled, urging his horses forward. As he drove away, leaving the boy to gape after him, he felt a twinge of guilt at having taken out his frustration on the lad.

6

Simone pulled her cap over her ears and hunched deeper into her coat, trying to ignore the raw wind from the river. Through the fogged windows of Hewlett's Exchange she could see Obadiah, smiling broadly as he gathered his cards and passed his hat.

Soon he joined her on the *banquette.* "Afternoon, Jean-Paul. Good crowd today."

"If I had known you'd take to a life of gambling, I never would have taught you those card tricks," Simone greeted him sourly, swinging around to head toward the market.

"I wasn't gamblin'. I was entertainin'," the Negro boy said, defending himself, as he fell into step beside her.

The pair cut across the Place d'Armes toward the bustling open market, above which towered the masts of the great sailing ships. On busy Levee Street, they dodged the heavy traffic and received a friendly nod from the *gaufre* man, the seller of fine thin cookies.

As they passed, a noisy dispute poured from a produce booth where a Slavonian vendor argued with a Creole housewife. A few feet away, an egg-seller hawked his wares, occasionally tossing an egg on the ground to prove its freshness. Stepping over the oozy mess, Simone was glad it was February, not July.

When she became aware of a party of Creole girls approaching, dressed in satins and velvets, accompanied by their maids and several young gallants, Simone turned. "Let's get out of here," she muttered.

"Guess you don't like gals yet, eh, Jean-Paul?" Obadiah grinned as they retraced their steps.

"Not much," was the curt reply.

"Someday you will," the other boy predicted.

"Don't count on it."

As they neared the square, Obadiah caught sight of a man nailing a sign to a post. "Come on," he urged, grabbing his friend by the arm and racing across the street, narrowly missing being run down by a clattering dray.

"What's so important that you'd nearly get me killed, Obie?" Simone demanded, yanking free when they stopped before the poster.

"Since you been teachin' me to read, I gotta see what's on every sign." After studying it a moment, he requested, "Read it to me, will ya? I ain't good enough yet."

"It doesn't have anything to do with us," she answered crossly. "It's about a masked ball to be held at the Orleans Ballroom next week."

"Aw," Obadiah sighed in disappointment. "I was hopin' the circus was comin' back to Congo Square. I sure liked the last one."

"Better than they liked you after you outfoxed the three-card monte dealer," Simone snorted.

"Learned from the best." He grinned and asked for the hundredth time, "Where'd you learn about cards, Jean-Paul?"

"Here and there," she answered as she always did.

"I can't understand it. How come you don't never talk about yourself? Alls I know is you come to New

Orleans from Bayou Teche, you can read and write, and," he added, "you play a mean game of poker. You're always beatin' Claude and them fellers, but I ain't figgered where the money goes, 'cause you're still wearin' them same baggy pants you was wearin' when you come."

"Sounds like you know a lot to me," Jean-Paul countered, then changed the subject. "Mam'selle Lisette's cook invited me to stop by this afternoon for hot gingerbread. You want to go?"

"What're we waitin' for?" the other boy asked, diverted by the promise of food.

As they walked to rue Dauphine, Simone's thoughts turned to the ball. She was right when she told Obadiah that it had nothing to do with them. But she allowed herself a brief flight of fancy, imagining herself in a white gown, with beaux lined up to dance with her. She had never had a season, never owned a ball gown or even a dress as nice as the ones worn today by the girls at the market. For an instant she felt a flash of jealousy, but she put it behind her when she and Obadiah presented themselves at Lisette's kitchen door for the promised treat.

"*Bonjour*, Jean-Paul," the *filles de joie* greeted the boy as he sauntered toward the madam's apartment, having left Obie to his fill of gingerbread. "How are you, *mon petit*?" The women enjoyed the lad's visits to the house on rue Dauphine. Though he was shy, Jean-Paul was polite, and they adored him for it.

"There you are, *chère*." Lisette looked up from her knitting and smiled when Simone entered. "I was hoping you would stop by. You've heard about the masque next week?"

Slumping in the chair across from her, Simone replied around her gingerbread, "I saw the sign this morning."

Lisette's needles stopped their movement as she

frowned reprovingly at her young friend. "Just because you masquerade as a boy does not mean you should act like one here, Simone."

"You're right." The girl sighed and sat up. "Every day, it seems harder to slip back and forth between Jean-Paul and me."

"I know," Lisette sympathized. "But I want you to practice being a young lady while you are here today because—" Putting her knitting aside, she rose and held out her hand. "Come with me."

She led Simone into the bedroom, where an exquisite white ball gown was spread on the bed. Trimmed with white lace and rose-colored ribbon, it was a frothy, feminine confection.

"What is this?" the girl asked in puzzlement.

"Your dress for the ball," Lisette answered eagerly. She opened the chiffonier and pulled out a pale pink petticoat. "And your petticoat and slippers," she said, holding out a pair of *peau de soie* shoes dyed to match the ribbons on the gown.

"It . . . it's all very beautiful," Simone stammered, "but I cannot go to the ball."

"Why not?" The woman cocked a skeptical eyebrow.

"For one thing, I'm supposed to be hiding."

"What better place to hide than behind a mask?" Lisette picked up a white satin half-mask from the dressing table and placed it beside the dress.

"I'd be recognized."

"I don't think so. You've changed, filled out just in the time I've known you, and now your hair is black instead of brown."

"And it's short," Simone reminded her.

"Easily remedied." The woman dismissed that objection with a wave of her hand. "I've ordered a hairpiece dyed black."

Simone looked wistfully at the ensemble on the bed, but she shook her head. "I'd never be able to carry off the masquerade."

"Simone Devereaux," Lisette exclaimed, "you have been posing as a boy for nearly nine months. Don't you think you could pass for the lovely young woman you are?"

"What if Marcel is there?"

"He won't be," Lisette said confidently. "I hear his mother is ill again, and he plans to stay with her until after Easter. Do go, *chère*. It's your chance to be the belle of the ball, at least for one night."

Simone was tempted. "What if someone asks my name?"

"Don't tell them. I've bribed the doorman to let you in without being announced."

"Alain de Vallière might be there," the girl protested.

"You're going to have to face him eventually. He has been here almost every day since November, looking for you. I don't need to remind you, you've had more than one narrow escape."

"And what do you suggest I do if he confronts me?"

"Smile and flirt and dance with him," Lisette answered promptly. "Go and have fun. You've had little enough in your life."

Warring emotions were evident on Simone's face as she lovingly fingered the lace of the gown. Picking up the mask, she held it in front of her face and looked in the mirror. At the ball she would be only one among many wearing masks.

When she faced Lisette, the other woman knew that she had won.

"*Très bien.*" Simone surrendered with a tentative smile. "I'll do it. And *merci beaucoup*. It seems you've thought of everything."

"Not quite everything," her friend disagreed. "I forgot to have a cloak made, but I have a short cape that will be perfect for you. Try the gown on, and we'll plan the conquest of every male in New Orleans by a mysterious, raven-haired beauty."

"Your *sentiment de fer*, your feel for the blade, is good, young friend," Serge told Jean-Paul, "but you must remember to keep your derriere in line with the rest of your body." He prodded the lad's hip gently with the buttoned tip of his foil.

"*Oui, maître.*" Simone nodded, wasting no time on girlish embarrassment.

"That's enough for today. I must go, but you may continue to practice if you wish," Serge announced, looking around the nearly deserted *salle*. A pair of fencers engaged in loose play in one corner, and a couple of his students, weary after their exertions, ambled toward the door.

The fencing master departed with a smile for his scrawny assistant as Jean-Paul concentrated on the muscle control necessary to keep his upper body straight, his knees slightly bent, and the offending portion of his anatomy tucked firmly in.

"Keep it in," a bold voice advised.

Simone glanced over her shoulder to see Alain leaning against a post, watching. "I don't need *you* to tell me that," she snapped.

"I thought you might appreciate some guidance from someone older and more experienced." He shrugged indolently.

"That's you, of course," she sniped, nettled by his criticism.

Alain's eyes narrowed. Time and time again Jean-Paul had provoked him, and he had often thought of teaching the boy a lesson. Today was the day for it.

"Since you've become such an expert under Serge's tutelage, why don't you show me what you've learned?" He donned his mask, his dark eyes challenging the boy through the wire mesh.

Simone hesitated only a moment. Much could be learned from practice with a good swordsman, and

Alain was one of the best. She would undoubtedly be beaten, but she vowed to give him more than he bargained for.

Putting on her own mask, she returned his salute. From the moment their blades engaged, Jean-Paul fenced aggressively, advancing on Alain with energy and speed. The big man parried his thrusts easily but allowed him to move forward unhampered. When the boy gathered himself for a lunge, Alain sidestepped neatly, reaching around to slap his foil across Jean-Paul's derriere.

"That's not fair!" the youngster yelped. Springing backward, he glared at his opponent.

"Keep it in," Alain counseled, grinning, as Jean-Paul rubbed his smarting backside.

Serge's assistant resumed his stance and began to fence more cautiously. Again Alain fought defensively, retiring just out of reach, inviting his opponent to make a *flèche*, a quick, short run. As Jean-Paul passed, Alain delivered another slap across his buttocks with his foil.

"You're cheating!" Jean-Paul howled, wheeling on the man.

"I'm reminding you of the *maître*'s lessons," Alain explained patiently. "And teaching you a lesson of my own."

"What's that?" the boy bawled.

"To respect your elders."

Enraged, Jean-Paul glared at him through narrowed green eyes, then charged mindlessly, all finesse forgotten in his anger.

Once again Alain applied his foil, but with less vigor than before. He wanted to curb Jean-Paul's insolence, not beat him. Yet the lad showed no signs of quitting.

When his small opponent resumed his stance, Alain saluted politely. "I'd like to give you more of my time, Jean-Paul, but I have an engagement this evening."

As he walked away, his voice drifted back to the

boy, "You really must work on your temper, young friend. It gives your opponent a definite advantage."

Simone watched her guardian go, tears of humiliation and rage rolling unheeded down her cheeks.

That night when Simone stepped from her bath, Lisette gasped in horror. "*Chère*, what happened to you?"

Simone twisted to examine her bruised buttocks in the dressing-room mirror. "I crossed swords with Alain today. He was set on teaching Jean-Paul a lesson," she said crisply as she wrapped herself in a towel.

"I've known Alain de Vallière for years. I've never known him to lose his temper quite so drastically," the woman said dubiously.

"I seem to have that effect on him."

"Indeed you do."

Lisette led the girl to a low stool beside the fireplace and began to towel her short hair dry.

Simone stared pensively into the fire, then sighed. "It is not enough that I make Alain lose his temper without even trying," she said sadly. "You know what is worse, Lisette? He makes me so angry, I go out of my way to provoke him at the *salle*."

"Provoked or not, it's not right to beat an innocent boy," Lisette said disapprovingly, picking up a comb.

"He didn't beat me." Simone was surprised by her own defense of him. "He only slapped me with his foil as the maître does at times, though I must say Serge doesn't do it with quite so much relish."

"Well, if Alain ever lays a hand on you again—"

"I don't think he will," Simone said.

"Hmmm." Holding a dozen hair pins tightly between her lips, Lisette gave only that enigmatic answer as she arranged the hairpiece on the girl's head.

Next, taking up a bottle of lotion, she rubbed Simone's rough hands until at last she acknowledged defeat. "These are not the hands of a genteel young lady."

"*Non,* they are the hands of a twelve-year-old boy."

"Never mind. I have lace gloves you can wear. Now come and I can help you into your dress."

"You are *très jolie, ma petite,*" Lisette said admiringly, as she hooked the back of the splendid evening gown. "Ah, I almost forgot." Picking up a circlet of pink roses from the dressing table, she placed it on Simone's head and affixed it to where the hairpiece joined her hair.

"Now turn around and close your eyes." When the girl had complied, Lisette led her to the full-length mirror. "Open them. Now, are you not *magnifique?*" she asked softly.

Simone stared at her reflection in disbelief. It was true, she realized. For the first time in her life, she was beautiful.

The gown Lisette had chosen for her was perfect, elegant in its simplicity. The white satin bodice left her shoulders bare, shirring in graceful drapes from the modest décolletage to the rose-colored sash at her narrow waist. Her sleeves ended in a cascade of white lace gathered with ribbons at her elbows.

Her glossy black hair was drawn back from the forehead and held in place by the rose circlet. A few loose tendrils curled around her face, as if to emphasize her femininity. Her color was heightened by her excitement, and her lips reflected the rose of the ribbons trimming her gown.

"I've never felt so pretty," Simone breathed.

"You're more than pretty, *chère,* you're beautiful," Lisette said with satisfaction. "Now the finishing touches." She brought out a fan and a pair of short white lace gloves.

"There is one more thing," Simone remembered suddenly. She picked up the boy's shirt she had been wearing and pulled her mother's necklace from the pocket.

"Wonderful!" Lisette fastened it at once around Simone's neck. "I've never seen a pearl so lovely. *Et, voilà.*" Simone stood still as Lisette placed a cloak over her shoulders and instructed, "Let me fetch Jude to walk you to the ballroom. I don't want you wandering around alone at night."

When she returned with her big doorman, Simone was waiting, already wearing her mask. Jude bowed politely and opened the doors to the garden, gesturing for her to precede him.

A cold, damp wind from the river whistled through the narrow streets as they walked silently to the ballroom. Drizzle had left the wooden *banquettes* slick, so they made their way carefully. At a small gate in a wall facing onto rue Orleans, they stopped, and the big Negro said politely, "I will come back for you in three hours, mam'selle. If you're not here, I'll wait."

Muted music drifted from inside as Simone crept through a shadowy, deserted courtyard. Leaves crackled underfoot, and water dripped in huge cold drops from barren tree limbs above. She glanced toward the ballroom, whose bright windows seemed to beckon her.

The side door, nearly invisible in the darkness, would open onto the long hallway that ran along the front of the building. Praying it was not locked, she tried it. When it opened, she stole into the dark hall.

A pool of light spilled through an open door halfway to the main entrance of the ballroom, and the rumble of masculine voices emanated from within. Stopping a few feet away, she peeped into the gaming room, where men gathered around the fireplace sipping from snifters, their masks pushed up carelessly over their foreheads. Others, tired of the ball, played cards at small tables. Stealthily, Simone slipped past to the foyer outside the ballroom.

Framed by the doorway, the doorman did not leave his post, but he nodded silently toward the cloakroom, where Simone doffed her cloak. When she returned to the foyer, he nodded again slightly and moved to one side. She paused apprehensively for an instant, then stepped into the ballroom, which was alive with music and color as couples swirled around the floor to the strains of a waltz.

Alain leaned against a marble column, surveying the ballroom. Even in idleness, his gaze was penetrating as he watched the dancers, considering whether he should go home. His boredom was replaced by mild curiosity when he noticed the doorman eyeing the crowd as he slipped aside to admit someone unannounced. What the devil could the man be up to?

The answer came when a vision appeared in the doorway. Uttering a surprised oath under his breath, Alain launched himself from the column and hastened to the girl for whom he had searched.

"My dance, I believe, mademoiselle." The handsome Creole presented himself with a bow, drawing Simone into his arms and onto the dance floor before she could object.

Held in his arms, Simone was afraid to look up past his crisp white shirtfront. Had he witnessed the near-physical jolt of gladness she had felt when she saw him striding toward her? Even now her knees were so weak, they barely supported her.

As he stared down at her bent head, the fragrance of roses wafted up to Alain, intoxicating him. "Don't you have anything to say to me after all this time?" he asked huskily, drawing her eyes to his and holding them with a burning intensity.

"What would you like me to say?" she asked breathlessly.

"You could tell me you're glad to see me. I've been looking for you for three months. Where have you been?"

"Why would you waste your time looking for me when I told you the last time we met that I cannot see you?" she challenged softly.

"You told me," he murmured, his lips close to hers, "yet here you are in my arms again."

"*Oui*, here I am." Her words came as a sigh as they spun around the dance floor, whirling among the dazzling prisms thrown off by the chandelier, oblivious to the other people in the huge room.

His back to the dancers, Fabrice Chauvin stood talking with Claude Galvez and Eugène Moreau.

"*Mon Dieu*!" Claude stared wonderingly over Fabrice's shoulder.

"What a beauty," Eugène breathed, his eyes following the couple as they swept around the dance floor.

Curiously, Fabrice turned to see what they regarded with such awe, and his jaw dropped in amazement. There, clasped in the arms of her hated guardian, was his *petite cousine*.

"*Pardon, mes amis*." Fabrice excused himself and headed toward the handsome couple as soon as the music drew to a close. All around him he could hear muted conversation. The question of Simone's identity was on everyone's lips.

When he reached them, the elegant young man bowed. "Mademoiselle, may I have the honor?" he asked, trying to ignore the way de Vallière's hold on her waist tightened possessively.

Alain's expression darkened when Simone accepted. "I'd be delighted. If you'll pardon me, Monsieur de Vallière." She slipped from his grip and was led onto the floor by Fabrice.

"Simone Jeanne-Marie Pauline Devereaux," her cousin began severely as soon as they were out of the other man's earshot, "what do you think you're doing?"

"Dancing with you, *cher cousin*, and enjoying myself immensely," she answered lightly.

"You know very well what I mean," he growled. "Are you mad to come here? Someone is sure to recognize you."

"No one but you," she assured him. "My father fell

from grace with *les bonnes familles* long ago. No one will know his daughter. Not even Alain has recognized me."

"Not yet. Claude and Eugène are also here. They could recognize you as Jean-Paul," he argued, not daring to state his true fear. What if Marcel Baudin appeared?

"Believe me, Fabrice, if either of them approaches me, I shall make sure that Jean-Paul is the furthest thing from his mind," she assured him with newfound confidence in her feminine allure.

Fabrice exploded in a loud whisper, "How long will you go on with this foolish masquerade? I keep hoping you'll give it up before you're discovered and your reputation is completely ruined. And now you trade one disguise for another. This is more dangerous than your boyish posturing. Why can't you just come home to LeFleur, where you'll be taken care of?"

"I can take care of myself, Fabrice. I learn more about defending myself every day."

"You speak of defense," he snorted. "I know you well enough to know you've probably decided to challenge Marcel yourself."

"Not until I'm good enough," she admitted.

"Baudin is one of the most skillful swordsmen in New Orleans. If you even *consider* challenging him, I will expose Serge's assistant as a girl," he threatened.

"You will not, Fabrice, because you vowed you would not."

He was aghast at her temerity. "Listen to reason, Simone," he urged.

"Don't shout. The music is about to end, and everyone will hear you."

"As a male cousin," he lowered his voice and continued insistently, "I have the right to counsel you."

"As a female cousin, I have the right to ignore that counsel." Smiling sweetly, she moved away from him.

"May I have this dance?" two voices asked in unison

behind her. As Fabrice stalked away, rigid with displeasure, Simone turned to see Claude and Eugène glaring at each other.

Simone responded teasingly, "What we have here is a most unwieldy combination for dancing, messieurs. Shall we simplify matters by agreeing that I will dance with one and then the other?"

They stared at her in mute admiration. Then Eugène found his voice. "But who will be first, mademoiselle? Will you choose?"

"Oh, dear." She gazed flirtatiously back and forth between them. "To choose would be difficult indeed. Perhaps there is another way—a peaceful way," she added hurriedly when she saw Eugène touch the hilt of the *colchemarde*, the sword cane, he wore at his side.

"We could flip a coin," Claude suggested, eager to please.

"*Très bon*," she approved. "Do you have one?"

Claude drew a gold piece from his pocket and flipped it. "Heads or tails, Moreau?" he asked as he slapped it on the back of his hand.

"Tails."

When he withdrew the hand that covered it, Claude's face fell. "Tails it is."

The band struck up a brisk reel as Eugène led the girl to the dance floor, and he almost wished he had not won after all. The next dance, Claude's dance, was sure to be a waltz.

The couple finished the reel, breathless and flushed, and Eugène returned Simone glumly to her next partner. He had been his most charming, and the mysterious girl had remained impervious to his appeal. He only hoped she would rebuff Claude's advances as coolly, for his friend was disgustingly successful with the ladies.

He would have been overjoyed by the couple's conversation if he had been able to eavesdrop while they waltzed. Simone told Claude no more than she had told

Eugène. He was still trying to find out her name when their dance ended and the girl was surrounded by a dozen admirers, each clamoring for a dance. Oblivious to the two sets of brown eyes following her around the floor, Simone danced and laughed and flirted.

Finally both Fabrice and Alain headed toward her. Fabrice reached her first, nearly flinching under Alain's cold stare as he claimed another dance with his cousin.

"Will you please go home, Simone?" he began at once. "You've had your fun. And your charade is becoming more dangerous each moment. De Vallière just stalked off to the gaming room, his face as black as thunder."

"What have I to do with that?" She shrugged carelessly.

"I'll tell you what. His eyes have not left you all night. You're playing with fire."

"So are you," Simone answered, catching sight of Zaza Pellarin's petulant young face. "Your intended is not pleased with your behavior either."

"She's not my intended," the young man muttered.

"Perhaps not yet," Simone said, "but she is the girl your father wants you to marry. This dance is nearly over. Go and ask her for the next."

"She is a child. Besides, you cannot expect me to dance with one girl and think of another," Fabrice grumbled. But he released her just the same.

"*Non*, that would be unchivalrous, and I would be forced to meet you under the Oaks," Simone teased, preparing to walk away.

"You know I would meet you anywhere, anytime you like," the young Creole replied, suddenly serious.

"As would most of the men in this ballroom," Alain's voice cut in. "I've been trying to convince her of that since last spring."

"Last spring?" Fabrice repeated dumbly.

"Why, Monsieur de Vallière, where have you been?" Simone turned to Alain hastily, evading her cousin's

question. Startled by the murderous glare Alain directed at Fabrice, she stammered, "Wh-where is your
mask?"

"I must have left it in the gaming room. No matter.
The next dance is mine, is it not?" His tone made it a
statement.

"*Oui*." She stepped at once into the big Creole's
arms, hoping to divert his attention from her cousin.
"*Pardon*, M'sieur Chauvin."

Alain's face was grim, and he said nothing as he
swept Simone around the dance floor. Finding a door
open slightly to admit a breeze into the overcrowded
ballroom, he waltzed her through it and into the chilly
courtyard.

"What are you doing?" she asked nervously.

"I want to talk to you."

"I do not think we have anything to talk about."

"Spare me your game playing, *ma petite*. And don't
tell me you don't play them. I've watched you all night,
leading the young dandies on, flitting from partner to
partner, flipping coins when you could not decide
which young gallant to favor, using me—"

"Using you?" Simone cried indignantly.

"*Oui*, to make young Chauvin jealous."

She nearly laughed aloud. "I was under the impression you wanted to dance with me."

"*Oui*, if for no other reason than to get some
answers from you. And I will have them." Without
warning, he reached over and untied the ribbons that
held her mask in place. She grabbed for it as it
dropped, but Alain captured her hand and said huskily,
"You're as beautiful as I remembered."

Feeling exposed, Simone pulled away from him. "I'm
going in. I don't think it wise to be alone in the dark
with a ladies' man."

"And just what makes you think I'm a ladies' man?"
he asked softly, stepping to block her escape.

Remembering just in time that he had confirmed

that fact to Jean-Paul, she quickly changed the subject. "Just like the first time we met, you do not care if I freeze," she snapped, wrapping her arms around her body to keep warm.

"You didn't freeze that night," he reminded her. "Your blood ran hot, and you cannot deny it. I'm not going to attack you," he growled when she stared up at him in alarm, her face bathed by the light from the ballroom. Taking off his jacket, he draped it over her bare shoulders and added gruffly, "I won't let you freeze either."

Her rose-scented perfume wafted to him as she settled the jacket around her. "*Merci,*" she murmured, though she still eyed him warily.

"Come here." Placing a hand against the small of her back, Alain moved her to stand in the shelter of a wall, missing her grimace when his hand brushed a bruise he had inflicted on Jean-Paul earlier.

Uncomfortably aware of the man's nearness, Simone backed away at once but found herself in a corner. Not again, she thought desperately, casting around for an escape.

She would never get past him unless she took him by surprise. In fencing, a feint could confuse your opponent and leave him open to an assault. Tonight a feint would be her deliverance from Alain.

But when she looked up at him, towering over her, she felt a qualm at her plan. He would not be easy to trick. Perhaps if she could flirt with him, get him to let his guard down, she could flee. But how could she do that when she found it so difficult to think? His legs pressed against her skirt as his big body shielded her from the wind, and she could feel the warmth radiating from him. The winter wind ruffled his dark hair and carried his spicy fragrance to her.

"Now, my love," he murmured, placing his hands on the wall on either side of her head, "you're going to tell me everything there is to tell about you."

"Surely not everything," she demurred, playing for time.

"Yes, everything."

"But, monsieur, that could take a very long time." She tilted her head to look up at him seductively and was disconcerted to find him braced on muscular arms, bending so his lips were close to hers.

"The longer the better." With tantalizing leisure, he planted light kisses at the corners of her mouth. "In fact," he whispered against her lips, "I don't care if it takes all night."

Now! Simone thought. Alain was not ready for any sudden moves. All she had to do was to duck under his braced arms and run. But then his mouth slanted across hers in fiery possession.

Too late, she thought hazily as he straightened, his mouth never leaving hers, and slid one of his arms under the jacket to cinch her waist and draw her close. Pressed against him, she shared his heat, his breath, his heartbeat, and all thoughts of escape fled.

With an unconscious whimper, she stirred against him, seeking instinctively to mold herself even closer to his hard length. Her hands skimmed his ribs as she slipped her arms around him, her fingers delicately tracing the hard muscles of his back.

Locked in his embrace, Simone did not feel the cold or the dampening mist in the air. Only a cheer from inside roused her from her enthrallment.

Alain drew back and smiled at her. "It is time for the unmasking, *mon amour*. Won't you tell me your name?"

Simone's sleepy green eyes widened. Damn him. He had made her forget her intention to escape. She had lost her opportunity to feint. The only thing left to her was to retire, quickly. Shoving hard against his chest, she broke free and spun to disappear into the darkness.

Wrathfully, he charged into the shadows behind her and was drawn up short by the soft snare of his jacket hanging on a tree limb. Yanking it out of the way, he wadded it in his big hand and looked around, but he could not see the girl. He searched the dark courtyard, discerning, at last, the gate in the wall. He threw it open and stepped out onto the *banquette*, but the street was deserted. She was gone, and he still did not know her name.

Muttering dire curses, he put on his jacket, irrationally spurred to greater fury because it smelled sweetly of her perfume. Then he stalked along rue Orleans into the night.

7

The day after the ball, the Vieux Carré buzzed with gossip. Everyone seemed to know at least one undisputed fact about the mysterious girl, and, at the *salle,* Claude and Eugène discussed her at length.

"No one remembers seeing her before," Eugène pondered with a frown.

"If they had seen her, they would have remembered. Who could forget those glorious green eyes?" Claude asked dramatically, unaware those very eyes glared at him from the equipment room.

"You never had a chance with her." Eugène smirked.

"As if you did, once de Vallière claimed her," Claude retorted.

"The lucky fellow. He disappeared into the courtyard with her, and they never returned," Eugène said with a knowing smile.

The cad, Simone fumed; Alain could have at least gone back inside to spare her reputation. Her cheeks burning, she picked up a soft cloth and set to work with special vigor, oiling the leather of the masks stored there. Maybe the same oil that kept the leather pliable would soften her hands.

"Not that it matters," she muttered under her breath. "I won't be playing the lady again any time soon." It was probably just as well, she thought. She had discovered last night that Alain was not the only one she could not trust. She could not even rely upon her own traitorous body.

She had realized, too, that she couldn't hide from him forever. But how could she face him? In the beginning, when she had met her guardian while wearing her feminine garb, she had enjoyed bearding the lion, but now she was tangled in the web of her own deception. And he was going to be furious when he found out.

Simone shuddered involuntarily at the thought of his dark eyes flashing with anger. Any ire he had exhibited in the past would pale in comparison. She was beginning to wish she had never begun this course of action.

She felt so confused. She had hated Alain since she was thirteen, but now . . . Her hands slowed in their activity as she recalled the feel of his lips on hers, the heat of his gaze. How could she surrender herself to his guardianship when he was obligated to find a husband for her?

By early afternoon, Simone's nerves were frayed, and Alain still had not appeared at the salle. Looking for projects to keep her busy, she took Serge's sword to her room for polishing. There, she hid from Alain and from her own emotions.

Alain marched into the house on rue Dauphine, a black velvet cloak over his arm.

"Yours, I believe," he spat, holding the garment out to Lisette when she turned to greet him.

"How did you . . ." She swallowed the rest of her question when she saw the forbidding look on his face.

"Is she here?" he demanded hoarsely.

"No."

"But she was here though, last night after the ball, wasn't she?"

"Only for a moment," Lisette admitted.

"She was probably afraid I had followed her," he muttered. "I thought about it, but I was too angry. I swear, Lise, that girl is driving me mad."

"Why don't you tell me what happened?"

Draping the cloak over the back of the settee, Alain sat down across from Lisette. "I claimed her for a dance the moment I saw her. When I had a chance, I took her into the courtyard and . .." He trailed off uncomfortably.

"And?" the woman prompted.

"And before I knew it, the little fool had run away from me again," he snapped.

"Why do you suppose she would do a thing like that?" she asked mildly.

"How the hell do I know?" Alain roared, jumping to his feet to prowl the room. Forcing himself to speak in a more moderate tone, he confessed, "All right, I kissed her."

"I see." Lisette's eyebrow rose in silent disapproval.

"She kissed me, too," he said defensively. "Then, with no warning, she ran. I was furious. In fact, I'm still angry. When I realized this morning that she had gone without a wrap, I went to the ballroom and explained that my sister had left her cloak there after the ball. The doorman gave me the only one in the cloak room." He picked up the cape in his big hand and stared at it bleakly. "I took it to the *modiste* whose label was inside, and who do you suppose she told me had ordered it?"

"I am sorry, Alain," Lisette murmured.

"I had hoped it would lead me to her. Instead, it leads back to you, here where I found her. You must help me. I have to see her."

"We've been over this before," the woman said gently.

"I'm not asking you to break your word." He caught and held her eyes compellingly. "You don't have to tell me anything. All I want is for you to arrange a meeting between us."

Lisette stared at her old friend in disbelief. The anguish on his face told her quite plainly he was in love. Alain de Vallière, in love. Astonishing.

Did Simone love him, too? Lisette turned it over in her mind. They certainly struck sparks off each other. Perhaps if they could resolve their differences, they would find happiness. And if Alain wanted to marry Simone, as she suspected, the girl would have both his love and all the protection she would ever need from Marcel Baudin.

"If I agree to arrange this meeting, do you promise not to behave like some rutting stallion?" she asked the man frankly.

"Of course." A frown knit his brows. "What do you take me for?"

"You seem to have uncommon difficulty keeping your hands off her," she reminded him mercilessly. "If you promise to treat her gently, I will have her here tonight so you can speak to her."

"I promise not to touch her," he agreed. "I just want to talk to her.

"*Bonsoir, chère,*" Lisette greeted Simone when she let herself into the apartment from the garden. "I see Obadiah managed to get my message to you."

"*Oui*, but I'm not sure it is a good idea for me to be here." Raking her cap from her head, Simone moved to stand in front of the fire. "I almost didn't come, but I wanted to apologize for being so irresponsible. Did Jude get your cape back?"

"It's safe and sound in my wardrobe," Lisette answered soothingly. "There's a nice hot bath waiting, and I have a surprise for you."

When Simone saw another feminine dress spread upon the bed, she said regretfully, "You shouldn't have bought this, Lisette. You know I cannot afford it until my father's debts are paid."

"I can," the madam announced, "and I wanted to buy it."

"You're very sweet." Simone turned a dazzling smile on her friend. "But if you stop and think, you'll remember I have no place to wear lovely clothes. When I go out, I must wear my veil and widow's weeds."

"Then you'll wear this when you're here," Lisette said with an air of finality. "Now have your bath, *ma petite*. After our *café*, we'll play dress-up."

Grinning in affectionate exasperation, Simone conceded to her dear friend's wishes.

Though she had been reluctant to stay, she was soon glad she had agreed. As she soaked in hot water, her tensions slipped away. Relaxed, she donned a robe and joined Lisette beside the fire.

"You were in such a hurry last night," Lisette said casually as she poured the coffee, "I didn't get to hear anything about the ball. Did you have fun?"

"*Oui*." Putting aside the disturbing memory of Alain and his fiery kiss, Simone told her friend of her adventures at the masque, her green eyes dancing merrily.

"Oh," Lisette cried when the girl dropped a butter knife, "my old nurse used to tell me that if you drop a knife, you'll receive a gentleman caller."

"I receive gentlemen every day." Simone smiled wryly. "But even the ones who were eager to dance with me last night come only to practice their fencing with Jean-Paul."

"That wouldn't be their excuse if they could see you now. You look so pretty, they would never recognize a certain boy of their acquaintance. I can hardly wait to see you in the dress. Do you really like it?"

"Very much. You always choose well for me."

"I have something else, a small gift," Lisette said,

pulling a dainty lace cap from her pocket. "It's the latest fashion from Paris. I thought you might enjoy it."

"I've seen these in the shop windows." Simone hurried to the mirror to try it on. Lisette thought her excitement was so completely female it was hard to remember that she spent most of her time masquerading as a boy.

"What was that noise?" Frowning, Lissette rose suddenly. "Did you hear a crash? I must see what it was. Why don't you try on the dress while I am gone?"

When Lisette closed the bedroom door, Simone slipped the dress over her head and went into the dressing room to stand before the full-length mirror. She had worked her way up the numerous pearl buttons from the hem of the gown almost to the low, square-cut décolletage when a light rap sounded on the door.

"Come in," she called. "What do you think?" she asked without looking around.

"I think you're beautiful," a familiar male voice answered caressingly, "as I have from the first time I saw you."

Simone whirled in alarm, her fingers fumbling as she hastened to finish buttoning her bodice. Alain stood in the doorway to the parlor, as he had the night they had met. Although the length of the room was between them, she retreated a step, warning, "Don't you come near me."

A pained expression on his face, he nodded. "I promise to stay away, if you promise to come into the parlor, where we can talk."

"I don't . . ." She changed her mind about arguing when he stirred restively. "*Très bien*, sir, but I hold you to your word."

"On my honor." Bowing, he stepped back to permit her to pass.

Simone preceded him into the parlor and sat on a chair beside the hearth, where she watched him warily. He took the chair opposite her, leaning forward so his elbows were propped on his powerful thighs. For a long, silent moment, he seemed to be memorizing a pattern in the Turkey carpet. At last, he said carefully, "First, mam'selle, I apologize if my behavior last night caused you alarm. I usually don't act in so impetuous a manner."

"I see," she said coldly, staring at a space somewhere over his shoulder. "I just bring out the worst in you?"

He frowned at her. At first glance, the girl looked demure in her floral gown and lace cap, but a stubborn set to her jaw, and a chest that heaved most distractingly under the thin fabric of her gown, belied that impression. He could see she was not going to make this easy for him.

"I took you into the courtyard because I wanted to talk to you," he resumed doggedly, "to get to know you."

He paused, but she said nothing. "I know almost nothing about you, not even your name. But I understand you are alone in the world, and I would like to help you."

"Are you saying you would like to be my protector?" Her voice was flat.

"In a manner of speaking, yes."

"You doubt my ability to take care of myself?" Her hostile green eyes met his challengingly.

His dark gaze did not waver. "I don't think you should have to take care of yourself, *ma petite*."

"You would give me all a woman could want, dress me in silks, shower me with jewels?" she responded sarcastically. "I've had that sort of offer before, m'sieur, and I want no part of it."

"Just a minute," he broke in, white-faced with anger, but she would not be silenced.

"Men!" she exploded. "You think any woman who is not married or under the protection of a family is fair game."

"I didn't say that," Alain snarled, outraged at her accusation.

"*Non*, but every time I have been alone with you,

you have tried to force your will on me," she countered.

"I will not be accused of that," he thundered, jumping to his feet to pace the room. "I will admit I've kissed you, and I've enjoyed it. But I have never forced myself on you."

"Don't shout at me!" she shouted, rising to face him.

"Then don't accuse me of more than I've done." He came to tower over her.

She stood her ground as if daring him to break his promise. "You have never done more because you were never given the opportunity, Monsieur de Vallière," she informed him icily.

While he watched, mute with anger, she stormed over to the bedroom door, pausing to say tauntingly, "I suggest you get a hold on your temper before you leave. You really must work on it. It gives your opponent a definite advantage, or so I've heard."

Then she stepped into the other room and closed the door behind her. He grimaced in vexation when he heard the insulting click of the lock.

Jamming his hat onto his head, he nearly trampled Lisette, who lingered in the hall.

"It did not go well?" she asked unnecessarily.

Alain's answer was an inarticulate growl as he passed her.

"Where are you going?" the madam asked.

"To get drunk."

Lisette winced when the front door slammed with such force that the glass in it rattled. Then she turned with dread to face Simone's ire for arranging this ill-advised meeting.

Alain slumped over a table in a seedy bar, the first one he had come to after leaving Lisette's house, and poured himself another whiskey. His wrath had subsided a bit, and now he mulled over the conversation he had just had with the most provoking female he had ever had the misfortune to meet.

Why wouldn't she listen to reason? he brooded. How could he court a girl when he couldn't even find out her name? Though she tempted him beyond sweet sanity, she obviously did not share his feelings. She ran away every time he went near her.

He didn't care, he told himself. He didn't care if he ever saw her again. He tried to convince himself by mentally tallying her faults. She was stubborn and independent and prickly.

Stubborn and independent and prickly? His brow furrowed, Alain closed his eyes and attempted to drown out the raucous sounds around him as he dredged his memory, but he could not recall whence that ready—and apt—description had sprung.

Drawing deeply on his drink, he reminded himself that she twisted everything he said, using his own words against him.

Suddenly he set down his drink so hard that the bottle bounced on the table. Those words—he had spoken them only yesterday, to Jean-Paul.

"Jean-Paul," he mumbled wonderingly. He looked enough like the girl to be her brother. How else would she know what he had said at the *salle*? If she were the sister of that surly lad, it would explain her animosity toward him, which he had found inexplicable until now.

Purposefully, Alain stood and tossed some coins onto the table. Then, swaying slightly, he left the tavern.

The pounding on the door made Simone start from a restless sleep. She was groggy, weary, and drained after the confrontation with Alain and an emotional scene with Lisette that had ended in tearful forgiveness.

When the hammering continued, Simone burrowed her head deeper into her pillow. Who could be so ill-mannered as to wake her in the middle of the night?

"Open up, Jean-Paul," Alain ordered through the door.

"I should have guessed," she groaned to herself. Sitting up in bed, she shouted, "Go away! The *salle* is closed."

"I want to talk to you."

"Talk to me tomorrow," she yelled, punching her pillow with every syllable. Damn the man, why didn't he leave her alone?

The pounding ceased, and Alain crooned dangerously, "You young *coquin*, I warn you. If I have to break this door down, I will."

He sounded as if he meant what he said.

"*Un moment.*" Jumping up, Simone pulled on her trousers, tucking in her nightgown, hoping it looked like a shirt. She had no time to bind her breasts, and her wadded nightgown made her baggy pants balloon bizarrely. She prayed the man would not notice either oddity in the dark. Schooling her face into a scowl, she opened the door a crack and asked curtly, "What do you want?"

"I want to know what her name is and where I can find her." Shoving the door open, Alain strode into Jean-Paul's bedchamber and looked around as if he expected to find someone lurking in the shadows.

"Where you can find who?" Simone snapped. She retreated a step when the big man swung toward her, his broad shoulders seeming to fill the tiny room.

"Your sister!" he roared.

"My what?" she hooted.

"Don't play games with me, boy. She plays enough for all of us."

"I don't know what you're talking about. I don't have a sister."

Alain stared at Jean-Paul closely through the darkness. "I think you're lying. If you were not so much younger, I'd believe you were her twin."

"You watch who you're calling a liar, you big lummox," the boy answered hotly. "Especially when you smell like a distillery and are so drunk you can't see straight."

"I am not drunk, and I see much more than I did. Are you going to tell me what I want to know, or do I have to shake the truth out of you?"

"Not without a fight." Simone dived for Serge's sword, which still lay on her table.

"Oh, no you don't." Alain lunged for the boy, his weight carrying both of them to the floor in a tangled heap.

Crushed under the Alain's powerful body, Simone lay still for a moment, trying to regain her breath.

"*Nom de Dieu,*" Alain muttered in confusion, feeling the unexpected softness under Jean-Paul's ill-fitting clothes. Lifting his head, he tried to discern the features of the face so close to his.

Suddenly erupting in a screech of outrage, the slender form beneath him began to thrash and buck wildly, jarring his teeth with every bounce. Small hands knotted into fists pounded on his back.

"Be still, you little wildcat," Alain grunted, trying to secure her flailing limbs. Bringing up one knee, he managed to capture one arm at her side. She gasped at the feel of him against her groin and fought all the harder.

Suddenly the rip of fabric could be heard, and Simone felt the cold night air on her bare breasts. She stifled a moan of frustration and redoubled her efforts to escape Alain's restraint. Strengthened by panic, she nearly threw him off.

Capturing both arms at last, he brought them above her head and held them in a tight one-handed grip. Outstretched on top of her, he lay still for a moment, panting.

Taking advantage of his seeming weariness, Simone began to struggle again.

"Don't." His grip on her wrists tightened, and his

voice was ragged against her ear. "Don't move that way
or we will both be sorry."

Something in his tone made her cease her writhing.

Sliding his free arm beneath her, the man rolled her
into a pool of moonlight and pinned her beneath him
again.

The light was behind him and Simone could not see
his face, but Alain saw his captive clearly. The green
eyes, so familiar, glittered in the moonlight as she
glared up at his shadowy form. Alain knew now that
the same mouth that had sneered boyishly at him was
just as capable of returning his kisses. The fine-
ly-chiseled features that were pleasing in the young
boy were strikingly beautiful in the girl.

And there was no doubt Jean-Paul was a girl. Alain's
eyes drifted downward to the smooth breasts, which
resembled polished white marble in the moon's glow.
In the shadowed crevice between them nestled an
object that shot sparks of green fire even in the dimness. Curious, he reached for it.

Flinching at the brush of his fingers on her skin, the
girl turned her head away. As Alain held up the band of
emeralds and looked at it, casual interest gave way to
stunned realization. It was Nicholas Devereaux's wedding ring.

"Simone!" he breathed, staring down at her disbelievingly. How could he have been so blind?

"Look at me," he commanded gently. When she
would not, he cupped her chin in his free hand and
turned her face toward him. Tears had left silvery
streaks on her cheeks. Even as she bit her lower lip and
fought to maintain her composure, she looked fragile,
vulnerable, and startlingly familiar.

"Why didn't you tell me?" he whispered.

"Why didn't you just leave me alone?" she countered in a strangled voice.

"I couldn't." Compelled by a rush of feeling, he bent
toward her. When she would have turned her head, his

hand cupping her chin held her fast, and he kissed her tenderly.

Simone became very still, hardly daring to breathe. This kiss was not like the others. His lips on hers were so gentle and sweet that she felt an ache deep inside. And when they left hers, she lay motionless, her eyes closed, feeling for a moment terribly empty and alone.

Was he mad? Alain wondered, staring down at her pale face. This was Simone, his ward, the little girl he had known since she was a child. But she was a child no longer. And if he didn't control himself now, she would be a woman before another hour passed.

Rising, he helped her to her feet and led her to sit on the edge of the bed. Then he closed the door and busied himself lighting a lamp. Anything to keep from touching her.

When he had collected himself, he turned to face her. She, too, seemed to have composed herself. Her expression cool and her chin high, her only concession to the situation was the shaky hand that clutched the tattered front of her nightgown.

"Why don't you tell me why you are here, living in a *salle d'armes*, disguised as a boy?" he began calmly.

"I am learning to fence."

"Enough evasions and lies, Simone. Virtually everything you have told me since the night we met has been one or the other." He went on when she would have protested, "Just tell me what you are doing here. You may as well. I'm going to find out."

She glared at him defiantly for a long moment, then she sighed. She was as tired as he of the deceptions and the scenes between them. Reluctantly, she told him everything—Marcel's attack, his search for her, Georges Chauvin's plan, her decision to hide, Serge's kindness, Lisette's friendship.

"But why did you hide from me when I returned? Didn't you know I would have helped you?"

"*Oui*, you would have helped me." She laughed bitterly. "Right into a marriage I did not want. Wasn't that your duty—to find a husband for Nicholas Devereaux's prickly daughter? Well, I did not care to be a responsibility for you to discharge efficiently. Isn't that how my father put it in his letter?

"Or would you prefer the way you said it yourself? 'The sooner I'm free of that obligation, the happier I'll be,'" she mimicked his words perfectly. "If our paths never crossed, M'sieur de Vallière, I supposed we could both be happy."

Alain was silent, accused by his own words, aching at the hurt he heard in her voice, pain he had caused. He realized how many times Jean-Paul must have overheard his frustration with his missing ward. He wished he could take back every word.

"Simone," he said tentatively.

"Please," she said irritably, "I'm not interested in anything you have to say."

"You'll be interested in this," he predicted with a wintry smile. Lounging against the table, he crossed his arms on his chest. "You *are* my responsibility and I *will* take care of you."

"I can take care of myself," she lashed out. "I don't need a guardian, a protector—*or* a husband."

"No, I suppose you can go on living here, as a boy, forever."

She glared at him, even angrier because she knew what he said was true.

"Besides," he said gently, "I wouldn't leave you to Baudin's tender mercies."

"Marcel has gone home. He's not expected back for weeks."

"When he does return, he won't find you here. You are coming to my house."

"I will not stay, unchaperoned, in the home of an unmarried man," she announced primly.

Alain bellowed with laughter. "You have lived,

unchaperoned, among a number of bachelors for the better part of a year."

"I can't just leave. What about my job?" she argued. "Serge will look for me."

"You are going to write him a letter and tell him you've found long-lost relatives upriver."

"But my friends will wonder what happened to me."

"They will believe what Serge tells them."

"What about Lisette?" she demanded stubbornly.

"I'll let her know you're safe."

"You have all the answers, don't you?" She frowned up at him. "Then tell me this, Alain, do you think you're strong enough to 'take me in hand'?" She threw more of his words back at him, her tone dripping sarcasm.

His jaw set grimly, he said, "I am going to try."

"I will not stay at your house," she insisted.

"Then I'll put Batiste on guard." Alain named his sturdy black servant Simone's jailor. "He will guard you day and night. You will never see beyond the walls of your bedchamber unless you give your word as a Creole gentlewoman that you will not try to escape."

The threat gave her pause, for she had seen his powerful slave, his back crisscrossed with scars from old beatings. Such a man must be dangerous indeed. At last she said grudgingly, "I give my word."

"*Très bien*. Gather what you will need for tonight." As he watched her move around the room, still gripping the front of her nightgown, he added casually, "There is one other thing, Simone. I will challenge Marcel when he returns."

"This is my fight," she said hotly, wheeling on him.

Alain's face was stony. "Not anymore."

Picking up her cast-off jacket, he helped her into it as politely as if she were dressed in satins and lace. "Come, I'll send Batiste for the rest of your things before morning."

As they walked to Alain's house on fashionable

Esplanade, he observed Simone carefully to see she did not bolt, his taut control belying the maelstrom of emotion he felt. How could he have been so stupid? Both of the females he had sought, the black-haired beauty and his ward, had been under his nose all the time, all wrapped up in an untidy package named Jean-Paul. And how could he have been so blind, he wondered, watching the girl beside him. She was beautiful.

Unlocking a door cut into a larger carriage gate, Alain led Simone into a spacious courtyard bordered on three sides by the house and its outbuildings and on the fourth by a high wall. Outside the main house, a staircase mounted to a gallery, along which were ranged the sleeping quarters. He showed her to an elegant parlor on the lower floor, and, reminding her of her promise, left to awaken Batiste.

When Alain returned, he led Simone through the courtyard and up the stairs, setting forth his rules. "You will use my room. Since it's hardly proper for me to sleep under the same roof, I'll stay in the garçonnière." He gestured across the courtyard toward the apartments set aside for the boys of a family. Stopping abruptly, he scowled at her. "What's so funny?"

"That you worry about improprieties," she answered with ill-concealed amusement. "My reputation will be ruined when people learn I'm staying, unchaperoned, in a bachelor's home."

"The innuendo would be far worse if word got out you were living in a *salle*," he snapped.

"I agree." She laughed aloud. "I fear I am already a tainted woman."

"Don't say that," he warned dangerously, throwing open the door to his bedroom. "Let me get a few things. Batiste will move the rest of my clothing tomorrow. You may have the run of the house and the courtyard, Simone, but do not set foot in the passageway, on the gallery, or in the alley where you might be seen until I have had time to even the score with Marcel."

"I won't be a prisoner," she protested, following him from the chiffonier to the doorway.

"No, you won't," Alain agreed perversely. "Here, sleep in this." He handed her a shirt.

"You're treating me like a prisoner, or a child," she stormed.

"Not a child." He stopped and stared at her, a blaze of desire flickering in his brown eyes before he turned away.

Uneasily, Simone tugged the front of her jacket together.

"*Bonne nuit, ma petite,*" he said softly. "Sleep well. You are safe now."

Sinking down on the bed, Simone stared despairingly at the door he closed behind him. She had just traded freedom for safety, and she did not like the bargain she had been forced to make.

8

The soft sound of a door closing roused Simone. Lifting her head groggily, she looked around. She was alone in an unfamiliar room—Alain's bedchamber.

She fell back onto the pillow, feeling weary even after her rest. Her emotions had been in such turmoil last night that she had thought she would never sleep. But apparently she had, and well into the day. She listened for the early-morning cries of the street vendors, but all she heard were muffled voices and the clatter of pans from the kitchen.

If Alain was ready to face the day, so was she, she thought determinedly, sitting up. But when she surveyed the room, she discovered the clothing she had worn was gone.

I gave my word I wouldn't try to escape, she thought crossly. He didn't have to take my clothes to be sure.

She was still frowning when there was a light tap on the door. Before she could respond, it opened and Alain's large figure filled the doorway. He carried a valise in one hand, and in the other he balanced a saucer and a steaming cup of coffee.

"*Bonjour,*" he called cheerfully.

"Do not come in here until you tell me where my

clothes are," Simone ordered, tugging the covers up over her chest.

"I've brought you some." Disregarding her command, he walked over to the bed. "And *café au lait*."

"*Merci*." She accepted the cup, watching as he set the valise at the foot of the bed. Rummaging in it, he pulled out one of her own gowns.

She regarded him incredulously. "Where did you get—"

"From your landlady. She saved a few of your possessions from the auctioneer, and when she learned I was your guardian, she gave them to me. These should keep you until I can buy some a bit more fitting."

"More fitting for what?" she asked tautly.

Realizing he had hurt her pride, Alain said softly, "Simone, I'm your guardian. You need new clothes, and I want you to have them."

"You want to dress me so I will attract a husband," she charged, throwing back the blankets and jumping up to confront him. "If you think you're going to marry me off to the first suitor who comes along, Alain de Vallière, you can forget it. I want to choose my own husband, a man who will love me forever."

He stared down at her in stark silence. She had voiced the problem with which he had grappled during the long, sleepless night. It was his duty—and his dilemma—to see Nicholas's daughter married. Simone was his ward, damn it, and still very young. But she was all woman, and he could not forget the taste of her lips or the feel of her body against his.

Stop, he commanded himself silently, knowing he should leave. With effort, he turned and walked toward the door, saying over his shoulder, "I assure you I will always strive to do what is best for you. I want to care for you, to keep you safe."

"By keeping me locked away?" Simone demanded scorchingly. Oblivious to the scantiness of her attire, she followed.

"I don't want you out and about until I've settled with Marcel," he said, turning again to face her. It was a mistake. He felt the familiar stir in his loins as he tried without success to ignore the enticing view of her bare calves below his shirt.

"You promised you wouldn't treat me like a prisoner," she protested.

"I also promised to keep you safe," he countered.

"I do not believe Marcel would kill me."

"No, but he could kidnap you and make your life a living hell. Once we duel, he will understand you are in my care, or he will die." Distracted by the defiant face lifted toward his, he said huskily, "I don't want him ever to threaten, or touch, you again."

Unable to stop himself, he laced his fingers in Simone's short, tousled hair while his thumbs traced circles on the slim column of her neck where her pulse fluttered wildly. It was so tempting to lean forward to steal a kiss.

Suddenly remembering himself, he yanked his hands away. "For God's sake, girl, cover yourself," he groaned. "What are you trying to do to me?"

He knew by the way her face colored Simone had not remembered she was wearing nothing more than his shirt.

"I am not trying to do anything but talk to you," she spat, throwing the door open. "If you'll recall, you are the one who came into my room. And now you can leave." Placing her small hands against his chest, she shoved him out onto the gallery.

Alain blinked in surprise as the door slammed in his face. His jaw working with anger, he swung around to stare out at the courtyard. He gripped the banister in white-knuckled hands, railing silently against the entire situation.

He wanted her so badly he ached. But in all his experience with women, he had never seduced a virgin, and he wasn't going to start with his ward, he told himself harshly. He inhaled deeply, hoping to clear his head and rid himself of the fragrant scent of her, which seemed to linger in his nostrils. How he was going to live under the same roof with her, he did not know.

Deliberately, he turned his mind to business. Though he intended to win his duel with Marcel, Alain wanted to set up a trust for Simone. Arrangements must be made, in case his plans went awry: instructions to be left with Dominique Cuvillion, his attorney; Jean-Paul's letter of resignation and an apology to be delivered to Serge; and a call to pay on Lisette. Slapping the rail decisively, he set out.

On the other side of the door, Simone fumed. How would she endure seeing Alain day in and day out? He always made her angry, and she never knew where she stood with him. One moment he looked as if he were going to kiss her, the next he acted as if he thought *she* was going to ravish *him*. She knew he thought of her as an obligation, yet when he had spoken to her, his voice had been vibrant with warmth and caring. He was high-handed, and he insisted on fighting her battles, but his touch had been gentle. How she hated the man and the confusion he caused her.

Her shoulders slumped dejectedly when she heard the clanking of the front gate. He had probably gone to interview potential husbands for her, she brooded, to find someone to take her off his hands. But her wrath had burned itself out, and all she felt now was sorrow at the thought.

Dispiritedly, she went to the washstand and found that the water in the pitcher was warm. So she *had* heard a door close earlier, she thought as she scrubbed the sleep from her eyes.

She unpacked the valise Alain had left for her, discovering the black dress she had worn to Nicholas's funeral, as well as her undergarments and stockings and shoes. Rebelliously, she rejected the frock Alain had spread on the bed for her and donned instead the heavy black dress. As she drew a comb through her hair, she decided it stuck out as badly on Simone as it had on Jean-Paul.

Downstairs, she halted uncertainly under a massive fig tree in the courtyard. Through the doorway of the kitchen, she could see Batiste, the muscles of his powerful back rippling under his shirt as he kneaded bread dough. The servant was even brawnier than his muscular master. Though intent on his task, he must have sensed her presence, for he looked over his shoulder.

"Morning, miss," he addressed her politely, his voice rumbling from deep in his massive chest.

"*Bonjour.*" She smiled tentatively.

"Did you sleep well?"

"*Oui, merci.*" She stepped nearer, encouraged by his amiable greeting.

"I'm Batiste Joseph," he said, wiping his flour-dusted hands on a towel. "Alain asked me to look after you."

"I know," she answered shyly from the doorway. "I'm Simone Devereaux."

Nodding at the cup she carried, he asked, "Would you like more coffee?"

"I can get it. I'm not really accustomed to being waited on."

"Then I think you must become accustomed to it." He smiled unexpectedly, his teeth flashing white in his ebony-skinned face. "'Lain says I'm to take care of you. I'll cook you an omelette while the dough rests." Taking her cup, he refilled it and returned it to her. Then he began to prepare her breakfast.

Simone lingered, unwilling to be banished from the familiar comfort of the kitchen. Batiste did not seem so bad after all, certainly not the surly warden she had expected.

Without turning, he suggested, "If you're going to wait, perhaps you'd like to sit down." He gestured toward a tall stool in the corner.

Simone perched on the seat while he cooked. For a time, the only sound in the kitchen was the sizzle of frying bacon. Then she asked, "Did you bring hot water to my room earlier?"

"Did I wake you? I think I'll have to practice if I'm to become a good lady's maid." He grinned over his broad shoulder.

"Valet, cook, baker—I think you're already a man of many talents." She grinned back. Shaking his head in private amusement, the big man returned his attention to his cooking. This Simone was lovely and spirited, just the way Alain liked them. No wonder he was in such a quandary, having her under his roof.

"How long has Monsieur de Vallière owned you?" Simone asked conversationally.

"He doesn't own me," Batiste replied.

"I . . . I'm sorry. I just assumed . . ."

"That's all right. Everybody assumes. If they didn't, I'd probably be sold right back into slavery by some bounty hunter, papers or no papers."

"I suppose that's true," Simone agreed reluctantly, "but it's sad to contemplate."

"There are many sad things in the world, little one," Batiste said gently. "My life was a lot sadder before Alain. He bought me when I was half dead, beaten by an overseer. Everyone, including 'Lain's own family, thought he was mad to buy me. But he hauled me home—"

"To Bois Blanc," Simone supplied, dredging up the name of the de Vallière plantation from distant memory.

"That's right," Batiste confirmed as he set a tray for her. "He taught me to speak French and to read and write. When I was healed, he gave me my manumission papers and wished me *bonne chance*."

"But you didn't go?" She hopped nimbly from the stool.

"No, as a free man, I am Alain's willing servant. And his friend."

"It sounds as if you both benefit from this arrangement," Simone observed.

"Indeed." Batiste regarded her with approval. The girl was wise beyond her years.

"How did you come to have Joseph as your last name?" she asked, taking the tray from him.

"I chose 'Lain's middle name. It was my first act as a free man."

"Alain Joseph de Vallière." Simone smiled as if she had just learned a delightful secret.

Batiste watched her trim, graceful figure as she walked across the chilly courtyard to the dining room. Roused from his bed last night, he had seen how anxious Alain had been. He had observed his testy employer this morning. Now that he had seen the source of both moods, he understood. And he was overjoyed.

Perhaps the big Creole had finally met his match in this little thing who had masqueraded as a boy, stood up to her guardian, and ejected him from his own bedroom this morning. Batiste chuckled. Though he thought he knew how 'Lain felt about the girl, he did not know yet how she felt. But something told him life was going to be very interesting in this house from now on.

"And her waist is only about this wide." Alain's big hands measured a narrow span in the air before he concluded sheepishly, "Well, you know."

"Please, 'Lain"—Lisette rolled her eyes—"I've been buying Simone's clothes for her for months."

"I know." He sighed. "I just want everything to be right for her. But I want the wardrobe quickly," he directed. "Price is no object. Did I mention that?"

"Several times." She cocked an eyebrow in exasperation. "I told you, I'll go to my dressmaker's this very morning. In the meantime, I have a couple of Simone's dresses here. Shall I send Jude over with them?"

"*Oui, merci*," he agreed, preparing to leave.

"Alain"—the woman halted him earnestly—"you do know that if I had realized Simone was your missing ward, I never would have promised to keep her secret from you?"

"I know."

"Why did she hide from you?" Lisette could not resist asking.

"Thanks to something she overheard me say at the *salle*, Simone has the idea that I want nothing more than to marry her off," he confessed with a sigh.

"And you haven't been able to make her understand that's the last thing you want?"

He shook his head.

"You love her, don't you, 'Lain?"

"*Oui*, though how I fell in love with such an impossible female, I'll never know."

"Have you told her how you feel?" she asked.

"*Non!*" he shouted. Then, seeing her surprise at his vehemence, he explained in a more moderate tone, "This is a real dilemma, Lise. Even though I love her, I can't do anything about it."

"Why not?"

"Because I'm her guardian. How would it look if I pressed my attentions on an innocent girl? I don't want anyone, least of all Simone, to think I took advantage of her."

"Don't you think she knows her own mind?" Lisette argued.

"Any advances I made now would be inappropriate," Alain maintained stubbornly.

"Having her in your home without a chaperon is inappropriate."

"No one knows she's there. I want to keep it that way until Marcel and I have had a chance . . . to talk."

"So you are going to challenge Marcel?"

"Better me than Simone, don't you think?"

"You think she would?" the woman asked, aghast.

"Of course, she would. That is another reason to keep her at home and out of trouble."

"Then when you've settled with him?"

"Once she is safe, I'll introduce my ward to *les bonnes familles*. No one need know about the *salle*; we'll tell everyone she has been living in the country."

"Do you know what you're suggesting, 'Lain?"

"That I introduce her to the most eligible bachelors in Louisiana," he answered harshly. "Simone has the right to choose whom she will marry. She feels very strongly about that. And now that I know the woman she has become, I do too."

"But—"

He cut her off with an impatient gesture. "She is young and inexperienced. I cannot ask her to marry me until she knows what she wants." He did not add that the thought that it might be another man made his stomach roil.

Lisette eyed her friend sympathetically. "What if she wants you?"

"I am hers," he said simply.

That night, in Alain's bedchamber, Simone dressed for dinner in the dainty gown she had tried on at Lisette's house. Had it been only last night? Her entire world had changed since then.

Alain's immense copper bathtub stood on the hearth, the water it held now cold. After Jude brought her clothes and a promise from Lisette to call the next day, Simone had decided to concentrate on being a girl again. She was through hiding her feminine attributes.

She had spent a long time in the tub, washing her hair until it began to show traces of its original rich brown. Fluffing her short, glossy hair with her fingers, she allowed it to dry in curls around her face.

As she slipped into a gossamer chemise and stockings, Simone reveled in the slide of silk against her skin. Then she donned a stiff petticoat and the feminine dress. As she buttoned the long row of pearl buttons up the front of the gown, she examined her reflec-

tion in the mirror and was pleased with what she saw.
Alain could not fail to notice she was a woman.

He noticed. A self-conscious blush stained Simone's
cheeks when she saw the admiration in his dark eyes.
"*Bonsoir, chère,*" he greeted her as she descended the
staircase. "You look lovely."

"*Merci.*" Her blush deepened when he kissed her
work-roughened hand.

"Come, Batiste has prepared a feast for us." Offering
his arm, Alain escorted Simone to the elegant dining
room, where the polished table reflected the crystal
chandelier overhead.

True to his word, dinner was indeed a feast, and
Alain was a charming host. They laughed and chatted
easily, as if the explosive scene between them that
morning had never occurred. At last, he said seriously,
"I never had a chance to tell you, Simone, how sorry I
was when I heard of your father's death."

"*Merci,*" she whispered with a lump in her throat.
Desperate not to cry, she quickly changed the subject.
"When I was talking to Batiste today, I remembered the
name of your family's plantation. Bois Blanc, isn't it?"

"White Wood," he confirmed. "You have a good
memory." Fishing in his pocket, he added, "And so do
I." He laid a bag of lemon drops on the table. "Are
these still your favorite?"

"Oh yes. Thank you." Touched by his gesture, she
beamed at him, and Alain's heart stood still.

"Do you," He cleared his throat, disturbed to find
his voice unsteady. "Do you remember what you asked
me when I left that first time?"

"Who would bring me candies," she recalled with a
smile.

"And teach you to fence," he amended.

"It seems you've done both, m'sieur." She surprised
him by laughing. "And I confess I prefer the candies."

"So do I, *chère.*" His deep chuckle mingled with
hers. "And I greatly favor Simone over Jean-Paul."

Smiling crookedly, he asked, "Since we're going to be living under the same roof, can we declare a truce? I promise I will be an exemplary friend."

After a moment, Simone smiled ruefully and said, "I am willing to declare a truce." Privately she wondered if friendship meant Alain would never touch her, never kiss her again. Though she should not care, she did, but she could not let him know. She shrugged carelessly. "Perhaps friendship will come in time."

So will love, *ma petite,* if I have anything to say about it, Alain thought with satisfaction. *"Très bien,"* he said heartily, rising to help her from her chair. "Tell me, do you still play the card games Nicholas and I taught you?"

"Perhaps if you refresh my memory," she suggested innocently. "It's been so long."

"It will come back to you," he assured her. Blissfully ignorant of Jean-Paul's participation in many all-night card games with Claude and friends, he led Simone into the parlor.

Near midnight, Alain lingered in his study next to the room where his ward now slept. Outside, the wind had risen and thunder rolled in the distance, but he was warm in front of the fire, sipping a brandy.

His long frame draped over a chair, he marveled at his discovery of Simone and wondered what had happened to the child who had pestered him all those years ago, chattering to attract his attention, sulking when that attention was brief. Since he had found her last night, he delighted in every moment spent with her, in every new facet of her personality revealed to him. He hadn't even minded being fleeced quite professionally in a game of *bourrée.* She was Nicholas's daughter, after all, he chuckled to himself.

Suddenly the night sky outside the window was split by a blinding bolt of lightning, and thunder cracked overhead, eliciting a cry from the next room.

Instantly Alain was on his feet, racing through the

wind-lashed rain along the gallery to the bedroom door. As he entered, the room was illuminated by stark white light, and the thunder sounded again close at hand.

Simone sat bolt upright in bed. "Stay back!" she shouted wildly.

"I came to see if you were all right," he answered. Then, realizing she was still asleep, he went to her, uncaring that he left a trail of water across the floor. "Wake up, Simone," he said softly, "you're having a bad dream."

"Don't make me hurt you," she pleaded, recoiling in horror from a scene only she could see. "So much blood! What have I done?"

Sitting beside her on the bed, Alain reached out to touch her shoulder, but he met with a flailing punch that nearly unseated him.

"I'll never be your mistress!" she cried desperately. "Never!"

"Simone, my poor little love," he murmured sadly, "wake up." He managed to capture her thrashing arms and shake her gently.

Drawing a shuddering breath, she opened her eyes to look at him dully. "Alain?" She touched his face as if to be sure he was there. "You're wet."

"I came when I heard you cry out. You were having a nightmare, *chère*."

"It really is storming. I was dreaming of the night . . ." Her voice trailed off pitifully.

"It's all right. You don't have to be afraid," he whispered. Unmindful of his wet clothes, he drew her against him, stroking her hair comfortingly. "I am here now."

A strangled sob escaped her, and abruptly Simone buried her face against his chest. While she wept, Alain cradled her in strong, protective arms and for the first time since her father's death, she did not feel alone.

* * *

"Isn't this one beautiful?" Simone asked excitedly. Holding a soft green dress in front of her, she waltzed around the bedroom, skipping through patches of the spring sunlight pouring in through the windows and the door on the gallery.

"Very pretty," Lisette approved as she unpacked more boxes.

Parcels from the shoemaker were stacked on the slipper chair, assorted hat boxes littered the bed. The bed was a jumble of splendid colors and textures as dresses and evening gowns, frilly chemises and stiff petticoats, an opera cape and a riding habit were added to the heap.

"'Lain must have liked the perfume you wore the night of the ball," Lisette said. "He bought you more."

"I liked it, too." Simone pirouetted past and took the bottle from her friend's hand.

"Why don't you try on that green dress while I put these things away?" Lisette suggested. "If we hurry, I'll have time to see how you're progressing on your needlework."

Simone spun away to close the door at once. As soon as she had changed, she said eagerly, "I'll put the rest away later, Lisette. Come downstairs now and let me show you what I've accomplished since our last lesson."

When the woman had visited for the first time a couple of weeks before, she had discovered that, though Simone could sew, she did not know how to embroider. Immediately, she set out to teach her. Both of them now looked forward to the quiet interludes when they chatted companionably.

After they were settled in the parlor, Simone asked, "Lisette, how long have you known Alain?"

"All his life." The madam was concentrating on unsnarling her thread. "His family and mine were neighbors."

"I can't imagine Alain as a child."

"He was a terror," Lisette said solemnly. Then she

smiled. "And out of the three de Vallière boys, he was my favorite."

"I didn't know Alain had brothers." Simone regarded her with surprise over her embroidery hoop.

"Two brothers and two sisters. But only Pascal, Alain's older brother, is left. The same epidemic that killed my family took its toll on his as well." Lisette bent over her work in exaggerated concentration.

"I'm sorry," Simone murmured.

"It was a long time ago," Lisette said briskly. "That year was hard for the de Vallière family. Madame de Vallière died as well, leaving Alain's father a very bitter man. I don't think he's said a kind word to his sons since."

"So that is why Alain lives in New Orleans and not in the country."

"There's nothing for him at Bois Blanc. Pascal will inherit the plantation, and he doesn't want Alain there."

"Why not?" Simone asked indignantly.

"Pascal has always been sickly. He's resented Alain's strength and vitality from childhood. Later he despised him for his business acumen. So, rather than fight with his brother, 'Lain seldom goes home. He has made a life for himself, managing the family interests here in New Orleans."

"Poor Alain, he hasn't known much love in his life, has he?"

"He's known a little," Lisette answered. "I'll always love him because he's been the best friend I've ever had. He stood by me when no one else would."

"I think you've been a good friend to him, too, Lisette. And I'm sorry if my masquerade caused any strain on your friendship."

"Alain understood that I had given my word to you. He's an honorable man. I'm just glad it's over."

"Glad what's over?" the man asked from the doorway.

"Winter," Simone lied, her face coloring tellingly. She had not heard him come in.

"So am I," Alain said, moving to stand beside her

chair. "Especially when I find you looking like a spring day. Is that a new gown you're wearing?"

"*Oui*. My new clothes came today." Simone sprung up at once and twirled ingenuously for his inspection. "Do you like it?"

"It's lovely." His voice was vibrant. "Do *you* like it?"

"*Oui*, I've never had such beautiful things."

"Everything is perfect, just as you wanted," Lisette assured him softly.

He smiled at the words, beaming all the more when Simone impulsively tiptoed to kiss his cheek and murmured, "*Merci*, Alain."

"My pleasure, *ma petite*." His arms closed around her, and he held her against him for a moment. "And you smell good, too."

Simone was flustered when he released her. Why did he have this effect on her? All he had done was give her a brotherly hug, and her heart was pounding.

Seeking to cover her discomfiture, she said crisply, "As much as I love all you bought me, I think you spent too much money. I don't know how I'll ever be able to repay you."

"I don't expect you to. It is my money to spend, at least until the next card game. I'm beginning to be sorry I taught her," he complained good-naturedly to Lisette.

At the sound of the bell at the gate, his face clouded. "Who could that be? I'm not expecting anyone. I'm afraid you must go upstairs, Simone," he said apologetically. "We cannot risk anyone seeing you."

The girl's good mood was swept away by the realization that she was little more than a prisoner in Alain's house. His generosity and all her new clothes could not change that fact. Sorrowful and silent, she left the parlor.

A few steps behind her, Lisette said, "I will see myself out the back way and come tomorrow."

The women were scarcely out of sight when Alain

went to answer the door. "Serge, sorry to keep you waiting," he greeted his friend, who waited on the *banquette*. "It took me a moment to remember Batiste is out at the market. Come in."

Her door slightly ajar, Simone listened to the voices drifting up from the courtyard. Recognizing the fencing master's voice, she smiled nostalgically, missing him and his kindness.

"Would you care for some *café*?" Alain was asking.

"*Oui*, and let us sit out here. It's such a beautiful day."

After a moment, Simone heard the men settle in the courtyard.

"Since you have not come to the *salle* for weeks, I decided I must call on you," Serge said lazily.

"Business affairs have occupied me," Alain explained.

"More likely affairs of the heart have occupied you," the other man teased. Leaning toward his friend, he sniffed. "You have about you the distinct fragrance of perfume, *mon ami,* the scent of roses. Is it true you've taken Lisette Dupré as your mistress?"

"What makes you think that?"

"It's what everyone says. You are the envy of the *salle*. She is a rare beauty indeed, and very unobtainable, until now. But then, you always had great luck with the ladies."

Alain glanced uneasily toward the gallery. He could not tell if Simone's door was closed or if it stood open a crack. Suspecting the latter, he said, "I've had no greater luck than you, *mon ami.*"

"You're too modest." Serge laughed. "You stole that dancer in Paris from under my nose quite nicely. What was her name?"

"Hélène," Alain mumbled uncomfortably.

"Nor have I forgotten the innkeeper's daughter," Serge accused humorously.

"Innkeeper's daughter?" Alain frowned, unable to place that conquest.

"Don't tell me you've forgotten Manon. Or what about—"

"Surely you haven't come to catalogue my idle flirtations," Alain interrupted.

"Idle flirtations?" Serge exploded in laughter. "The pretty gypsy —Carmen, wasn't it?—would have killed for you."

Out of the corner of his eye, Alain saw Simone's door close.

"What did you come for, Serge?" he growled.

"To ask if you will practice with me before the assaut d'armes in May," Serge replied, somewhat surprised by his friend's brusqueness. "You're the only opponent who truly tests my skills."

"I heard there was to be a tournament for the maîtres d'armes. I'd be glad to help," Alain agreed, remorseful at his impatience.

"*Merci beaucoup*." The fencing master rose and bowed politely. "*Pardon*, my friend, but I have several private lessons this evening and I must get back to the *salle*."

Mounting the stairs to the second floor a little later, Alain knocked on Simone's door and called, "You can come out now."

"I prefer to stay in, *merci*," she informed him through the closed panel.

"I thought you would like to hear about our caller."

"I know it was Serge."

"Don't you want to hear about our conversation?"

"I heard all I need to know about your 'idle flirtations.'" The door was flung open, and Simone glowered at him.

Alain fought back a smile. "They happened long ago, *ma petite*. There's no reason for you to be jealous now."

"Jealous?" she hissed. "Why should I care whom my guardian sees? Though why my father ever decided to hand my future to a ne'er-do-well, a ladies' man—"

"That's the second time you've accused me of being

a ladies' man. Just where did you get that idea?" he interrupted.

"You told me so yourself, outside Lisette's house."

"When you were Jean-Paul. Now I remember. You provoked me into that."

"It was still fine talk for a boy to hear," she shot back.

"Accusing me of loitering in front of a whorehouse was fine talk for a girl to speak," he thundered, out of patience at last.

She glared at him, incensed that he was right. "You, sir," she said haughtily, "are a cad and a *roué*, not a suitable guardian for a young lady."

"And you, mam'selle, are a complete hoyden. Your taste of freedom obviously did not agree with you. It proves what I've always said. You need someone to take you in hand."

"Well, it won't be you!" she yelled.

"Not tonight anyway," he agreed, his voice deceptively mild. "I fear if I tried to take you in hand now, I would strangle you." With that, he turned on his heel and disappeared into his study.

9

It was wash day in the Vieux Carré, and the river-scented wind carried the Monday morning odors—the mingled scents of soap, bluing, and starch and the aroma of red beans cooking on wood stoves in every household.

Peeping over a stack of clean towels, Simone climbed the stairs to the garçonnière. She smiled at Batiste over the railing as he heated water in washtubs near the kitchen and waited for her to bring the soiled linens from Alain's room.

The day was warm, and in the fig tree a bird was chirping cheerfully. The big servant also sang, his voice deep and soothing. Simone listened, her bad mood of the night before dissipating with the morning fog.

At the top of the stairs, her steps faltered. She did not know why she should be nervous. Alain had gone hours before, leaving his door and the louvers of his jalousie window open to the breeze. During the past few weeks, bored with idleness, she had often helped with the chores, but this was the first time she had gone into Alain's room.

Her feet made no sound on the thick Turkey carpet as she entered. Balancing her burden of towels, she pulled back the curtains that billowed softly over the open windows. Sunshine streamed into the orderly room. The narrow tester bed was rumpled and unmade, but no clothing or shoes cluttered the floor. The only thing that seemed out of place was a towel crumpled beside the bathtub on the brick hearth.

Humming, Simone hung clean towels on the back of the washstand. Quickly she stripped the linens from the bed, trying not to notice the imprint of Alain's head on his pillow or the scent of him wafting from the sheets as she wadded them into a bundle and laid them at the foot of the bed.

She went to pick up the towel from the floor, anxious to leave. Just being there made her feel vulnerable somehow. She must not soften toward Alain when there were still battles to fight. Her guardian was charged with finding a husband for her, after all.

As Simone stood beside the mantel, her eyes fell upon a sword lying there. It looked like . . . it was! Smiling incredulously, she picked up her father's sword and turned it over in her hand. She had feared it was lost forever.

"I know you were angry last night, but that's no reason to ambush a man in his own room," Alain teased from behind her.

Simone turned to see him on the landing. "I didn't hear you come up," she greeted him breathlessly, wondering how such a big man could walk so quietly.

Removing his hat, he stepped into the room. "Would you accept that as a peace offering?" He nodded to the sword she held.

"I may have it? Really?"

"Really," he replied. As he walked toward her, he carelessly pitched his hat toward a rack on the wall, where it caught neatly on one of the pegs.

"*Merci*, Alain." Forgetting the harsh words they had

spoken last night, she smiled radiantly. "How did you get it?"

"I told you I got a few things from your landlady." He stood so close to her that the toes of his polished boots disappeared under her full skirt. "What are you doing in here, *chère*?" he asked softly.

"I came to get your linens for the laundry." She ducked swiftly to scoop the towel from the floor with her free hand as if to offer proof.

"Ah yes, the laundry," he murmured, taking it from her when she rose and tossing it onto the sheets.

Still he did not touch her, but Simone suddenly wished he would.

His dark eyes roved over her approvingly, taking in her rolled sleeves and the apron she wore over her housedress.

"What a pretty picture you make, Simone," he complimented her, "very feminine and very domestic. Almost wifely."

At his choice of words, her green eyes darkened to the color of a tempestuous sea.

"Wait," he commanded quietly. "Before you storm away from me again, there's something I've wanted to say since the night I discovered you hiding at the *salle*."

"*Oui*?" Trepidation mixed with unexpected anticipation as she watched him.

Alain flexed tense shoulder muscles and searched for the right words. "I just want you to know, Simone, I would never make you marry against your will. I promise you'll be able to choose your own husband."

She looked at him blankly for a second. He was telling her what she had wanted to hear since she had learned he was her guardian. But just now, when he had stared at her with that gleam in his eye, she had felt butterflies in her stomach that had nothing to do with their conversation.

What was wrong with her? she asked herself as she

did almost every time he came near. Why did he cause her pulse to race and her breath to grow short? And why did she feel such absurd disappointment at his words?

"*Merci*," she said flatly, scooping up the bundle of soiled linens. Her heart was pounding, but she forced herself to appear calm. "You must excuse me. Batiste is waiting. The water is probably hot by now."

"Of course." With a rueful expression, Alain watched her hasty departure. He thought he had given her one of her heart's desires, yet she acted as if she could not escape his company fast enough. He would never understand women, and this one in particular.

Scowling, he walked out onto the landing. In the courtyard below, Simone turned suddenly, her bundle still slung under one arm, and brought the sword up in front of her face in a graceful fencer's salute. "Thank you for my father's sword, 'Lain," she called up to him. "It means a great deal to me."

Alain stood on the gallery, overlooking the narrow street and smoked a slender black cigar. Simone had already retired, using the excuse that she wanted to rise early to assist Batiste with the ironing. To listen to her, you would think the big black servant could not lift a flatiron without help from his *petite amie*.

Slouched against a post, Alain tried to shed his irritation. He inhaled deeply, savoring the scent of the night and of his own tobacco.

Suddenly his eyes narrowed as he peered through the darkness. Fabrice Chauvin lurked across the street, watching the house again.

Alain swore under his breath. He had known the young Creole was suspicious and it was painfully obvious that Fabrice was in love with Simone but he was letting emotion cloud his reason. In his determination to find out if his cousin had been discovered and taken in hand by her guardian, it had not even occurred to him that he might lead Marcel directly to her.

Alain considered going down to the street and trying to explain his actions and his motives to Fabrice. But he knew that, given the slightest proof of his suspicions, the young hothead would challenge him to a duel—a complication Alain did not choose to add to his difficulties. In the end, he went inside and closed the door, leaving Fabrice to his vigil.

"Have patience, *chère*," Lisette urged from the bench beside the fountain in the courtyard.

"I've been patient." The girl paced, her skirt swirling with each turn. "But I've been locked away here for three months."

"It is not Alain's fault that Marcel has not returned," Lisette reminded her.

"I know," Simone said crossly. "It's just that I feel so restless. I want to scream at Alain because he goes out and leaves me. And that happens more and more. When he is here, he is considerate, but it seems lately he goes out of his way not to be with me."

Not to be *alone* with you, Lisette corrected silently. Only yesterday she had listened to Alain complain of a similar restlessness. He was not happy when he was away from Simone, yet he was afraid of what he might do when he was with her.

That was the reason he had furnished the girl with a practice foil and a fencing mask. He had even returned Jean-Paul's clothes to her so they could practice fencing in the courtyard these warm evenings. According to Alain, they practiced until both were exhausted and drenched with sweat. Then Simone went up to her room to bathe and to bed, while he prowled, unable to sleep. But the practice seemed to make her happy, he confided, and it helped him keep his hands off her.

How simple it would be, Lisette mused, if she could

tell each how the other felt. Alain was too stubborn to admit his love to Simone, and Simone was too stubborn to admit hers even to herself. One day they would learn. Perhaps even today, she thought with satisfaction, hearing his tread in the passageway.

"Ladies, *bonjour*," Alain greeted them brightly. "Did you come prepared today, Lisette?"

"I did," she confirmed. With a mischievous glance at Simone, she set her hat securely on her blond head.

"Batiste," Alain shouted toward the kitchen, "is the picnic basket ready?"

"It is." The big man appeared with a mammoth hamper. "I was about to bring the carriage around."

"*Très bien*." Alain took the basket and said carelessly over his shoulder, "Then you're the only one who isn't ready, Simone. Run and put on your widow's cloak and veil."

"We're going out?" The girl looked thrilled.

"If you don't keep us waiting all day." He frowned playfully.

When she had hurried away, Alain turned to Lisette. "You are sure you don't mind playing chaperon?"

"Only for you, *mon ami*. But I tell you, if you can no longer control your baser instincts, you've become a weak man indeed." She shook her head in mock exasperation.

"I do wish Marcel would return," he acknowledged, only half in jest. "This arrangement causes me the tortures of the damned."

"You may suffer them awhile yet. Marcel's cousin, Charles Greaux, told me the reason he hasn't returned is that Madame Baudin is near death. He said Marcel is quite distraught. He's always been very close to his mother."

"True," Alain muttered, "though he once killed a man who called him a mama's boy."

When Simone returned, Alain's open landau was waiting, and Lisette was already settled on the seat.

"Where are we going?" she asked excitedly as Alain handed her in.

"To Lake Pontchartrain, where it is cool and private." He took the seat across from the women.

With a sharp whistle, Batiste urged the horses forward. The twin bays seemed to catch the spirit of the day and trotted smartly out of the carriage gate.

As the rig rolled down Esplanade, Simone spied a crowd of men headed along Barracks Street toward The Shades, a popular dueling spot under a stand of massive trees.

"Someone is dueling?" she asked unnecessarily.

"Undoubtedly. There have already been several differences of opinion regarding the *assaut*." Alain shrugged.

"The *assaut*?" Simone gasped. "How could I have forgotten? Why aren't you there, 'Lain?"

"Because I'm going on a picnic at the lake." His eyes caught hers through the veil and held them.

"Don't you want to be there to encourage Serge?"

"I've helped him practice and prepare, but today he has plenty of encouragement. He's surrounded by adoring admirers and won't miss me. I wanted to spend the afternoon with you, and Lisette," Alain said quietly.

Jostling off the road, the picnickers found an isolated stand of pines in the midst of a meadow. The lake was out of sight beyond the trees, but the water could be heard lapping softly at the shore.

Batiste spread a blanket on a lush bed of clover dotted with yellow dandelions and began to unpack the hamper. Taking off her cape and veil, Simone wandered to the water's edge, enjoying the spring day. Lake Pontchartrain stretched out to the horizon, its blue water glistening in the sunlight. Though she had seen it many times, she was always awed by its vastness.

On her way back, she gathered wildflowers, using her bonnet as a basket. She joined her friends, placing her bonnet on the blanket as a centerpiece for their makeshift table.

After lunch, Batiste took a fishing pole and went down to the water. Almost at once, Lisette sat up and announced, "Even the sun filtering through the leaves is too much for me. If I don't want to burn, I had better remove myself to the carriage. Batiste put up the top so I could nap in comfort. Wake me when you're ready to leave."

Simone watched her go, suddenly self-conscious when she felt Alain's gaze upon her. He lay on his side near her, braced on one elbow, admiring the way the breeze ruffled her short hair, lifting it gently from the nape of her neck.

"You look like a flower yourself in your pretty yellow dress, *chère*," he said lazily, watching her weave chains of dandelions and clover. "What is that you're making?"

"A garland." She held up the short length for his inspection.

Alain smiled knowingly. "My sisters used to make these. They would weave them to be as long as their beaux were tall."

"I don't have a beau," she answered, looping the ends of the chain together so it became a small band of flowers.

"Come now," he teased, "isn't there anyone you love?"

"*Non*." She seemed engrossed in her handiwork.

"Perhaps you haven't found him yet," he murmured, taking the garland from her. "I think you'll find that man who will love you forever."

"Perhaps." She watched as he draped the flower chain around the crown of his hat, which lay beside him on the blanket.

"How will you recognize this paragon when you see him?"

After a moment, Simone answered, "I suppose I'll

know him by his gentleness and his strength."

"Well, my romantic little friend, it sounds to me as if you're looking for a saint," Alain snorted, rolling to lie on his back. "Men are flesh and blood, and sinners in the bargain, with very human traits like pride and temper." With that remark, he threw his arms back to cushion his head and closed his eyes.

Simone was about to reply that he had done an adequate job of describing himself when she realized that *her* description fit him, too. She was rocked by an unwelcome revelation. She loved Alain de Vallière. Drawing a shaky breath, she almost groaned aloud.

There was every reason she should not love him. First among them was that he did not love her. To Alain, she was a ward, the girl he had known from childhood, a burden to be unloaded on a fiancé. He was arrogant and hot-tempered.

But the reason which suddenly loomed largest in Simone's mind was Marie LeVeau's dire warning. She could almost hear her words, "You will bring danger to those you love." No, she could not, would not, love Alain.

At the edge of the thicket, the horses blew and stamped. Other than an occasional bird song and a venturesome insect buzzing near Simone's ear, but no other sound marred the stillness of the afternoon. Absorbed in her thoughts, she was silent while Alain napped.

But Alain was not asleep. Through slitted eyes, he watched Simone as she sat beside him, her feet tucked beneath her. He wondered what had brought the melancholy expression to her face. When her gaze swept him, he closed his eyes and felt the brush of her skirt against his hip as she shifted slightly to face him.

Alain was so handsome, and he didn't look nearly so fierce in repose, Simone thought. When he was awake, that rugged visage looked so stern. But now his lips curved slightly, as if he were having a good dream, and his thick dark hair fell to his forehead in tousled curls. He looked approachable and almost as young as the first time she had met him.

"If you like what you see, *chère*, why not have a closer look?" he drawled. Opening his eyes, he stared directly into her surprised green ones. Without warning, his arm shot out and crooked around her neck, yanking her down across his chest, wedging his hat between the blanket and her.

"Alain!" She planted her palms on the ground on either side of him and attempted to push away, but his other arm encircled her, anchoring her against him. "Let me go."

"Shh, you'll wake Lisette." He nodded toward the carriage. "You don't want your chaperon to find you in a compromising position."

"Then let me up," she demanded a little less loudly. His lips were very close.

"When you tell me why you've been watching me for the past five minutes," he insisted.

He held firm against her sudden flurry of movement until Simone panted, "I thought you were asleep, you conceited—"

"Ah, and you'd been watching with such tenderness," he teased, his arm tightening around her squirming figure.

"You're crushing your hat," she whispered, trying to divert his attention.

"You're the one lying on it," he pointed out, whispering himself. The hush of their voices made it seem as if they were in an isolated, private world. "That Panama is one of my favorites, you know. It will cost you most dearly, my love."

Though she stiffened against him, he drew her down slowly to meet his lips. Gently he kissed her, feeling her lips warm under his and the tension leave her rigid shoulders.

He thought fleetingly that he should release her

when he had stolen his playful forfeit, but he could not. After a taste, he longed to savor her lips more fully. And when those lips parted, naturally, willingly, to invite his tongue into her mouth, Alain feasted on the sweetness of her kiss.

Simone was lost in sensation, encompassed in the heat of Alain's passion. She did not know when her hands stopped bracing her against the ground and moved up his sinewy arms to clutch at his broad shoulders. She felt, only felt, and she reveled in his touch as his big hand skimmed her ribs and lingered to cup her breast.

When his mouth left hers to trail kisses down her neck, Simone fought for self-control, and sanity began to return, bringing with it all the reasons she could not love him. Determinedly, she pushed away from his questing lips.

"You must let me go," she begged raggedly.

"Simone, what's wrong? You're trembling." He sat up, cradling her in his arms. "I did not mean to frighten you, my own. Don't you know I would never hurt you?"

"I . . . I know." Pale and shaken, she freed herself from his embrace. She wished she could explain that every kiss, every caress, hurt, because she could never have him as her own. And that if she was frightened, it was not because of Alain, but because of her unwanted response to him.

Masking his chaotic emotions, he picked up his hat and commented lightly, "I don't think we did it any great damage after all. If you will fold up the blanket while I find Batiste, it's time we were going home."

He set out for the shore, his face grim below the gay flowers decorating his Panama. He paused just out of Simone's sight to collect himself. After her response to his kisses, he could not believe she found him repulsive. So what had changed her willingness to withdrawal? Did she suddenly remember the old days, think of him as an older brother? God knew, his thoughts about her were far from brotherly. And God knew, though he would not force himself on her, he wanted her.

"What a hell of a situation," he growled to himself and went to look for Batiste.

Summer arrived in New Orleans with blazing sun, swarms of gnats and mosquitoes, and the threat of yellow fever. As the days lengthened, tempers grew shorter, and the occupants of the house on Esplanade were not immune to the relentless heat.

Since the picnic, Alain and Simone had been wary of each other, neither mentioning what had occurred between them. Forcing himself to feign indifference, Alain was brusque with Simone, sparking her temper and setting off a series of clashes. At last he had given up in disgust and nearly exiled himself from his own home.

Late one night as he neared his house, his step slowed and he squinted through the darkness toward his front gate. Had he seen a shadowy form as the moon disappeared behind the clouds? Was it Fabrice Chauvin, perhaps? Or even Baudin's man?

Easing into the shadows himself, Alain stole along the *banquette*, but when he reached a place where he could view the front of his house clearly, there was no one to be seen. Feeling a little silly, he let himself into his gate. Waiting for Marcel was wearing on him. He was beginning to see things, Alain chided himself.

His steps were sure and silent as he made his way toward the garçonnière. Then a movement in the dark courtyard caught his attention. Perhaps he had not been seeing things after all, he thought grimly. Someone was lurking near the fountain.

He backtracked soundlessly to approach from behind. As he crept closer, the fragrance of roses wafted to him on the night wind, and he knew, before the moon broke through the clouds, that it was Simone.

He halted, torn by indecision. For nearly three months, he had gone out of his way to avoid her, but seeing her in the moonlight proved irresistible. Softly he called, "What are you doing out here, Simone?"

Startled, she turned. "Oh, Alain. I couldn't sleep. It's too hot." She whispered to keep from awakening Batiste.

"It's too hot for almost everything," he growled, noticing the way she clutched her modest robe closed.

"It's still a beautiful night." She eyed him consideringly, trying to judge the reason for his ill humor. When he met her gaze without smiling, she said woodenly, "I should go."

"No, stay," he commanded. "Please," he amended with a dry smile.

They were silent, the tinkling of the fountain the only sound. At last, Simone drew a pleasurable breath and murmured, "I like it when the night smells of honeysuckle."

"It is lovely." Alain leaned against the trunk of the fig tree and watched her.

"It's nice to see you when you are not angry, 'Lain," she said with a tentative smile.

"It's nice to see you when you are not aloof," he countered bluntly.

She ignored the invitation to spar, choosing instead to placate him. "I know the past few months have not been easy for you."

If he had known what exquisite torture it would be, Nicholas would never have named me guardian, Alain thought bleakly.

"I still wish you did not feel you must challenge Marcel," Simone continued earnestly.

"There's no other way to protect you, *mon amour*." Alain allowed himself the endearment, but he would not touch her. "What Marcel seeks is not justice, but revenge . . . and you."

"I know," she sighed sadly.

How he longed to hold her, to reassure her, but he could not bear to have her reject his tenderness again. "I realize this hasn't been easy for you either," he told her stiffly. "You are lonely here, I know, but it won't last much longer."

"*Non.*" Simone nearly choked on the word. What was wrong with her? For months she had been miserable, locked away in Alain's house, but now she found she hated the thought that her captivity would end, separating her from the captor she had come to love.

"You will be happy again soon," Alain was saying through clenched teeth, "free to meet new people, make new friends. You'll be besieged by suitors." He felt as if the words were being torn from him. "So many you won't know how to choose."

She stared up at him, stricken.

"What's wrong now?" he snapped when he saw the tears glistening in her eyes. "Isn't that what you want?"

"I don't want suitors, and I don't want to choose." She whirled and raced across the courtyard, her naked legs flashing in the moonlight through the opening of her robe. Her bare feet whispered on the treads as she ran up the stairs.

His face dark with wrath, Alain was a step behind her when she opened the door to her room. Grabbing her wrist, he spun her to face him. "Damn it, Simone, first you want to choose your husband, then you don't want to choose at all. I don't understand."

"I didn't expect you to."

"What do you want of me?" he snarled.

Unexpectedly a dam burst within Simone, and words poured out. "I want you to love me or hate me, but stop being indifferent to me. If I cannot have you, I want to be free of you and the confusion you cause me. Just leave me alone."

"What do you think I've been doing, you little fool? I have stayed away, trying to ignore the desire that gnaws at me every time I see you. Do you know what it has been like having you here, within reach, yet unreachable? Unlike the man of your dreams, I am flesh and blood, so I suggest you go into your room now, *petite*, and close your door. And lock it, for I'm no saint," he concluded dangerously.

"And I'm not a child," she raged, refusing to retreat. "I am a woman, Alain de Vallière, and I want to be treated like one."

"My pleasure," he said hoarsely, driven to the brink of fury by her words. Sweeping her up into his arms, he kicked the door fully open and carried her into the bedroom. "Is this what you had in mind?"

Breathless, aroused, and a little frightened, Simone could not find her voice to answer as she was borne to the bed in strong arms.

Placing one knee on the bed, Alain put her down with surprising gentleness, then stretched out on top of her. She could feel his full length pressing against her as he braced himself on his elbows so he would not crush her, his forearms forming a tender cage on either side of her head as he dipped his head to kiss her.

"Is this what you wanted, *chère*, to be treated like a woman?" The anger was gone from his voice.

He watched her intently through the darkness. Almost fearfully, she met his dark eyes. Staggered by the yearning he saw, Alain lifted her to meet his fiery kiss. His mouth slanted across hers, taking insistent possession. She responded with an intensity to match his own, wrapping her arms around him.

After a moment, he drew back to look at her in wonder. Her face had lost its earlier uncertainty, and she looked up at him, her eyelids heavy with desire. Trailing kisses along her jaw to her ear, he asked huskily, "Do you want me, Simone?"

"*Oui*," she whispered, her fingers feathering lightly along his spine, creating delightful spasms of sensation.

"And I want you," he murmured, his breath stirring her hair. "I have wanted you from the first moment I saw you at Lisette's. But when I learned you were a virgin, I couldn't take you. Just as I can't take you now, though all of me cries out for relief." He rolled to lie beside her on the bed, struggling for control.

Simone lay still, rigid at his rebuff, as he sat up and said hoarsely, "If I take you this way tonight, I fear you will hate me, and yourself, in the morning. And I don't think I could bear it."

Looking down at her, he knew he had to go before he gave in to what his body demanded. "We will talk in the morning, my darling, when I—and you—can think straight. *Bonne nuit.*"

His lips brushed her forehead, and then he was gone, leaving her miserable and aching with a strange, hollow emptiness.

Simone hoped she was too late for breakfast and for Alain's promised talk. She was not sure she could face him after her brazen behavior the night before.

"*Bonjour*, sleepyhead," he greeted her in the dining room.

"*Bonjour.*" She sank into her chair without meeting his eyes.

"I was beginning to think I would have to wake you if I wanted to speak to you before I left for the day." His tone was casual as he filled a coffee cup and slid it across the table toward her.

"*Merci*," she muttered, staring down at it with exaggerated interest.

Alain watched her toy studiously with her spoon, then he ordered softly, "Simone, look at me."

Reluctantly, she lifted her troubled gaze to his and found his eyes held concern, not judgment. In fact, he said approvingly, "You look lovely this morning."

"*Merci*," she said, suddenly shy.

"We need to talk, you and I," he said.

"I'm sorry about last night, Alain," she blurted out.

"I'm not." He smiled unabashedly. "Now I know you want me as much as I want you. And I do want you, Simone, for my wife."

"Your wife?" She stared at him through wide eyes.

"*Oui*. I love you. Will you marry me?"

She wanted to cry out in joy, to accept at once. But she could not. The words of the voodoo queen returned to haunt her. Loving Alain would bring danger to him. "I . . . You must give me some time, 'Lain."

"If you wish." He had thought, somehow, after last night it would be easier. Rising, he kissed her lightly on the mouth. "Think on my proposal while I'm gone, and know that I love you."

"I will," she promised, reaching out to smooth his lapel in an unthinking, intimate gesture.

He captured her hand and kissed the palm tenderly. "Until this evening," he murmured, unable to resist another kiss in farewell.

"Until this evening," she echoed breathlessly as he departed.

It was not until Alain walked away from the house along the sunny *banquette* that he realized she had not said she loved him.

Throughout the day, Simone pondered her problem, deciding at last that she was not a superstitious person. Voodoo magic made no difference. She loved Alain.

She prepared a special meal, dismissed Batiste for the evening, and dressed in a pale green silk gown she knew Alain would like. When she was ready, she started downstairs to await his return.

Passing his study door, she heard voices and stopped. The deep voice could only be Alain's. She hadn't heard him come in. The other voice belonged to

Serge, and he was saying, "Why did you never mention you had found your little ward?"

"It never came up," Alain answered blandly. "What did Baudin say?"

"He agrees to meet at dawn at the Dueling Oaks, but he insists first blood is not enough."

"Then it will be to the death."

Simone threw the door open and glared at the two men, who turned to her in surprise. "Why didn't you tell me Marcel was back, Alain?" she demanded.

"He only returned today." He set his drink on the mantel and walked toward her.

"And you wasted no time in challenging him. Please don't fight him. I don't want you to."

"Serge, this is the reason I didn't mention finding Simone." Taking her arm, he led her to stand before the fencing master.

Serge regarded her incredulously, then in amazement. "Jean-Paul," he breathed. "But . . . but . . . No wonder you did not want anyone to know, Alain! The girl could be ruined after living in my *salle*."

"You do not have to talk about me as if I am not here, maître," she informed him even as she curtsied politely. "*Bonsoir*. It's good to see you again."

Serge smiled ruefully. "I must say, you've become an even finer lady than you were a fencer, little one. And curls and gowns become you more than swords. But why ever did you come to my *salle*?"

"I was trying to evade Marcel Baudin's notice, and Alain's."

"You did not do so well in the latter, I think. Though I must say, you had me fooled. I feel like a buffoon to have mistaken a pretty girl for a little boy."

"I'm sorry. I did not mean to insult you."

"Have no fear, mam'selle. I would not challenge a woman to satisfy my wounded dignity. Besides when you fight, you are a—"

"A spitfire?" she supplied coldly. "I believe that's

what you once called me. If you'll pardon me..." She
stalked from the room.

"Jean-Paul had big ears," Alain told the bewildered
man, "and he listened to many of our conversations.
My own words still come back to haunt me."

"It seems to me, *mon ami*, that you have a bigger
problem than Jean-Paul's ears. I will see myself out and
leave you to deal with *la belle* Simone. Until dawn, at
the Oaks."

10

When Serge had gone, Alain's thoughts returned to his confrontation with Marcel. He had met the handsome Creole in Exchange Alley that morning. Marcel had returned to New Orleans only the day before. Fresh from his bedside vigil with his mother, who had lingered beyond all expectation, he was restless and irritable.

"What do you want, dc Vallière?" he had snarled when Alain hailed him.

"You and I have a matter of some importance to settle, Baudin, on the field of honor," Alain said without preamble.

"I have no idea what matter you mean." Marcel's silky voice had been menacing nonetheless.

"You have made repeated threats toward my ward, Mademoiselle Simone Devereaux."

"Your—your ward? You bastard! You've been hiding her all the while I've looked for her, haven't you?" Marcel screamed in rage. "I'll meet you under the Dueling Oaks, and I'll kill you. Simone is mine."

"She belongs to no one, yet," Alain rapped out. "But I hope to make her my wife."

Marcel laughed insinuatingly. "I said I would make her my mistress, and I will. But even I wouldn't seduce her with fraudulent promises of marriage."

"I intend to marry her, Baudin," Alain said stonily.

"Not if you're dead, de Vallière."

"My second will call on you this afternoon," Alain had responded coldly. Then he had gone into the *salle d'armes* to ask Serge to serve as his intermediary in the complicated negotiations that followed a challenge. Finally he had visited his attorney, Dominique Cuvillion.

Though he was now weary, Alain could not rest until he reassured Simone. As he tried to collect himself, mentally rehearsing what he would say to her, he faltered. His own fate was too uncertain to press for an answer to his proposal now. But just once he longed to hear Simone speak the words he wanted to hear. He needed to know she loved him.

Hearing a light tread outside, he opened the study door to discover her, wrapped in a black cloak, stealing down the stairs. She stared at him guiltily as he stepped out onto the gallery and demanded, "Where do you think you're going?"

Lifting her chin resolutely, she returned his fearsome glare. "I am going to see if I can talk some sense into Marcel."

"Are you mad?" Alain was at her side on the stairs in an instant. "You would hand yourself over to him after all you've been through—all we've been through—to keep you safe?"

"If it will keep him from killing you." She gnawed a bloodless lower lip to keep her composure.

"Thank you for your unflagging confidence in me," he snapped, "but you are not going anywhere." Dragging her upstairs, he thrust her into her room. "You will stay in this house if I have to sit on you to keep you here."

"You overgrown simpleton!" She ducked under the arm blocking the door and nearly escaped.

"Ah, tender words from my beloved, how sweet they are to the ear," he muttered grimly. Catching her by the wrist, he yanked her back and closed the door. "Get rid of this," he advised, loosening the tie at the neck of her cloak and watching the garment fall to the floor. "You are not going anywhere."

"You don't understand," she seethed, prying at his fingers.

"No, I don't," he said flatly. By simply flexing his arm, he hauled her close to his chest so her feet almost left the floor. "How can you think I would allow you to live in fear of Marcel when I have it in my power to protect you? For months we've waited for this. After tomorrow, you'll be free."

"Or you'll be dead." She dissolved unexpectedly into deep, wrenching sobs. "Marie LeVeau told me I would bring danger to the ones I loved. Don't you see, Alain? I cannot let you go."

The scowl on his face was gradually replaced by the dawning of hope. He relaxed his grip on Simone's arm but did not release her. Placing his other arm around her shoulders, he drew her against him gently. "Are you telling me that you love me?"

"Of course, I love you," she wept. When he freed her wrist, she slid her arms around his waist and buried her face between the lapels of his jacket.

"I love you, too, *mon amour*," he murmured. "Don't cry, not over some silly voodoo nonsense."

"Alain, I do not want to take the chance that Marcel might kill you." Her voice was muffled against his broad chest.

"He won't kill me, especially now that I know I have every reason to live." Tilting her face toward him, he kissed each eyelid lovingly, savoring the salt of her tears, before seeking her mouth.

When Alain's lips left hers at last, Simone drew a calming, hiccuping breath and nestled closer. Smiling fondly, he went to sit on the edge of the bed, pulling her onto his lap and wrapping an arm around her waist. She regarded him uncertainly for a moment and, reassured by the tenderness she saw, twined her arms around his neck and lifted her face for another kiss.

Joyfully he obliged her and felt a shudder of arousal when her tongue met his, timidly at first, then with more boldness. He laid his big hand against the smoothness of her cheek, his thumb tracing delicate circles on her chin.

He leaned back on the bed, never allowing his lips to part from hers, then rolled so she lay next to him. His hand drifted downward, pausing to stroke the warm, soft skin of her neck before sliding down to the pliant mounds below.

At the intimate touch, Simone gasped, her breath mingling with Alain's, and laced her fingers in his hair. Her body arched reflexively, and her tingling breasts, seemed to swell and strain against the bodice of her gown. Even through the thick layer of satin, his hands on her body were like fire, and they moved lower and lower, igniting a desire that had only smoldered before tonight.

Awed by her response to his caresses, Alain drew back to gaze at her. Her lips were swollen, evidence of their passion. She opened heavy eyelids and looked up at him.

"Please don't stop," she whispered entreatingly.

"Do you know what you are asking?" He nearly choked on the question, but he had to ask it. She was so young, so innocent.

"I know." Her fingertips traced his mouth. "And I believe what you say, that all will be well tomorrow. But when you go, I want you to be certain of my love."

His dark eyes riveted hers with a look that made her tremble, not from fear but anticipation. Rising, he pulled her up to stand beside him and began to undress her, his fingers made clumsy by uncharacteristic nervousness. Stepping behind her, he cursed under his breath as he fumbled with the long line of hooks down the back of her dress. She felt the cool evening air on her skin when the gown gaped open. Leaning against him, she reveled in his touch as he trailed his fingertips over her shoulders to the exposed curves of her smooth, firm breasts.

Slowly, deliberately, Alain removed her dress. By the dim lamplight, Simone could see the passion in his eyes as she stood before him in only her undergarments. She sought to free him of his jacket and waistcoat, her inexperience exciting him more than proficient dexterity ever had.

Untying the ribbon that held her petticoat in place, he pushed it down over her hips, so it fell to the floor with a whisper of sound. Taking her hand, he helped her step out of it and led her to sit on the bed. He stood beside her, his eyes never leaving hers, as he untied his cravat and dropped it.

Simone's breath caught in her throat when he removed his shirt, baring the well-defined muscles of shoulders and arms and the impressive mat of black chest hair, which tapered into a line that disappeared into his trousers, leading her eye to the bulge that clearly showed his need for her.

She smoothed his dark hair tenderly as he knelt beside her and removed her shoes. Slowly, he unfastened her garters and rolled her stockings down, his hands caressing her calves. When his intimate task was completed, he rose and pulled her again to her feet, removing her camisole and pantalettes.

Carefully, Alain laid her on the bed and removed the rest of his clothing. The planes and angles of his body gilded by lamplight, he looked down at her.

"*Dieu*, you are beautiful," he breathed wonderingly.

"So are you," she answered, her voice husky with desire.

He joined her on the bed, his expert hands remembering their skill as passion mounted and his mouth claimed hers in ardent possession. She returned his kisses hungrily, molding her body to his, touching him everywhere as he touched her, giving back instinctively as much pleasure as she received.

She shuddered and a moan escaped her when he slowed his explorations and poised to enter her.

"Gently, my own," he whispered against her ear, "it will only hurt for a moment."

"I'm not afraid," she answered, and indeed she was not as she began to experience sensations she had never dreamed of.

Holding her against him, Alain pushed his way gently into her waiting, welcoming warmth. As desire burst into white-hot flame, the world around them melted away, leaving only the heat of passion to consume them, to meld them into one.

A long time afterward, as they lay together, limbs intertwined, near sleep, Simone murmured, *"Je t'aime,* 'Lain."

"And I love you," he whispered, his arms tightening around her. He lay awake for hours, grateful for the gift of herself that Simone had given him and hopeful that she would love him for the rest of their days.

Simone stirred, a mild, unfamiliar soreness in every part of her body. "Alain," she murmured, the memory of the night just past bringing her fully awake. She reached toward his side of the bed, but he was not there, and the sheets were cold.

Sitting up, she peered through the *baire* at the dim room. The heavy draperies over the windows made it impossible to tell whether it was night or day. Getting up, she drew on a robe and rushed downstairs in the muted predawn light.

Hearing a sound from the kitchen, she entered hopefully and found a grim-faced Batiste.

"He's gone," he said before she could ask.

"Why didn't he wake me?" Her voice quavered unreliably.

"He said when he looked in, you were sleeping. He hoped to be back before you knew he had gone."

Simone regarded Batiste uncertainly for a moment. He did not know what had happened last night. Alain had not told even his faithful servant.

"Batiste, we could—" she started.

"I know what you're going to say, little friend," the big man interrupted. "It would do no good to follow Alain to the dueling field, and probably harm. I promised him I would keep you here if I had to lock you in your room."

"That is not necessary. My word is my bond," she answered stiffly.

"Don't be angry," he beseeched. "I'm Alain's friend, and yours. But I, too, gave my word."

"I know." She sighed. "But what are we to do? Sit here and worry?"

"Try not to worry. Alain is the best swordsman I know besides Maître St. Michel. You go and put on your prettiest dress for welcoming him home while I cook breakfast."

"*Très bien.*" Simone's heart was heavy as she trudged up to her room, but Batiste was right. Alain would soon be home again, and all would be right with her world.

Listlessly, she washed and dressed. When she went to the bureau for her hairbrush, her eyes fell upon an envelope, addressed to her, and a slender velvet box she had not noticed before. With trembling hands, she opened the envelope and withdrew a note in Alain's bold hand.

Simone, my own love,

By the time you read this note, I will have gone to meet Marcel under the Oaks. I know you did not wish it, but I could not do otherwise for you, for us.

If my skill with the sword fails me, I will die a happy man, knowing you return my love. Though defeat is bitter to contemplate, I have left instructions for your security, and Batiste will protect you to his last breath.

Rest assured, mon coeur, that I have every intention of returning to you the victor, having won for us a long and contented and peaceful life together.

Please accept my gift to seal our engagement and to signify my love for you. Emeralds mean lucky in love, you know, and how fortunate I am to have loved you.

Your adoring Alain

Opening the box, she found a magnificent emerald and diamond necklace with earrings to match. Unable to contain her emotions, Simone threw herself down on the rumpled bed she had so recently shared with Alain and wept until no tears were left.

Batiste made no comment when she returned to the kitchen, red-eyed and pale. After breakfast, they sat in the courtyard, waiting.

As the oppressive minutes ticked by, Simone was deluged with a flood of memories: Alain holding her as they waltzed; Alain parrying skillfully as they fenced; Alain, his rugged face alive with tenderness, as they made love.

She started violently when the bell sounded at the front gate. Batiste was on his feet at once.

"Stay here," he commanded, disappearing down the passageway to the street. Through the wrought iron gate, he could see three men on the *banquette*.

"Where is de Vallière?" Marcel Baudin greeted Alain's servant haughtily.

"He left before dawn to meet you at the Oaks," Batiste answered, his brow creased with concern.

"He never showed up," Marcel asserted, looking to Charles Greaux, his second, and his henchman, Guy la Roche, for agreement.

They nodded, and, emboldened by the company of others, Charles added, "Perhaps he had second thoughts and turned back."

"Not Alain," Serge said from behind them. He had arrived in time to hear the snide remark. "Something is wrong."

Batiste regarded Alain's second worriedly and asked, "You did not see him on the road?"

"*Non.*"

"I demand to see Simone," Marcel interrupted arrogantly.

"M'sieur Alain sent her away," Batiste lied.

Marcel's icy blue eyes narrowed at the servant. "I know she is here. Get out of my way or I will walk over you."

"You may try, sir," Batiste said, drawing himself up to his considerable height.

"You'll find it difficult to walk over both of us." Serge added his support, stepping beside Batiste.

"I am willing to try," Marcel snarled.

Charles stared at him disbelievingly. Sometimes he wondered if his cousin were mad. He had been willing to serve as second in a duel, but he would not take on the best fencing master in New Orleans for a woman he did not even know.

"Temper, Marcel," he cautioned him, catching his arm when his cousin would have drawn his sword.

The blond-haired Creole whirled on his unfortunate relative, but the distraction proved to be what he needed. Gradually the haze of red cleared from his vision, and the pounding in his head lessened. After a breathless moment, he collected himself and addressed Batiste. "Tell Simone to pack her things. When de Vallière forfeited the duel, he lost all claim to her. She is mine now, and I intend to have her."

"You would have to fight me for her," the servant informed him, unperturbed by the menace in Marcel's voice.

Seething with fury, the Creole considered running de Vallière's insolent slave through, but he thought better of it with Serge standing by. Instead he pivoted and stalked away, trailed by his bodyguard and his anxious cousin.

When the three had gone, Batiste and Serge went to the courtyard, where Simone waited, white-faced and tense.

"You heard?" Batiste asked.

She nodded, looking back and forth between the men. "What could have happened?"

"I don't know, but I mean to find out. I'll search the road to the Dueling Oaks. If 'Lain is there, I'll find him."

"I will go with you," Serge offered at once.

"I would appreciate it if you'd stay with Simone," Batiste told him.

"No one needs to stay with me," she announced. "Let me change clothes, and we can all go."

Both men looked pained at her suggestion, but it was Batiste who spoke.

"*Petite amie*, I promised Alain I would protect you," he said gently. "If I don't find him right away, we must get you out of here before Marcel Baudin returns."

"If I put on Jean-Paul's clothes and—"

"You would not be safe." Serge sided with Batiste. "Don't you see, mam'selle? Marcel already knows you are here. If he saw Jean-Paul emerge from Alain's house, he would see through your masquerade at once."

"He's right," Batiste agreed quickly. "You must save that disguise in case you need it later. If I find Alain, this conversation will have been for nothing. But, as it is, we're wasting valuable time. Both of you must wait here for me."

"*Oui*, but Batiste," Serge suggested tactfully, "I would feel better if the mam'selle had a lady friend to keep her company."

Despite the gravity of the situation, Batiste fought back a smile at the man's unexpected delicacy. "I'll stop at Mademoiselle Duprè's on the way out of town." He nodded encouragingly at the girl who watched him, seemingly numbed. "Try not to worry, Simone."

Before she could speak, Batiste was gone.

After Lisette arrived, tense and solicitous of her friend, there were more hours of waiting. Serge paced while the women sat silently. Everyone rushed to the passageway when they heard the carriage gate open. Batiste appeared, leading Alain's horse. In his hand was the man's battered hat and, at his side, attorney Dominique Cuvillion

"I fear something has indeed happened to 'Lain," the servant said at once. "I found his horse wandering and his hat in a thicket where there were signs of a fight."

"Have you sent for the police?" Simone asked.

"M'sieur Cuvillion did." Batiste nodded toward Alain's bookish lawyer. "We decided it was better that he report Alain's disappearance. I was questioned. That's what took so long."

"What did the police say, monsieur?" Simone asked the attorney.

The young Creole's thin, pinched face looked dazed as he stared at Simone through his spectacles in open amazement. She was the most beautiful girl he had ever seen. Her green eyes were large in her pale face, and her hair, cut short for no reason he could imagine besides illness, made her look fragile and ethereal. There had been few women in his life, and Dominique felt an unfamiliar stir of protectiveness toward this one.

When Alain had come to him yesterday, he had been baffled by the man's very specific instructions regarding his little ward: She must be kept hidden. This lovely young woman must be the ward in question, but if Alain thought her a child, Dominique mused, he must be blind.

The proper young man was scandalized to realize Simone had been living in the household of a bachelor. Even now she was unchaperoned but for a manservant, a prostitute, and a fencing master—hardly suitable companions for a girl who looked fresh and innocent and extremely distraught. His heart went out to her, and he did not care if it ever came back.

"Did the police say they would search for him?" Simone was asking urgently.

"*Oui*, mam'selle." Recovering himself, Dominique searched for words that would soften the blow, but there were none. Running his fingers through his prematurely thinning hair, he explained gently, "They believe your guardian may have been the victim of foul play. They plan to drag the bayou nearby to see if they can find his body. I—I'm sorry."

Simone sat down heavily, tears brimming in her green eyes.

"Mademoiselle Devereaux," Dominique said urgently, "I have bought some time before the police come. You must not be here when they do. Though I do not understand why, Alain was adamant that you must be kept safe from discovery from any hint of scandal, and from Marcel Baudin. Is there perhaps somewhere you could go?"

"She could come to my house." Lisette spoke for the first time since the lawyer's arrival.

"I hardly think that suitable," he sputtered. Turning back to Simone, he asked, "Are you not related to the Chauvins of LeFleur?"

"I can't go there," Simone replied dully. "The danger to them would be too great."

"Will you please explain to me what is going on?" the attorney bade indignantly.

Haltingly, Simone recounted a sketchy story of her flight from Marcel and the reason for it, though she omitted the fact that she had disguised herself as a boy and hidden in Serge's *salle d'armes*.

"I see why Alain was keeping you hidden," Dominique said slowly when she had finished, "but surely Baudin can be reasoned with. Let me go to him and see if I can buy your father's IOU's."

"That is kind of you, Monsieur Cuvillion, but I don't have the money."

"But you do, mademoiselle."

She stared at him uncomprehendingly. "I don't understand."

Now Dominique told half-truths, the story Alain wished Simone to hear. "A sizable amount of money has been invested for you. You see, more than enough money to pay your debts came from the auction of your possessions, and there was a modest bequest overlooked in the reading of the will. Monsieur Fusilier didn't know where to find you, so he turned it over to Alain, who invested it quite wisely. The original amount has more than doubled by now. The interest alone should keep you comfortably for some time, even after I buy back your father's IOU's."

"Then do what you can, monsieur," she requested, scarcely reacting to his news before she turned to Batiste. "Isn't there anything else we can do, anywhere else we can look?"

Lisette stopped Dominique as he prepared to leave. "I wish you *Bonne chance*, monsieur, but I do not think Marcel will ever leave Simone alone."

"I am told I'm very persuasive," the attorney replied, looking down his aristocratic nose at her. "If anyone can free her of his threat and save her from debtors' prison, I believe I am the one."

His confidence was severely shaken, however, a few hours later when he met with the furious Creole.

"Tell Simone I don't want her money," Marcel raged. "Tell her I want her. I demand payment in full. Do you understand?" he screamed. "She will pay!"

Alarmed, Dominique returned to the house on Esplanade.

"Were you followed?" Batiste greeted him.

"I'm not a complete idiot," the lawyer snapped, his muddy brown eyes resting on the black man with dislike.

At that moment, Serge emerged from the study, where he had been watching the street, to report, "La Roche is watching the house."

Dominique was nearly sick with remorse. "Any word of Alain?" he asked, looking woeful when Batiste shook his head.

"There is only one way out of this," the young Creole concluded. "I must challenge Baudin."

"Absolutely not," Simone refused.

"I think it is my place to do so, Mademoiselle Devereaux," he said fervently, "since your guardian is not here."

"Why you?" Serge protested, descending from the gallery. "Why not Alain's second?"

"Stop it, both of you," the girl commanded, causing them to stare at her in surprise. "I won't allow either of you to challenge Marcel. Too much damage has been done already. Let us not add your deaths to it."

"Then we must get you away from him, away from New Orleans altogether." Serge mused, his mind as agile as his body.

"I have a friend, l'américain, who owns a small steamboat, a bayou packet," Lisette volunteered suddenly. "He'll be leaving New Orleans tonight for a couple of weeks. If he took Simone with him, she would be safe until we can learn what has become of Alain or can make other arrangements for her."

Though nearly paralyzed by sorrow, Simone was about to remind them of her continued presence when

Dominique cut in excitedly, "A bayou packet? He could take her to Paradis, my plantation on Bayou Lafourche."

"I cannot leave until I know what has happened to Alain," Simone argued before everyone started talking at once.

In the end she was overruled, and Batiste crept out of the house under cover of darkness to deliver a note to the captain of the steamboat moored at the Canal Street Wharf.

"He'll do it," the servant announced when he returned, "but we must hurry."

"Serge hitched up Alain's coach," Simone said, "and he's waiting now at the front gate to let Dominique in when he returns with his carriage."

"Everything is ready," Lisette concurred. "Simone's trunk is loaded. I'll send Jude for the rest of her things in the morning."

"Good." Batiste nodded in approval.

"Here comes M'sieur Cuvillion." They heard Serge's muted call, then the creak of the big gate before it was obscured by the cadence of the horses' hooves on the drive. Dominique alit from a compact open carriage, built for speed and tonight to be used as a decoy.

"Is everything ready?" he whispered.

"*Oui*," Lisette answered for all of them as she donned a cloak and pulled the hood up to hide her blond hair. Simone kissed her cheek, then watched as Dominique helped her into the carriage, his thin face showing his concern at the prospect of their mad moonlight drive.

Before he climbed into his carriage, the young Creole caught Simone's hand and kissed it ardently. "*Au revoir*, mademoiselle," he murmured. "Take care of yourself. I will see you at Paradis."

"*Oui*," Simone agreed sadly, "and *merci*, all of you." Her vision blurred with tears, she walked with

Batiste to Alain's closed coach while Serge ran to unlock the carriage gate.

When it was open, Dominique urged his horses forward and his carriage thundered from the drive. Before it had traveled a single square, another rig raced from the darkness in pursuit.

11

"*Damn it, Tom,* we can't hold our steam much longer. Why can't we get underway?" the river pilot asked his captain again.

"Because we're expecting another passenger," Captain Franklin answered patiently. Lounged against the railing of the *Bayou Queen*, his tiny claptrap stern-wheeler, he grinned over his shoulder at his grizzled companion. "What's your hurry, Zack?"

"Same as usual," Zachary Cameron retorted. "We're behind schedule before we've even cast off. But looks like we don't have to wait any longer," he commented, his eyes on a closed coach arriving at the head of the dock.

Three people alit: a graceful mulatto man Tom did not recognize; Batiste, the ebony giant he had met earlier; and a woman, wearing a hooded cape.

"What do you know about this passenger?" Zack asked, watching the three unload their meager baggage onto the levee.

"Nothing, except that she's a friend of Mademoiselle Dupré's." Tom stood erect and headed for the gangplank when he saw the mulatto climb back onto the driver's box and drive away.

"I know you've got a soft spot for the ladies, Tom, but I can't believe we're runnin' behind for a whore," Zack groaned in exasperation.

The captain's blue eyes rested on the pair mounting the gangplank. The huge black man hauled a trunk on his back, bending under the weight. He seemed to lean over the tiny woman protectively, as if he could shield her with his bulk.

"This one's not a whore. Lisette says she's a gentlewoman," Tom replied, unperturbed when Zachary snorted and set off for the wheelhouse.

"Captain Franklin, thank you for waiting," Batiste greeted him. "This is my mistress, Mademoiselle Simone Devereaux."

"Captain Thomas Jefferson Franklin, ma'am." Tom swept off his cap and bowed elegantly. "Welcome aboard the *Bayou Queen*."

"*Merci*." The woman's voice was almost a whisper, refined and obviously Creole. Unable to see the face inside the dark cowl, Tom could tell nothing more about her. She was silent while her manservant handled the arrangements for their travel. As the boat pulled away from the dock, Batiste secured a cabin for her and agreed to help cut and load wood at each stop along the run to pay for his own passage.

When their business was concluded, Tom watched Batiste lead the woman up to the boiler deck to her cabin. Once she was inside, the negro glanced at the captain, as if daring him to send him to steerage, and spread a blanket on the deck. Then he lay down, blocking her door with his body.

In the cabin, drained and weary, Simone waited for sleep that would not come. At last she sat up in her narrow bunk and flexed her aching shoulders. Unable to sit still, she rose and paced the tiny cabin, forcing herself to face the question she had refused to consider since Alain's disappearance. Was she responsible for what had befallen him? Had her love brought danger

to him? It was true he had not been killed on the dueling field as she had feared, but where was he? She
would know if he were dead, she told herself fiercely.

She would feel it. He must be alive. He must.

As the predawn light crept through the louvered
windows on deck, Simone opened her trunk and took
out the dress on top. One was much the same as another. She had brought ordinary clothing, refusing to pack
her mourning costume. She would not even contemplate grieving for Alain. She could not conceive of his
death.

Unable to bear the confinement, she decided to walk
on deck, but when she opened her cabin door, she
tripped over Batiste. Half-asleep, her mighty guard was
on his feet in an instant, thrusting her behind him and
swinging to block any possible assault.

"Batiste, wake up." She shook his arm gently.

Blinking at her, he said gruffly, "Don't scare me like
that."

"I only wanted to go for a walk."

He tossed his blanket just inside the cabin and
closed the door. "All right," he rumbled, yawning, "let's
walk."

Batiste peered at Simone with concern as they
strolled. Even in the dimness, he could see she was pale
and listless. He knew she had not slept much last night,
for he had heard her crying when she thought no one
could hear, and it had nearly broken his heart.

"How long before we get to Paradis?" she asked suddenly.

"Three or four days, if this ruin of a boat doesn't
strand us somewhere." The big man grimaced when the
curses of the engineer reached them over an abrupt
clanking of the engine.

"So we may have word of Alain in as little as a
week?" she asked when the ruckus died down.

"Perhaps," he answered, "but I think you must prepare yourself for the worst, *petite amie*."

"You think he is dead, too, don't you?" Simone stared out at the rosy sunrise, her hopeful smile fading.

"I don't want to think so, but *something* has happened to him."

"I know," she agreed with a sigh, "but I cannot give up."

"Then don't." Batiste smiled reassuringly. "We'll trust that all will be well soon." He had more than one reason to hope so. If Alain had been murdered, he, as a black man with ready access to de Vallière, would almost certainly be suspected, and he had worsened his situation by leaving New Orleans. Not that it mattered. He would keep his promise to care for Simone.

From up in the pilothouse, Tom saw his passenger's face for the first time. Even from a distance, he could tell Mademoiselle Simone Devereaux was young and beautiful and very sad. Beside her giant black servant, she looked fragile, but there was pride and mettle in her bearing. Though the captain watched for her through the day, he did not see her again.

Simone woke late the next morning, but she felt rested for the first time in days. Then she realized what had awakened her. The boat was not moving.

She dressed hurriedly and went out on deck, opening her door carefully, but Batiste was not at his post. Momentarily blinded by the sun's glare, she paused to allow her eyes to adjust. Down on the riverbank, she saw her big friend laboring with a gang of men to cut and load wood.

"Good day, Miss Devereaux," a pleasant voice said from nearby.

Simone's first impression when she turned was of a winning smile and a pair of sapphire-blue eyes that crinkled at the corners. The young man's face was handsome and likable. Below the engaging smile with its even white teeth was a dimple in his chin.

The captain had removed his cap to greet her. His black hair was thick and curly, and one unruly tendril dipped down on his bronzed forehead, giving him an even more youthful appearance. He was not as big or solid as Alain, she thought, unconsciously measuring him against the Creole, but he was taller than average, and the body beneath his sturdy work clothes was lithe and trim.

"Bonjour." She could not help but return his infectious grin.

"Captain Franklin, at your service, ma'am," he introduced himself. "We met briefly when you came aboard."

"Oh, yes, Thomas Jefferson Franklin, a very American name. I remember." She extended her hand uncertainly. She was not sure how a lady greeted a Kaintock. She had never met one, as a lady.

Tom's smile widened even more, if that were possible, and he kissed her hand politely. "Are your accommodations to your liking?"

"They're very nice, thank you."

"And are you enjoying your trip?"

"Oui, merci. I take it from your accent, *Capitaine,* that you are not from Louisiana?" she inquired before he could ask another question.

"No, ma'am. I'm from Virginia. I take it from your accent that you are?" He joined her at the railing, oblivious to Batiste's dark stare from the shore.

"I'm from New Orleans. But tell me," she requested hastily to forestall further questions, "how did you come to be named for a great president?"

"The Franklins always name their sons after Revolutionary War dignitaries. Thomas Jefferson was a great hero of my father's. He saved the best for last."

"So you're the youngest?"

"Yep. I have three older brothers."

"And they're also named after Revolutionary heroes?

"George Washington, John Hancock, and Samuel Adams," he confirmed. "My father is Paul Revere. And I have a cousin Ethan Allen.

"You laugh," he accused teasingly when she giggled.

"Our family reunions sound like roll call at the Continental Congress."

The sound of the whistle drowned out their laughter as the men on shore began to file up the gangway.

"If you'll excuse me, looks like we're about done here." Tom nodded politely. "I'd be honored if you'd join me in my cabin this evening for dinner, ma'am."

Simone's vivacious face sobered. "Thank you, but no."

"Perhaps another time," he suggested. Then he strode forward to oversee the crew's work.

"Perhaps," she murmured, awash in remorse. For a moment she had put aside her sorrow and enjoyed a lighthearted chat with the captain. But somehow she feared that if she forgot Alain for an instant, all hope would be gone. And that must never happen.

Joining her, Batiste asked, "Did the captain bother you?"

She looked up at him in surprise. "No, he was just making conversation. Why?"

"Alain asked me to look after you. If a man pays you unwanted attention, I'll chase him away."

"The captain only talked to me. Save your protection, *mon ami*, until there's something to protect me from."

The next morning, Simone stood beside the railing outside her cabin. She breathed deeply of the scents of the river and the wood smoke from the steamboat.

"Good morning, ma'am," Tom called. "Join me for a stroll?"

Simone considered refusing, but the morning was sunny and warm, and Tom Franklin smiled so appealingly. She took his arm, and they set off around the deck.

While they walked, she learned Tom was something of a black sheep in his family. Realizing he was more interested in westward expansion than in farming, his father had given him a choice: Stay and inherit acres of Virginia farmland, or go and accept a small bequest. To

Paul Revere Franklin's dismay, his youngest son had chosen the money and gone to seek his fortune.

Tom had gotten as far as the Mississippi. At his first sight of the broad river and the rudimentary steamboats that plied her, he had fallen in love. Taking a job on one of the boats, he had labored to learn the river.

"After several years," he concluded, returning Simone to where Batiste waited, "I was able to buy this boat. And the *Bayou Queen* is just the beginning." His blue eyes shone with enthusiasm. "A couple of months ago, I bought another packet, the *Cajun Queen*. She isn't in as good shape as this one." He glanced over his shoulder distractedly when Batiste snorted behind him. "I'll have her running soon, though, and we'll double our cargo capacity. One of these days there'll be a whole fleet," he said, gesturing toward the crown painted on the smokestack, "the Queen fleet. We'll run the lower river from St. Louis to New Orleans."

When the attractive captain took his leave, Simone feared he would ask her to dinner again, but his behavior remained exemplary and he left her in peace.

In the days that followed, she did not forget her problems, but the farther the *Bayou Queen* steamed from New Orleans, the farther they seemed to recede. Tom's contagious good humor was a welcome respite after months of turmoil and unhappiness, and his effortless charm seemed to put even the wary Batiste at ease.

When they left the river for the Bayou Lafourche, the mood on the packet became slow and easy. During the sultry days, alligators and snakes swam lazily underwater and waterfowl took to the air, disturbed by the chugging steamboat.

One day, unwilling to swelter in her cabin, Simone walked on the deck with the young captain.

"See those planters?" He nodded toward several passengers who loafed on the stern, pitching coins at bubbles churned up by the paddlewheel. "They always do that when they're bored," he chuckled. "I figure if I rigged up some sort of basket underneath the wheel, I could rake in the coins at the end of each run, and in a year or so, I could probably buy another steamboat."

"You're incorrigible," Simone reprimanded, laughing.

"Yes, ma'am, but I'm told all I need is a good woman to straighten me out." He smiled, but his eyes were serious.

Uncomfortable, Simone looked away, toward the pilothouse. "Is that your friend, Zachary, who glares so fiercely from up there?"

Tom's eyes followed the direction of her gaze. "That's him, all right." He waved at Zack and received a nod in return. "He's not really fierce. He just looks that way."

"You've known him a long time?"

"He taught me what I know about the river. He's been traveling it since he left Kentucky nearly forty years ago."

"In New Orleans, we call all Americans Kaintocks, but I don't think I've ever seen one who was really from Kentucky."

"Well, Zack is the real thing," Tom said, chuckling when Simone glanced up at the man apprehensively. "Kaintocks are a little rough by Creole standards, but we're not so much different than anyone else. Though I haven't been able to get many folks here in Louisiana to believe it."

"Perhaps they'd understand it better if you told them in French," Simone suggested.

"They might," Tom conceded. "Think you might teach me some?"

"I could try."

He grinned unabashedly. "The pretty phrases, too? You never can tell when I could need to woo a Creole gal . . . for business reasons, of course."

"Of course." She tried to hide a smile.

"Since we reach Paradis in the morning, you'd better

start my lessons right away," he recommended lightly. "It's going be a strain, even for a fellow who learns as fast as I do. You may have to work straight through to bedtime." His teasing ended on a tentative note. "Will you have dinner with me tonight?"

Feeling unexpected regret that the trip was so near its end, she surprised herself by agreeing.

When Tom called for Simone that evening, he had dressed carefully in an elegantly tailored broadcloth suit, and he thought her resplendent in a rose-colored gown. Proudly, he escorted her to his cabin, stopping just short of the door to glare at Batiste, who followed.

"Is there something you want?" Tom asked mildly.

"Just to be near if Mam'selle Simone needs me," the big servant rumbled.

Scowling, the captain opened the door for Simone and watched her guard post himself on the deck outside.

"Batiste is very protective of me," Simone apologized as Tom closed the door.

The good-natured Virginian had already forgotten his pique. "I know it's not customary for a gal to be unchaperoned," he said, leading her to the most desirable seat in the cabin, a threadbare easy chair. "Would you care for some wine?"

"*Merci*," she accepted. Loath to explain the reason for Batiste's vigilance, she sipped her wine and encouraged Tom to talk.

He delighted in her presence, and their dinner conversation was lively.

The hour was late when they emerged from the captain's cabin, and although Batiste was no longer in sight, Tom knew he was close by. Unperturbed, he took Simone's hand and walked her to her cabin.

Outside her door, Tom stopped. "I don't know what you're running from, darlin'," he said softly, "but if I can ever help you, all you have to do is ask."

"*Merci*," she whispered gratefully as he politely kissed her hand and bade her good night.

As Tom strolled back toward his cabin, Batiste watched with approval from the shadows. He had heard the captain's words and was pleased at their new ally.

Dusk was falling over Paradis as Simone bent over her sewing. She did not mind helping around the house; it passed the time and seemed to please her hostess, Dominique's aunt, Marie-France.

Simone remembered the day two months earlier when the *Bayou Queen* had tied up at the landing here. Rotund and frowning, Marie-France had met them on the dock, accompanied by Remi, her aged black scarecrow of a butler.

Without a doubt, the old woman had found her unexpected guest objectionable. Her disapproval had been visible on her face as she turned her cold, slate-colored eyes on the girl with the unladylike hair and the huge black manservant. Why had Dominique sent them to Paradis?

Marie-France had found the answer in her nephew's letter, but she hadn't liked it. The American captain provided an excuse for her annoyance. Because he had performed a service for her family, she was obligated to invite him to dinner, but she clearly did not want to.

Tom had refused the woman's grudging invitation, adding, "But I'd like to say good-bye to Simone and Batiste, if you don't mind."

So relieved was Marie-France that he would not be staying, she overlooked his use of the girl's first name and his camaraderie with a common slave.

"Très bien," she agreed, "come up to the house when you are ready, mademoiselle, and I'll show you to your room. Remi will see to your man."

The captain had extended his hand to the powerful servant. "So long, Batiste. Take care of your little friend."

"I will, Cap'n." The black man smiled as Tom shook his hand. "Thank you for your help."

Turning to Simone, the Virginian laid an awkward, calloused hand against her cheek. "I still don't know what you're running from, and I'm not sure what you've run to. But my offer of help stands. If you ever need me, tie this to the landing, and I'll stop." He thrust a fine linen handkerchief into her hand.

How often Simone had wanted to signal him in the days that followed. Once her unwanted guests were settled, Marie-France had informed them she had no time for entertaining. She lived at Paradis with a small staff of servants, keeping house for her bachelor nephew, which she would do until he married his betrothed, Bernadette Blanchard, a neighbor's daughter.

Simone had tried from the first to be helpful, but Marie-France never seemed to approve. Dominique's aunt was aghast to learn that Batiste was a free man and owned a shotgun. However, she came to accept his offerings to her table with a good appetite.

In the end, it was Simone's skill with a needle that broke through the old woman's reserve. She embroidered linens for her and mended a lace tablecloth. Now she was sewing winter clothes for the slaves while Marie-France canned, hot work even in mid-October.

A steamboat whistle sounded at the landing, and excited voices reached Simone all the way at the back of the house. Laying her work aside, she hurried to see who had arrived. Marie-France and Remi were already at the landing. Seeing that the smokestack rising high above the bayou was not painted with a crown, Simone felt a stab of disappointment that it was not the *Bayou Queen*.

While she watched, a gangly man disembarked from the boat and hugged Marie-France. Dominique! Perhaps he had brought news of Alain. Simone set off at a run.

When Dominique saw her skimming across the green lawn toward him, her skirt billowing, his heart stood still. She was even more beautiful than she had been in New Orleans. Fresh air had put the color back in her cheeks, and her face was animated with eagerness. Could it be that she was glad to see him?

"Simone!" He hurtled down the steps to meet her. Catching her hands in his, he smiled warmly. Then, remembering himself, he asked, "I may call you Simone, mayn't I?"

"*Oui.*" Simone freed her hands, acutely aware that Marie-France's rheumy eyes rested on her with renewed hostility.

"And you must call me Dominique. You look lovely."

"*Merci,*" she thanked him almost impatiently. "Have you brought word of Alain?"

"Nothing that cannot wait, I'm afraid," he said. Glancing back at his aunt, he missed the sorrow on Simone's face. "Here comes my aunt with Capitaine Juneau. You and I will talk later."

"Did you stop to visit Bernadette?" Marie-France addressed her nephew loudly as the captain escorted her across the lawn.

"*Non.*" Dominique was not eager to discuss his fiancée in front of Simone.

"You should have stopped, Dom. The Blanchards, the family of my nephew's betrothed, are our closest neighbors," the old woman explained, mostly for Simone's benefit. "You know they would have lent you a horse to come the rest of the way home, *cher.*"

"I was in a hurry to be here," the young man responded, hoping to pacify her.

"How sweet." A pleased smile lit the old woman's face. "You can always ride over tomorrow, *oui?*"

"If there's time," he answered uncomfortably. "This is to be a short trip."

Through the long dinner, Simone waited miserably, but Dominique did not reveal his news. At last, when he escorted her into the parlor for coffee, she asked in a low urgent voice, "Please, Monsieur Cuvillion . . ."

"You agreed to call me Dominique," he protested, patting the hand she curved over his arm.

Simone could feel her patience ebbing. "*Très bien*, Dominique. Will you please tell me what news you bring of Alain?"

He led her near the window while Marie-France poured coffee in front of the fire. Reluctantly, he muttered, "The police still have not recovered his body, but—"

"But?" she prompted sharply.

"Quietly. I do not want Tante Marie upset," he insisted, his myopic brown eyes darting toward his aunt, "Alain's clothes washed up on the levee a little below town a couple of weeks ago. Though it is hard to be certain, there appeared to be bloodstains on them."

Simone's face paled. "But why . . ."

"I don't know," he said gently, "but I think we must accept the sad truth. Alain is dead."

"I cannot believe it," she whispered painfully. "I won't."

"I do not want to admit it any more than you. Alain was my friend for many years. But the proof can hardly be questioned. He is surely dead."

"I must go back to New Orleans." Simone drew a steadying breath.

"*Non*," Dominique said firmly. "Baudin is there. Since his mother's death, he has nothing to distract him from his search for you. And from what I understand, he has been in an explosive mood. He was hardly off the boat before he killed another man in a duel. His sixth or seventh."

"His fifth," she corrected absently, ignoring the man's look of horror that she should know such a statistic. "Lisette wrote me about it last week."

"I thought now that you're back among decent people, you would have broken your ties with Mademoi-

selle Dupré, Maître St. Michel, and their kind."
Dominique frowned, uncaring that his aunt squinted
toward them curiously.

"What kind is that?" Simone's murmur was ominous. "Have a care what you say, m'sieur. We are talking about friends of mine."

He stared at her in astonishment. He had known the
demure girl must have great inner strength to survive
all she had been through, but he had never seen an
external sign of it. He was not sure he liked it, but
decided perhaps she was simply upset about the news
he had brought.

"I meant only that they're hardly suitable companions for a girl of *les bonnes familles*," he soothed her.

"Improper they may be, but they helped save my
life."

"I helped save you, too, Simone," he reminded her
with a hurt expression.

"You did, and I appreciate it." Her anger at the man
who gazed pleadingly at her disappeared, but she had
to get away. Curtsying politely to the other occupants
of the room, she requested, "If you will pardon me, I
would like to retire. *Bonne nuit*, mam'selle, *Capitaine*,
Dominique."

Both aunt and nephew watched her depart, uneasy
for different reasons.

Marie-France's disquiet stayed with her the next
day, unabated until she saw Dominique onto the packet for New Orleans, away from the girl's allure. Standing on the landing beside the obese old lady, Simone
watched the boat disappear around the bend and tried
not to show how relieved she was that Dominque was
gone.

Simone pulled her woolen shawl tight against the
November chill and placed another log on the grate.
The afternoon was overcast and dreary, the cold wind

making a tree limb creak in complaint against the window frame.

"Steamboat comin'," a slave shouted outside.

She hurried to the window. An unfamiliar sternwheeler was slowing and edging toward the dock. Simone was about to turn away when she saw the gilded wooden crown suspended between the double smokestacks. A crown meant a Queen boat, and a Queen boat meant Thomas Jefferson Franklin was putting in at Paradis.

She did not even stop to don a coat. Clattering downstairs and out the front door, she raced across the lawn, outstripping Marie-France, who shouted, "Where do you think you're going?"

"To meet Capitaine Franklin," Simone called over her shoulder.

"L'américain?" the old woman asked distastefully and slowed her step.

Tom leapt to the landing as Simone arrived. "You're pretty as a picture, gal," he greeted her, taking her hands in his. Stepping back, he looked her over warmly. "Country living agrees with you."

"It's good to see you again," she answered, suddenly shy. The captain was more handsome than she remembered, and his pleasant face was lit with an elated smile. Looking away, she saw Marie-France approaching without haste.

Simone reclaimed her hands hastily and said, "Capitaine Franklin, you remember Mademoiselle Cuvillion."

"I do indeed. A pleasure to see you again, ma'am." Tom swept his hat from his head and bowed.

"*Bonjour, Capitaine.*" Marie-France did not offer her hand. "What brings you back to Paradis so soon?"

"Letters, ma'am. One for you and one for Miss Devereaux." He presented the envelopes with a flourish.

"*Merci.*" Marie-France pocketed hers at once. "I

suppose your schedule will not allow you to join us for dinner?"

"Since this is a shakedown cruise, I don't really have a schedule, ma'am. I'd be delighted to stay, if you'll have me."

"Of course," she acquiesced stiffly. "Simone, see to our guest while I make arrangements with the kitchen. *Pardon, Capitaine.*"

As the couple neared the house, they were hailed by Batiste. Excusing herself while the men visited, Simone withdrew a short distance to read Lisette's letter.

There was still no word of Alain, her friend wrote. Marcel was frustrated in his search, but he continued to look for Simone. Lisette believed the scarred Creole was mad, but those foolish enough to comment on his erratic behavior found themselves facing him under the Oaks. It was odd, she added, that when Dominique had challenged him to a duel, Marcel had declined.

So Dominique had challenged Marcel after she'd asked him not to. Simone seethed, knowing the young lawyer was alive only because of Marcel's whim.

"Is anything wrong?" Tom asked, coming to stand beside her.

"*Non.*" Shoving the letter into the pocket of her apron, she smiled. "Come. If I know Marie-France, she will be waiting with sherry in the first parlor.

The old woman was indeed waiting. She sat rigidly erect, the ribbons of her spinster's cap tied tightly under her double chin, obviously disapproving of Tom and his friendship with Simone. Small talk was strained and the call to dinner a relief.

When they returned to the parlor after dinner, Marie-France dominated the conversation, speaking of *les bonnes familles.* Her manner clearly telling Tom he was an outsider, she lapsed finally into scornful silence.

Recognizing her game, Simone set out to make the

man feel welcome. "Tell me about your new boat, Capitaine," she encouraged.

"Isn't she a beauty?" He regarded the girl gratefully. He might not know *les bonnes familles*, but he knew steamboats, and he was delighted to tell Simone about his new *Creole Queen*. "A packet her size is better suited to the river than the bayou. And not only is she bigger than my other boats, she's faster and luckier, too. I won her in a poker game."

"You won her?" Admiration mingled with incredulity in Simone's voice.

"A pair of fives beat a pair of fours." He grinned broadly when she laughed with pure delight. He bit the inside of his cheek to keep from laughing at the horror on Marie-France's face.

"Do you always bluff?" Simone asked, still chuckling.

"When I can get away with it," he admitted with a twinkle in his blue eyes, "and sometimes when I can't. Last week I lost the money I was saving for the new boat I'm having built. She'll be bigger than the *Creole Queen* and more luxurious. But I guess she'll wait until I win again."

"I have not played cards in such a long time." Nicholas's daughter sighed wistfully.

"I happen to keep a deck with me at all times," Tom answered challengingly, pulling it from the pocket of his jacket.

"I think it is time for bed," Marie-France announced. Rising, she began to gather her things.

"You go ahead," Simone insisted politely. "I'll be up in a while. If you like, I'll lock up so Remi doesn't have to wait up for me."

Her objection done away with before she could make it, Marie-France marched out wrathfully, her lips tight. The girl took no notice, pulling a handful of buttons from her sewing kit to use as chips.

Simone enjoyed the card game, laughing aloud at Tom's bemused expression as she shuffled, performing the sleights of hand her father had taught her. She won steadily, and the captain decided he had never been taken so smoothly in all his twenty-six years, but he did not care. Their time together was relaxed and companionable, and it ended all too soon.

Simone walked him out, across the veranda and onto the moonlit lawn toward the boat. Gripping her elbow to steady her on the dew-wet grass, Tom drew her into the shadows under a great oak tree and turned her to face him. Holding her arms in an easy grasp, he kissed her gently.

Accustomed to casual flirtation, Tom was unprepared for the storm of feeling that coursed through him. He drew her closer, savoring the softness of her lips.

Simone's head whirled with wonderment. How could the mere touch of his lips take her breath away? Where was her loyalty to Alain? Was she wanton? Traitorous?

Her questions remained unanswered, unexamined, as Tom's kiss deepened and she forgot all but sensation.

Shaken, they parted at last, both uncertain what to say or do.

Recovering himself first, Tom caressed her cheek with a tender hand and murmured, "I think I've wanted to kiss you since the first time I saw you on the bow of the *Bayou Queen*."

"Please don't say that," she implored. "I—I'm not ready for—"

"It's all right," he interjected soothingly, kissing her chastely on the forehead. His hands gently slid down her arms as he released her. "In time, you'll be ready, and I aim to be here when you are."

He strode toward the boat, his voice drifting back to her. "I'll be back, darlin'. Don't forget me while I'm gone!"

After a night haunted by dreams of Alain, Simone was awakened at dawn by the *Creole Queen*'s whistle.

Standing at her window, she watched as the boat steamed away from the Paradis landing, the roiling waters of the bayou matching the disturbing churning in her heart.

12

The mood at Paradis was cheerful as Marie-France supervised the twining of a garland in the chandelier in the foyer. The scent of pine mingled with the aroma of cider from the parlor as Simone helped prepare for the arrival of Dominique's sisters and their husbands and broods for Christmas.

Simone was looking forward to the holidays. Celebrations shared with her father had been meager but festive, and *réveillon* at Lefleur and the exchange of small gifts on Christmas Day were her fondest childhood memories.

Suddenly the front door opened and a gust of cold wind swept in.

"Robert, you great baboon!" Simone heard Marie-France squeal. "Take your cold hands off of me."

"A fine way to greet your favorite brother," a male voice chided.

"My only brother," the woman retorted. "Give Remi your greatcoat and come in."

The voices grew louder, and Marie-France appeared in the doorway to the parlor, carrying a candied pineapple, the bachelor's contribution to family dinner.

Behind her was an elegant, silver-haired man who stared with delight at Simone.

"Simone, this is my brother, Robert," Marie-France announced decorously. "He'll be with us for Christmas. Robert, I want you to meet Simone Devereaux, the ward of one of Dominique's clients."

"A pleasure, mademoiselle," Robert said heartily, kissing her hand. "You must call me Nonc' Robert as the other young people do."

"If you will call me Simone." She was immediately at ease with the older man, recognizing him at once as the *fainéant*, or the loafer, of the Cuvillion clan. Almost every Creole family had one; Nicholas had counted many among his friends.

"*Café, chère*?" Marie-France asked him.

"*Oui*, and a bit of brandy to warm me, if you have it." Robert smiled disarmingly at his prim sister. Catching himself before he sat on a sewing basket, he picked it up and peered inside. "This is your work, Simone? What are you making?"

"Bean bags for the children."

"How very kind of you. I take it you don't yet know the little ruffians," he commented dryly.

"Robert, how can you say that about your own family?" Marie-France protested.

"You know it's true, *chère*. When Olympe and Colette and their clamorous progeny get here, there won't be a moment's peace."

"Try to behave yourself," she scolded, though he had voiced thoughts close to her own.

"I always try to behave, *ma soeur*. I just fail so miserably at it, it's hardly worth the trouble." He winked merrily at Simone. "But for our lovely guest's benefit, I will take the trouble."

Marie-France wasted no time in seeking Simone's assistance. "Would you be Robert's dinner partner during his visit? Play cards with him, keep him busy. When he is bored, he, er, imbibes rather freely."

"I'd love to," Simone answered, happy to provide a service for her hostess. And Nonc' Robert was already her favorite Cuvillion.

When Dominique returned to Paradis just before Christmas, she was doubly glad that she had agreed to the arrangement. Her duty gave her an excuse to avoid being alone with the young lawyer. His too-frequent touch and possessive manner disturbed her and she felt the Cuvillion women closing ranks against her when they observed his pursuit of her.

Dinners, which, in Creole fashion, went on for hours each night, became a misery. Seated at the head of the table, Dominique insisted Simone sit at his left, with Nonc' Robert at his right. As host he prevailed, but Simone could feel Marie-France watching her balefully from the other end of the table.

Throughout the meals, the young man's weak brown eyes, magnified through his spectacles, tried to hold hers. Each time he passed a dish to her, his fingers brushed hers lingeringly. And several times, speaking so only she could hear, he repeated the story of his role in her rescue, seeming just as amazed at his bravery in the fifth telling as he had in the fourth.

"I wish you could have seen Baudin's face when he discovered the woman in my carriage was not you," he chuckled again on Christmas night.

"Shame on both of you," Nonc' Robert boomed suddenly, causing his nephew and nieces to regard him indulgently.

"Shame, Dom," he repeated playfully. "You tell Simone secrets and leave me to find solace in my wine glass."

Simone observed Robert warily. His patrician face was flushed, and his speech was slightly slurred. Dominique had monopolized her company, and she had not paid enough attention to the old man.

She turned a dazzling smile on him and said quickly, "But, Nonc' Robert, the entire time I conversed with my host, you were never far from my thoughts. I kept wondering when you might be ready for a game of cards before the fire."

Out of the corner of her eye, she saw Marie-France relax, certain Simone could cajole her brother away from the table and the wine.

"In a moment, *chère*. A toast first." Robert got to his feet unsteadily and lifted his glass. "Each Christmas we gather here. Each Christmas the faces remain the same, if a little older. This year, I propose a toast to Simone, the lovely new addition to our holiday celebration. May it be the first of many."

Marie-France and Dominique's sisters glared at the inebriated man, while the husbands squirmed uncomfortably, aware of their wives' upset. Simone blushed and stared down at the table, feeling the hostile eyes of the other women upon her.

By the next morning, it was apparent that the Cuvillion women intended to exclude Simone whenever possible. They ostracized her from conversation, their voices dying when she entered a room. At last she asked Marie-France to be allowed to leave Paradis on the first available packet.

But Robert's sister was intractable. "I will not release you from your promise, Simone. It's true Robert made a fool of himself last night, but for the first time in memory, he apologized this morning. I expect you to keep him in line until the day after Epiphany, for that is when he plans to leave. In the meantime, do nothing to encourage Dominique. He is betrothed."

"It seems my very presence here encourages him," Simone said bitterly. "That is why I must go."

"When Robert is gone, you may go when and where you wish," Marie-France answered.

Heartsick, Simone knew she must honor her word. In the rainy days that followed, she tried even harder to maintain her distance from Dominique and to ignore the hurt she saw in his eyes.

Just before New Year's, the family was invited to a ball at a nearby plantation. Simone selected her gown carefully, choosing a modest dress, almost plain in its simplicity.

Dominique was admiring when she descended the staircase, but before he could step forward to claim her, Marie-France seized his arm. "Will you escort me to the carriage, Dom, and be my gallant on the ride to the Picards'? I promise to release you from that duty when we arrive, for I know you will want to spend your time with Bernadette."

"Bernadette?" the young man repeated dumbly, his eyes on Simone. "Of course, Bernadette," he winced when his aunt pinched his arm.

At the Picards' home, they found a country ball attended by Creole neighbors for miles around. It was unlike the elaborate *masque* she had attended in New Orleans, but Simone enjoyed it, forgetting for a while her troubles.

After dancing with her host, she hastened to Nonc' Robert's side, but she was not allowed to stay there. One partner after another claimed her. She danced with young and old, trying not to notice how Dominique's eyes followed her even when he danced with Bernadette Blanchard, a plump, pretty girl who gazed up at him in adoration.

At last the moment arrived that Simone had been dreading: She spied Dominique crossing the dance floor toward her.

She turned to his uncle desperately. "You haven't danced with me once, Nonc' Robert. Would you think me bold if I asked you?"

"Not at all, *chère*." He seemed flattered by her request. "The young gallants have kept you so busy, I did not think you had time for an old man."

"I do when he is the handsomest man here," she flirted safely.

"Ah, if only I were thirty years younger." Smiling, he led Simone out onto the dance floor.

When Dominique halted in his tracks, frowning, Marie-France held her breath. She gasped quietly when he walked behind his uncle and tapped him on the shoulder.

"Dominique." Robert glanced back at his nephew in surprise.

"I was on my way to ask Simone to dance, Oncle, but you were too fast for me. I've not danced with her once this evening. May I presume upon you to surrender your partner?"

Simone's heart sank when the older man conceded with a conspiratorial smile, "Gladly, my boy."

"You should not have done that," she protested as Dominique swept her into the circling dancers.

"But I did." He held her close, oblivious to his aunt's scowl and the hurt on Bernadette's face. "Why have you avoided me all evening, Simone?"

"I haven't avoided you." She nearly missed a step, endeavoring to distance herself from his clinging embrace. "You've been busy with Bernadette, and I have been quite content with Nonc' Robert."

"You've danced with every other man in this room," he accused.

"*Oui*, everyone has been very kind, considering I'm a visitor."

"Is that what you think?" Dominique asked, his voice tender. "They could not wait to dance with you because you are the most beautiful, the most charming woman here."

"Now you are being kind," Simone murmured, wondering whether the dance would ever be over.

"I'm very fond of you, you know." The young man's watery brown eyes searched her face for a response.

"Dominique, please, your fiancée is staring." Simone caught sight of Bernadette over his shoulder as they whirled around the floor.

"Let her stare," he said recklessly, uncaring of anything but the girl he held in his arms.

The moment the music drew to a close, Simone broke from the young Creole's grasp and hurried to where Marie-France sat, her face grim under her lace cap.

"Your behavior is disgraceful, mademoiselle," the old woman hissed, "allowing my nephew to hold you so closely."

"I'm not responsible for his actions," Simone snapped, out of patience at last. "Would you prefer that I had made a scene so everyone could witness his rather unwise advances toward me?"

"*N-non.*" Marie-France was taken aback by the girl's vehemence.

"I sought to repay an obligation when I agreed to stay on at Paradis. I assure you I have done nothing to encourage your nephew," Simone said hotly. "It seems tonight you must choose between Robert's indiscretions and Dominique's," she added when the woman's eyes went to her brother, who added to the contents of his punch cup from a silver flask. "I want to go upstairs now."

"You are right." Marie-France sighed reluctantly. "It would be best if you retired."

"*Merci*. I'll make my excuses to Madame Picard." Simone stalked away, shaking with fury.

Pleading a headache, she went upstairs to the wing of the house allocated for the women's use during the ball. As she opened the door to the bedroom she shared with three other women, she heard footsteps behind her.

"Simone, wait," Dominique called softly.

"Go back downstairs at once, sir," she ordered in alarm. "You know what people would say if you were found in the women's wing."

"I must talk to you," he insisted stubbornly.

Feminine laughter came from down the hall, and shadows floated behind a half-open door. Grabbing her hand, Dominique ducked into Simone's room, pulling her behind him.

She prayed none of her roommates had retired early. When she surveyed the moonlit room, she was relieved to find they had not. "You are going to ruin both of us," she snapped.

"Shh, someone is just outside." Listening at the door, he gestured urgently.

Simone froze when she heard soft giggles and the rustle of petticoats as the women passed through the hall on their way back downstairs.

When they had gone, she turned to reason with Dominique and discovered he was watching her, his gaze as limpid as the moonlight pouring through the window.

"I had to talk to you," he whispered.

"Dominique, I don't care how innocent a conversation you intend, if people knew you were in my room—"

"Are you afraid to be alone with me, Simone?"

She hesitated, then said carefully, "What I fear is that you are going to be very sorry for this later."

"I don't think so. And the risk is worth it if you will promise to marry me." He took a tentative step toward her.

She stared at him in amazement. "Marry you?"

"Of course. Don't you know I love you?"

"But I don't love you, and I never let you think I did," she said gently, deciding truth was the best course. "I cannot marry you. Besides, you are betrothed to a lovely girl."

"Bernadette was chosen for me. I don't want her. I want you." He held out his hands in supplication. "It doesn't matter if you don't love me yet, Simone. Love can come after marriage. It happens all the time."

"Then it could happen if you married your intended."

"I will never feel for her what I feel for you," he maintained. "Marry me, Simone."

"I cannot."

"Is it because Alain is not here to give you permission?"

"No!" she protested hotly, her cheeks reddening.

"Ah, I see the problem," the young attorney said knowingly. "Many wards become infatuated with their guardians. But it passes, Simone. I promise if Alain were here, he would approve our union."

Her eyes filled with tears, Simone shook her head and retreated step.

"All I ask is that you think on my proposal and accept this as a token of my love," he insisted, producing a dainty golden locket from his pocket.

She stared at the necklace dully. "I can't accept this."

"If you will not take it to seal our engagement, consider it a gift of the season. I have not yet told my aunt, but I must leave the day after tomorrow, and I won't be here for the exchange of gifts on New Year's."

"Dominique—"

"When I return for Epiphany, I will expect your answer," he cut her off. Then, capturing her face between moist, uncertain hands, he brushed her lips with his. "Until morning, *chère*," he whispered and was gone.

Still clad in her ball gown, Simone lay across her bed and pondered her problem miserably. She was bound by her word to stay at Paradis until Nonc' Robert departed, but she did not know if she could do so without hurting Dominique.

Two days later, the young man rode to Donaldsonville to catch a packet to New Orleans. With a sigh of temporary relief, Simone watched his horse trot through the hazy December morning toward the Mississippi.

On the day after New Year's, a message arrived from Dominique. He was still finishing his business and might not arrive in time for Epiphany, but he would come as soon as possible.

Simone's discomfort was not alleviated by the news. Dreading the hurt her rejection would cause him, part of her longed to be gone from Paradis before he returned; another did not want to leave without making things right between them.

Epiphany crawled by as Simone apprehensively awaited Dominique's return, but he never arrived. Early the next morning, Olympe and Colette and their families piled into their carriages and departed, taking Robert with them.

When they were gone, the house became quiet and the mood, dismal. Freed of her commitment, Simone decided to leave as soon as possible and explain to Dominique later. Almost as soon as the coaches had disappeared down the narrow lane, she sent Batiste to put out the signal flag for any passing steamboat. Marie-France watched without comment before stamping into the house.

During the afternoon, the old woman was called away to a difficult birth in the slave quarters. Simone's melancholy lifted somewhat when the sun broke through the overcast. Putting on a jacket, she wandered to the landing. No boats were in sight. On impulse she tied Tom's handkerchief to a steel ring on a piling, then strolled to the back of the house, where she found Batiste mending fishing nets under a mimosa tree.

"Saw you out at the landing." He grinned as she approached. "Any boats yet?"

"*Non*," she muttered. She stopped near him and listlessly poked her toe at the long brown seed pods that littered the ground below the tree. "I'm afraid the first one that comes will carry Dominique."

"You don't wish to face him because he is in love with you?" Batiste said.

"*Oui*, and nothing I say seems to change his mind. I think I must write what I feel in a letter and get away from here quickly."

"I agree." He nodded. "Where shall we go, *petite amie*?"

"Do you still want to go with me?" She looked at him discerningly.

His strong black fingers ceased their activity, and he gazed up at her, surprised by the question. "Of course I do."

"I would release you from your promise, Batiste," she offered.

"Only Alain could do that. But I would go with you anyway, and I'll stay with you as long as you need me."

Through tears of gratitude, she murmured, *"Merci, mon ami."*

"But the question still stands," he went on practically. "Where will we go?"

"Back to New Orleans, I suppose."

"That could be dangerous for both of us," he counseled. "Marcel Baudin searches for you and the law for me."

"The law?" She stared at him in consternation.

"M'sieur Cuvillion says I am wanted for further questioning. Since the police now believe Alain was murdered, they naturally suspect me. M'sieur Cuvillion will not tell them where I am because he wishes to keep you out of the investigation. If we go back to New Orleans, I fear both of us will have to live in hiding."

"I suppose we could go to Texas," she suggested dubiously. "So many people are heading there these days. Still, we must go to New Orleans to get my money. I don't like living on charity."

While she talked, Simone picked up a mimosa seed pod and slashed the air with it, testing its rigidity and strength. With a sudden impish grin, she saluted Batiste with the stubby, unwieldy "sword." To her delight, he rose and found himself a "weapon."

Assuming the *en garde* position, they began to duel, their seed-pod swords buckling and wobbling. Simone had not realized that Batiste was a skillful fencer, but he had trained with Alain. He fenced effortlessly, laughter rumbling deep in his massive chest as she kicked her skirt out of the way and advanced. She giggled when her sword began to sag limply.

Abruptly Batiste ceased his sport, his face subdued, his arms falling limp at his sides. Simone turned and saw Dominique behind her, his pinched face white with rage.

"What do you think you're doing?" he choked.

"Fencing," she said coolly, trying to maintain her temper in the face of his.

"It's a fine thing to come home and find you cavorting around the grounds with a freed slave," he lashed out.

"Simone meant no harm," Batiste defended her.

"You!" Dominique turned a wrathful gaze on the black man. "I expect you off this property at once or I'll beat you within an inch of your life."

"Just a moment," Simone said hotly, grabbing his coat sleeve.

"And you, go to your room," he commanded, wheeling on her. "I will speak to you when I've had time to compose myself."

"You'll speak to me now. What right have you to order me around?"

"The right of a future husband. And your behavior does not become a Cuvillion," he answered, his voice rising.

"Future husband?" she shouted. "I told you I would not marry you. Besides, although you seem to have difficulty remembering it, you already have a fiancée."

With a pained expression, Dominique looked around to see if any of the slaves who worked nearby had heard, then said in a more moderate tone, "I told you I would break the engagement. I love you, and I want to protect you and your reputation. That is why Batiste must go. He has overstepped the bounds.

"Don't say anything else," he cautioned her wearily. "We will talk later. I'm going to the garçonnière now. Remi says my aunt may be away well into the night. We should not sleep under the same roof without a proper chaperon. I will see you at dinner."

He left Simone, speechless with anger, under the mimosa. When she looked around, Batiste had disappeared, leaving his nets unmended.

"I told Remi and I'm telling you, I'm not coming down to dinner," Simone informed Dominique through her closed door.

"Please, we must talk," he pleaded. Not in his wildest imagining would he have recognized the slender lad who stood poised on the other side.

"I haven't had time to compose myself yet," she replied icily, borrowing his words from the afternoon.

"Come out, *chère*," he cajoled. "I cannot bear your anger. Everything I have done has been for your own good."

"For your own good, Dominique, leave me alone."

He must have sensed that her ire was about to erupt again, for he departed, and she heard him trudge downstairs.

Simone paced before the fireplace. She must leave Paradis, for she could not marry Dominique. She could not marry anyone. She was promised to Alain. And if, God forbid, Alain was gone . . . then she must live her own life.

Her preparations for departure were complete, but she waited, clad in Jean-Paul's clothes, knowing Batiste would return for her.

Just then, a light tap sounded at the French doors. Flooded with relief, she hurried to open them.

"I was beginning to worry," she whispered to the man crouched on her balcony.

"I wouldn't leave you, little friend." Stepping into the bedchamber, Batiste nodded approvingly. "I see you're ready to go."

"When we left New Orleans, I didn't know why, but I brought these along," she said, plucking at her baggy clothes. She had not believed how difficult it was to

don them again. She had stuffed her hair into a stocking cap, vowing not to crop it again unless it became
absolutely necessary.

"Are you ready?" He waited at the door to the balcony.

"One more thing." Simone placed the notes she had
written to Dominique and his aunt on her pillow. She
had expressed her appreciation to Marie-France for her
generosity and enclosed money with a request that she
forward her belongings to Lisette's house. She could
imagine Dominique's disapproval when he heard of it.

In the note she wrote to him, Simone tried to rebuff
him gently. With thanks for his kindness, she enclosed
the locket he had given her.

"Let's go," she murmured, picking up the bundle
containing a few of her possessions.

The pair eased themselves onto a tree limb near the
railing and climbed down to the lawn. Stealing through
the shadows to the bayou road, they set out toward the
Mississippi.

After a cold night of hiding in a barn, Simone and
Batiste cut across open fields to the River Road, a little
south of Donaldsonville. Before long, they heard the dis-
tinctive churning of a paddlewheeler. Climbing the levee,
they waited until it came into sight around the bend,
then both began to wave wildly.

"Is it . . . ?" Batiste wondered aloud, his eyes fixed
hopefully on the steamboat.

"It is!" Simone shouted gladly. "It's the *Creole
Queen*!"

"Cap'n Franklin," Batiste bellowed across the water
as the boat slowed and nosed toward the riverbank.
Sleepy passengers poured onto the deck in various
stages of dress, abandoning their morning toilettes for
fear the rumors were true—that steamboats were little
more than floating volcanoes. When they found, to

their relief, that they were not sinking, they lined the railing to watch as new passengers were taken on.

Simone spied Tom on the hurricane deck, and she knew he had recognized Batiste when he vaulted the ladder to the lower deck and hurried forward to where the gangplank was being readied. Tom's steps faltered when he recognized the smaller of the travelers, and he stared at Simone in disbelief. Since he had kissed her, he had been unable to get her out of his mind. Now she was here, but what a sight she was—rumpled, dressed as a boy, with a stocking cap pulled over her ears. Still, her green eyes were unmistakable.

"Thanks for stopping, Cap'n," Batiste said as soon as he was aboard, the "lad" in tow. "You remember my master, M'sieur Jean-Paul?" he asked, gesturing toward Simone, who stared at her feet.

"Sure do. How are you, Jean-Paul?" Tom played along.

"Still shy," the servant explained when the youngster mumbled unintelligibly, his chin firmly tucked against his neck. "His widowed mother just died."

"Sorry to hear it," the captain responded appropriately, knowing his passengers were listening. "Y'all going to family in New Orleans then?"

Batiste nodded. "We have money for M'sieur Jean-Paul's passage. I can help wood up, in exchange for steerage."

"Reckon we always need another hand," Tom ruminated agreeably. "Ask the first mate down on the main deck for a hammock. I'll take Jean-Paul to my cabin till we find accommodations for him. This way, young man." He strode toward the companionway, leaving Simone to follow.

The moment he closed his cabin door, the captain said severely, "I don't know what you're up to, Simone Devereaux. And I don't care, now that you're here," he added, his frown giving way to a smile.

Wrapping his arms around her, he planted a kiss more of relief than of passion on her lips. Before she could object or respond, he released her.

Simone blinked in surprise, then removed her cap so her brown hair tumbled to her shoulders and grinned at him. "I'm glad to see you too, Capitaine."

"I've been worried sick about you," he said gruffly. Dropping into his shabby armchair, he pulled her down so she perched on his knee. "I stopped at Paradis this morning when I saw your signal."

She looked stricken. "I'm sorry. I forgot all about the handkerchief when Batiste and I left."

"In the dead of the night, from what I hear. Did your hasty departure have anything to do with the master there?" His voice was deceptively mild, but when Simone looked at him, she saw uncharacteristic anger smoldering in his blue eyes.

"Nothing happened. He . . . he just decided he wanted to marry me," she assured him quickly.

"I can understand that, even seeing you dressed as a boy." He chuckled when she shot up from his lap. "What are your plans now?"

"We haven't really decided. I have some money in New Orleans. Batiste and I thought we might make a start somewhere else."

"I'll take you anywhere you want to go," Tom offered earnestly.

"That's not necessary."

"Maybe not to you, but when I left Paradis, afraid I'd never see you again, I realized . . ." He rose and began to pace the cabin. "Hell, I don't know how to say this."

Stopping, he turned to her. "I love you, and I want you to be a part of my life. All my work, the whole Queen fleet, won't mean much if you don't share it with me. I hope it was Cuvillion you were set against, darlin', and not marriage, because I want to marry you."

Simone stared at him in astonishment, but her mind was working. After a moment, she replied carefully,

"I'd like to share your life and your work. But not as a wife—as a partner."

"A partner?" he echoed incredulously.

"I like you a great deal, Tom, but I don't love you."

"Perhaps you just don't know it yet," he advised pleasantly.

"I can't marry you," she went on in a rush. "But I believe in your plans for the future. I'll give you every cent I have toward the completion of your new steamboat . . . if you'll let me operate a gambling salon aboard it. Of course, we would split the profits equally."

Tom looked at her. The plucky little Creole was serious.

"The games would be honest, of course," she continued. "None of the sleight of hand I showed you at Paradis."

"But what about all the running and hiding you've been doing?" he asked with a perplexed frown.

"I can continue to keep my identity a secret. I have a plan. We could call the casino Carnival and decorate it as if it were Mardi Gras. The dealers, the croupiers, even I would wear half-masks as part of the decor."

"It's not a bad idea," Tom admitted. "But I'm not sure you'd be safe."

"Let Batiste and me worry about that," Simone said firmly. "If you agree, I have one stipulation."

"First you expect me to agree to a hare-brained scheme where you're hiding right out in plain sight, and then you make stipulations?"

"Only one. I want your word you'll never be a customer in the casino. You, er, have been known to lose," she concluded delicately. "I have no desire to have anyone else as a partner if you were to lose the Queen fleet."

"Can't I just hire you to manage a casino so you don't have to hand over your life savings?

"I want to own a part of it," she persisted.

"What if it doesn't work? What if I manage to lose your investment?" Tom tried to reason with her.

"You won't," she answered confidently. "If you want me to stay, it's the only way. Will you take me as a partner?"

"It's a good idea," the captain muttered, more to himself than to her. "It won't take much to get the new boat ready. The design wouldn't even have to be changed to add a casino."

With a mighty sigh, he surrendered. "You are the stubbornest woman I've ever met. But you got yourself a partner, darlin'. We'll make a fortune."

13

The morning was clear and bright when the *Creole Queen* nosed into the teeming Canal Street dock. Up in the pilothouse, Zack Cameron squinted at his pocket watch with satisfaction and pronounced, "Right on time."

On the bow, he could see Tom directing the crew to prepare for landing. Shifting to look at the hurricane deck below, he saw the girl, clad in boy's clothes, a stocking cap covering her luxuriant brown hair. Her big shadow was at her side.

Unaware of the pilot's scrutiny, Simone scanned the densely forested western shore across the roiling water. Although she had lived in New Orleans all her life, she had never experienced the thrill of arriving by boat.

On the more populous east side of the river, the shoreline was reinforced by sturdy embankments built of rich brown dirt, levees that stood between New Orleans and the muddy, churning Mississippi. Over centuries the river had cut a deep curve in the terrain, so it almost encircled the town. It was no wonder, she mused, that New Orleans was called The Crescent City.

She drew a deep, appreciative breath. The atmosphere was a heady mixture—fecund river smells, the faint aroma of spices, and the fragile perfume of fragrant flowers that wafted from somewhere upriver. It was good to be home.

When the paddlewheeler was in place, it gave a mighty shudder and released a billow of steam into the blue sky. A plank was lowered as the bell sounded, alerting passengers to go ashore.

"Wish you'd let me go ashore with you," Batiste fretted.

"You know you will be safer on the boat," she answered firmly.

"I'd feel better if you stayed, too."

"I have business to conduct," she explained again. "I'll be safe at Lisette's. Her last letter said she was certain Marcel was no longer watching her house. Even if he were, he has no reason to suspect Jean-Paul and I are the same. And don't suggest again that you could disguise yourself, Batiste. You are too large to hide."

"I know," he acknowledged glumly. "Is the captain still irritated at you?"

"*Oui*," Simone answered with a sigh. "He can't understand why I masquerade as a boy when he brought my trunk from Paradis. I tried to explain it was safer for the time being, but—"

Grinning, the big man interrupted, "He said..."

"'You're the stubbornest woman I've ever met,'" they recited in unison, laughing.

As Simone clattered down the companionway, her voice drifted back to Batiste, "Tell Tom I will meet him at Lisette's tomorrow evening as we planned."

"Jean-Paul, welcome back," Simone was greeted by the girls when she entered the house on rue Dauphine. "We feared we would never see our little gentleman again."

Drawn by the excited voices, Lisette flew from her

suite and rescued the lad from the chattering circle of females.

Closing the door to her apartment, she hugged Simone. "It is good to see you, but what are you doing back here, *chère*? I thought you were safe at Paradis."

"Safe from Marcel, but not from the marriage-minded Dominique," Simone responded wryly, kissing her friend's cheek.

Lisette's brow quirked, and she laughed. "*Mon Dieu*, Simone, you do have problems with men."

"I don't know what happened," the girl said sheepishly. "I did not encourage him." She raked the cap from her head, and her brown tresses fell to her shoulders.

"I know what happened," Lisette declared. "You're even more beautiful than when you went away. I see the change in your face, and I suspect the body you're hiding under those clothes tells the whole story."

"It was harder to disguise myself this time," Simone admitted. "I'm terribly uncomfortable."

"Then you must change. Your things are in the dressing room."

"I hope you don't mind that a small trunk will also be arriving," Simone called as she walked through the bedroom.

"I don't." Lisette watched with amusement as the girl loosened the confining wrapping from her upper body and drew a deep, grateful breath.

When she had changed into a robe, Simone joined the woman in the parlor. "Is there any news of Alain?" she asked, settling before the fire.

"Still nothing." Lisette's gray eyes were sad. "After his clothes were found, the investigation virtually halted. It's as if he vanished from the face of the earth."

"Do the police still suspect Batiste?"

"They suspect everyone and no one. Is Batiste with you?"

"I couldn't get rid of him if I wanted to," Simone

answered with a smile. "I did convince him to stay with
Tom for now."

"Tom Franklin?"

"He picked us up below Donaldsonville and brought
us to New Orleans."

Lisette did not miss the slight glow in Simone's
green eyes when she spoke of the young captain, and
she felt pleased at the renewed signs of life in this
young woman who had known so little pleasure and so
much grief. The madam had always liked the brash,
likeable Virginian, trusting him enough to enlist his aid
to spirit the girl from New Orleans. She had not anticipated an attraction between them, but perhaps it was
the best thing. Feeling a twinge of disloyalty to her old
friend, Lisette forced herself to put it aside. Poor Alain
was dead, and Simone must go on with her life.

She listened with approval as her friend told of her
newly formed partnership with Tom and their plans for
the Queen fleet. The women visited well into the night,
making up for all the talks they had missed.

The next morning, Simone resorted to her old sub-
terfuge of mourning attire and went to the bank. On
learning that she proposed to close her account, the
bank president argued and cajoled, for he felt he owed it
to the memory of his old friend Alain de Vallière to look
after his ward. But he could do little to sway the determined young woman, other than convince her to hold a
portion of the account in reserve for emergencies.

That evening, Simone twirled in front of Lisette, her
full skirt belling around her. "How do I look?"

Simone's white satin evening gown was trimmed
with rich white lace. A bright green ribbon bordered
the low décolletage, and a ruffle of lace cascaded over
her breasts, swaying softly when she moved. Her shoulders were bare, as were her arms, and at her neck and
earlobes blazed the emerald jewelry Alain had given
her, green stones to match her emerald eyes. Her hair
was drawn back, sleek and elegant, but her excited

smile belied the sophisticated image she presented.

Before Lisette could answer, a knock sounded at the door. She smiled as Simone scurried for a last look in the mirror. Smoothing her skirt and patting at her hair, the girl nodded her readiness.

"Mademoiselle Dupré, you're even prettier than the last time I saw you," Tom greeted Lisette, pecking her on the cheek before turning to Simone, admiration in his blue eyes. "So are you, sugar—a *lot* prettier."

Simone's breath caught in her throat as he smiled. Gone was the careless, windblown captain of the river. Tom's raven curls had been tamed. His fashionable suit was expensively tailored of crisp black broadcloth. A white shirt contrasted with his sun-bronzed skin, and golden cufflinks glittered at his wrists. Amid the luxuriant ruffles on the front of his shirt was tucked an impeccable silk cravat, its blue stripe the same sapphire hue as his waistcoat and his smiling eyes. His trousers fit his muscular thighs as if molded to them, and a pair of polished black leather boots completed the picture of elegance.

While the two stared at each other across the quiet room, Lisette cleared her throat delicately and said, "I think I'll check on my guests now. Why don't you make yourselves comfortable? Tom, there's bourbon for you in the decanter."

"Thanks, Lise," he muttered distractedly, his gaze never leaving Simone.

When the door clicked shut behind her, Tom gestured toward the settee. "Let's sit down."

When they were settled, Simone asked, "You haven't changed your mind about having me as a partner in your new steamboat?"

"No."

"Then here is my investment." Taking a wad of bills from her reticule, she thrust it into his hand.

His eyes widened. "G-good Lord," he stammered, "I can't take all this, Simone."

"I kept back enough to live on," she argued. "The man at the bank insisted on it."

Tom's jaw dropped at that admission. Then he closed his mouth, and his lips curved in a wondering smile. "You're the damnedest girl I've ever met," he uttered softly. "I never know what to expect of you. You turn me all around and shake me up. And the hell of it is, I'm beginning to like it."

"I'll bet you say that to all your partners," she teased.

"Every one so far." Leaning back, he regarded her seriously. "We've got to do some reconsidering here. This is as much money as I have tied up in the new boat *and* the packets. I propose that you either take back a good portion of it or become my full partner."

"I'd own half of Franklin Steamboats?" she mused thoughtfully.

"Franklin and Devereaux Steamboat Company, if you say yes."

"Just Franklin is fine. I'd prefer to be a silent partner."

"Can't say I'd like it if you were too silent, darlin'. I'm getting used to your sass."

Ignoring his teasing, she extended her hand. "I will be your full partner, Tom, but I don't think you know what you're letting yourself in for."

"I can't wait to find out," he murmured. Taking her small hand in his, he brought it to his lips instead of shaking it as she had expected. "You and I are going to do just fine together."

The next morning, Tom took Simone to meet his attorney. His eyebrows shot up when she emerged from the bedroom in full mourning costume, but he said nothing when he saw her to his rented carriage. As he'd said he never knew what to expect from her.

As the carriage rolled across Canal Street toward the American Section, Simone asked, "Where are we going?"

"Settle down, little Creole." Tom halted the rig

beside a two-story wooden building on the wide thoroughfare. "I promised Batiste I'd protect you from the Kaintocks."

"But you're a Kaintock."

"You don't need protection from me. I suspect it's going to be the other way around," he grumbled, helping her down from the carriage.

"Welcome back, my boy." Hiram Anderson, Tom's stout and balding attorney, greeted them jovially in the anteroom to his office.

"Hello, Hiram." Tom beamed as the attorney pumped his hand. "I'd like you to meet Miss Simone Devereaux, my new partner."

"P-partner?" Hiram sputtered, turning to the woman who was lifting the veil away from a young and pretty face.

"How do you do, Monsieur Anderson," she greeted him in charmingly accented English. "Tom has told me so much about you."

"How do you do, Tom," he said to his client, "may I see you in my office?"

"Not without my partner," the captain answered mildly.

Exasperation was plain on the attorney's ruddy face. "As you wish. Come in, both of you."

When they were seated, Hiram faced them across the desk and demanded, "Tom Franklin, what in tarnation—begging your pardon, ma'am—have you done? Have you been bluffing with a pair of deuces again?"

"Not since I lost the money to finish my boat," Tom admitted candidly. "To answer your question, Hi, what I've done is to sell half of Franklin Steamboat Company to Miss Devereaux."

"Half . . . as in equal?"

"Isn't that what it usually means?" The young man frowned.

"But, Tom, a woman in business?" Hiram's voice

was pleading. "It just isn't done, especially not in Louisiana."

"Monsieur Anderson," Simone cut in pleasantly, "many things are not done because they have not been tried. Why shouldn't I be Capitaine Franklin's silent partner? Because I know nothing of cargos and engines? It was not my knowledge of those things he needed. He needed money to finish his boat, and I gave it to him."

Hiram stared at her mutely, unable to argue with her logic.

"And she gave me some great ideas, Hi. I tell you, we're going to make a fortune," Tom interjected eagerly. "Steamboats aren't just for carrying freight and a few passengers. They've become floating hotels. Simone made me see that we could take it even a step further. My boat—*our* boat is going to be big, three full decks high, not including the hurricane deck or the pilothouse. Why shouldn't a boat that large have a casino with square deal games and the prettiest hostess on the river?"

"You're proposing Miss Devereaux run this establishment?" Hiram asked disbelievingly.

"*She's* proposing she run it," Tom corrected ruefully, "and she's already told me I can't play there." Chuckling when the attorney stared at the girl in awe, he added, "I know she looks like a frail little thing, but she's got a will of pure iron."

"I'm afraid he is right," Simone affirmed with a dazzling smile. "I know it may take time to become accustomed to a woman in commerce, but consider this: If I keep Tom from bluffing with a pair of deuces, we may indeed, as he says, make a fortune."

"Perhaps my wife has been right all along," Hiram muttered. "She said all Tom needed was a good woman. I'll draw up the partnership papers right away."

After their meeting, the couple drove to the shipyard outside of town to inspect the new boat. They picked their way through seeming chaos to the huge, unfinished shell of a paddlewheeler. Supported by massive steel horses and still without its enormous sidewheels, the steamboat resembled a building uprooted from its foundation. Pieces of the paddles were stacked beside the hull, and two steel cylinders lay on the ground, smokestacks waiting to be set over the engine room.

The noise in the yard was deafening, but the din was soon replaced by the murmur of voices as the workmen drifted toward lunch.

"Come on," Tom said, taking Simone by the hand, "they won't be back for a while. We can explore."

He led her up a steep, swaying gangplank to the main deck of the deserted shell, where the pungent scent of oil lingered over shiny newly installed machinery.

Together they climbed the curving staircase on the bow to the boiler deck, the second level. They passed the long rows of cabins, which flanked the ladies' lounge, on their way to the cavernous area set aside as the Grand Salon, the common area and dining room of the big boat. A carved wooden bar occupied the center of the room, waiting to be installed.

On the third deck, they found themselves at the doorway of the unfinished space that would become the casino. Amid the sawdust and unvarnished timbers, Simone tried to imagine what it would look like.

"Do you want to see your new home?" Tom asked, guiding her up another companionway to the open hurricane deck that covered half the length of the boat. Forward were spacious cabins and toward the stern, the pilothouse rose yet another floor.

The January wind whipped at Simone's clothing and made her veil flutter wildly in front of her face. Removing her bonnet, she gazed about, thinking she had never been so far from the ground. She could see the river stretching out for miles in either direction, and behind her were acres of marshland.

"I'm going to live up here?" she breathed, enchanted by the thought of all she would see as they cruised the river.

"This deck is reserved for officers, and owners. It'll be very private. Come tell me if you like the cabin I chose for you."

She followed him to the forwardmost cabin, which looked out over the bow of the great boat.

"What do you think?" he asked, watching her with pleasure.

"I think it's wonderful." She turned her face to the wind. Her hair came unbound and whipped around her flushed face.

"I don't know when I would've—*if* I would've—finished her without you," Tom said. "I'd like to name her for you. I want to call her *Emerald Queen* . . . for your green eyes. That is, if you don't mind," he finished shyly, as if embarrassed by his sentiment.

"I'd be honored." Tiptoeing, she kissed him on the cheek, backing away before the flicker of longing in his sapphire eyes could kindle a deeper burning.

In the days and weeks that followed, their life settled into a busy routine. Simone turned her attention to furnishing the boat, quickly realizing that completing construction would account for only a small part of the *Emerald Queen*'s expenses. She worked hard, determined to make the boat a success from the beginning. Tom met with the shipbuilders and chandlers and hired the crew, stewards, maids, cabin boys, even an orchestra.

Simone usually spent her evenings in Lisette's suite, alone if the madam was busy. She had banned Tom from visiting every evening, disturbed by the restrained passion in his sleepy blue eyes and confused by her reactions to it.

Sitting with Serge before the fire one evening, she was pondering the emotions Tom roused in her when the maître's voice interrupted her reverie.

"I'm sorry, what did you say?" she asked, shifting her distracted gaze to him.

"I asked whether you wanted to finish our game or not," he repeated patiently, gesturing toward the chess board between them. "I think perhaps your mind is too full of your '*mericain*."

"He's not my *américain*." Simone focused on the pieces with exaggerated interest.

"He would like to be."

Giving up her pretense, she gazed at her friend with tears in her eyes. "I know," she answered. "But I cannot forget Alain."

Leaning back in his chair, Serge regarded the girl seriously. "I know you grieve for Alain, *ma petite*, but you're so young. I think even he would want you to live—and love—again."

"Perhaps," she whispered with a sad smile. "Someday."

Near the end of March, Tom and Simone went to dinner at the Andersons' apartment above Hiram's law office. They had often visited with the older couple and their shy daughter, Barbara, in the past two months. Simone had taken a special liking to Hiram's wife, Dulcie, a vigorous, big-boned woman.

When the party was assembled in the parlor, Hiram lifted his glass and said, "I believe tonight is something of a celebration. According to my calendar, construction of the *Emerald Queen* should be at the halfway point. Is that right, Tom?"

"Should be," Tom clarified gloomily, "but I can't see how she'll be done in time."

"Don't look so sad, Capitaine," Simone chided, laughing. "Haven't I told you? In New Orleans, pleasure sometimes pauses for business."

"She's right," Hiram affirmed. "And somehow, business still gets done."

"Well, I wish the work crew would pause more often for business and less for lunch. I'd like the boat in May, as promised, but at the rate they're going, it'll be Christmas before we can take to the river."

Aside from that moment of gloom, the evening passed pleasantly, and in the dark cab on the way home, Tom put his arm around Simone, pulling her against him so she fit in the crook of his arm, her head on his shoulder. For a time they were silent, the only sound the clopping of the horses' hooves on the cobblestone streets.

"Simone," his voice was a whisper in the night.

"*Oui*?" She tilted her face toward him slightly and discovered his lips were close to hers, so close she could feel his warm, sweet breath on her face. His eyes were shadowed as he gazed down at her. Dipping his head, he kissed her with aching sweetness.

When his mouth left hers, he whispered against her ear, "I love you."

"Tom . . ." She stirred in his arms.

"Shh." He drew her close so his chin rested lightly on top of her head. "I don't expect you to say anything. I know you're confused. I can see it in your eyes."

"I don't know what I feel," she confessed. "I don't think I'm ready to love or to be loved."

"There's not much you can do about the latter." He chuckled ruefully. "Maybe not the former either. I keep telling you, you love me, honey. You just don't know it yet. Guess I'll put off proposing again to give you a little longer to think."

Simone was grateful that he did not press her, but her relief battled unexpected disappointment the rest of the way home. Though Tom held her close, he did not try to kiss her again.

Hand in hand, the couple walked to the garden gate Simone continued to use as her entrance and across the dark patio into Lisette's empty apartment.

Tom waited until Simone lit a lamp. "I suppose I'd

better go. We have a lot to do tomorrow."

As he started to leave, she said softly, "Tom, thank you for understanding."

He turned to her, his pleasant face somber. "I don't understand," he said distinctly. "I just know things between us are the way they are for a reason. If I could change them, I would. As it is, I'll just love you and wait."

Her green eyes filled with tears. "I don't mean to hurt you."

"You haven't hurt me, Simone." He was beside her in one stride, his hands on her shoulders. "The last two months, working on the boat with you, have been the happiest of my life."

The end of his declaration was lost against the tempting softness of Simone's mouth. Though he had not intended it to happen, when he stared down at her, he could not resist. As he pulled her to him, his lips seeking hers, she was rigid for an instant, but then her resistance began to melt, leaving her body soft and yielding in his arms.

Tearing his mouth from hers with effort, he held her close. His forehead pressed against hers, he cast about for his composure.

"Unless you've changed your mind about loving and being loved, I've got to go," he muttered. "Now." Drawing a steadying breath, he released her and stepped back.

Simone also retreated, shaken. "I—I'm sorry."

"I'm not." Tom smiled wryly. Simone's lips were puffy from his kiss, and her eyes were dark with desire, but the turmoil she felt was clearly visible on her face.

Touching her cheek, he murmured, "See you tomorrow, darlin'."

She watched him disappear through the garden gate and fought the urge to call him back. What kind of woman was she? she agonized. She had given herself once to a man, certain she could feel such yearning only for him. But a moment ago, in Tom's arms, she had felt a stirring she had never expected to feel again. She did not love Tom as she had loved Alain, but she could no longer deny her feelings. She wanted the American captain as much as he wanted her.

14

The night sky glittered with stars, and the May breeze carried on it the scent of the river as a slight figure in loose clothing and a straw hat passed through Exchange Alley. Though it would be her last visit with Serge for some time, Simone was pleasantly excited. In two days, the *Emerald Queen* would leave New Orleans.

At the Canal Street Wharf, the great steamboat waited, rising above the waterline like a floating white palace trimmed in gilt. Her paddleboxes were painted bright green, and a golden crown was affixed between smokestacks fifty feet high. She was splendid, even more beautiful than the partners had imagined.

Absorbed in her thoughts, Simone paid little notice to her surroundings as she walked along rue Conti until a voice hissed her name from nearby.

Her heart pounding, she was on her guard immediately, if belatedly. A man stood before her on the *banquette*. Lit from behind by a streetlight, his face was not visible. A tall opera hat and an elegant cloak further masked his identity.

"I thought it was you," Fabrice growled. "Where have you been?"

Simone relaxed slightly and snapped, "Keep your voice down, Fabrice."

"Is that all you have to say to me?" Her cousin scowled down at her. "I've looked everywhere for you. I was afraid Marcel had kidnapped you—or killed you—before you deigned to send your cryptic little note to *maman* to let us know you were still alive."

"I'm sorry, Fabrice. I couldn't let anyone know where I was."

"Not even your own family?" he exploded.

"It was too dangerous," she explained patiently. "How are Tante Viviane and Oncle Georges, and you?"

"They are well. I'm engaged," he answered grimly. "And I want you to come home to Lefleur, where you belong."

"I don't belong there anymore, Fabrice, if I ever did."

"If you think I am going to allow you to resume your masquerade at the *salle*—"

"I don't," she cut in.

"Then why are you wearing those clothes?"

"This is temporary. I am leaving town in a few days."

"I demand an explanation," the young Creole said indignantly.

"I'm not going to stand in the middle of the street and discuss our family business, Fabrice."

"Then come where we can discuss it in privacy."

"Aren't you late for the opera?" she asked when the church bells tolled the hour.

"What? Ah, *oui*." Her cousin looked down at his formal attire as if surprised by what he was wearing.

"Why don't we meet tomorrow evening?"

"Where?"

Unwilling for anyone, even Fabrice, to know her hiding places, Simone named a discreet restaurant.

"*Trés bien*. I'll arrange for a private dining room.

Nine o'clock—and don't come dressed as Jean-Paul."

"I won't."

"Perhaps I should walk you wherever you are going," he suggested swiftly when she started to leave.

"*Non, merci*." She kept walking. "I'm a big boy. I can take care of myself."

Marcel hunched on a bench, the green-eyed prostitute he had engaged for the evening forgotten upstairs. He had excused himself for only a moment, but as he walked along the hallway between the private dining rooms, he had heard a disturbingly familiar voice.

"Simone!" he whispered. But from which room had the voice come? He could not burst into a private room, so he positioned himself in the bar near the foot of the stairs to wait.

He had been waiting for some time when Fabrice Chauvin ushered a cloaked woman through a crowd of new arrivals and out the door to the street. Her head was bent so her hood concealed her face, but Marcel knew it was Simone.

A gleam in his pale eyes, he shoved his way through the crowd and followed. Fog rolled in from the river, wisps forming halos around the lamps along the narrow street. Not far away, Fabrice was helping his companion into a closed coach.

"Chauvin," Marcel called, striding toward him. "I'd like a word with you."

Fabrice's face paled when he saw him, but he maintained his composure. Closing the carriage door, he greeted the blond Creole in a tight voice, "*Bonsoir*, Baudin."

"*Bonsoir*," Marcel responded amiably. "I saw you inside, but you got away before I could say hello."

Fabrice realized miserably there could be only one reason Baudin wanted to speak with him: He had seen Simone. "How are you, Marcel?" he asked, trying to delay the inevitable, hoping his resourceful cousin would think of a way to escape detection.

"I am well. I haven't seen you for a while. I heard you are engaged. Is that your lovely fiancée in the carriage?"

"Er, no," Fabrice muttered glumly.

"Une *fille de joie* then, perhaps?" Marcel asked with a knowing smile. "A last fling before wedlock?"

Fabrice seized upon the insinuation. "You won't say anything, will you? Zaza is so young, and her family is old-fashioned. I don't think they would understand."

"I won't say anything, if you'll introduce me to your friend," Marcel said slyly.

"Another time perhaps." Fabrice reached for the door latch.

"Now." Marcel laid a detaining hand on his arm.

Unable to delay any longer, Fabrice opened the coach door and muttered, "Mademoiselle, may I present Monsieur Marcel Baudin."

When no answer came from the dark interior, both men peered inside. Simone had gone, leaving the door on the other side of the carriage open. It swayed silently on the breeze.

"Where is she?" Marcel snarled.

"I—I am as mystified as you, m'sieur," Fabrice stammered.

"Where is Simone?" the fair Creole roared.

"You know she has been missing for more than a year," her cousin countered.

"Don't lie to me," Marcel snapped. "I know the slut was living with de Vallière."

"What?" Fabrice's eyes were round with disbelief.

At the other man's obvious shock, Marcel scoffed, "Don't tell me you are surprised by your petite cousine."

"I . . . I watched the house for weeks," Fabrice answered in a strangled voice. "I never saw her."

"*Non*, she and her lover were very clever," Marcel

sneered. "But she doesn't have de Vallière to protect her any longer. Where has she gone now, Chauvin?"

"I don't know," Fabrice said weakly.

Marcel scrutinized his face for a long moment, then, apparently satisfied, he snarled, "Tell Simone when you see her that nothing has changed. I will have her." With that, he pivoted and marched away.

Feeling shocked and betrayed, Fabrice got into his carriage and was driven away.

Marcel paused on the *banquette* and looked around for his bodyguard. Perhaps la Roche had found the girl, he thought hopefully, though he doubted it. The stocky Cajun was strong, and he followed orders, but he was slow-witted. Presently Guy la Roche came into view, running down the street toward him.

"Me, I think she's the girl you seek," he greeted his employer, puffing.

"Where is she? Why didn't you bring her back?"

"I lost her," the Cajun admitted, shamefaced. "But she ran fast for a girl, yes. I kept her in sight for a time, but when I turned onto rue Dauphine, it was as if she had vanished."

"Rue Dauphine?"

"*Oui.*"

"Come." Marcel strode toward his carriage. "We're going to pay a call on Mademoiselle Lisette Dupré."

"Perhaps Marcel didn't see you," Lisette suggested hopefully as she followed Simone through her suite, picking up garments as the girl shed them.

"Perhaps, but I have a terrible feeling." Simone stepped out of her petticoat. "I must go before I bring danger to you."

"I know you said Marie LeVeau told you you would bring danger to the ones you love, but—"

"Look what happened to Alain," Simone interjected soberly as she secured her hair on top of her head. "I no sooner admitted I loved him than he vanished without a trace. You risked Marcel's wrath when you helped me escape, and you do so every time you provide refuge for me. My family cannot protect me. Batiste and Serge have offered to fight him, but, as *gens de couleur*, they would hang if they lifted a finger against him." Hastily, she donned Jean-Paul's trousers over her pantalettes. "The sooner I'm aboard the *Emerald Queen*, the safer we will all be."

"What about Tom?" Lisette asked. "You care for him, I know."

Simone stared at her, her green eyes as hard as the jewels they resembled. "Tom doesn't know about Marcel, and I don't want him to know."

Wisely, Lisette did not pursue the subject. Tossing Simone's clothes onto the bed, she helped her with the wrapping around her upper body. "Even though you're leaving here tonight as Jean-Paul," she said through a mouthful of pins, "I want you to let Jude walk you to the wharf."

Before Simone could answer, a great commotion came from the front of the house.

"You can't go in there!" Jude bellowed.

"Try to stop me and die!" a familiar voice roared, nearly drowning out the pounding footsteps in the hall.

The girl's face blanched. "Marcel," she whispered. "I knew it." She shoved her bare feet into the heavy boy's shoes and grabbed her shirt from the doorknob where it hung.

Suddenly the door was thrown open and the wild-eyed Creole strode into Lisette's suite. A slender form stood poised in the bedroom. Though partially dressed in a boy's clothes, the figure was undeniably female . . . undeniably Simone.

"No!" Marcel bellowed, his face flushed with rage. In a rush, everything became clear to him. The object of his obsession had been hiding right under his nose!

As he charged toward her, Simone ducked through

the French doors into the courtyard. Marcel tried to hurl himself after her, but his way was blocked by the willowy, determined Lisette.

"Catch him, Jude!" the madam shouted to the doorman. Wheeling, Marcel met Jude's assault with the strength of a madman, clubbing him with the hilt of his sword. Returning to the hall, he raced toward the door at the end, which opened onto the courtyard.

In the dark garden, Simone made her way surely to the back gate. Her hand was extended toward the latch when it opened and Guy la Roche stepped through, his sword drawn, fog swirling around him. Unarmed, she looked around for a weapon, but she found none.

Smiling, la Roche cajoled, "Where is the girl, little boy? You tell me and I will not harm you, *non.*"

"Simone!" Lisette appeared in the door from the parlor and tossed her a fireplace poker. "This is the best I can do."

Marcel's bodyguard looked puzzled when the boy caught the tool and, using it as a sword, began to advance. La Roche met the attack with surprising agility, but still his small opponent advanced.

Simone tried to circle, to reach the gate. If she could slip into the alley, she could outrun the thickset man. Dimly she was aware of Marcel's frustrated pounding on the door he had found locked. Her back against the brick wall, she fenced desperately, knowing she was tiring. The poker was clumsy and unwieldy, and it was becoming harder and harder to block la Roche's thrusts.

Suddenly she felt a searing pain in her side and a spreading liquid warmth soaking into the wrapping she wore beneath her flapping shirt. The poker felt so heavy in her hand, she could hardly hold it. Lifting her eyes to her opponent, she saw the triumphant spark in his eye—abruptly extinguished when Lisette felled him with a well-aimed flowerpot from across the garden.

"*Merci!*" Simone called and ran out of the gate.

Unaware the girl had been wounded, Lisette waited until she was certain she was gone. Then she went to the door and unlocked it. Marcel nearly toppled into the courtyard when the door opened.

"Where is she?" he choked in rage.

"Where is who?" Lisette looked around the dark garden.

"You know damned well I mean Simone."

"There is no one by that name here, m'sieur."

"You've been hiding her. I ought to kill you!" he screamed.

"I would think twice before making such a threat, especially in front of so many witnesses." Lisette gestured upward.

Marcel turned. The blood rushed to his head, roaring when he saw, in nearly every upstairs window, curious faces peering down at the courtyard. The pounding in his ears was so great he nearly did not hear the madam speak.

"None of them is sure what happened here tonight," she said softly, "but if you don't go and take your friend, I'll be happy to tell them."

The pounding eased, and Marcel realized she was waiting for an answer. "I will go," he said, "but I'll be watching you."

"Do not bother," Lisette said, her gray eyes cold. Then she turned and went inside.

Simone staggered, staying close to the shadowy buildings. The fog was becoming thicker; it could not be far to the river. She had come this far unnoticed, but she feared she would faint before she could reach the boat. She was light-headed and her thinking was becoming more and more muddled when she stumbled into the ropewalk that angled toward the wharf. With relief, she recognized it. Only a little farther to Canal Street.

Placing one foot in front of the other with effort, she lurched toward the lights at the other end of the passage. She blinked, trying to clear her vision, as a shape materialized in the darkness some distance away.

"Obie," Simone croaked just before her legs gave out.

The Negro boy raced to the fallen figure, facedown in the swirling fog. His eyes widened when he turned Simone gingerly. "Jean-Paul! And you ain't a boy at all," he breathed wonderingly. "You're hurt. We gotta get you to a doctor."

"Must get . . . to . . . the *Emerald Queen*," she whispered, her pale face rigid with pain.

"The new boat? At least it's close. Come on." Pulling her to her feet, Obadiah looped her arm around his neck and gripped it tightly, his other arm wrapped around her waist. Half-carrying, half-dragging Simone's limp body, he took her to the wharf.

"Help, somebody! Anybody!" he shouted as they neared the gangplank.

Tom emerged from the engine room, where he had been inspecting the mechanical marvels of his new steamboat. When he saw the pair on the dock, his smiling face grew taut with shock.

"Simone!" He raced down the gangplank and scooped her into his arms. She looked as if she were bleeding to death, but she was conscious. "What happened, darlin'?" he nearly wept.

"Hard to parry with a poker." She smiled weakly. "Get Batiste. He'll know what to do.

"*Merci*, Obie," she murmured, then her head lolled over Tom's arm.

Tom stared down at her, panic-stricken until he saw the pulse fluttering in her throat. "Come with me," he told Obadiah grimly. "I want to talk to you."

The urchin followed as the captain carried the wounded girl the length of the huge boat and up three flights of stairs without slowing an instant. And as he went, Tom bellowed for Batiste.

On the hurricane deck, he shouted up toward the pilothouse, "Tell the engineer to start building steam. We're taking her out."

"Tonight? But, Tom, we've only got a skeleton crew and no provisions," Zack leaned out the window to argue.

"We've got all we need for this run," Tom yelled. "Get on that speaking tube and get some steam. I want to leave within an hour."

"You're the captain." Shaking his head in exasperation, the old pilot pulled his head back inside the wheelhouse.

"Wait here," Tom ordered Obadiah.

In his cabin, the man laid Simone on his bed, unmindful of the velvet spread. Taking a knife from his pocket, he cut away her ruined shirt, paling when he saw the blood-soaked wrapping beneath. Carefully, he slid the blade under the bindings and sliced through them and the camisole she wore.

The wound was a long gash in the smooth white skin of her side, but it was not deep. Yanking a handkerchief from his pocket, Tom attempted to stem the flow of blood until Batiste could arrive.

The big black man entered without knocking, evidence of his distress. "Where is she? What happened? This is my fault," he groaned, seeing his mistress's still figure outstretched on the bed. "I should've been with her."

Wasting no more time with recriminations, he knelt beside her and examined the wound.

"Is she going to be all right?" Tom asked hoarsely.

"She will be when we get the bleeding stopped and clean the wound," Batiste answered, reaching for the wooden case of medicines he had brought with him. "But she won't be doing any more sword fighting for a while."

"Thank God," Tom said, nearly weak with relief.

"Don't worry, Cap'n," Batiste reassured him, his competent hands already at work. "The blow was lessened by the binding she wore, and it looks as if the blade glanced off a rib. She will be sore, but it's not a bad wound. Biggest problem is that she's lost a lot of blood."

"If you won't need me for a minute, I have to see to a few things." Tom paused at the door. "Batiste, I have to know. Simone isn't running from the law, is she?"

"No, Cap'n. She's running from something over which the law has no control." The girl moaned then, and Batiste turned his full attention to her.

Pondering the big man's words, Tom went to speak to Obadiah.

"She's gonna be all right, ain't she?" the boy asked anxiously the moment he saw the captain.

"Yes. Thanks for bringing her here. Did anyone follow you?"

"Didn't see nobody."

"I'm grateful to you, Obie. That is what Simone called you, isn't it?"

"Simone. So that's who she was all the time." Obadiah grinned. "I knew Jean-Paul wasn't 'xactly what he seemed."

Tom laughed in spite of himself and offered his hand. "I'm Captain Franklin."

"Obadiah Prejean." The boy's toothy smile widened as they shook hands.

"How can I repay you, Obadiah?"

"I . . . I'd like a job, sir, on the *Emerald Queen*. I'm a free person of color," he added quickly. "I figure there ain't much of a future blackin' boots and doin' card tricks."

"Did Simone teach you the tricks?"

"Yes, sir."

"Then there's no future at all. You're liable to end up a young, good-looking corpse."

"Oh, you've played cards with her, too," Obie said knowingly.

"Took me for every button I had," Tom answered cryptically. "All right, Obadiah, go get your things, but make it fast. And, Obie . . ." He delayed the lad long enough to hand him a coin. "Send the first urchin you see to Lisette Dupré. Have him tell her her friend is all right."

"Yes, sir." Obie saluted smartly and clattered down the companionway.

A little later, Tom descended from a hurried conference with Zachary in the pilothouse and returned to Simone's side. Her face was ashen and her breathing shallow, but she slept peacefully. Batiste was gathering his vials of medicine and placing them in his case when Tom entered.

"How is she?" the captain whispered.

"Sleeping, but she's already got a fever. Will you stay with her while I make a tisane? Only be a few minutes."

"Of course." Tom pulled his dilapidated chair next to the bed and watched Simone while she slept. Who had done this to her? He had known she was in some sort of trouble, but who would want to harm her? She looked so small and vulnerable in the big bed that he wanted to hide her away where trouble would never find her.

Feeling the vibration when the paddlewheels began to turn easing the gigantic boat away from the pier, the captain relaxed. Obadiah must have returned.

When Simone moaned and thrashed in her sleep, Tom was on his feet in an instant, his hand on her brow. She was burning up with fever. Her breathing had become ragged, and she began to shiver. He chafed her slender arms between his hands, trying to warm her, and wondered where Batiste was.

Just then the big man returned, carrying a cup. His brow furrowed with concern, Batiste bent over his patient and forced a little of the fluid between her lips.

Simone opened dull green eyes. "Bat," she mumbled, "he found me."

"It was bound to happen, *petite amie*, if we stayed in New Orleans."

"Thought I was safe at Lisette's," she said with effort.

He put the cup to her lips again. "Drink this and rest."

She obeyed, then closed her eyes without seeing Tom nearby. But he saw a tear slip from the corner of one of her closed eyes and run down into her hair. After a moment, she said sleepily, "Do you think Alain would understand, Batiste? I've tried to be strong since he . . . but . . . I'm tired . . . of being strong . . . of being alone."

"You're not alone, little one," the big servant murmured. "You have me."

"And me," Tom echoed quietly. Simone did not hear. She was already asleep.

Simone awoke to sunlight angling through first one window, then another, as the boat followed the river's course. She opened her eyes slowly and lay still, not daring to stir. Memories of the night before were hazy, but she felt a throbbing in her side that verified the nightmare.

She looked around to discover Tom dozing beside the bed, unshaven, dark circles under his eyes. His weary, rumpled appearance and battered chair looked out of place amid the luxury of the *Emerald Queen*. She was aboard the magnificent steamboat, she knew that. But how?

Hoisting herself up on her elbows in an attempt to sit up, Simone gasped aloud at the pain. Tom awoke and catapulted himself from his seat.

"What are you doing, darlin'? Don't try to get up." Easing her back on her pillow, he sat on the bed beside her and held a cup of water to her lips. "Here, drink this. You must be thirsty. You ran a fever last night."

"How did I get here?" She frowned up at him as she tried to recall what had happened after she left Lisette's.

"Obadiah found you and brought you aboard."

"Obadiah Prejean?"

"The one and only." Tom nodded with a grin.

"What a surprise I must have been to him." She smiled wanly.

"You're a surprise to everyone, darlin', especially me. You surprised me witless last night, when I saw you bleeding all over the dock."

"I'm sorry." She reached up and smoothed his tousled black hair.

Capturing her hand, he asked grimly, "Who did this, Simone? Tell me, and I'll take him apart with my bare hands."

"That wouldn't do any good." She withdrew her hand. She would not let Tom risk his life at the hands of an expert New Orleans swordsman.

"It would sure as hell make me feel better," he fumed.

"Please, can't we put what happened behind us?"

"I don't even know what happened," he said painfully, "because you don't trust me enough to tell me."

"I trust you. I just do not want you to be in danger."

"God save us from stubborn women," Tom muttered. "And you're the stubbornest one I know. Listen, darlin', nothing is more important to me than your safety." He laid his hand on her cheek, his thumb tracing her lips. "I want to take care of you."

"It seems you've been doing that."

"It was my pleasure . . . mine and Batiste's."

"*Merci*." Realizing for the first time that she was naked under the blanket, she blushed and changed the subject. "Shouldn't you be in the pilothouse? I can tell we're moving. I'm glad I didn't ruin our plans for a trial run this morning."

"We left New Orleans last night. If we hold our speed, we ought to be in Natchez by early afternoon."

"We weren't supposed to go all the way to Natchez. The *Emerald Queen* hasn't even been christened yet," she protested.

"We'll christen her later. We had cargo to deliver."

"What cargo?" Simone asked skeptically.

"Some plows, some yard goods—"

"That doesn't sound like much."

"There's an upright piano for a cathouse, too," he added defensively.

"No passengers?" Her green eyes were shrewd.

"Not this trip."

"So I did ruin our plans," she muttered. "You left early because of me, didn't you?"

"We needed a shakedown," Tom countered reasonably. "You'll be glad to know Zack says she handles like the jewel she is.

"I'm going to go find Batiste now," he said, rising, "and tell him you're awake. He'll want to change that dressing."

"Would you ask him to bring me a robe?"

"Why?"

"I've taken your bed. I'm not going to take your clothes. And I am not moving to my own cabin stark naked."

"You're not moving anywhere, any way, until Batiste says you can," Tom said stubbornly.

She glared up at him. "I don't know why you brought me to your cabin in the first place, Tom Franklin, but if you think I am going to—"

"You might wait till you're invited, Miss Devereaux," he interrupted heatedly. "I don't expect you to share my cabin, but I do expect you to get well. You'll stay here until Batiste says you can be moved."

"I'm getting up as soon as I am able," she announced with a defiance that belied her weakened condition. "We still have to put the finishing touches on Carnival."

"We won't be opening the casino right away," he informed her, "and I'm not sure you should be a part of it when we do."

"We made a deal," Simone snapped, sitting upright, heedless of the pain, "a business deal."

"That was before I knew your life was in danger," he argued. "Do you think I'm going to let you risk it for business?"

"It's my life." Her expression was mutinous.

Tom's blue eyes narrowed, but his voice was mild. "You must be feeling better, sugar, or you wouldn't be so damned cantankerous."

"*Mere de Dieu*!" she seethed. "You *'méricain coquin . . .*" Emerald eyes clashed with sapphire.

"Damn it, Simone, if you're going to holler at me, at least do it so I can understand." Frowning, he left, closing the door on an impassioned outpouring of French.

The *Emerald Queen* was moored in Natchez at dusk, swaying softly with the current and bumping gently against the wooden dock.

Ensconced in her own cabin since the afternoon, Simone could be still no longer. She rose stiffly and went to the window in her small parlor to look out at Natchez-Under-the-Hill, the roughest town on the Mississippi.

At the end of the pier was a huddle of rough wooden buildings brightly lit from within. They were backed by a high clay bluff, which seemed to curve over the rude settlement. Gazing upward, Simone saw what seemed to be another town perched above, separate and somehow superior. Over the water, Simone could hear faint music and the sound of a woman's shrill laughter.

A light rap sounded at her door, and Tom entered, staring in vexation toward the empty bed. Turning, he located Simone, her long nightgown a white blur in the shadows by the window.

"What are you doing up?" he asked gruffly, leading her by the hand to her bed where he tucked the covers firmly around her legs. Then he sat beside her, his back propped against the headboard and his legs outstretched on the velvet coverlet. Crossing his arms on his chest, he asked, "Are you still mad at me?"

"I wasn't really angry with you," Simone answered quietly. "I'm sorry I lost my temper."

"It's all right." He put a comforting arm around her,

mindful of her injury, and pulled her to rest against his side.

They sat in silence as the night deepened and the candle beside the bed guttered. Drowsily, Simone nestled with her head on Tom's chest, listening to his even breathing. He was so still, she thought he had fallen asleep.

"Simone, who is this Alain you spoke of while you were delirious?" he asked, his voice floating to her on the darkness.

Her breath caught in her throat, but Simone forced herself to answer calmly. "He was someone I cared for very much. He was my . . . guardian when my father died."

"Was? You mean he's dead, too?"

"*Oui.*" Her voice quavered, and she felt the ache of unshed tears at the back of her throat.

Tom placed a kiss against her hair. "You poor little thing," he murmured, "you've had some hard times, haven't you? And nobody to take care of you. It's all right now. I'm going to take care of you from now on."

A flood of emotion, dammed since Alain's disappearance, finally broke. Simone wept against Tom's shoulder until she had no more tears. Then, cradled in his arms, she slept peacefully for the first time in months.

15

"*Evening, Cap'n,*" *Batiste murmured* as Tom stepped out and closed Simone's cabin door softly behind him.

"I fell asleep sitting with her," the captain said when he discerned the servant in the darkness.

"You had a long night last night."

Joining Batiste at the railing, Tom asked, "You know I love Simone, don't you?"

"I know."

"I'd fight for her, but I don't know who to fight. She won't tell me, and I don't know what to do to win her trust." Tom shook his head, his face bleak.

"I believe Simone would trust you with her life, Cap'n, but she doesn't want you to fight her fight," the big black man responded. "She believes she brings danger to anyone she cares for. She is protecting you the only way she knows how, outside of leaving you."

"You think she cares for me?" Tom's voice held a note of cautious hope.

"My little friend is the only one who truly knows her own heart," Batiste answered.

"I don't think she does yet," the Virginian muttered

more to himself than to his companion. After a time, he asked, "I'll have to let her open the casino if I want her to stay aboard, won't I?"

"If you wish to keep her respect. You gave her your word."

"I know, but—"

"Cap'n, she'll be safer with you and me on this boat than she has been for a long time. And you will have her at your side."

"That'll do for now," Tom murmured, ambling toward his cabin.

The next morning, Simone awoke with a ravenous appetite. After she had attacked her breakfast with gusto, Batiste examined her wound and pronounced her well enough to walk on deck.

"Is the *capitaine* around?" she asked, seemingly casual.

"He's everywhere," Batiste replied with a chuckle, "in the wheelhouse, in the boiler room, and everywhere in between."

But Tom was nowhere to be seen when Simone strolled the hurricane deck that afternoon. Peering down the companionway, she saw Obadiah draped over the railing on the deck below. "*Bonjour,* Obie," she called.

Lifting his head, he looked around queasily. Silhouetted against the sky, the girl looked pretty and fresh in her simple dress and bonnet. You'd think she'd never been sick in her life, Obadiah thought crossly, much less wounded in a sword fight.

Straightening with care, he answered, "Hello, Miss Simone. You look a lot better today than the last time I saw you."

"I wish I could say the same. Are you ill?"

"You stay up there." Obie gulped deeply when she started to descend. "And please don't tell Cap'n Franklin I'm seasick."

"He wouldn't mind," she sympathized. "It's no crime to suffer *mal de mer*."

"Seems pretty ungrateful after he gave me a job."

"Tom gave you a job?" she asked with genuine pleasure.

"As a waiter." Obadiah looked wretched at the thought of food.

"I would rather have you with me in the casino."

"You better take that up with him." Clutching a post, the boy sagged against it.

"Is there anything I can do?"

"Jest lemme die in peace," he requested hoarsely.

"Before I go, Obie . . ." She lingered. "*Merci beaucoup* for rescuing me."

"You're welcome," he gagged, then bolted forward out of sight.

"Don't think we're gonna make a river man of that boy," a gruff voice said behind Simone.

She turned to find Zachary Cameron standing behind her. Neither had seen the other at close range before, and they inspected each other silently for a moment.

The pilot was a compact, bowlegged, barrel-chested man. His face was dour and had probably always been homely. His nose, which had obviously been broken, was off-center, giving him a rather sinister look. Under bushy brows, his sharp hazel eyes scrutinized Simone.

With all the certainty of a first impression, Zack guessed the girl was as intelligent as she was lovely. And she was very pretty.

"You must be M'sieur Cameron, Tom's good friend," she guessed with a smile.

"Zack," he corrected, sweeping his cap from his head. Through sparse iron-gray hair, his pate shone white in contrast to his tanned face. "And you must be Miss Simone Devereaux."

"*Oui.*" She nodded graciously.

"Would you do me the honor of a promenade around the deck?" he invited, unexpectedly gallant.

"If we go slowly." Simone accepted the arm he

offered. "I'm glad to meet you at last, Zack. Tom has told me a great deal about you. You are the *Emerald Queen*'s pilot?"

"One of them. Ulysses Rabalais has the helm now." He nodded toward the wheelhouse, where the dapper Cajun waved and flashed them a brilliant smile.

"You and Tom have known each other for some time, *oui*?"

"Seven years. Met him when he was fresh from the East. Taught him what he knows about the river—what he was willin' to learn, anyway. Tom's a bright feller, but he's more interested in engines and contraptions than in readin' the water and pilotin'. Still, I'm mighty fond of him." Stopping, Zack leveled an appraising stare at Simone. "That's why I've been wantin' to talk to you, young woman, to see if you're worth a hill of beans."

"A hill . . ." She blinked at him in surprise.

"I'm not much with words, miss." He grimaced at his own bluntness. "I want you to know Tom Franklin is a good man with more heart than sense. I've known him long enough to see he's in love with you. I reckon there's a brain behind those green eyes of yours, so I'll tell you straight. A gal hurt him real bad once and I don't wanna see it happen again."

The wave of anger Simone had felt when Zachary started to speak receded. This brusque man was concerned for his friend.

"I wouldn't hurt Tom," she protested. "I have become very fond of him. After all, he saved my life twice."

"Don't tell me what you're feelin' is gratitude." He scowled.

"I don't know what I feel," she replied. "I—I like Tom. I enjoy his company. But I, too, was hurt, M'sieur Cameron. I do not think I will love again."

"You're honest. I'll give you that," Zachary said.

"The question is, am I worth 'a hill of beans'?" she

reminded him dryly as they reached their original position on the deck.

He offered a rare smile. "I reckon you're all right with me, even if you don't know what you feel. You'll figure it out in time," he said, unknowingly echoing Tom's opinion. Touching a finger to the brim of his cap, he strolled back to the pilothouse.

That evening, Simone dressed for dinner in her cabin, choosing a pale pink gown she thought Tom would like. Still unable to lift her arms without hurting her side, she left her hair down, brushing it until it gleamed and curled on her bare shoulders.

She was ready when her guest rapped on the door. Fresh from his bath and smelling of soap and bay rum, Tom stepped into the cabin. His face showed signs of recent shaving, and the hair at the nape of his neck curled damply against his stiff white collar.

Following his nose to an elegantly set table, he uttered two words hopefully, "Fried chicken?"

"I remembered it was your favorite."

Pulling the bottle from the silver wine cooler, he glanced at it, his eyebrows lifting. "Champagne?"

"My favorite," she answered with a grin. "Come, let's eat."

Neither brought up the subject that was on their minds during dinner. But before the man could tell Simone he planned to keep his word about the casino, she began, "Tom, I've been wanting to talk to you all day, about Carnival. Won't you let me run it?"

Though he had known all along what her game was, the captain was suddenly unaccountably hurt. "Is that what this was all about, Simone?" he asked harshly. "Wining and dining me so you could get your way?"

She cringed inwardly but defended her actions. "I wanted you to be in a good mood before—"

"Before you went to work on me," he finished flatly. Wadding his napkin, he tossed it onto the table and rose. "You could've saved your feminine wiles. I made my decision last night."

"You made your decision?" Simone's wrath was incandescent. She did not allow him to elaborate before she was on her feet. "Of all the high-handed, tyrannical—"

"Let's talk about low-down female tricks," Tom hollered back as he paced the cabin. "And I actually thought you were beginning to like me a little!"

"How dare you shout at me," she yelled, dogging his steps. "I'll have you know, I do like you, Thomas Jefferson Franklin, more than a little."

Whirling in midstride, he caught her in his arms as she bumped into him. "How much do you like me, darlin'?" he asked, grinning.

"Not much at all right now," she snapped, straining in his embrace, but he did not free her.

"You said 'more than a little,'" he insisted softly, nuzzling her ear. "Is that a lot?"

"I didn't say that," she whispered. She would have shied away from his touch, but a warm, delicious languor stole over her as he trailed kisses down her jaw, stopping just short of her lips.

"Would you say you care a great deal for me?" His tongue teased the corner of her mouth.

"No, I wouldn't," she whispered, her arms twining around his neck as she tilted her face toward his. "I won't."

"This is the kind of argument I like to have with a woman," he murmured, bending to kiss her.

Her anger forgotten in the bliss of strong arms sheltering her, offering her safety and so much more, Simone returned his kiss, moaning softly and gripping his shoulders when his lips moved down her neck to the sensitive base of her throat. As he dipped to nibble at the pale flesh exposed above her décolletage, she swayed toward him, feeling as if her breasts were swelling and straining against the bodice of her dress.

"Simone," he whispered, stroking her cheek with the back of his fingers, "I love you." He ached to make her his own.

Opening eyes hazy with building passion, she smiled and murmured, "I lied. I do care a great deal for you."

She had not said she loved him, but Tom's spirits soared, and he could wait no longer. Lifting her into his arms, he carried her into the bedroom and set her on her feet beside the bed.

"Simone?" he whispered hoarsely, offering her one last chance to change her mind.

"It's all right, Tom," she assured him.

"Turn around, then," he instructed softly. When she obeyed, he unlaced the back of her gown and began slipping it down. It ensnared her arms close to her body, and before he freed her, he bent to feather kisses down her spine. When his mouth returned to her shoulders, she leaned back against him, feeling him warm and solid behind her and the brass buttons of his waistcoat deliciously cold through her lacy camisole.

He lifted her dress over her head and dropped it onto a chair. "Stay right here." Stepping into the parlor, he returned with a candelabrum, which he placed on the table beside the bed. "I want to be able to see you."

"I want to see you, too," she whispered, standing before him in her petticoats and flimsy undergarments.

"What's wrong?" she asked with dread when he openly winced.

Tenderly, he touched her side, where the stark white bandage was visible through her camisole. "Simone, I—"

"You won't hurt me," she murmured. She stepped around him, her full petticoats swaying, and helped him out of his jacket. He faced her, striving to control the rush of desire that swept over him as she unbuttoned his waistcoat with enticing slowness.

After she had removed it and turned her attention to unknotting his cravat, Tom untucked his linen shirt and removed its studs. Beneath it, the smooth, hard planes of his body were burnished by candlelight. His torso was flat and muscular, bronzed by the sun. Above his hard belly, a thick mat of black hair covered his chest.

Drawing Simone to him, he tugged her camisole up, sweeping it smoothly over her head when she lifted her arms. Molding her arms so they wreathed his neck, he held her, reveling in the feel of skin against skin. He rubbed against her gently, the crisp hair on his chest brushing her sensitive breasts.

Cupping a breast in his hand, he bent to caress it with his mouth as she arched against him, shuddering at the heat of his lips, her hands working the shirt from his muscled shoulders.

His mouth returned urgently to hers, and he untied the tapes that held her petticoats and pantalettes in place. He pushed them down, his hands sliding sensuously over her hips, her thighs. His fingers hooked in her garters, taking her stockings with him in a downward progression as he traced the path with kisses.

When she stood naked before him in the flickering candlelight, his eyes drifted over her appreciatively. "You're so beautiful," he said, his low voice rife with intimacy.

Her green eyes glowing at the warmth of his words and touch, she sat on the bed while Tom stripped off the remainder of his garments and stood before her. Below his line of his belt, his skin was white, and his legs were lithe and well muscled. As if mesmerized, Simone's eyes were drawn to the evidence of his arousal before traveling slowly upward to meet his. Unembarrassed, she met his sapphire gaze. Then, without a word, she held out her arms to him.

He stretched out beside her on the bed, rolling her to face him. His hand caressed her breast, then glided along her body, skimming her ribs, lifting to miss the bandage, descending to stroke the curve of her hip.

She molded herself to the hard length of him and

gasped and clutched him tightly when his hand found the moist, warm center of her.

"I want to love you, but I don't want to hurt you. I know a way that will be good for you," he whispered, rolling them so he lay beneath her.

She cried out in surprised pleasure when he thrust upward to fill her. Instinctively, she drew her knees up and moved with him, rising above him, rising with him toward ecstasy she had never known.

Panting, drenched with sweat, content beyond compare, the lovers wrapped their arms around each other, and eventually they slept.

Simone awoke slowly, suspended in rich sensation. She burrowed deeper into the rumpled sheets, drawn by the weight beside her. Then, suddenly, her lashes fluttered open. Tom lay beside her, encircling her in a sleep-heavy embrace. One of his legs pressed across her stomach and twined down between her legs. The lean hardness of his torso and limbs against her was a vivid contrast to the warm softness of him that moved against her hip, seeming to possess a life of its own.

A smile flitted across her drowsy face. Last night, she had discovered a fulfillment she had thought she would never feel again. The numbness she had felt these many long months had finally abbed away, to be replaced by simple, unquestioning happiness Tom's presence.

Tugging gently to free her hair where his shoulder captured it against the mattress, she shifted to look at him. Nestled against her arm, he slept, looking youthful, even vulnerable. Watching him, Simone felt the stirring of tenderness. She *did* care for him. But she must not fall in love, she told herself, smoothing back the familiar errant curl from his forehead.

At her touch, his eyes opened, crinkling with a sleepy smile. "Good morning, darlin'," he murmured. "How are you this morning? I didn't hurt you last night?"

"*Non.*" She returned his smile.

"Good. I never want to hurt you." He lay back on his pillow and slipped his arm beneath her so she was cradled on his shoulder, her face against his neck.

After a moment, he said, "I was trying to tell you something last night, Simone, but you wouldn't give me the chance." His arm tightened around her when she stirred at his side. "No, I want you to listen. Before I came here I had already decided that I wouldn't argue if you wanted to run the casino. But you must promise me two things."

"What?" she asked guardedly.

"One, that you never leave this deck without a mask or some sort of disguise. And two, that you'll keep Batiste with you as a bodyguard at work."

"Is that really necessary?"

"You want to keep your partner happy, don't you?" he countered lightly. "And three—"

"You said two," she interrupted. Lifting herself on one elbow, she stared down at him accusingly.

"I forgot to mention the most important one," he informed her without remorse. "If I ever have reason to believe you're in danger, I want you to leave the river. We'll find someplace safe for you, but I won't have you taking unnecessary risks."

"All right," she sighed in resignation.

"Now, to other important items of business . . ." he announced, pulling her down so he could kiss her soundly. "Will you marry me?"

"I told you—"

"But after last night . . ." he interrupted.

"Is that why you made love to me, so I would marry you?"

"I wanted you. I still want you. But more important than the desire I feel for you is the love," he told her earnestly. "You won't admit that you love me, but I know you do, Simone. I can tell by your eyes and your lips and your touch."

"Tom, I can't—"

"Shh, you don't have to say the words." He silenced her with a kiss. "Just show me."

One warm September evening, the *Emerald Queen* steamed away from Helena, Arkansas, a pleasant town situated on a bluff overlooking the Mississippi. The crew was assembled on the capstan, singing and waving to the crowds on the levee, while the captain strolled through the long, narrow Grand Salon.

Usually busy, the huge room that ran almost the entire length of the boiler deck was nearly deserted, a quiet oasis aboard the bustling boat. For an instant, the serenity was intruded upon by rapid, jarring notes as an adventurous tot swiped at the keyboard of the piano beside a small bandstand. Before the sound had died, the child was gone, pursued by a long-suffering older sister.

The chords faded, leaving only the buzzing of flies around the lazy ceiling fan and muted voices coming from the bar. Planters discussed the price of cotton and cane, their quiet conversation punctuated by the staccato sound of dice thrown at the end of the bar. None of it seemed to disturb the old men who catnapped in wicker armchairs in shady corners.

"They say that, behind her mask, Mademoiselle Emeraude is the most beautiful woman on the river." The youthful male voice caught Tom's attention.

"I thought you said no one had ever seen her face," a girl challenged, speaking very low.

Tom glanced around for the source of the conversation, his eyes falling on four girls and a pair of young men huddled around a table. Not far away sat two Creole women, obviously the girls' mothers, each with an eye on her daughters as they chatted.

"No one has seen her face, except perhaps the *capitaine* of this boat or her huge black slave," the second young man explained.

"Wouldn't it be romantic if the *capitaine* and Mademoiselle Emeraude were in love?" One of the girls sighed.

"Romantic, but unlikely," the first Creole snorted.

"Why?" she asked. "He's handsome and very charming."

"Emeraude has broken hearts from New Orleans to St. Louis. She spurns all admirers."

"What good is being scandalous if you are not also fickle?" another girl reasoned.

"Quiet, Minette," cautioned the others in unison. "You don't want your *maman* to hear."

Unnoticed by the group, Tom left the Grand Salon. Pausing at the railing, he stared out at the rugged shoreline. The *Emerald Queen* had made the run to fur-rich St. Louis more than a dozen times now. Since their second trip upriver, they had had to turn away passengers, and he had to admit, much of their success was due to Simone. Travelers enjoyed the grandeur of the majestic paddlewheeler, but it was Carnival with its gambling, its Mardi Gras ambience, and its beautiful masked hostess, that truly drew them.

Simone seemed to thrive as the enigmatic Mademoiselle Emeraude. She had been given the nickname by a lovesick Creole swain, and it had stayed with her. She cultivated a shroud of secrecy, recognizing that it was as valuable to their endeavor as Tom's easy charm. Besides making her popular, the mystery surrounding her kept her safe. Known only to the *Emerald Queen*'s trusted officers, she did not mingle with the customers. And passengers were not permitted on the hurricane deck.

Going to Simone's cabin, Tom found her sipping a glass of lemonade, still clad in the boy's pants she wore when fencing. Turning to her Gisèle, her new maid, he drawled, "You got another glass of that lemonade, Dimples?"

"*Oui.*" The girl giggled and scurried to get some for

him. The daughter of a gambler, her father's death had left her destitute and unable to pay his IOUs. Reminded of her own situation, Simone had rescued the girl and been rewarded with a loyal servant and friend. Gisèle also adored the captain and fervently wished her mistress would marry him.

"You and Batiste been practicing again?" Tom asked unnecessarily as he sat down across from Simone.

"The casino was not in use."

"I can't understand how a gal so little and soft and sweet got to be such a hellion with a blade."

"I can't understand why a man from a fine Southern family does not understand the *Code Duello*," she retorted genially. When she had tried to explain it to him, he had asked quite reasonably why the duelists couldn't simply flip a coin.

"What about their honor?" she had countered, aghast.

He had shrugged. "Either you have honor or you don't. What good does it do to fight over it?"

Even now, she shook her head at the memory.

"Thanks, Gisèle." Tom accepted a frosty glass from the maid. "You know, I just came from the Grand Salon, where your mistress was the topic of the day."

"Mam'selle is always the topic," Gisèle bantered.

"Was I tragically deformed at birth or tragically disfigured by small pox today?" Simone asked with a wry smile.

"You were tragically in love with me." Tom grinned. "Another in a long list of calamities." He sipped his lemonade, then said seriously, "Thought you'd like to know, Simone, a couple of your old favorites came aboard in Helena."

"Garth and Stoddard," she guessed at once, her green eyes darkening ominously.

"The 'Colonel' and his capper," the captain acknowledged. "Figured you'd want to keep an eye on them.

"How I hate sure-thing players." She expelled her

breath in a puff. "These two are skillful cheats. Do you think I can catch them this time?"

"Yep, and when you do, I'll be ready."

The night was hot, even on the river. Simone's head throbbed when she emerged from the office with Batiste. Her headache was not helped when Carnival's band began to play a noisy polka, the latest rage. She spied the obese Garth and his scruffy shill, Stoddard, at one of the poker tables. The dealer caught her attention, looking relieved when she positioned herself inconspicuously to watch the game. After a few moments, she nodded, and Tom, who stood near the door, disappeared into the darkness outside.

With expansive goodwill, Garth placed the deck of cards he had shuffled in front of Stoddard to be cut.

"No need, Colonel." The scrawny man pushed the deck back toward him. "No need whatsoever, sir. Just run 'em."

But before Garth could pick up the deck, Simone placed her hand over it.

"*Bonsoir,* gentlemen," she greeted them amiably. "You do not mind if I take a look at this deck of cards, do you?"

"What seems to be the problem?" Garth blustered. "There's nothing wrong with those cards."

"They do not seem to be nailed or marked in any way," Simone conceded mildly, "but I could have sworn I heard a riffle shuffle."

"You're outta your mind," Stoddard objected.

"Shall we see how the next deal would have gone?" Leaving the deck on the table, she dealt the top four cards to each of the other players. The fifth, a king, she placed in front of Garth. She dealt four more to the other players and the fifth, another king, to the squirming Garth. When the cards were dealt, a full house—three kings and two aces—lay in front of him.

"That doesn't prove anything!" he bellowed.

"Does this?" she asked, swooping forward to pull an ace from Stoddard's vest pocket.

The room, which had grown silent, erupted into angry shouts. Batiste gripped Garth by the nape of his neck, and the dealer grabbed the other. Followed by an irate crowd, they hustled the crooked players out of the casino to the stern. In the wheelhouse, Tom had already slowed the *Emerald Queen*'s engines. The paddlewheels bit into the current to hang close to shore.

Some captains marooned cheats on sandbars in the middle of the river, but sure-thing players found aboard the *Emerald Queen* received a dunking in the muddy water of the Mississippi and were left behind, near shore but sometimes miles from any town.

When Garth and Stoddard were thrown into the river, the fat card shark dived underwater to avoid the hail of bullets that followed such an ejection on most boats. Cursing, Stoddard found his footing and slogged ashore.

"'Tis sure I'll not be wanting to get on the wrong side of ye. Mam'selle Emeraude, is it?"

Simone turned. Tall and broad-shouldered, a man lounged against the railing, watching the unscrupulous duo haul themselves onto the river bank. By the dim light from inside, she could see his chiseled profile . . . which looked so very familiar.

"'Lain?" she whispered, her face paling behind her mask.

Suddenly the paddlewheels increased their speed, causing the boat to lurch forward, bucking against the current. Simone stumbled, reaching for the rail and missing. The man lunged to catch her, stepping into the light that poured through the doorway to the casino. Sinewy arms wrapped around her waist and held her against a powerful body.

The eyes observing her so closely were hazel, not brown like Alain's. Glints of auburn shone in his wavy hair, and he wore a carefully trimmed moustache above a devilish smile.

Making no attempt to release her, he laughed. "Though I've always been something of a ladies' man, I can't recall ever having *this* particular effect on a woman."

Planting her hands against his chest, Simone straightened and pushed away from him. "*Merci*, Monsieur . . ."

"Hennessey. Devlin Hennessey," he introduced himself. "Dev to me friends."

"You must pardon me, Monsieur Hennessey. I think perhaps I've had too much excitement this evening."

"Maybe a promenade under a moonlit sky would calm ye?" he asked, offering his arm with a charming smile.

"*Non, merci.*"

"Would ye walk with me if I told ye I'd wanted to meet ye since I first saw ye this evening?" he asked, his voice serious.

Acutely aware of his nearness, Simone retreated a step. She was reassured to hear whistling and footsteps on the companionway. Tom was returning from the pilothouse. As he stepped into the light, he frowned toward the couple on the dark deck.

"*Capitaine*," she hailed him gladly, "I want you to meet—"

"Hello, Hennessey," he greeted the other man flatly.

"Evening, Franklin," Devlin Hennessey responded with a cool nod.

Simone looked back and forth between the men, who regarded each other with obvious dislike. "You know each other?"

"We met once over a poker table," Devlin explained.

"Remember when I lost the money to finish the *Emerald Queen*?" Tom asked.

"'Twas a fair game," the Irishman absolved himself. "And ye still managed to build the finest boat on the river."

"Got myself a partner," Tom answered, looping a proprietary arm around Simone's waist.

The other man's eyebrows rose, and he smiled ruefully. "So she's rich as well as beautiful. Yer a lucky fellow indeed to have such a 'partner.'" Bowing, he said, "Ye'll excuse me, mam'selle. 'Twas a pleasure to meet ye."

When he went inside, Simone removed Tom's hand from her waist and wheeled on him. "What was that all about?"

He seemed surprised by her annoyance. "I didn't want Hennessey to bother you. Unless you want him to," he concluded accusingly.

Simone massaged her temples in an attempt to relieve her aching head and snapped, "I don't want anyone to bother me."

"Are you all right, darlin'?" he asked with a concerned frown.

"My head aches," she muttered. "I'm going up to my cabin."

When Gisèle had helped her undress, Simone threw herself across her bed and buried her head in her pillows, trying to block out the music from below, but she could not sleep.

It was not only her head that hurt, she discovered despairingly. Her heart ached . . .at the memory of Alain.

How careful she had been not to think of him. And no wonder. The pain was too great, even after all this time. She remembered his kiss and the feel of his hands on her body as if they had been together only yesterday. She remembered their promises, and their hopes. She remembered a lifetime of loving him. She had thought she had put the past behind her. But deep inside she knew it was the memory of Alain that kept her from giving wholly herself to Tom . . . or to any man.

Simone finally slept and did not awaken until the

boat whistled, signalling its arrival in Memphis. Rising sluggishly, she bathed and dressed. In the light of morning, she examined her feelings of the night before. The handsome gambler had caught her eye only because of his resemblance to Alain. Now that she realized that, she would have no further problem with him.

There was a light rap at the door, and Tom stepped into the suite, holding out a bouquet of flowers. "You look beautiful this morning, darlin'. Are you feeling any better?"

"Much better, *merci*."

"I came to see about you last night, but you had gone to bed. I'm sorry about that little scene with Hennessey," he said hesitantly. "I acted like the cock of the walk. I . . . I don't know what got into me."

"I know what got into you. You were jealous. But you didn't need to be."

A relieved smile lit his face, and he bent to kiss her cheek. "I love you, Simone. Get some rest, and if you'd rather not come down tonight—"

"Don't worry. By tonight, I will be — how do you say it?—as fit as a fiddle."

"I'm going to make a Kaintock out of you yet." Tom grinned and ducked out the door.

That evening, Simone descended the spiral staircase to the office, pausing to speak to Virgil, her right-hand man in the casino. When she stepped out, she saw Dev Hennessey. His broad back was to her as he leaned over the roulette wheel to place his bet. She had not been mistaken last night, she thought, drawing a quick breath. In profile, he looked very much like Alain.

As if he knew she were there, he glanced over his shoulder, and his hazel eyes met hers. Nodding casually, Simone veered across the dance floor in the opposite direction. But before she had taken two steps, Dev was at her side.

"Ah, me dance partner. I've been looking for ye,

mam'selle." He swept her into a waltz before she could protest.

Seeing Batiste move to come to her aid, Simone motioned him to stay. She glanced around with dread, unable to spot Tom. She hoped he, too, would stay wherever he was. She would handle the presumptuous Devlin Hennessey. Attempting in vain to step out of his grip, she said, "I am sorry, but I don't dance with customers."

"Careful, love, ye'll make me tread on ye with me big feet."

She smiled in spite of herself, for he was an excellent dancer. But she insisted, "Monsieur Hennessey, you must release me. I meant what I said. I do not dance with customers."

"I think ye dance quite nicely with customers," he disagreed unconcernedly. "And ye should, with good customers."

"What exactly makes a good customer?" she could not refrain from asking.

"A good customer loses, of course," he said promptly. "And I've a mind to lose a great deal tonight. Maybe even me heart."

"Monsieur Hennessey—"

"Dev, me sweet, Dev." Skillfully, he danced her onto the dark deck. Releasing her, he led her to the rail, where they could look out over the moonlit river.

"I must go inside." Simone glanced uneasily toward the door.

"If yer looking for yer 'partner'"—Dev's voice was heavy with irony—"I think I saw him go down to the boiler deck some time ago, like the trustworthy captain he is, to see to his passengers in the Grand Salon."

"All the more reason I should return to the casino," she said firmly, turning to leave.

Dev caught her arm and drew her closer to him. "Why'd ye try to avoid me, Emeraude?"

"I was not trying to avoid you." Her protest seemed

loud, and she realized the orchestra had taken a break. Sweet mandolin music drifted up from the main deck, where the steerage passengers were gathered on the bow.

"If ye don't mind me saying so, yer a terrible liar," Dev murmured, his face close to hers. "Do ye belong to Franklin?"

Glaring up at him, she pried at his fingers. "I don't belong to anyone."

"Good." He released her abruptly. "That means there's a chance for me."

"What it means, m'sieur," she said, drawing herself up, "is that I am my own woman."

"And a fine one, too." Devlin chuckled as he followed Simone back into the casino.

Tom stepped from the shadows at the head of the companionway and stared after them. Climbing to the hurricane deck, he stood at the stern, grappling with unaccustomed, unpleasant jealousy as he stared at the *Emerald Queen*'s wake in the moonlight. He loved Simone and knew, though she never said it, that she loved him, too. He had been patient since that night at Paradis. Over the past two years he had watched her blossom from girlhood to womanhood, and he had loved every step of that development. But, damn it, how much longer was he supposed to wait?

Other men had flirted with Emeraude, but for the first time the captain was apprehensive. He sensed the gambler was different. Maybe he had been wrong to make no claim on her, Tom brooded. He did not share her bed, except when invited. He had not even proposed for months. What good was this waiting?

"Get a hold on yourself, boy," he muttered. It was only a matter of time before Simone realized she loved him. In a few days they would reach St. Louis, and Hennessey would leave the *Emerald Queen*. Then

Tom could forget this hateful emotion gnawing at him.

Wearing a rare expression of resignation, the captain returned to his passengers, bypassing the casino with Simone—and Devlin Hennessey—within.

16

Awash in spring sunshine, Simone and Tom stood in front of their New Orleans office, a squat wooden building, and surveyed their freight yard as mule-drawn drays came and went. At their dock, the *Creole Queen* was being loaded. They could hear the creak of her winch over the clamor in the yard.

Tom gazed around with satisfaction. Franklin Steamboats now had offices in New Orleans, Memphis, and St. Louis. Their three packets plied the bayous. Last May, a second mammoth steamboat, the *Queen of Hearts*, had been christened, and another, *Fortune's Queen*, was being built.

His partnership with Simone was more profitable than he had imagined. What was even better was that she seemed content with her life on the river and with him. And Tom was delighted with her—his partner, his lover, his best friend . . .everything but his wife.

"Who'd have thought we'd fill up so much space so quickly?" Simone was saying ruefully.

"Good thing the lot next door is available. We can build another building, maybe two," Tom mused.

"And what will we use for money, Thomas Jefferson

Franklin? Three steamboats in three years has eaten up most of our cash. You're not planning on taking a loan from a bank?"

He winced at the very thought. "The banks wouldn't touch us when we were starting out, and now we're going to return the favor. Why pay them interest on a loan?"

"Turnabout is fair play." Mischievously, Simone finished the speech she had heard a dozen times before.

As they ambled toward the freight-yard gate, they waved to Obadiah, who labored on a nearby loading dock.

"I'm glad we found a home for the seasick sailor," Tom said. "And he's doing a fine job."

"*Oui*," Simone answered distractedly. Though the mourning costume she wore was hot, a pleasant breeze blew in off the river. "Don't order a cab, Tom," she said. "Let's walk to the boat."

"I guess we've got time." The man made a great show of checking the sapphire-studded watch Simone had given him for his birthday the week before. "All right, darlin'," he said, offering his arm, "let's promenade like the fashionable folks."

It was less than half a mile to the Canal Street wharf, and, along the way, steamboats of all sizes lined the levee. While they walked, the couple heard a familiar whistle and gazed upriver.

"Oh, look, here comes the *Queen of Hearts*."

"Ahead of schedule, too," Tom said proudly. "What a fine fleet we have, Miss Devereaux."

"They are impressive," she acknowledged, "but I think our next boat should be another cargo vessel."

"Our next boat," Tom crowed. "I like the way you think, partner."

"Haven't you always told me to think big?" she asked with a grin.

"Yep, we'll make a fortune."

"Come on." She tugged him toward the *Emerald*

Queen's gangplank. "If we are to afford this big thinking, we should start our next run."

Tom balked, his good humor vanishing when he
saw Devlin Hennessey climbing the curving staircase
to the boiler deck. "What do you suppose he's doing
here?"

"Probably going upriver. That's where the boat is
going," Simone answered lightly, knowing he disap-
proved of her friendship with Dev.

"Why do you waste time on that riverboat Romeo?"

"Dev has been a good friend to me," Simone responded briskly. "He's one of the few people I've trusted in the
past few years, and he's never given away my identity."

"I know," Tom admitted grudgingly, "but he might
spend some time in New Orleans. They *do* have gambling here, you know."

Gisèle met Simone at the door of her suite. "*Bonjour*, mam'selle," she greeted her. "Who do you suppose I saw as I came aboard?"

"Dev Hennessey." Untying her bonnet, Simone
raked veil and hat off in one, impatient move.

The maid's face fell. "How did you know?"

"Tom and I saw him too."

"I wish Ethan Franklin would pursue me half as
much as M'sieur Hennessey chases you," Gisele said
romantically. Then, taking Simone's hat, she sighed,
"Poor mam'selle . . ."

"What do you mean?"

"It is easy for me," she said. "I know the man for me.
I have only to convince him of it. But you must choose
between the *capitaine* and Monsieur Hennessey."

"Why should I have to choose?" Simone frowned at
her.

"Because they are both in love with you," Gisèle
explained patiently. "Surely you can see that."

"I cannot. I'm very fond of Tom, but Dev is just a
friend."

"Someone should explain that to him," Gisèle

replied primly. "Someday, I think, you will have to choose between them."

"Perhaps someday, not now," Simone firmly closed the subject.

The *Emerald Queen* did not leave New Orleans until after sundown. As she steamed upriver, the moon hid behind the clouds, and the night was as dark as Tom's mood. He kept to the pilothouse all evening, avoiding not only Simone and Dev in the casino, but also the passengers in the Grand Salon.

"What the hell?" the captain growled crankily when his black study was interrupted by the faint banging of pans and shouts in the distance. Throwing a window open, he leaned out to hear, "You aig-suckin', two-laigged child uva swamp rat, gol-danged brass-button fancy man!"

"What it is, hein?" Ulysses asked from his position at the wheel.

"Keelboat, running without lights," Tom answered through gritted teeth.

"Why dontcha watch where yer a-steerin' that floatin' teapot?" the belligerent holler drifted up to the wheelhouse.

"You slack-jawed, lop-eared, pug-ugly, pernicious son of Beelzebub!" Tom roared, finding the perfect opportunity to vent his spleen. He leaned far out the window to bellow back the tapestry of colorful language.

Behind him, Ulysses barked orders to the engine room. When his captain stopped for breath, the pilot picked up the thread, swearing passionately, partly in French, partly in picturesque English.

The *Emerald Queen* passed the keelboat with no worse consequences than the starboard wheel chewing up their oar. When the excitement was over, Tom looked out over the hurricane deck, much cheered. Suddenly the moon peeped out from behind the clouds, and he saw Simone and Dev at the top of the companionway, staring in open amazement toward the pilothouse. He felt a perverse satisfaction when they parted without a quiet moment together.

He was still smiling when Dev climbed up to the wheelhouse.

The gambler sat on a bench, propping one foot on the seat nonchalantly. "I never knew anyone to curse such a blue streak since me pa," he remarked to nobody in particular.

"*Merci*," Ulysses answered at once with pride, "but Capitaine Tom, he has a fine turn of phrase as well, *oui*?"

"*Oui*." Dev laughed. "If I didn't know better, I'd say he sounded upset about something."

"Having our paddlewheel break a broadhorn's tiller into lucifer matchsticks was a might unsettling," Tom drawled mildly.

"Unsettling, eh? I wouldn't want to be around if ye were truly riled," Dev said with a lazy grin.

"Wouldn't particularly advise it," Tom replied curtly.

"What makes ye especially mad, Cap'n?"

"Irishmen who ask damn-fool questions."

"Then I'll ask ye one more and be on me way," the gambler replied, rising. "Since yer not easily nettled, ye don't mind that I'm courting Simone, d'ye?"

"She's a big girl," Tom said stiffly.

"Not very," Dev countered with a smile, "but 'twas all I wanted to know." He departed, and Tom's black mood returned.

"Well, what do you think?" Tom's voice echoed in the vast, empty hall.

"I think it's beautiful," Simone pronounced with a sincere smile.

"Yep." He looked around the marble-floored foyer with pride. "It's one of the oldest places in the American Section, but it's been well kept."

"Why didn't you tell me you were buying a house?" She slid her hand into his, and they wandered through the cavernous rooms.

"I just decided to do it," he answered with a shrug. "The old lady who owned it wanted to move to Mobile to be with her daughter's family. The time was right. The price was right. I even inherited a butler in the deal."

"Why on earth do you need a butler?" she asked, laughing.

"Next best thing to a wife." Tom drew her into his arms and grinned down at her. "I still haven't filled that position. Would you care to apply?"

"Excuse me, sir." A very proper English accent cut through their banter. The couple turned to see an old man peering down his rather long and pointed nose at them from the doorway. "Some gentlemen are here to deliver a bed."

"Thank you, Wakefield," Tom replied solemnly and released Simone. His expression matched exactly the one worn by the aged butler. "Would you show them to the master suite?"

"Very well, sir," Wakefield said politely. "Will you be staying the night?"

"I'll be staying on the boat. We leave tomorrow for St. Louis, and I won't be back for nearly a month. You will look after things while I am gone, won't you?"

"You may depend on it, sir." Wakefield bowed as deeply as age allowed, then departed. If he wondered about the curious behavior of his new employer and the radiant young woman clad in mourning, his impeccable decorum did not give him away.

As their carriage rolled toward the gate, Tom glanced back at the elegant house and murmured contentedly, "A home of my own. I haven't had one for a very long time."

"It is lovely," Simone complimented his choice. "I hope you'll be very happy here."

"I'd be happier if you were here with me." Shifting so he looked her in the eye, he reminded her, "You never answered my question."

"What question?" she asked, even though she knew.

"Whether you'd care to apply for the job of wife—my wife."

"I don't know," she responded lightly, hoping to tease him from his serious mood. "What does the position pay?"

"I'm not joking, Simone. I'm asking you to marry me."

"Tom," she chided gently, "we've been through this again and again. Our life on the *Emerald Queen* is happy just as it is."

"But I want to be more than business partners. I want to be partners in everything. Simone, I love you."

"I can't marry you." She regarded him with genuine distress. "I'm sorry."

Sighing in discouragement, Tom faced forward and took her hand in his. "I didn't mean to upset you, darlin'," he said quietly. "I said I'd wait for you until you were ready, and I will. But I'm going to keep proposing till you admit you love me and say yes."

Tears brimmed in Simone's green eyes as he carried her hand to his lips and kissed the fingertips.

"You're the stubbornest woman I've ever met, Simone Devereaux," he said hoarsely, "but I think I can outlast you."

Aboard the *Emerald Queen*, Lisette, a regular visitor when they docked in New Orleans, waited in Simone's cabin.

"Lisette, I was afraid I wouldn't get to see you this trip." Simone hugged her friend gladly.

"I would have been here sooner," the madam said, "but the roof has sprung a leak right over one of the bedrooms."

"Ah, the hazards of operating a business in your home, eh, Lise?" Tom teased when she turned her cheek for his kiss.

"You never change, Tom," she scolded, rolling her gray eyes. "I don't know how Simone puts up with you."

"I don't either," he answered, grinning at Simone as she sat down beside the blonde woman. "I'm just glad she does. I'll leave you two to visit, but I'll see you before you leave, Lise. In the meantime, ask Simone where we went this morning."

When he had gone, the madam turned to her friend expectantly.

"Tom took me to see the house he bought," Simone explained.

"Tom bought a house?" Lisette's eyebrow lifted expressively.

"In the Garden District. It's beautiful."

"Why don't you marry him, *ma chère*?" the woman asked abruptly. "I know he has asked you."

"Many times," Simone admitted. "And I have considered it, but something keeps me from it."

"Voodoo nonsense?" Lisette said crisply. "Unless there is someone else . . . Gisèle mentioned a gambler?"

"Since my maid knows so much of my private life, did she tell you Dev proposed and I refused?" Simone retorted.

"Don't be upset," Lisette coaxed. "She cares as much for you as I do. *Is* there someone else?"

"Just Alain," Simone confessed with a sigh. "Days, even weeks, go by and I do not think of him, and then suddenly . . ."

Lisette looked pained. "'Lain is dead and gone, *chérie*. I think—" She shut her mouth abruptly. "Never mind what I think."

"Tell me," Simone requested. "I want to hear."

"I think," the woman replied slowly, "that Tom loves you very much. And I think you love him. You just haven't admitted it yet."

"Now you sound like him," Simone said with a dry smile.

"Then he is a wise man and a patient one to wait

while you struggle with your feelings. If he waits long enough, I think you'll marry him."

After a long moment of silence, Simone murmured, "Perhaps . . . someday."

Sipping a brandy, Tom watched through the open door to the bedroom as Simone arranged her hair. The radiant fire of diamonds flashed in the lamplight, and he was pleased to see she wore the bracelet and earrings he had bought for her from his share of the first year's profit.

He rose when she joined him, admiration shining in his blue eyes. "You look lovely as always," he complimented her huskily.

"*Merci*." She beamed up at him. "And you are very handsome in your new suit."

"Thank you, ma'am. I have something new for you to wear, too," he said, drawing a slender box from his pocket. "I should've given it to you in January, on the anniversary of our partnership, but we were busy getting ready to launch *Fortune's Queen*. Since the Andersons' dinner tonight is a belated celebration . . ." He handed the box to her.

"Oh, Tom!" She gasped when she saw the blazing diamond choker.

"As much as I like those emeralds, I thought you might enjoy a change," he suggested shyly.

"Oh, yes! Help me put it on." She turned so he could unfasten the clasp of her emerald necklace while she removed the earrings.

Planting a kiss on the nape of her neck, he obeyed. Then he clasped the diamond necklace around her neck and bent to whisper in her ear, "Do you really like it?"

"I love it." She rubbed her cheek against his and murmured, "But you should not pamper me so."

"I'm glad I have you to pamper," he answered, turning her to meet his kiss. Clutching his lapels, she swayed against him, her body molded to his. Tom thought about carrying her into the bedroom and forgetting the dinner party. "I wish we didn't have to go anywhere tonight."

Her heart pounding, Simone also considered missing the soiree, but it was, after all, being held in their honor. Taking a deep breath, she reminded them both, "Business before pleasure."

"There is not another Creole like you in South Louisiana," Tom groaned as he released her.

At the dinner party, they learned there was a double reason for celebration when Hiram proudly announced the engagement of his daughter, Barbara, to his junior partner, Jeremy Nash.

When the guests had exclaimed and many toasts were drunk, Dulcie leaned toward Simone and whispered tipsily, "Wouldn't it be nice if the next engagement we celebrated was yours and Tom's?"

Simone's hopes that no one had heard that remark were dashed when Hiram boomed, "You two are partners in everything else. Why not in marriage?"

"I've proposed till I'm blue in the face," Tom retorted good-naturedly. "I figure when Simone is ready, she'll let me know."

"You'd make Simone propose to you?" Barbara gasped in shock.

Tom turned a poker face toward the horrified young woman and asserted innocently, "It's her turn."

"Behave yourself, Tom," Simone commanded, smiling.

"Oh." Barbara laughed uncertainly. "You're joking, Captain Franklin. Sometimes I cannot tell."

"Neither can Simone . . . sometimes," he claimed teasingly, but his blue eyes were pensive as they rested on the woman he loved.

* * *

"*Vingt et un*," Emeraude said, turning up her cards, "and the house wins."

"You're damnably lucky, ma'am," one of the players complained. "If I didn't know what a square deal player you are, I'd wonder."

Turning her masked face toward him, the woman said coolly, "As you say, m'sieur, I am a square deal player and damnably lucky."

"Indeed," he stammered when Emeraude's hulking black shadow stirred restively behind her. "I couldn't agree more," he added as he gathered his chips and hastily departed.

Simone glanced up at Batiste when he rested a warning hand on her shoulder. Behind his mask, he scowled toward the door.

Turning warily, she saw through the press of people a familiar figure—Marcel Baudin. The moment she had dreaded had arrived.

The blond man was still handsome, the scar on his forehead detracting little from his good looks. In fact, it gave his face a certain sinister appeal. He carried himself arrogantly, his pale eyes seeming to burn with a fervid intensity as he surveyed the room and its occupants. Quite unexpectedly, they caught and held the green eyes of a masked woman at the *vingt et-un* table, the famous Mademoiselle Emeraude. He began to push his way through the crowd, set on meeting her.

Her hands shaking, Simone picked up the cards and began to shuffle them. She tried to behave as if nothing were wrong, hoping no one noticed the strained expression she wore.

At the bar, Tom noticed. He glanced toward the door to see what she watched with such uneasiness and saw a man making directly for her. Downing his bourbon in one gulp, the captain strode toward the table. Batiste relaxed slightly when he approached.

Bending, Tom whispered to Simone, "Anything wrong?"

"*N-non.*" She looked up at him, her green eyes large behind the slits in her mask. "Why do you ask?"

"Because you're as white as a ghost." Pulling out a chair, he asked the players, "Mind if I sit in for a few hands?"

Over the top of her mask, Simone's eyebrows arched in amazement. In all their time on the river, Tom had never broken the ban she had placed on his gambling.

Marcel presented himself. "*Pardon*, mademoiselle, you are the famous Emeraude?"

"I am called Emeraude," she forced herself to answer calmly.

"I am Marcel Baudin of New Orleans." He bowed, then continued smoothly, "When I heard the most beautiful woman in Louisiana hides behind a mask, I was intrigued. I had to meet you."

"We are pleased to have you aboard the *Emerald Queen*, Monsieur Baudin," Simone said with a gracious smile, "but I'm sorry. I cannot talk now. I must deal."

"Can you not find someone to take your place?" Marcel pressed. "You are a beautiful woman, and I will not be happy until I have danced with you."

"Then you're doomed to a life of misery," Tom cut in unexpectedly. "We have a rule that Emeraude doesn't dance with customers."

"Who are you?" Marcel swung on him belligerently.

Tom was not intimidated. "Captain of the *Emerald Queen*."

"Surely, *Capitaine*, there are some rules that were made to be broken." The Creole smiled confidently.

"Not this one," Simone declared. "I'm sorry, Monsieur Baudin, but I cannot dance with you."

Taking her refusal with ill grace, Marcel snarled, "You *will* dance with me."

"No, she won't," Tom said definitely, rising. "And if you keep bothering her, I'll stop and put you off on a sandbar, as sure as you're standing there."

Marcel's face was mottled with suppressed rage, but

he bowed stiffly and conceded, "I will talk to the lady later."

Tom watched as the Creole stalked toward the bar, then he said to the others at the table, "Looks like I won't be sitting in, after all, boys, but I need to borrow your dealer." He motioned for Virgil to take Simone's place.

"Keep an eye on that one," Tom murmured as he passed Batiste.

The couple was scarcely in the office before the captain demanded, "What the hell was that all about?"

"What?" Simone was taken aback by the anger on his face. His eyes were two chips of blue flint.

"Who was that scoundrel?"

Simone opened her mouth to tell him, but she could not. Tom would surely insist on fighting Marcel, and, just as surely, he would be killed. She would not allow Marie LeVeau's prediction to come true again. It didn't take voodoo to know it. And she would not bring danger to Tom.

"Someone who wanted to dance with me." She shrugged carelessly. "What's wrong, *cher*?"

"Did you see his eyes? He's crazy." Braced against the edge of the desk, the captain raked his fingers through his curly hair in a harassed gesture. "I don't want you to go back to Carnival tonight or any night while he's aboard."

"Don't be silly. Tomorrow night in Vicksburg we'll have not only passengers but townspeople who come for an evening's gambling. They want to see Emeraude. I will not let that man chase me from my own casino. And I will not argue about it," she warned.

"You are—"

"The stubbornest woman you've ever met," she finished for him. Stepping over his long legs, she kissed him on the forehead.

Flinging an arm around her waist, he hugged her and muttered against her hair, "You're the sassiest, too. Just be careful."

That night after Carnival closed, Tom descended from the wheelhouse to see about Simone. When he rounded the cabin section, he found Batiste lying on a pallet in front of her door. Silently, the captain went to his cabin without waking her or her sentinel.

The next night, Simone went to the casino with Batiste as usual. They paused in the doorway, the petite woman and her huge bodyguard, and surveyed the room. It was packed and becoming more crowded by the moment, but neither saw Marcel among the gamblers. Perhaps he had gone ashore for the evening, Simone thought hopefully. Free of his pale-eyed scrutiny, she strolled between the tables, stopping at each to visit her clients, gently refusing each request for the pleasure of a dance.

"Mademoiselle Emeraude." Virgil approached and handed her a piece of paper.

Looking down at it, she asked, "Where is he?"

"Over there." He pointed to a young man slumped drunkenly in his seat at the poker table. "I tried to explain, but he wouldn't listen."

"It's all right," Simone assured him. "I will speak to him.

"Monsieur Melançon?" The young man tried to focus bleary eyes on the vision who smiled so engagingly at him. "I must speak to you about your IOU. I fear we cannot accept your family plantation as collateral."

"But it's some of th' fines' cotton land in L-Louisi- . . . Pointe Coupee Parish."

"Which is why you would feel great regret if you woke in the morning without it. Why not go with Virgil to the dining room before you retire to your cabin?" Simone suggested smoothly. "He is friends with the cook and can get you anything you like."

"Even gumbo?" the young man mumbled as Virgil hauled him to his feet.

"The very best gumbo," Virgil assured him, half-carrying him from the casino.

As Simone crossed the room toward the bar, she heard a voice sneer, "You made a fool of yourself, Bill. I told you she wouldn't dance with you."

She stopped in her tracks. The scoffing intonation was just the way Eugène Moreau had sometimes sounded when he patronized Jean-Paul so long ago. How she had hated it.

Nearby two young men, barely out of adolescence, sat at a table. The older was saying, "You wouldn't listen. I told you about Miss Emeraude. She doesn't dance with customers, and, even if she did, she wouldn't dance with you."

The younger man's chin rose pugnaciously. "You take that back, Roy, before I call you out to settle this with fisticuffs."

"Any time you think you're big enough, Billy Boy," his elder taunted.

"*Pardon*, messieurs." Simone glided to stand beside them. Directing her attention at the younger lad, she said, "I did not have time before, but I would be delighted to dance with you now."

"You . . . you would?" he stammered, his face aflame.

"*Oui*." Smiling and hoping no one noticed she broke her own rule, she held out her hand. They left Bill's brother with his mouth ajar.

"You sure showed Roy, Miss Emeraude," Bill said admiringly. "He thinks he knows everything, and if you try to argue with him, he gets hot as a firecracker."

Suddenly Marcel appeared at their side, his face dark with wrath, and seized Simone by the arm. "I thought you didn't dance with customers."

She looked around desperately, spying Batiste across the room with Tom. The instant she caught the big man's eye, he began to push his way through the crowd, the captain on his heels.

Reassured that help was on the way, Simone pulled

from Marcel's grip and said coolly, "As a rule I do not, monsieur, but tonight I broke the rule."

He stared at her in mute rage, then he whirled on the hapless Bill and began to choke him.

In a split second, Roy had vaulted the table and thrown himself on Marcel's back, trying to pull him off his brother.

"Get away or I will kill you!" Marcel shouted over his shoulder.

"Not till you let go of my little brother!" Roy yelled.

Straightening with a roar, Marcel yanked from the older boy's hold and wheeled on him, his eyes alight with maniac fury.

Simone looked desperately for Batiste. He was elbowing his way through the crowd that had congregated to watch the confrontation.

"Monsieur Baudin," Simone caught his arm as he advanced on Roy. He did not even look at her as he shook her off. His pale eyes were fixed on the object of his current fury.

The young man retreated. "Stay back, I warn you," he ordered nervously. When Marcel did not halt, Roy reached under his jacket and pulled out a small pistol.

"Go on," he shouted, shakily pointing the weapon at him. "Get out of here."

"Do you think you can frighten me?" Marcel laughed quietly. "I've killed a dozen men in duels, and I have never been wounded, not even scratched. You cannot hurt me." He walked slowly toward Roy, who backed off another step.

"I tell you, I'll shoot," Roy warned, but the Creole continued to advance.

When Marcel was at point-blank range, Roy pulled the trigger. Nothing happened.

"The cap misfired," someone murmured as the young man stared at the pistol in his hand in horror.

"You see, I am invincible," Marcel crooned, smiling.

Then, without warning, he flung himself at Roy.

Before Marcel could harm the young man, Batiste captured the Creole from behind. He carried him, kicking and cursing, to the deck and flung him over the side.

"Now you are both invincible and wet," Emeraude's bodyguard called as Marcel foundered, cursing and screaming, in the muddy water beside the dock. "You'll find your luggage on the landing, sir. You are not welcome aboard the *Emerald Queen*."

Tom might have echoed Batiste's words to Baudin when he saw Devlin Hennessey scramble to board the *Emerald Queen* the next morning.

Smiling brightly, the gambler raced up the gangplank just as it was being pulled aboard and called, "Top of the mornin', Cap'n."

"What are you doing here, Hennessey?" Tom greeted him coolly.

"Looking for a good poker game. I thought I'd try me luck on the *Emerald Queen,* where the food is better, the beds softer, and the women lovelier."

"Women?" Tom frowned.

"Woman," Dev corrected unabashedly.

"When we didn't see you for a while, I thought you either got killed in a crooked card game or got smart enough to leave Simone alone."

"Sorry to disappoint ye on both counts. I couldn't stay away any longer. I have to see Simone. How is she?"

Tom glared at him through narrowed eyes. "I'm warning you, Hennessey. If you do anything to hurt her . . ."

"I wouldn't hurt her. I'm in love with her, too. 'Tis the reason I'm back." He grinned at Tom's obvious irritation. "What's the matter, Cap'n? Can't ye do with a bit of friendly competition?"

"Did better without it," Tom snapped, and he stalked away without a backward look.

The *Emerald Queen* churned through the night, causing waves to slap softly against the sleeping riverbank. Zack maneuvered the great steamboat through treacherous currents, dodging newly formed sandbars, performing his job with skillful ease.

The decks were dark and deserted. Only Tom lingered on the bow of the main deck, smoking, fighting a continued battle with jealousy. All night he had watched Hennessey with Simone. She had welcomed Dev back cordially, showing him nothing more than friendship. Still, the doting attention the gambler paid her had irked the captain.

Tom propped one booted foot on an oily coil of rope and leaned against a deck post, frowning when he felt the paddlewheels slow. Up ahead, he spied what looked to be a logjam in the water. The *Emerald Queen* approached it slowly, carefully. Suddenly a call came from the stern. "Pirates!"

Tom swore under his breath. He hadn't heard of river pirates along this stretch of the Mississippi in years, and they usually attacked keelboats or tiny packets, not huge steamboats.

As men poured from the forecastle and the passenger cabins, armed with knives, swords, pistols, and tiny derringers, Tom ran to the stern to see several deckhands fighting off the pirates who approached either side of the huge boat in dugouts. A cry went up from the bow as more swarmed from the "logs" onto the deck.

"Fire!" Tom shouted when a lantern was knocked from its post and rolled among the cotton bales. Tossing a couple of the burning bales overboard, he recruited several passengers, pointing toward some buckets. "Use river water to douse the bales," he ordered, "or the boat'll go up like tinder." They set to work immediately forming a bucket brigade.

Through blinding smoke, Tom saw pirates streaming up the companionways and ladders to the other
decks.

"Simone!" He roared her name as his personal battle
cry. He had to be sure she was safe. Reaching the stairs
to the boiler deck, he raced up them, throwing pirates
down as he passed them.

On the second deck, the captain found his crew
fighting amid the smoke. Coughing and choking, he
saw Hennessey and Virgil, back to back battling the
intruders.

Tom fought his way to the companionway, seizing a
pirate who was attempting to climb to the third deck.
As he dragged him down, the man's head bounced on
every tread until he landed in a heap at the bottom.
Tom scrambled over him to the next deck.

Finding it deserted, he hoped none of the raiders had
reached the hurricane deck and the cabins. But he heard
the sharp report of a rifle as he was about to clamber up
the companionway and was forced to dodge as a pirate
plummeted from the deck above. Stepping over the
dead man, he scaled the ladder cautiously.

Ulysses leaned out of the pilothouse, a rifle in his
hands. Through the window, Zack could be seen at his
post, steering the *Emerald Queen* past abandoned
dugouts.

"Simone!" The captain raced toward her suite. The
door to the deck stood open. Stepping in, he saw no
one was inside, but heard sounds of battle in the casino
below.

His feet barely skimmed the steps of the spiral staircase as he whirled down it. He dashed from the office
at its foot into Carnival, where he found Simone, wearing a long white nightgown and armed with her father's
sword. She and Batiste battled four pirates among the
gaming tables and roulette wheels. Three others mis-
creants lay unconscious on the floor.

Nearly limp with relief, he watched the pair herd their opponents to the far end of the room, where Gisèle stood on the billiard table, cue in hand. The maid hit the intruders over the head when they were close enough, then coolly tallied her score.

Suddenly Simone cried, "Tom, behind you!"

Tom spun to find a muscular raider creeping through the door from the deck, his knife drawn. Simone's shout diverted the pirate's attention long enough for Tom to spring. The captain seized the hand holding the knife but could not break the hold. Locked in a struggle of muscle and will, they staggered out on deck and disappeared from Simone's view.

"Tom!" she screamed, trying to work her way toward the door through which he and his adversary had gone. But a wiry, gap-toothed man entered the casino through the opposite door. Pleased at finding a helpless female, he gripped her wrist and whirled her around. His smile disappeared when she faced him with a sword.

"Put that down, girlie," he said, releasing her arm. "You don't wanna hurt yourself with that thing."

"I'd rather hurt you," she countered grimly, taking the *en garde* position.

"I hate to do this," he said almost sadly, pulling a pistol from his belt. "Hate to ruin that pretty face of yours."

Before he could aim, Simone struck his wrist with the flat of her sword. Crying out at the numbing blow, he dropped his pistol. His beady eyes narrowed as she backed him against the wall. Like a trapped animal, he looked around furtively, suddenly seizing a billiard cue from a rack nearby.

He came out of his corner, swinging the cue with all his strength. She tried to parry his attack, but when the stick made contact with her blade, it jarred her very bones, and her sword did little damage to the cue. She retired a few steps.

"Come on, girlie," the pirate sneered. Circling her, he poked at her with the cue. "Ain't you gonna teach me some fancy fencing?"

"*Très bien*," she muttered. "The first lesson is never to leave your side uncovered." Performing a *flèche*, she backed the man against the billiard table. Then, with a quick balestra, she ran his shoulder through. His enraged howl of pain was cut short when Gisèle added another to her score.

Satisfied Batiste was finishing off his opponent, Simone dashed out on deck in search of Tom. Her eyes streaming from the smoke, she saw two figures locked in combat against one of the paddleboxes. Tom's attacker had lost his knife and now tried to bend Tom backward, to force his head through the slats where the huge paddle turned. Simone's breath caught in her throat. He would be crushed!

Tom managed an upper cut to the man's jaw, knocking him back. Straightening, he readied himself to aim a powerful swing, but suddenly his opponent was not there. Instead Tom saw Simone, smoke-stained and bedraggled, her hair cascading down her back. Standing at the head of the companionway, her face set and grim, she gazed at the deck below.

She had caught the man offguard when she pushed. Now he writhed, cursing and clutching at his leg, as the ebbing battle swirled around him.

"Simone." Tom touched her shoulder gently.

"My own." Her face crumbling, she turned to him and sobbed, "I thought he was going to kill you."

He enfolded her in his arms. "Are you all right?"

"*Oui*," she wept. She lifted her face toward him, the tears making startling white streaks in the soot on her cheeks. "But I would never be all right again if something happened to you."

His arms tightened around her. "It's all over now," he whispered, stroking her hair.

"I love you, Tom," she said simply.

"I know, darlin'," he answered, smiling down at her tenderly. "Didn't I always tell you so?"

As they kissed, neither saw Dev Hennessey climbing up from below. But halfway up the companionway, he saw them. With a sad smile, he backed down the steps.

17

From the guest room of Tom's house, Simone watched as leaves skittered across the lawn, carried on the January wind. Her wedding day had dawned cold and cloudy, but even the ominous weather did not alter her joyful mood.

"I hope it does not rain," Gisèle fretted. "Rain on your wedding day is an ill omen."

"It won't." Simone smiled. "Wakefield will not allow it. Calm down, Gisèle. You're making me nervous."

"You should be nervous," the maid answered, fussing with Simone's lace veil. "You're the bride."

"You are the maid of honor, and you're nervous enough for both of us," her mistress retorted.

"I think I should go down to the parlor and see whether all the guests have arrived," Gisèle suggested.

"How is everyone getting along?" Simone asked, conscious of the oddly mixed group that waited downstairs—Kaintock, Creole, and Cajun, black and white.

"Your Uncle Georges is waiting to give you away. Your *tante* is crying, and the wedding has not even begun," the maid chuckled as she departed.

Alone, Simone stared out at the roiling clouds, her

thoughts on a day four months before, the day after the pirates' attack. . . .

Poised on the deck outside Tom's cabin, Simone had debated whether or not to knock and wake him. She knew he had not returned to the *Emerald Queen* from the sheriff's in Helena until nearly dawn. She knew because she had not slept, wrestling with fear and memories and untold emotions, deciding at last to put the past—and Marie LeVeau's prediction—behind her. Marcel's visit to the boat and the pirate raid had been dangerous, but both times Tom had been unharmed. Her love might have brought peril to him, but it had saved him last night.

And it was love she felt for Tom. It was different from the love she had felt for Alain, but it was love nonetheless. Alain was gone. Tom loved her. It was time she admitted it to herself.

As she stood, reflecting, at the door, the cabin boy appeared with the captain's breakfast. Taking the tray from him, she knocked.

"It's open," she heard Tom call.

The air in the cabin was redolent of the scent of soap. Tom stood in the doorway to the bedroom, wearing only a towel around his hips and lather on his face. His blue eyes widened when he saw her. "Simone, what are you doing here?"

"Bringing your breakfast," she answered crisply, setting the tray down. "I need a moment of your time."

"By all means." He gestured grandly for her to enter the bedroom. "You don't mind if I finish shaving?"

"*Non.*" But her step faltered at the door.

"Sit down," he invited, pointing to his disreputable chair.

"I'm surprised you still have this," she said, regarding it dubiously.

"I don't get rid of things I like." He grinned at her and applied more soap and water to his unshaven jaw.

She perched on the edge of the seat and watched the

muscles of his shoulders flex under smooth brown skin as he shaved. His back tapered into narrow hips. His buttocks were lean and firm under the towel secured at his slender waist. Her eyes drifted down powerful thighs and calves knotted with muscle and covered with black hair.

Realizing that he watched her in the mirror, she asked nervously, "Did everything go all right with the sheriff?"

"Yep. It'll be quite a spell before those fellows bother anybody else." He resumed his motions, jutting his jaw as he scraped the lather from under his chin.

"I need to talk to you, Tom," she said all at once.

He nearly sliced his throat as he turned to gape at her. Had she changed her mind about what she had said last night? Had it been relief that made her say she loved him, and nothing more?

"I need to talk to you, too," he responded in a tight voice. "Ladies first."

Simone drew a deep breath. "Will you marry me?"

"You're proposing to me?" Tom asked with a giddy grin.

"It is my turn," she replied, trying not to smile.

He knelt beside her chair, gathering her into his arms. "You know the answer, darlin'. I've wanted you for my own from the minute I met you." Unmindful of the lather on his face, he kissed her.

Lacing her fingers in his damp hair, Simone returned his kiss with pleasure.

When they parted, he toweled the traces of lather from her face and teased, "When we're married I expect you to stay out of my shaving soap." Then he said seriously, "Knowing you love me and that you're willing to marry me makes what I have to ask a lot easier."

"What is it?"

"I want you to leave the river."

"All right," she agreed quietly.

"You will?" Tom's shoulders sagged in relief. "I was

afraid last night would look like a tea party when I asked this of you."

"No, I realize it's time for me to go, though I hate the thought of being separated from you so much."

"We won't be apart. Zack can take the *Emerald Queen*. He loves this boat."

"So do you. And you love the river. What will you do?

"I'm going to settle down and start a new life, with you."

When Simone emerged from Tom's cabin a long, loving while later, she felt as though she were floating on air. She came to earth abruptly, however, when she saw Dev lounging against the railing outside, waiting for her.

"Ye've the bloom of a woman in love about ye, me dear," he greeted her jauntily.

"Dev . . ." she began hesitantly.

"Franklin was right all the time," he said mildly. "Ye loved him and hadn't admitted it. I had hoped I might change ycr mind."

"If anyone could have changed it, it would have been you," she said softly. "But I do love Tom."

"Then be happy, Simone." He kissed her hand and was gone.

How lucky she was to have a man like Tom waiting downstairs to make her his wife, Simone thought now. Already her business partner, he had made her his partner in every way. Despite Louisiana's Napoleonic Code, he had arranged it so she would not only retain ownership of her own property, but also become an equal partner in his.

Once she had admitted it, her love for Tom had filled the many gaps in her life. She felt whole and truly ready to face the future for the first time since Alain's disappearance.

How odd to think of Alain on her wedding day.

When he had disappeared, she had felt certain she would die. Now their one night of love, with all its blazing intensity, was a distant memory. She still felt sad when she thought of Alain, and she knew she would never forget him, but it seemed time had indeed healed her. Alain was the past. Tom was the present and the future.

Simone and Tom were married among those who loved them. Serene and lovely, the bride stood before the priest with her adoring captain. Their eyes on each other, they repeated their marriage vows. Tom placed a gold band on Simone's finger, and she slid Nicholas's emerald band onto his.

After a wedding supper with their friends, the groom insisted he and his new wife spend the night in the bridal suite at the St. Charles Hotel. "A suite of rooms set aside for newlyweds," he mused. "If it works for a hotel, it ought to work for a steamboat."

"We'll make a fortune," Simone said in unison with him.

"We're still partners, aren't we?" he asked, grinning.

"In everything, *mon amour*."

Several hours later, wearing nothing but a blanket from the rumpled bed she had recently shared with her husband, Simone sat on the carpet before the fireplace in the bridal suite. Similarly clad, Tom sprawled beside her, his head in her lap, a drowsy, sated smile on his handsome face.

"Simone," he murmured, "can you reach my jacket?"

The garment was on the settee with various other articles of clothing rapidly removed when the couple was finally alone. She leaned slightly, careful not to dislodge his head from its resting place, offering him a delicious view of creamy white breast.

Plucking the jacket from the pile, she handed it to him. He pulled a document from the pocket and gave it to her. When she read it, her eyes glazed with tears.

"You bought LaVictoire?" she whispered. "My family's plantation?"

"Lock, stock, and sugar house," he acknowledged, sitting up to face her. "I got more interested in it every time you pointed it out—or what we could see of it—from the river. If it's agreeable to you, we're going to live there and grow sugar cane."

"Of—of course, it is," she stammered, still stunned. "But you know what they say about sugar, Tom; a man must be a rich cotton planter before he can even start as a cane planter."

"They've been growing cane at LaVictoire for about fifteen years now. I've seen the books. Cane has been more profitable than cotton for them the last ten years."

"It's still a gamble," she cautioned.

"When did that ever slow us down, darlin'?"

She mirrored his smile. "When do we leave?"

"I'll be going in the next few weeks. I may need to get crews working on the levee before spring thaw up North. We don't want to start our life there with a crevasse."

"Why can't I go with you?" she demanded.

"The house isn't ready. Simone, LaVictoire isn't the way you remember," he tried to explain. "It's in pretty sad shape."

"I don't care," she maintained. "Please, Tom, I don't want to be apart so soon."

"I don't like the idea either, but you'll be much more comfortable—" He broke off as she looked at him meltingly. "Oh, all right," he said grudgingly.

"You will take me with you?" she cried. Rising on her knees, she rained jubilant kisses on his face, losing her blanket in the process.

Tom's exasperated frown transformed into a smile as he lay back on the carpet, taking her with him. Discarding his own blanket, he caught her lithe, naked body against his and rolled, trapping her beneath him.

"I couldn't leave you," he murmured. "Who would I argue with?"

Remembering his words the first time they had made love, she responded huskily, "This is the kind of argument I like to have with a man."

In the fire's glow, Tom and Simone—partners, friends, lovers and, at last, husband and wife—merged, making love slowly, passionately, their cries of fulfillment mingling in the night.

Simone awoke, thinking how wonderful and natural it was to awaken beside Tom. He lay on his side, his arm wrapped around her waist, drawing her into the curve of his body.

"Morning, Mrs. Franklin," he murmured against her hair.

"*Bonjour, mon mari*," she answered with a contented sigh.

"What do you want to do on the first day of our marriage?"

"Stay in bed all day." She scooted even closer.

Chuckling, he nuzzled her neck. "The hotel wants its room back by noon."

"By noon?" She sat up, frowning.

"It's all right, darlin'." He grinned lazily and pulled her back down beside him. "There's still time to say a proper good morning to each other. . . ."

Several hours later, the newlyweds emerged from the hotel into a thundershower. Unprepared for rain, Tom turned his collar up and draped his greatcoat over Simone's head before they ran for the coach awaiting them.

"Simone Devereaux," Marcel whispered, staring at them from an office across the street. He had only glimpsed the woman and had not gotten a good look at her companion, but he knew it was Simone.

He ran out into the street and called after the coach, but his voice was lost in a roll of thunder. Rain poured down his face . . . just like the night five years ago when he had watched her gallop away from him.

"Simone," he muttered, rubbing his temples, trying in vain to relieve the merciless pounding in his head. "Just when I think I might forget, I see you again."

A few weeks after her mistress married, Gisèle finally convinced Ethan Allen Franklin that he loved her. They were married at the house on St. Charles Avenue, and Tom and Simone saw them off to St. Louis on a sunny morning in February. Tears pricking the backs of her eyelids, Simone watched as the *Emerald Queen* disappeared around the bend, making the trip for the first time without her owners aboard.

"Come on," her husband said comfortingly. Taking her hand, he led her to Franklin Steamboats' small dock, where he gestured toward the *Bayou Queen*, clean and shining with new paint. "There she is," he said proudly, "LaVictoire's own sternwheeler."

"She's beautiful," Simone said delightedly, waving to Batiste, who awaited them on deck.

"I couldn't scrap her . . . for sentimental reasons," Tom said. "So, if you'll step aboard, Mrs. Franklin, we're going home."

The next morning, they tied up at a brand-new landing along the Coast, a section of the Mississippi north of New Orleans. A freshly painted sign on the dock announced it to be LaVictoire. Simone strained to see the house from the levee, but it was still screened by overgrown trees.

"This dock was the work crew's first job," Tom explained, helping her down the raw lumber steps that led down to the dirt road beside the levee. "We had to be able to unload our worldly goods. I understand the furniture is still in the house, but I'm a man who likes his comfort," he added with a smug smile.

When she glanced back, Simone saw Batiste carrying Tom's dilapidated chair ashore, and she rolled her eyes.

On the whole, she was to say later, the chair was in better shape than anything else at LaVictoire. She could scarcely believe her eyes when they stood at the foot of the patchy *allée*. So much grass grew up through the drive, it was difficult to tell it from the weed-choked lawn. The house with its eight majestic white pillars, which she remembered so well from the portrait of her mother, was built along West Indian lines, with a hipped roof and three dormer windows. The lower gallery, reached by a pair of curving staircases called welcoming arms, ran completely around the house, and more than a score of windows and doors opened onto it.

But the roof had great holes in it, and, between the peeling pillars, both upper and lower gallery sagged. The hurricane doors were faded green, and one shutter was propped against the wall below a shattered window. Panes of glass were broken in the beveled fanlight over the weathered front door. The rest of the windows were shuttered tightly or boarded up, giving the house a dismal, neglected look.

"I told you, it was in sad shape," Tom muttered as Simone stared in horror.

"LaVictoire was the most beautiful house along the river," she choked.

"Do you want to go back to New Orleans until the place is fixed up, darlin'?" he asked worriedly. "Or we can sell it. We don't have to live here."

"No, this is our home now." Smiling soothingly, she took his arm. "We'll make it beautiful again."

Surveying the ruin dubiously, Tom mumbled, "Should've known a woman as stubborn as you would take to a challenge like this."

He escorted his wife to where an ancient white man waited with a handful of slaves in the head of the *allée*. They looked almost as shabby as the house.

"Captain and Mrs. Franklin?" the old gentleman wheezed. "I'm Alonzo Haley, overseer here."

"Monsieur Haley, do you not recognize me?" Simone cried.

He regarded her through weak, watery eyes. "You do look familiar, ma'am, but I can't rightly say."

"I'm Nicholas Devereaux's daughter."

"Little Simone?" He smiled reminiscently. "I remember when your pa used to bring you here to visit." His smile abruptly faded. "I heard about his death several years ago and I was sorry."

"*Merci*," she murmured.

"So you're taking care of her now." Mr. Haley offered Tom a surprisingly strong grip.

"I'm trying to," the Virginian drawled with a grin.

"The Devereaux were always good to me and mine. Your grandfather gave me a small farm, you know, Miss Simone—for my old age. Neither of us figured I'd still be here so many years later, waiting for the new owner at LaVictoire."

"You've tended LaVictoire all this time?" she asked in astonishment.

"Best I could. Last owner didn't even live here. I couldn't leave till I knew LaVictoire was in good hands. I know it isn't much to look at, Cap'n," he added, catching Tom's skeptical look, "but the fields are rich and fertile, and they were mighty productive for the last owner.

"Before you inspect the house," Mr. Haley continued, "these folks are what's left of the house slaves. Last owner closed up the place, you know, so they have been working in the fields." He nodded toward the cluster of Negroes. "The round un is Savannah, the cook, and those are her daughters, Rosette and Celestina. And the bright gal with the younguns is Sally. Her boy is Napoleon, and the gal is Josephine."

Wobbling slightly, Mr. Haley led the way up the less precarious-looking staircase to the house.

"And you thought Wakefield was old," Tom muttered in Simone's ear as the overseer fumbled blindly with the key.

The doors, swollen and warped, opened with a mighty groan when Tom rammed them with his shoulder. LaVictoire's new owners stepped into a huge, dusty foyer, where cobwebs festooned the chandelier.

They walked through musty, long-unused, high-ceilinged rooms. The moldings were chipped and gray, and stained sheets draped the furniture. Straw mats, used in summer, had been left on the floor and were now rotted, home to vermin. The flue had been left open in the first parlor, and dirt daubers had built a nest in the fireplace. After ascertaining the nest was deserted, Tom knocked it down and sent Napoleon for wood.

Simone wandered from room to room, opening shutters as she explored to admit the meager sunlight struggling through dirt-encrusted windowpanes.

"I think we'll start here in the first parlor, M'sieur Haley," she announced efficiently when she returned. "If we close off the second parlor"—she struggled with the huge *porte coulisse* door between the rooms—"I think we'll be comfortable sleeping here tonight. Could you ask the house slaves to come in, please?"

There began such a frenzy of cleaning as the house had not seen for years. Simone not only set the house slaves to work, she also recruited some of the *Bayou Queen*'s crew. The mistress of the house was everywhere as windows were washed, walls scrubbed, and woodwork polished. Rotting mats were taken away, cypress floors scrubbed. Locating the carpets stored for a winter long past, Simone was relieved to find they had been packed properly with tobacco leaves to repel insects.

Under Tom's watchful eye, the marble mantelpiece was cleaned, and a family of mice was chased from the settee. Delicate painting on china doorknobs emerged as the grime was removed. By the end of the day, the room was a clean, cozy refuge amid the ruin of LaVictoire.

That evening, the deckhands hauled a mattress from the *Bayou Queen* to the house. Tom and Simone spread it on the floor in front of the fireplace and dropped upon it, falling asleep at once.

It was still dark when Tom awoke to discover his wife dressing. "What time is it?" he asked sleepily.

"Nearly dawn. I'm sorry I woke you. I wanted to get an early start."

"I'd say the middle of the night is early enough," he grumbled mildly. "Where is it you're going?"

"To inspect the storehouse, smokehouse, and dairy. I saw the kitchen yesterday. Later I'll start the cleaning upstairs."

"Guess I won't be dawdling in bed with my bride." Tom rolled, wrapping himself in the blanket, and sat on the edge of the mattress, his knees to his nose. "I can see now a man can't be a planter and a gentleman of leisure at the same time, particularly if his wife won't cooperate."

With an indulgent smile, Simone bent and placed a kiss on his mussed mop of curls. "What are you going to do today?"

"Mr. Haley and I plan to inspect the levee to see if it needs to be reinforced. If it'll hold, we ought to be able to get to the house and the outbuildings. I'll set the field hands to work in the slave quarters. The cabins are shabby and their roofs leak worse than ours."

"Tom," Simone began tentatively, "I don't think I like being a slaveholder. Couldn't we free them?"

"I don't like it any better than you do," he answered, expelling his breath in a puff, "but the entire plantation system is built on slave labor. If we freed them, just out of the blue, do you know what havoc it would cause?

"First, the plantation would shut down, and I don't think we could afford to get it running again. Second, you know free people of color seldom stay free. If a bounty hunter or a crooked slave dealer gets his hands on them, their manumission papers aren't worth a damn. They could end up someplace a lot worse than

LaVictoire. And last, we can't unless we're prepared to move up North. We'd probably be run out on a rail by our new neighbors. They don't take kindly to Abolitionist talk in these parts."

"I don't think I'm an Abolitionist. It's just that I've never owned a slave and never thought I would."

"The best thing we can do, Simone, is to make sure ours are well treated." Tom got to his feet and began to put on his pants. "No beatings, no forced breeding, no tearing families apart. We'll make sure they're well fed, well cared for, and have good living conditions—starting today."

"You are right," she said reluctantly, kissing him before she left. "I just wish there was something I could do to change it."

"I imagine the slaves will be freed one day, darlin'," he called after her, "but I don't expect it in my lifetime."

Within a week of their arrival, the interior of the house was transformed. It smelled of soap and wax and polish. Glass sparkled and wood glowed. Most of the repair work was done, whitewashed moldings had been restored to their original positions, and a maker of plantation furniture had been consulted.

At Simone's right hand through it all was Rosette, a pretty slave who had grown up in the big house when the owners still lived there. She was familiar with its workings and very capable.

One day while they washed and dried dishes, Simone asked, "Would you mind moving to the servants quarters in the big house, Rosette?"

"I s'pose I could," the slave said reluctantly. "I'd be a real good lady's maid to you."

"I do not need a lady's maid," Simone answered, adding another saucer to the stack.

"Then what would my duties be?"

At her look of dread, Simone knew she thought she was being asked to serve as Tom's concubine. "I don't know how things have been done here before," she said slowly, "but neither I nor my husband would ask you to be anything other than a housekeeper."

"Housekeeper?" Rosette blinked in surprise.

"*Oui*. I need someone to help me, someone who knows LaVictoire and can teach me what I need to know, who can manage if I am away."

With dignity, the slave nodded. "I'll be your house-keeper, Mrs. Franklin. We'll make this the finest house on the river."

Simone stood on the gallery at dusk gazing out at the river. The trees that blocked the view had been trimmed, and in the distance, she could see the sparkle of the setting sun on the water. Leaning against a column, she turned her face to the breeze. Though evening approached, it was still warm, and the promise of spring was in the air.

She heard Tom whistling as he walked from the garçonnière where he had been inspecting the day's work. He did not see her, and she watched as he halted near the mounting block at the head of the *allèe* and surveyed the grounds with satisfaction, his hands on his narrow hips.

"I know that look," she called. "What are you plotting now, Thomas Jefferson Franklin?"

He grinned up at her. "Nothing more wicked than an evening promenade with my wife."

She hurried to join him, slipping her hand into his as they strolled over the lawn, where patches of dark, rich dirt still showed through. They ambled along the fence that now encircled the grounds. Stopping at the carriage gate, they admired the *allée*, newly paved with shells.

"Come with me," Tom urged, leading her across the road to the steamboat landing. Arms around each other, they watched the full moon rise over the treetops on the opposite shore and savored the night sounds—

the cry of a bird, the cacophony of tree frogs, the lap of the river against the pilings.

When they turned to go back to the house, the sight of LaVictoire took Simone's breath away. It loomed majestically at the end of *allée*, its twin staircases indeed "welcoming arms." The whitewashed columns seemed to glow in the moonlight. Lamps had been lit inside, and light poured from the windows along the galleries. The graceful fanlight above the door was ablaze with shards of color, lit from within by the crystal chandelier in the hall.

"Oh, Tom, isn't it beautiful?" she breathed delightedly.

"Beautiful," he echoed with pride. "Just like its mistress."

"You only say that because you love me," Simone teased.

"I do." His voice was serious.

Turning in his embrace, she linked her arms around his neck. "I love you, too," she whispered, thrilled by the desire in his eyes as he bent to kiss her.

"Come, Mrs. Franklin," her husband murmured after a moment. "It's been a long day, and I have plans for a longer night."

Arms intertwined, they crossed the shadowy lawn to the house.

18

During the spring, Tom and Batiste rode the fields with Mr. Haley. The aged overseer found Tom a fair student, but it was Batiste who showed the most promise when it came to farming. He and Tom managed to run LaVictoire smoothly after Mr. Haley left for his long-awaited retirement.

Simone developed her own routine, making the rounds of the storehouse and the infirmary each morning. With Rosette's help, she supervised the staff to keep the house immaculate and the garden, dairy, and smokehouse well tended. She often fell into bed at the end of the day exhausted, but she had never been happier.

When they could find the time, Simone and Tom went riding over the property or to visit neighbors. Tom bought his wife a docile mare, and for himself he purchased a gelding he named Hocus Pocus. The big bay was an ordinary-looking animal, but when challenged to a race, he magically became the fastest runner in three parishes, much to the Virginian's delight.

Simone and Batiste fenced behind the house during good weather and in the ballroom during bad. At first, they were a curiosity to the slaves, but soon everyone became so accustomed to the sight that only the children congregated during their practice—the children and Rosette who always found a reason to be near when Batiste appeared at the house.

Evenings were frequently spent entertaining. The Franklins' neighbors came first because they were curious, but later because they genuinely liked their host and hostess. Monsieur Guilbeau, their Creole neighbor to the north at pretty little Hideaway Plantation, had decided he was too old to care for convention and struck up an immediate friendship with l'américain, Tom. The Martins, neighbors to the south, were américains themselves with a houseful of marriageable daughters. Mrs. Martin, a plump, pleasant woman, was alert to bachelors at any party. The unlikely mix of people met often at LaVictoire and came to enjoy one another's company.

The plantation's pleasant, busy routine was uninterrupted until late spring, when Georges and Viviane Chauvin came to visit.

"If they'd just stop thinking of me as a Kaintock," Tom complained on the first night of their stay as he dressed for dinner. "I can't outdrink, outfight, or outshoot much of anybody, and I can't remember the last time I whipped my weight in bobcats."

"You can outcuss any man on the river," Simone said helpfully.

Tom ignored her. "Your uncle acts like he thinks I'm crazy. Think that's because I married his niece?" He grinned impudently. With a shake of her head, she pushed the wayward curl from his forehead and kissed his cheek. Then, taking his hand, she led him downstairs, where Georges and Viviane admired the portrait of Simone's mother hanging over the mantel in the parlor.

Over dinner, they spoke mostly of inconsequential matters. When Simone asked about Fabrice, her aunt replied, "He is in Europe. Most boys go when they are younger, but we wanted him to have the opportunity before he settles down. Besides Zaza is still in school at the Ursuline convent."

"He's marrying Antoine Pellarin's youngest girl." Georges was obviously proud of the match he had made. "Pellarin's a sugar planter. Do you know him, *Capitaine*?"

"No, sir, can't say that I do."

"I saw your fields when we arrived. Ribbon cane, is it?"

"Yes, sir."

"Looks good," Simone's uncle complimented him grudgingly.

"Thank you. I'm learning as I go along. And I started out with a very good teacher—Mr. Haley, the old over-seer. His son, Leon, is my sugar-maker."

"Well, if there's anyone who knows sugar, it's Alon-zo Haley and his boys," Georges said, warming to the subject. "They're known up and down the Coast."

"Tell me, Monsieur Chauvin—"

"Georges, please," he requested, "if I may call you Tom."

"Of course," the American agreed with an easy smile. "Tell me, Georges, what do you hear about the new centrifugal machine for separating molasses from sugar?"

Simone and her aunt smiled at each other across the table as the men launched into a lengthy discussion about cane.

The next morning while the men rode the fields, Simone took Viviane to see the summerhouse in a glade at the edge of the lawn. Though incomplete, it promised to be the coolest place on the plantation with its tiled floor and wooden benches. The entire structure was raised above the ground to catch the breeze from the river and to escape the clouds of gnats and mosquitos that plagued the area in summer.

"This is pleasant," Viviane said when they finished

their inspection. "Do we have time to see the chapel before we go in?"

"What chapel?"

"It's very tiny, almost a grotto," the woman explained. "I remember there was a path through the woods to the bayou that borders the property. It stood a short distance from the path."

"Do you think you could find it?" Simone asked excitedly.

"It has been years, but, yes, let's try."

The path was nearly obliterated by undergrowth, but they picked their way through the brush, finding at its end the tiny chapel with its family tombs amid an over-grown garden.

Dropping onto a bench, Viviane mopped her brow and looked up at her niece. "Your life seems happy with l'américaine, Simone."

"Very happy," she confirmed. "Tom is good to me."

"It's time you had some joy in your life, chère. It seemed for a while there was nothing but trouble for you. Now it is even safe for you to come home. Marcel Baudin is not in New Orleans, and he probably won't be for some time."

"How do you know?"

"All the Vieux Carré is talking. He nearly killed *une fille de joie*. . . ." She paused, her face flaming at the words. "I heard she had green eyes like yours. In the face of *le scandale*, his father called him home."

"You don't know for how long?"

"*Non*. But think of it, *chère*," Viviane urged. "You can come home. It has been so long."

Her niece smiled and shook her head. "At one time I would have leapt at the chance. But LaVictoire is my home now, *Tante*. I'm happy here with my American."

In the days that followed, Simone knew what she had said was true. Serenely, she watched spring slip into summer. In the fields, tender green blades emerged from the soil, growing from stalks laid out in rows. Soon the growth began to harden, stretching toward the hot Louisiana sun. By late summer, a sea of sugar cane stood as high as a man's head, its tasseled tops rustling in the humid breeze.

One morning as Simone weeded around the chapel, she heard a call from the bayou. Looking around, she saw Ardoin Naquin, an old Cajun who lived in the swamp, poling his pirogue toward shore.

"*Bonjour*, Madame Franklin," he called, tying the little boat to a willow at the water's edge. "You are out early today, *oui*?"

"*Bonjour*, M'sieur Naquin," she greeted him with a smile. "I decided to work while it was cool."

"Me, I wouldn't worry about the heat," Monsieur Naquin said. "Las' night I heard the bullfrogs sing. It's gonna rain today."

"Good. Plenty of rain makes more sugar in the cane," Tom called, ambling toward them along the path from the house.

"*Ah, Capitaine.*" The leathery old man smiled, a gold tooth glinting in the sun. "You learn good t'ings from M'sieur Haley."

Turning to Simone, he said, "I brought you somet'ing, chère." He reached into the pirogue and picked up a small bundle of black fur, setting it on the ground at her feet.

Blinking in the sun, a puppy looked around. He snuffled at Simone's slippers, then, growling ferociously, he attacked, only to slide off her toe. Picking himself up, he growled again and wobbled to sit down at her feet.

"He likes you, yes," the old Cajun said excitedly. "He'll protec' you."

"*Merci beaucoup*, m'sieur." Simone scooped the puppy up, holding him out for Tom's inspection. "What shall I name him?"

"He looks like a . . . Jupiter to me," her husband suggested, watching the wriggling puppy try to lick her face.

"What a big name for such a little fellow."

"He'll grow into it," Tom predicted. "Just look at those paws."

Before he could grow into his name, Jupiter was a clumsy animal, all feet and tail. He followed Simone everywhere. For anyone who approached his mistress, friend or foe, he was a menace, not because of his ferocity, but because he was always underfoot.

For that reason, he was banned from the ballroom when Simone and Batiste fenced. On a cloudy, muggy day in late summer, she could hear him whining piteously from the gallery. All the windows were open to admit a breeze, though none stirred. A number of black children hung on the windowsills, dividing their time between petting Jupiter and peering in at the fencers.

"*Touché!*" Simone cried, making a point. "Perhaps we should stop for today," she suggested when Batiste grimaced, obviously irritated with himself. "It's too hot anyway."

"Please. I need to talk to you, *petite amie*," he requested, his gaze sliding toward the corner where Rosette sat with a basket of mending. "Alone."

Leading him into the study, Simone asked, "What is it, *mon ami*? You've been distracted all morning."

"Rosette and I wish to be married," he blurted out, "and we need your permission."

"My permission?" The woman looked puzzled.

"She belongs to you," Batiste reminded her.

"I had almost forgotten," Simone said slowly. "Of course I give my permission—gladly."

"Thank you. There is one other thing," he added delicately.

"*Oui?*"

The powerful black man drew a deep breath and said, "You and I have been together a long time, little one. I don't want you to think I would break my vow—"

"Because you're taking a wife?" she asked softly.

"Batiste Joseph, you've been as good to me as family would be. I want you to marry Rosette and be very happy. I release you from your oath."

"I told you before, only Alain could do that. Besides, I want to stay. I've gotten used to your willful ways," the servant teased, trying to mask his sentiment.

"What is this?" Tom asked playfully as he entered the study from the gallery. "You look like the cat who ate the canary, Simone."

"Only because Batiste and Rosette are going to be married," Simone retorted with a broad grin.

"Congratulations!" Tom whooped. "I wondered when you'd get around to asking her." He pumped Batiste's hand, then regarded him seriously. "A man with a new wife needs a home of his own. The overseer's cottage—and the job—are yours, if you want them. I'll pay you the same as Mr. Haley was getting."

Batiste stared at the captain in disbelief. "I can ride the fields and supervise work gangs, but, as a man of color, negotiating with factors would be impossible for me."

"Not if they don't know it's you they're negotiating with," Tom answered imperturbably. "I already consult you on the big decisions, and I trust you to make them on your own. Just let those fellows think you're following my orders. If the idea doesn't stick in your craw, we can get around their prejudices and I'll have the finest overseer on the Coast."

Batiste considered for a long, silent moment before extending his hand. "I'd be honored to be your overseer, Cap'n."

"Done." Putting an arm around his wife, Tom drew her to his side and said, "I hope you and Rosette will be as happy as we are."

"That'd be about as much as a man could ask," Batiste answered with a smile, and he set off to find his wife-to-be.

In early autumn, the couple was married in the plantation chapel with Tom and Simone as witnesses. As a wedding gift, Rosette received her manumission papers from the master and mistress of LaVictoire.

As the days grew shorter and cooler, the plantation bustled with preparations for harvest. Although cane was left in the fields to ripen as long as possible, it had to be harvested before the first frost.

The sugar house was cleaned, and the coopers finished the barrels to hold the yield. In the big house, coats and jackets were sewn for every slave on the plantation. Now gangs of men were cutting wood to power the steam engines of the sugar mill.

One October night, the Franklins read in the parlor, the only sounds the crackle of the fire and occasional whimpers from Jupiter, who lay at Simone's feet, chasing rabbits in his dreams.

Tom looked up from his book. "We start harvesting tomorrow. That means long days. This is likely to be the last evening we get to spend together for a while."

Rising, Simone stepped over the big dog and went to curl up in her husband's lap. "I'll miss you, *mon amour*."

"You'll miss our poker games." He chuckled, shifting in his chair to accommodate her small form. "How much do I owe you now?"

"You nearly quadrupled my household allowance this month with your last double-or-nothing bet."

He laughed. "It'd be easier to give you the money, but it's more fun to cut the cards."

Simone laid her head on his shoulder, and they stared at the flames in companionable silence for a time.

"Darlin'," Tom said quietly, "are you happy here?"

Lifting her head, his wife stared at him in surprise. "You know I am."

"You're not bored or lonely, living in the country?"

"No." Then she asked, her voice uncertain, "Are you?"

"How could I be bored with a woman like you—

sharp mind, sharper tongue, and all the rest nicely curved?" He grinned, running his hand over her hip. "I just thought you might like to go down to New Orleans while I'm busy with the harvest."

Capturing his hand, she tucked it around her waist and said firmly, "My place is with you, Tom, especially when you'll be working so hard. We'll have fun later."

"Then we'll work hard through harvest and play hard when it's done. But now, madame," he announced, "we must sleep hard. I have a feeling it's going to be one hell of a week."

The next morning, after a hurried breakfast, the field hands were assembled at the edge of the ocean of cane, each carrying a big curved cutting knife. As they waded into the cane, one of the men began to sing, and the others joined in, finding a rhythm for their labor in the song. One slice near the ground, and the stalk was free; two quick strokes down either side, and the leaves were gone, another cut at the top, and the tassels of new growth fell to the ground. And so it went, hour after hour.

The cane was hauled to the sugar house for grinding to extract the juice. Smoke from the wood fires billowed from the chimneys as the steam machinery ground noisily, separating the juice from the bagasse, the cane pulp. Huge kettles of juice thickened into syrup over open fires. Slaves, sweating despite the autumn chill, fed the flames continually. They worked among the giant wooden hogsheads in which the thick syrup, *la cuite*, would be stored until it granulated. The part that did not granulate would be molasses.

Simone saw little of Tom for nearly two months. He rose before she did to be at work by dawn and returned near midnight to collapse into bed. She did not go to the sugar house, unwilling to be in the way. Harvest, grinding, and boiling were grueling tasks requiring close attention. The master of LaVictoire worked side by side with his men, feeding the grinder, tending the boiler, consulting with his sugar-maker.

When she did spend time with her husband, Simone worried over the dark circles under his eyes. But Tom was flushed with success, certain the harvest would be profitable and that cane was the business for him.

Just before Christmas, sugar making ended, and Ethan and Gisèle and their new baby, John Adams, arrived for the holidays. Their host rested for the first few days of their visit, but soon he and Ethan were embroiled in planning a house party for the first week of January. When Tom realized that his and Simone's wedding anniversary fell on Twelfth Night, nothing would do but that they celebrate both in a cheerful conglomeration of festivities, beginning the day after New Year's and culminating with a ball on Epiphany.

The guests at the Franklins' first house party were a lively group. Besides family and neighbors, Zack; the Andersons, the Nashes, and Jim Reynolds, Franklin Steamboats' manager in New Orleans, and his family arrived on the *Bayou Queen*. The only shadow on Simone's good spirits was Lisette's gentle refusal to visit with them openly now that she and Tom were a respectable married couple.

During the cold, cloudy days, the men hunted or fished while the ladies remained inside. In the evenings, everyone gathered in the parlor for music, singing, or recitations.

On Twelfth Day, a plum cake was served at breakfast. Dulcie found a bean in her slice and was crowned queen for the day. At the ball that night, she was installed on a dais to accept playful homage from the other guests. Nearby, Zack and Jeremy discussed the possibility of annexation for Texas while Ethan explained the workings of the telegraph to Betsy Reynolds.

"I'll tell you," Tom was saying to Hiram, "the screw propeller will make it possible for steamboats to cross the ocean. Paddlewheels are too unreliable."

"I can see that sailing ships will be obsolete one day," the attorney granted, "but screw propeller vessels are still unproven."

"They're testing them now in England. We could—"

"Make a fortune," Simone interrupted wryly, eliciting a laugh from Hiram. "I'm sorry to disturb you, gentlemen. But, Tom, don't you think you should make your toast to the queen now?"

Taking Simone's hand, he stepped to the center of the room and lifted his glass toward the dais. "Ladies and gentlemen," he called, "it is my privilege to propose a toast to Dulcie Anderson, the queen of our Twelfth Night."

When everyone had saluted the queen, Tom lifted his glass again. "And I propose a toast to Simone Devereaux Franklin, who became the queen of my life, one year ago today. Happy anniversary, darlin'," he murmured, kissing her as their guests applauded.

Simone worked sluggishly in the hothouse her husband had built for her. He had gone to New Orleans on business at the end of January, nearly two weeks ago, and she wished now that she had gone with him. She was lonely.

Tamping down the soil in the clay pots on the table in front of her, she hollowed out the center in each, remembering the rhyme Rosette had taught her. "Plant four seeds for one to grow: one for the blackbird, one for the crow, one for the cutworm, and one to grow," she chanted, setting a bulb in each pot, pushing them deep and covering them.

Suddenly a steamboat whistle rent the quiet.

"The *Bayou Queen*," Simone gasped, whipping off her apron and wiping her hands on it. She might not be at her best, she decided, but she would not take time to change. Patting at her straying hair, she raced to meet her husband, reaching the landing just as a deckhand leapt to secure the boat.

"Simone!" Before a gangplank was down, Tom had joined her on the dock. Smiling, he opened his arms, and his wife threw herself into them, wrapping her arms around his neck and kissing him soundly.

"Oh, Tom, I've missed you so," she whispered in his ear.

"And I've missed you." He swept her off her feet in a bone-crushing hug before he set her down and ordered playfully, "Let me look at you."

He inspected her, breaking into a broad smile. "Nope, you haven't changed. I'd know you anywhere, Mrs. Franklin. You've got a smudge on your nose."

"You haven't changed either," she said with a sniff, accepting the handkerchief he offered. "You still say the most flattering things. But I'm glad to see you. I was beginning to worry."

"Trouble with the boiler. The *Bayou Queen* is about on her last legs. But just wait till you see what I brought you." He moved from her line of vision so she could see the boat. The gangplank was in place, and a passenger was ready to disembark.

"Lisette!" Simone cried excitedly.

The women came together with a flurry of hugs and chatter.

"Tom convinced me to come, now that your other visitors have gone," Lisette was saying when he joined them with another guest.

"Sugar, this is Gabriel DeLatte, a maker of daguerreotype portraits. Monsieur DeLatte, my wife, Simone."

"*Bonjour*, Monsieur DeLatte. Welcome to LaVictoire," she greeted the slender young man graciously.

"Call me Gabriel, please," he requested with a charming smile. "After all, we are almost old friends, Madame Franklin. Your maiden name was Devereaux, no?"

"You're Maryse DeLatte's son!" she cried, recogniz-

ing him as the son of a quadroon *placée*. "I used to see
you on Sundays at Congo Square."

"*Oui*, before I was shipped off to France to be edu-
cated," the elegant octoroon acknowledged.

"I have this idea, darlin'," Tom explained as they all
trooped toward the house. "Instead of having our portraits painted, we're going to have daguerreotypes
made. It's the very latest thing. Just wait till you see.
Gabriel brought some samples of his work." He nodded
toward the bag the young man carried.

When she saw the samples, Simone discovered
Gabriel was an artist. The images he captured were of
living, breathing people, not stiffly posed mannequins.

Willing to humor her husband, she sat the next day
for the young man. Lisette kept her company, but the
process was long and required patience from both photographer and subject. Gabriel was unfailingly polite,
and it was from him that Simone learned of Tom's bigger plan. He wanted a visual record of plantation life,
from the planting of new cane to harvest and sugar
making. She shook her head, in disbelief. Still, her husband's passion for all things progressive was a small
vice in a good man.

When he had developed Simone's picture, Gabriel
pronounced the petite Creole woman not only lovely
but photogenic. He began to follow her on her rounds,
juggling equipment, insisting she freeze while he took a
picture. He even set up his camera at a distance when
she did not know it and took her picture while she
bathed Jupiter. The image was blurred, but it captured
the look of sheer determination Simone wore as she
wrestled the big dog into the tub.

"Look at it!" Tom whooped with laughter when he
saw it. "I told you, you're the stubbornest woman I've
ever met—and here's proof. This is the gal I love." To
her horror, he commandeered the daguerreotype and
cut it to fit in his watch cover.

She tried to wheedle the unflattering image from

him the next morning in the privacy of their bedroom, but she succeeded in doing nothing more than arousing his amorous instincts.

After lengthy, languorous lovemaking, she slid from the bed and went to the vanity. Propped against the headboard, Tom watched appreciatively as Simone piled her hair on top of her head, her firm breasts displayed to their fullest as she lifted her arms. He thought she had never looked more beautiful.

Going to the tub that awaited her on the hearth, she paused to test the water, her back to him. Even though they had just made love, her nakedness brought a tightening to his loins. Her smooth back tapered to a narrow waist; her buttocks were round and firm; her legs, slender and graceful.

Tom went to kneel, naked, beside the tub. "You're so beautiful, Simone," he murmured, pressing a kiss on her wet shoulder.

"I'm glad you think so, *mon amour*." She smiled at him tenderly. "I only hope you continue to like my figure as it changes. He frowned in puzzlement. "I have been waiting for the right moment to tell you," she said. "We're going to have a baby, Tom."

"A baby?" he repeated. Getting to his feet, he stared down at her incredulously. "But when . . . how?

"Toward the end of summer," she informed him, laughing aloud. "And I think the 'how' happened when harvest was over."

"You've got to take it easy, darlin'. Let's get you out of that tub before you catch cold." He lifted her from her bathwater before she could protest. Cradling her against his bare chest, he carried her, dripping, to the bed and laid her down gently. "We're going to take special care of you now. You can't work so hard. And you've got to give up fencing for a while. And horseback riding."

"And posing for daguerreotypes," she added firmly.

Tom's blue eyes gleamed. "What if—"

"Don't even say it, Thomas Jefferson Franklin. I will not have my picture taken in that condition, not for you or posterity."

"I wouldn't think of it, darlin'," he soothed his wife indulgently. "Besides, I have a picture of you . . . in my watch."

Marcel Baudin strode along rue Condé. It was good to be back in New Orleans on this fine summer day. Perhaps he should commemorate his return, he mused, pausing in front of a daguerreotype studio.

A bell jangled when he opened the door, and a tenor voice called from the back of the shop, "*Un moment, s'il vous plaît.*"

The fair-haired Creole wandered from picture to framed picture while he waited. He stopped short when his eyes alit on a familiar face. On a small easel was a portrait of Simone Devereaux. The blood rushed to his head, and the familiar, maddening pounding began.

When Gabriel DeLatte emerged from the workshop, smiling, Marcel grabbed him by the arm and dragged him to the easel. "Where did you find this woman?" he bellowed.

The photographer blinked in shock. "Madame Franklin?"

"Madame Franklin?" the scarred man repeated blankly.

"*Oui*, of LaVictoire." Gabriel wrenched his arm free.

"The Devereaux plantation . . . I should have known!" Marcel howled.

Gabriel was suddenly apprehensive. He had not asked permission to use the picture in his shop, but, then, he had not expected to be confronted by a madman. "Please, monsieur, I think you should go now."

His unwanted customer did not seem to hear him. He stared at the daguerreotype, as if mesmerized. "Simone is married?"

"Quite happily. Now will you go?" Gabriel tried to usher him to the door.

"She should have been mine!" Marcel roared. He clutched at his head with both hands. The world was enveloped in a red fog. He advanced on the octoroon, remembering nothing until he stood in the shambles of the studio. While the injured man moaned among his ruined equipment and displays, Marcel snatched up Simone's portrait and stormed out.

19

The bright October sunlight streamed through the open doorway of LaVictoire's chapel, illuminating dust motes dancing in the air. The baby cradled in his arms, the priest dipped his hand into the baptismal font and asked, "What is the name of this child?"

"Aurora Marthe Marie-Louise Franklin," Tom answered with a sheepish smile. "She'll always be Rory to me. I still say the name's bigger than she is," he muttered to Simone, who had insisted on naming the baby after both their mothers.

Anointing Aurora's mop of black curls, the priest intoned, "Aurora Marthe Marie-Louise, I baptize you . . ."

Silently, Simone offered a prayer of thanksgiving for her young family and for Zack and Lisette, Rory's godparents.

Lisette had arrived not long after the baby's birth, bringing with her the news that Marcel had been committed to an insane asylum.

He had gone completely mad, wrecking Monsieur DeLatte's shop and severely beating the slight photographer. Then he had rampaged up rue Condé, smashing shop windows and terrorizing passersby. When the police tried to restrain him, he had attempted to run one of them through with his sword. Only his father's influence had spared him the embarrassment of a public trial. Discreetly, Marcel had been whisked away to an asylum in North Louisiana.

"Why didn't you tell me about this before?" Tom had asked with an injured expression when Simone finally told him of her ordeal. "I would have protected you—or died trying."

"Which is precisely why I didn't tell you," she retorted. "Do you think I wanted to lose you?"

At that, his hurt had melted away, and he had managed a rueful smile. "I knew you loved me, honey, from the beginning."

Yes, Simone thought now as the autumn sun bathed her loved ones in gold, she had much for which to be thankful.

The following spring, Simone returned to New Orleans, a mature and captivating woman. The Franklin family, accompanied by Rory's nurse, Celestina, arrived aboard the *Dixie Queen,* their newest steamboat, as it steamed downriver for the very first time.

No longer in hiding, Simone attended the theater and the opera and the races. She and Tom attended balls on both sides of Canal Street. Though in demand as a dinner guest and a dance partner, she was always ready to slip away from would-be admirers and into the arms of the most desirable man present: her husband.

Simone was the talk of New Orleans. Her name might be mentioned over tea in the Garden District, over *café* in the Vieux Carré, and, one warm morning, over the clatter of Smoky Mary, the train that carried picnickers to Lake Pontchartrain.

"I heard she goes out without even a maid to accompany her," a woman confided to her friends.

In the seat in front of the three Creole women,

Simone glanced at her husband, but he did not seem to be listening.

"I understand," another contributed to the gossip, "that she receives Lisette Duprè as a caller quite frequently."

"To her home?" the third gasped.

"Just last week, Reynard, my eldest son, told me he saw her coming from Exchange Alley," the first woman interjected eagerly.

"What did he do?"

"He tipped his hat as a gentleman should. Apparently, she bade him good morning and said she was taking a shortcut from her bank."

The women shuddered delicately, and one of them clucked, "From her bank. Imagine a Creole lady doing such a thing."

"*Oui*," sighed another. "As if it was not enough that a Devereaux, one of *les bonnes familles*, married a Kaintock."

Simone smiled wryly. Years ago *les bonnes familles* had rejected Nicholas Devereaux because he was a gambler, and now they gossiped because his daughter had married an American. Let them say what they wished, she thought exultantly. Tom was a wonderful husband and father. Tucking her arm into his, she smiled radiantly up at him.

"What brings this on?" he asked, placing his hand over hers.

"Happiness, *mon cher*, happiness."

"You're not *so* happy here that you don't want to go home before the hot weather sets in?" he asked with apparent concern. "We have got cane to plant."

"I'll be ready to leave next week. We'll follow the fashion," she teased. "Summer in the country and *la saison des visites* in town, after harvest."

But harvest passed and summer came again before the Franklins returned to New Orleans.

While the *Bayou Queen* was edging up to Franklin

Steamboats' dock that hot July day, a sailing ship tied up just a mile downriver in the Vieux Carré, and a man disembarked.

The Louisiana sun beat down unmercifully, and heat shimmered from the tarred surface of the pier, but the big, broad-shouldered man seemed undisturbed by it as he hired a porter to see to his luggage. A quizzical frown on his bronzed, craggy face, he made his way through the crowd and halted on the levee. Somehow he had imagined New Orleans would have changed more in seven years; he should have known the city was timeless.

Striding purposefully to the Canal Street Wharf, Alain de Vallière booked passage on a steamboat bound upriver, a steamboat fancifully named the *Emerald Queen*.

"I don't know what possessed us to stay in New Orleans in August," Tom grumbled. Stepping from the tub, he began to dry himself sluggishly.

"You promised Tante Viviane we would be here for her charity ball," his wife reminded him as she donned her stockings.

"Well, the heat is enough to stymie a lovesick boar hog."

"How *do* you come up with such colorful language?" Simone watched as he rambled around their bedroom, showing no inclination to put on the formal clothing she had laid out on the bed for him.

"Colorful language is a natural talent," Tom said modestly. "All Franklins are born with it."

"So I've noticed," she retorted. "Rory called Tina a gol-derned dunderhead last week."

"She got her little mouth around that? I'm impressed." Looking thrilled, the captain began to dress.

When he finished, he went to fasten the tiny buttons on the back of Simone's blue gown. As his task progressed, he planted feathery kisses along her spine, bringing chills to her bare arms.

"Do we have to go to this ball?" he whispered against the smooth skin of her neck.

"We told Tante . . ."

"Couldn't we change our minds?"

"We promised." Sighing, she turned to straighten his cravat. Then she looked him in the eyes and offered suggestively, "But we could come home early."

"You're my kind of woman, Simone Franklin," he murmured with a lecherous grin.

"Simone, Tom, we had begun to think you weren't coming," Fabrice's young wife greeted them when they arrived at the St. Louis Hotel.

"We wouldn't have missed it, Zaza." Simone kissed her on the cheek. "Where is my aunt?"

"Dancing with Fabrice. Oh, look, there is my sister. Will you pardon me while I speak to her?"

"Of course. What's going on over there?" Tom asked, nodding toward a group of chattering, excited Creoles clustered nearby.

"I do not know exactly. Maman Viviane said that one of New Orleans's finest citizens has returned—'from the dead' as she put it. He is older, so I don't know him. But he is very handsome," Zaza added ingenuously before departing.

When she glanced curiously toward the crowd, Simone stiffened with shock. The blood drained from her face, and her knees threatened to buckle beneath her. *Alain!*

Closing her eyes, she drew a steadying breath. It could not be. Alain de Vallière was dead, murdered seven years ago. Her eyes must be playing tricks on her.

She opened them cautiously . . . only to discover that a pair of intense dark eyes watched her from across the room. As if scoffing at the doubts on her face, Alain nodded a silent acknowledgment, a contemptuous smile curling his lips.

"Simone, what's wrong?" Tom's voice reached her only dimly.

"The heat," she muttered, too stunned for coherence, "I must sit down for a moment."

Solicitously, her husband guided her to a chair and rushed to fetch her a cool drink.

Simone watched with dread as Alain detached himself from the crowd surrounding him and strode toward her.

"*Bonsoir*, Madame," he said calmly, bowing. "I trust you remember me. I am Alain de Vallière."

Acutely aware they were being watched, Simone responded graciously, though she looked around in vain for Tom. "I remember you very well, Monsieur de Vallière,"

"May I have the pleasure of this dance?" he asked with studied politesse, acting as if their feelings for each other and the promises they had made never existed.

"Alain, I—" Simone looked up at the tall Creole. His eyes were intense, challenging. He had not forgotten anything.

"For old time's sake?" he asked quietly.

Still in shock, Simone rose and took his arm. As she allowed him to lead her to the dance floor, she told herself it was only because this dance might be her only opportunity to speak to him privately.

Held decorously in Alain's arms, she gazed up at him, but he stared expressionlessly over her head, moving silently, mechanically.

"Are we not going to talk?" she ventured at last.

"There is really nothing to talk about, Madame . . . Franklin," he answered curtly. "That is your name now, is it not?"

"*Oui*," she murmured. "But—"

"I merely wanted to see, after all this time, how it would feel to hold you in my arms again."

"How is it?" Simone whispered, hating herself for asking.

"It is not as wonderful as the last time." He smiled blandly when she stiffened, and went on, "But then, nothing remains the same after so long. Fortunes won and lost, friends and lovers—even enemies—gone. Who would have thought *la belle* New Orleans would ever be overrun by Kaintocks and Yankees? *C'est la vie*," he said conversationally.

His insinuations began to penetrate the fog of her emotions. "Alain, try to understand"—she tried to control her quaking voice—"you've been missing for seven years! I thought you dead."

"And you suffered so," he taunted. "For a month or two. Did you find consolation living with Franklin on his boat?"

"How dare you?" She strained to pull away from him, but his arms tightened around her. "You return— after seven years with no word—and sneer at me because I made a new life for myself?" She was trembling, now. "I do not have to answer to you, sir. In fact, you might explain to me where *you* have been all this time."

"I might," he said carelessly, "but this is not the time or place. If you want to talk to me, *ma petite*, you can do it tomorrow. I've taken a suite here in the hotel. Everything has indeed changed—even my house. And all for the worse."

"Things have not changed so much that a woman can visit a man's hotel room," Simone responded icily.

"As you please, *chère*. You know where to find me."

Smoothly he danced her to the corner where her husband waited, a crystal cup in his hand and a perplexed frown on his face.

"There you are, darlin'," Tom drawled mildly when they joined him, but his wife discerned the irritation and concern in his voice. "You made a mighty speedy recovery. Aren't you going to introduce me to your partner?"

"Of course." Simone rapidly collected herself. "Tom, may I present Monsieur Alain de Vallière. Monsieur de Vallière, my husband, Capitaine Thomas Franklin."

"De Vallière . . . Alain de Vallière?" the Virginian asked enthusiastically. He pumped Alain's hand with one hand and balanced Simone's punch in the other. "I'm pleased to meet you, sir. I've heard your name in shipping circles recently, but I had no idea Simone knew you."

"Alain was my guardian, Tom," his wife said quietly.

"I thought you said your Alain was dead." He looked at her in surprise, missing the sharp glance the other man threw her.

"I thought he was," Simone replied through bloodless lips.

"You must have given her quite a start," Tom said to the big Creole. "No wonder she was feeling faint."

"I'm afraid I did. I imagine she could use that punch." Alain nodded toward the cup the other man held.

"Of course. Here you go, sugar." Handing it to his wife, he steered her toward a chair. "Sit for a minute and take it easy while I introduce Mr. de Vallière to some people. If you have a moment . . ." Tom regarded Alain questioningly.

"Of course. And call me Alain."

"If you'll call me Tom." The Virginian offered one of his easy smiles when Alain nodded in agreement. "You'll be all right, won't you, darlin'?" he asked Simone. "We'll only be a minute."

Simone's head ached, and she longed to be alone to examine her wildly mixed emotions at Alain's return. She had felt stunned—and weak with relief— to see him alive, but things were indeed different after seven years. Certainly she had changed, she thought. And, feeling his coldness toward her, she knew he had changed, too.

Sipping punch to calm himself, she watched Tom introduce Alain to Hiram Anderson and Jeremy Nash. But her mind kept richocheting around Alain's brazen invitation. How could he think she, a married woman, would go alone to his hotel room? And he had seemed so confident that she would.

"May I have this dance, *Cousine*?"

Fabrice stood before her. She had not even seen him approach. "Of course." Her lips curved in a smile that did not reach her green eyes.

"I'm sorry I was dancing with *maman* when you came in," Fabrice said as they joined the other dancers. "I wanted to warn you that de Vallière was here. Is it not amazing? After seven long years . . . ," he mused aloud.

"It was something of a shock." She attempted to keep her tone light.

"Is it . . . is it true that you lived in his house unchaperoned for a time?" he asked unexpectedly.

"Who told you that?" she asked with surprise.

"Marcel. He wasn't lying, was he?" Fabrice's brown eyes rested on her shrewdly.

"No, he wasn't," she replied, wishing her cousin did not look so hurt after all this time.

"De Vallière could ruin your reputation. People have long memories in New Orleans. Do you want me to talk to him for you?"

"Ah, *Cousin*," she said with a sigh, "do you still want to take on my problems for me? Is it not enough to care for your lovely wife?"

"I will do whatever I can for you, Simone. I'm learning to love Zaza, but I will never stop caring for you."

"I will fight my own fights," she informed him, adding softly, "if I can figure out what I'm fighting."

"It appears Alain has not told your husband of your . . . connection, at least," Fabrice said, glancing toward the men. "Tom seems to be his usual easygoing self." He had tried not to like l'américain, but Tom's effortless charm had worked as surely on him as it seemed to be working on Alain.

"*Oui.*" Simone glared resentfully at Alain. Towering over the others, he laughed and chatted with Tom.

When their dance was finished, Fabrice returned Simone to her corner. "Remember," he murmured before he walked away, "I am here if you need me."

Grateful for his support, even if it sometimes made her impatient, she watched Tom and Alain saunter toward her.

"Tom," she greeted her husband, "I'm sure Alain will excuse us. I'd like to go home now, if you don't mind."

"Of course, darlin'." He regarded her with concern. "You do look a mite peaked. I'm sorry I kept you waiting."

He turned to his companion. "Alain, it's a pleasure to meet you. Simone and I would like you to come to the house for dinner one evening soon. I'm sure y'all have a lot to catch up on."

"We do," Alain murmured meaningfully. Bowing, he kissed Simone's hand, holding it overlong. "*Bonne nuit, ma petite.* I look forward to our next meeting."

When Tom went to order their carriage, Simone unclenched her fist and stared bleakly at the key Alain had slipped into her hand. The key to his suite.

Despite her resolutions, Simone stood in the hallway outside the man's room the next morning, key in hand as she debated whether to go or to stay. The decision was made for her when Alain, unshave and clad only in a robe, opened the door to glare at her through bloodshot eyes.

"Why don't you dawdle there until everyone in the Vieux Carré has seen you?" he growled. Seizing her wrist, he pulled her inside.

"How did you know I was there?" Simone yanked from his grip.

"I saw you from the window." He would not tell her he had watched for her all morning after a long, sleepless night.

"Would you like a drink?" Standing at the liquor cabinet, the whiskey decanter in hand, he heard the rustle of her skirt behind him.

"Isn't a little early?"

"Not for hair of the dog." He poured a healthy shot for himself, then turned and said, "I knew you would come."

"Then you knew more than I did," she snapped. "I only decided this morning, out of respect for what was once between us."

"And what was that?" he inquired with a distant, wintry smile.

"I . . . I loved you," she answered in a strangled voice. She did not know what she had expected, but she had not foreseen the coldness of this stranger who stood so very near.

"Ah, yes," Alain said scornfully. "With all the passion your fickle heart could muster."

"I loved you so I thought my heart would break when you disappeared," she replied, glaring up at him with seething intensity. "Everyone told me you were dead. I refused to believe it. But when you did not return, finally I had to."

"So you could marry your American."

"So I could go on with my life," she amended, suddenly weary.

Alain stared down at her in silence. He would not comfort her. He could not. Since learning Simone had married another, he had numbed himself. He did not want to feel tenderness, compassion, even friendship for her. If he allowed her to penetrate his bitterness, he knew the raw, aching pain he would feel. He knew it well. He had lived with it long enough.

"What happened to you, Alain?" She broke the silence. "Why didn't you let me know you were alive?"

"Communication was hardly appropriate when I learned you had married. From what I hear, you eloped with your captain before I had even escaped from the West Indies. That's where I was taken," he answered her questioning gaze, "after I was kidnapped."

"But who? Why?"

"Surely you did not think I had abandoned you," he said. "I leave desertion to someone who has more stomach for it. You, for example."

"That is unfair," she protested hotly.

He scowled down at her before going to the window to rest his forehead against the cool glass and stare at the street below. "Was it fair that I was accosted by a band of ruffians as I rode to meet Marcel at the Dueling Oaks that morning? Or that I was knocked unconscious and stripped of my clothes? Was it fair that I awoke in irons, in the brig of a ship which was already well out to sea? Or when I was hauled to the captain's cabin, where Comtesse Marguerite—"

"Louis-Philippe's cousin?" A long-forgotten conversation popped into Simone's memory. "The woman whose husband you killed?"

"I did not kill him." He frowned. "How did you know about that, anyway?"

"I . . . Jean-Paul heard many things," she reminded him.

"Well, Marguerite was a vindictive bitch," Alain muttered more to himself than to Simone. "It seems the king thought a change of scenery would be good for her, so he ordered her to her plantation in the West Indies. She blamed me for her husband's death, for the loss of her life at court, and for the lack of a lover to share her bed.

"So I was given a choice. I could become her lover, or I could work in the fields of her plantation. Either way, I would be her slave. And one way or the other," he recalled, grimacing in distaste at the memory, "I would make restitution."

Smiling mirthlessly, he glanced over his shoulder at Simone. "What a romantic fool I was. Do you know what my choice was? I labored in her fields for three long years, knowing somehow, someday, I would return to you, my love. That knowledge alone kept me going under the inhuman conditions of the foul compound where we were penned like animals." For a moment he seemed lost in dire memories. But then he continued the grim tale.

"One terrible and bloody night, the slaves revolted. Even then, I was less interested in rebellion than in returning to you. Always you. I escaped in a boat, and, after drifting several days, I was picked up by a passing ship headed for Charleston. It was a long way home, but I was on my way." He paused.

"This is where the story becomes comical . . . one mishap after another." His voice was bitter. "The ship foundered in a storm, and I was rescued by a ship bound for France. Even though it was agony for me to realize how much longer it would take, I knew I would still get home. To you." He laughed mirthlessly.

"Who do you think I met in Le Havre before I sailed for home? Serge St. Michel. He lives in France now, you know. He was remarkably reticent when it came to you, but when pressed, he finally told me you had married your Kaintock. The soft-hearted *maître* even defended you," Alain said softly. "We got gloriously drunk together and before he knew it, I had sworn him to secrecy, forcing him to agree that under the circumstances, it would be better if you didn't know I lived."

"Then why have you come back?"

"My brother Pascal is dead, and my father is ill." He faced her, his expression stark.

How she ached for him. But what could she say? What could she do? She murmured her condolences and sadly prepared to leave.

"Don't go," he commanded harshly. "Don't you want to hear the end of my story? The king finally heard of his cousin's perfidy and my experiences, and he asked me to undertake the governor's position on the island I had only recently fled. The proposal held an ironic fascination for me, and, since I no longer had a reason to return to New Orleans, I accepted. For the past three years, I have been one of His Majesty's governors in the Caribbean, much to the benefit of my finances. Still, when my father summoned me two months ago, I decided to resign and return to Bois Blanc. End of odyssey," he concluded. "And here I am."

"You've been through a great deal," Simone murmured sympathetically.

"Spare me your pity, madame." Alain's face was a cold mask of arrogance. "I do not need it, Just as I do not need you."

"'Lain . . ." She searched for the proper words. "I'm sorry these things happened, but they weren't my doing. Surely you must see that. Why do you hate me so?"

"I don't hate you, *ma petite,*" he answered. He bent so his face was disturbingly close to hers. "Even though you betrayed our love, I don't hate you. I do not feel anything for you . . . beyond mild curiosity."

"What do you mean?" She stared up at him.

"I wanted to see if you were any truer to Franklin than you were to me." He smiled spitefully. "I see you are not."

Simone drew back her hand to slap him, but Alain caught it and pulled her roughly against him. His mouth slanted across hers in a fierce, demanding kiss.

Her green eyes wide in alarm, she struggled in his grasp, but Alain gripped her more tightly, his tongue plundering her mouth.

When she whimpered, he gentled his kisses, but did not stop the assault on her dizzied senses.

"Remember?" he whispered against her lips. "Remember when you gave yourself to me? Remember our night of lovemaking?"

Slowly, Simone succumbed to his persuasive caresses, his tender words. The years seemed to melt away, mingling past and present. Her will to resist her long-lost love crumbled. She closed her eyed and yielded to his heat.

Abruptly Alain set her away from him, sneering, "Just as I guessed. An unfaithful lover makes an unfaithful wife."

This time he did not try to stop her as she drew back her hand and slapped him. Then she fled, the sound of Alain's jeering laughter echoing in her ears.

20

Simone walked along rue Chartres, savoring the scent of the freshly washed *banquettes* and the aroma of breakfast cooking in a hundred close-packed dwellings. Though she was happy in the American Section with Tom, she missed mornings in the Vieux Carré. The cries of the street vendors, sometimes melodious, sometimes strident, were welcome sounds to her ears.

"Emeraude," a familiar voice called, "how are ye?"

"Dev!" Simone greeted the gambler with pleasure. "I'm fine. How are you?"

"All the better for seeing ye. Yer a winsome sight, Mrs. Franklin, in yer bonnet with flowers upon it."

"*Merci*, monsieur. You look rather handsome yourself."

"'Tis the air of respectability, I imagine." He made a great show of preening. "I just opened a casino of the better sort on Poydras. I could use a good dealer. . . ." he teased, falling into step beside her. "What are ye doing out and about this fine morning?"

"I've been to see my attorney."

"What a business woman ye've become, and still ye

manage to be the prettiest thing in all Louisiana." He leered playfully at her.

"You're a terrible flirt, Devlin Hennessey," she responded with a shake of her head.

"Aye," he agreed with a shameless grin. "'Tis good to see ye, Simone. Join me for a cup of *café*."

"One cup," she agreed. "Then I have to go."

They headed for a nearby café, where they sipped bitter coffee lightened and smoothed with milk and chatted. A short time later, they stepped out onto the sunny *banquette* and parted.

Simone had not gone five steps before another familiar voice said softly, "So I am not the only man Madame visits when her husband is not watching."

Looking around, she saw Alain standing in a doorway. With a knowing smile, he doffed his hat. Refusing to explain her actions to him, she drew herself up and marched away without a word.

She was still trying to put aside her anger when she arrived at Lisette's house. In the foyer, she marched through a clutter of crates and barrels, stepping back to allow Jude to pass with a huge box and a harried expression on his face.

In Lisette's barren suite, stripped of its familiar trappings, Simone found the woman bent over a barrel. From the barrel's hollow interior, Lisette instructed, "You can take the other crate now, but be careful."

"I came to help." Simone chuckled. "But I don't think I can handle that crate on my own."

Lisette straightened and turned. "Oh, chère, I thought Jude had come back. Will you help me pack my mother's china?"

Taking off her hat, Simone rolled up her sleeves and set to work. "I can hardly believe you're going to be our neighbor."

"When Monsieur Guilbeau offered to sell Hideaway to me, I could hardly believe it myself. I couldn't have been more surprised, or touched. He knows who I am and how I made my living, and he does not care."

"He is an unusual man," Simone said. "He liked you the few times he saw you at LaVictoire, and that was good enough for him."

"I like him, too." Lisette's gray eyes were suspiciously moist as she wrapped a teacup in paper. "He is a dear old gentleman, like a favorite uncle, wanting me to have Hideaway because he has no close family and wishes it to be in good hands. I cried when he told me. First because he was so sweet, and then because I knew I couldn't afford it."

"But you found he was not so interested in money, didn't you?"

"*Oui*, he sold it to me for a scandalously low price. All he wanted was the promise he could live in the garçonnière until his death. I'm so excited, I'm not even sorry to leave New Orleans."

"I won't be either."

Lisette looked at her sharply. "What's wrong, *ma petite*?"

"Oh, I just saw Alain again," Simone answered, a frown knitting her brows. "For the past month, I've seen him everywhere. At the theater, the racetrack, parties—everywhere. I look up and see his superior smile. Even if he is not present, people talk about him—on both sides of Canal Street. He's always polite, but just under the manners . . . I don't know . . . he seems to bait me."

"He has changed. There's a bitterness about him that was not there before," Lisette said with a sigh, remembering his first visit to her house after his return. She had wept with happiness to see her old friend, but when their conversation turned to Simone, she found he was not the man she had known.

"But, Alain," she had protested, "you must understand, when you first disappeared—"

"I heard it from her. I don't want to hear it again," he had snapped. "Spare me a defense of the faithless bitch."

"Did you want her to live for a dead man? Because that's what you were, Alain de Vallière—dead and gone." Lisette had quickly seen that he did not want to hear it, even if it was the truth.

"I wouldn't expect her to mourn forever, but I certainly didn't expect her to elope with the nearest available man," he had maintained unreasonably. "It is not as if she was without a protector. I left Batiste to care for her."

"You delude yourself if you think protection is the reason Simone finally married Tom Franklin." The woman decided she could do no less than tell him the truth. "Simone finally married Tom because she loves him. And he loves her very much."

"He is welcome to her," Alain had snapped, storming out as Lisette watched, helpless and deeply troubled for her friend.

Still troubled, the madam muttered, "*Oui*, he is much changed, Simone. Life was very unkind to him, and it changed him. It is sad, but he is not the man you once loved."

"*Non*." Simone turned her attention to packing and hoped Lisette would not notice the tears that had sprung to her eyes.

Returning home that afternoon, the first thing Simone saw was a creamy calling card on the table in the foyer. She picked it up and stared at it with chagrin. Alain de Vallière . . . What kind of game was he playing? Had he come to report her meeting with Dev? Or to tell Tom that he had once been her lover? Why couldn't he leave her alone?

"You just missed Alain de Vallière," Tom announced. He emerged from the study, carrying two-year-old Rory in his arms.

"So I see," his wife said coolly. Tossing the card back onto the table, she removed her hat before the foyer mirror.

"*Maman!*" Rory crowed, leaning precariously

toward her. Her green eyes, so like her mother's, danced with delight as she held out the doll she clutched in her pudgy arms.

"See what he brought Rory?" Tom struggled to maintain his grip on the squirming little girl. "She took to Alain like a bear to honey. Even gave him a famous Franklin smile."

"Did she?" Taking her daughter, Simone admired the new toy. "What a lovely doll."

"Nonc' 'Lain gave her to me," Rory informed her mother.

"He said that with its green eyes and black hair, the doll looked like Rory," Tom said, adding with a chuckle, "Guess she's supposed to be as mischievous as Rory, too. He said her name is Coco Robichaux. Isn't that the imaginary girl who makes good Creole children do naughty things?"

"*Oui.*" Simone smiled, though inwardly she fumed.

"Down," Rory demanded when she saw the butler approaching. "Coco wants to see Wa'field."

"Time for lunch, Miss Aurora." Wakefield smiled indulgently and offered a liver-spotted hand.

"My name is Rory," the child maintained stubbornly.

"Yes, Miss Rory." Chuckling, the butler led her away.

"Come with me, darlin'," Tom requested. "I need to talk to you."

Cold with dread, Simone followed her husband into the study.

As he pawed through the papers cluttering his desk, he said, "I wish you had been here earlier. Alain was sorry he missed you."

"But I saw him just this morning." Simone decided to counter any trouble the Creole might have tried to cause. "He said nothing of coming here."

"He didn't mention that, but he didn't stay long. He seems like a helluva nice fellow. I'd like to get to know him." Tom sorted through his papers, his mind on business, missing Simone's expression of dismay.

"Here we go." He seized a piece of paper. "The estimate for a new engine for the *Creole Queen*. We have to consider whether it's worth it to replace it or not. She's pretty old for a steamboat."

Accepting the sheet from her husband, Simone tried to concentrate on the numbers printed on it, but her roiling emotions would not allow it. She decided she hated Alain even more than she had at thirteen. But she could not let anyone, especially Tom, know how she felt.

Feeling his questioning gaze upon her, she looked up. "I agree. Even though we might like to, we cannot hang on to the *Creole Queen* just because she is a part of our past."

With a regretful smile, Tom moved around the desk to kiss his wife lightly on the lips. "Thank goodness you're in better shape than she is, darlin'. I'd hate to have to retire you."

In the weeks that followed, Tom and Alain sought out each other's company, much to Simone's consternation. Though it was time to go home, the Franklins lingered in New Orleans, waiting for the arrival of new equipment Tom had ordered for LaVictoire's sugar house.

When the equipment arrived at last, Simone insisted her family leave the city at once. As the *Bayou Queen* neared LaVictoire, Tom stood behind his wife, his arms looped around her waist.

"I used to think I couldn't be content unless I was on the river," he said quietly. "Now I know I am happiest at LaVictoire with you and Rory. It'll be good to get home."

She turned to him, her feelings clearly displayed on her face. "I love you, Tom."

"I love you, too."

For days after their return, Tom tried in vain to get his new equipment running. Colorful curses punctuated his frustration when he discovered he was missing a part.

He made a hurried trip back to New Orleans but was unable to get the part in time for the upcoming harvest. The plantation would have another sugar-making season without the benefits of a centrifugal separator. Tom did not say whether he had seen Alain, and Simone did not ask.

Fall was hectic at LaVictoire. While the men were busy with the harvest, Simone and Rosette hurried to make baby clothes for the child Rosette was expecting in December, and Simone threw herself into preparations for the holidays.

Ethan and Gisèle arrived before Christmas with John Adams and Patrick Henry, who was just two months older than Rory. At first, three-year-old Johnny tried to dominate the younger children. In the end, independent Rory became the natural leader, inciting her male cousins to mischief they would never have dared on their own.

The holidays were a delight that year. The Franklins bestowed Christmas gifts of fruit and clothing on all their slaves and a toy for each child. On New Year's Day, Tom and Simone were going over the arrangements for the Twelfth Night party, when he suddenly remembered an extra guest he had invited.

"You did what?" Simone snapped.

"I invited Alain the last time I saw him in New Orleans," he answered, surprised by her vehemence. "I know I should've told you, sugar, but I was busy with the harvest and forgot all about it. One more person won't really make a difference, will it?" he coaxed.

"I do not suppose it will." She sighed. "It's just that we've always arranged for even numbers of males and females so everyone has a dinner and dancing partner," she protested feebly.

"Don't worry, darlin', I'll dance with him. I'll even let him lead," her husband assured her with an outrageous wink.

The guests began to arrive the next day and were

greeted by Tom and Ethan and Gisèle. The hostess was in the overseer's cabin, where Rosette's labor had finally begun.

As the hours wore on, Batiste, who had taught Simone all she knew of healing, hovered underfoot. At last she sent him to wait outside, where he paced the porch. Between Rosette's contractions, Simone heard voices and glanced out the window.

Alain was approaching, and the big overseer had bounded out to meet him. Though Batiste had been overjoyed to hear that his former master had returned safely, nothing had lured him from the side of his pregnant wife. Now he was unmistakably happy to see the Creole.

The two big men embraced, then, seemingly embarrassed, they looked each other over and relaxed into their old bantering style.

After a while the talk became serious. "So you thought I was dead, too?" Alain asked soberly.

"Wasn't much else to think, 'Lain. We searched, the police searched. M'sieur Cuvillion brought word about your clothes being found . . . well, that seemed as close to finding a body as anyone was going to get."

"So you both gave up and threw in with Franklin," Alain said, faintly accusing.

"We did what we had to do," Batiste answered. "And Cap'n Franklin was a godsend. Neither of us was safe in New Orleans. I was a suspect in your murder, and Baudin was hounding Simone. He caught up with her one night, and his bodyguard wounded her in the side."

"What?" the Creole breathed disbelievingly. "This is the first I've heard of it. Dieu! Sometimes I wish Marcel had not been committed. He has much to answer for."

"Simone is safe now. That's all that matters. She's got a peaceful life here, 'Lain. I think she'd just like to forget the past."

"She can't forget any more than I can," Alain said bitterly.

"She's happy, 'Lain," Batiste replied with a note of warning in his voice. "Cap'n Franklin is a good man, and he's good *to* her."

"I know, *mon ami*," the other man sighed, a bleak expression on his face. "I know."

Simone shivered as the men moved out of earshot.

The next morning, she joined her guests at breakfast, apologetic for her absence the previous evening, but wearing a bright smile. During the night, Rosette had presented Batiste with a healthy freeborn son named Alexander.

Sensing that Alain had taken his conversation with Batiste to heart, Simone relaxed somewhat. He was courteous and cordial, charming the other guests, and, when he spoke to her, his comments were no longer pointed. Still, she often felt his dark eyes upon her, and she was careful not to be alone with him.

One sunny January afternoon during the holidays, Alain entered the house through the back door, carrying Rory on his shoulders. His hands gripped her legs to steady her as her little fingers twined in his dark hair.

Seeing Simone in the deserted dining room, he halted in the doorway. Preoccupation with dinner preparations replaced the guarded expression she usually wore around him. With the haughty mask removed, he saw warmth and vulnerability in her face. She started and looked up when Rory called, "Look, *Maman*. I'm riding."

"So you are." Walking toward them, Simone smiled up at her daughter. "Have you been bothering M'sieur de Vallière?"

"This is *mon* Oncle 'Lain." Rory hugged him in rapturous affection, wrapping her arms around his head so he could not see.

"Easy, Rory," Alain commanded, laughing as he lifted the child's clinging arms from in front of his face.

"She hasn't been bothering me," he told Simone. "She's been teaching me how to fence."

Simone's cheeks colored slightly at her daughter's unwitting audacity, but before she could speak, Rory piped, "*Maman* fights with swords."

"I know," Alain said softly. "I've fenced with her on starlit summer evenings."

Simone's reluctant gaze was drawn to the man's face as he looked at her with the first real warmth she had seen in his eyes since his return.

Simone's flush deepened under his scrutiny, and she looked like the girl Alain remembered so well. He fought the urge to bend his head and kiss her as she stared up at him, her green eyes dark with inner turmoil. The couple stood motionless for a moment that seemed suspended in time.

Fortunately, Rory broke the mood. "You can't fight with her," she insisted, oblivious to the undercurrent of tension between the adults. "She only fights with Batiste."

The mask fell into place, and Simone became the efficient hostess again, excusing herself to check on the centerpiece.

Alain watched as she disappeared into the butler's pantry, then he shook his head as if to clear it. Thinking he was playing with her, Rory chortled with delight and demanded he do it again.

In the pantry, Simone listened as her giggling daughter was carried down the hall to the parlor.

How could Alain have such an intense effect on her after all this time? she asked herself fearfully. How could he affect her at all, when she loved Tom? Stabbing cut flowers into a crystal vase, she vowed not to be alone with Alain ever again.

At dinner that night, Alain was all a hostess could wish in a guest. He was charming and witty; his conduct toward the ladies was courtly and gracious. Gently he discouraged Mrs. Martin's advances on behalf of her daughter Nell. He listened politely to Dulcie's rambling account of her last trip to Boston, and he discussed rising property values with her husband. In his behavior toward his hostess, he was scrupulously proper.

But the evening passed at a snail's pace for Simone, and she wished she could be anywhere but in the same room with Alain.

Coffee was served in the parlors. The *porte coulisse* doors were thrown open, and, in the formal first parlor, Gisèle played the piano softly. Tom and Alain stood talking by the fire in the second parlor. At a nearby table, Dulcie, Barbara, and Mrs. Martin were engaged in a favorite pastime, telling fortunes with cards.

"Monsieur de Vallière," Dulcie beckoned him, "why don't you come and let us foretell your future?"

Smiling, the big man pulled out a chair and sat down. "I cannot say I believe in fortune-telling."

"You might be surprised," Barbara insisted as Dulcie laid out the cards. "Sometimes the cards can be amazingly accurate."

"I see love," Dulcie announced excitedly, "and possibly marriage with a beautiful woman."

"Then you are seeing my past, Madame Anderson," Alain corrected dryly. "I loved a beautiful woman once, but I will never do so again. And the very thought of marriage strikes terror in my bachelor heart."

"Do not say such a thing, Mr. de Vallière. Someday another young lady might suit your fancy," Mrs. Martin interjected, casting a sidelong glance at Nell. "You never know, you might marry yet."

"*Oui*, madame, you never know," Alain agreed carelessly.

On the settee, Simone and Lisette exchanged knowing smiles. That nonchalant remark signaled the commencement of an assault by the Martin mother and daughter on Alain's bachelorhood, and, for a moment, they felt sorry for him. Then, realizing the campaign would keep him occupied, Simone sat back complacently to watch. She was disconcerted to discover that he also covertly watched her.

On the morning before Twelfth Night, Simone donned a pair of boots and slipped out into the overcast morning before her guests awoke. Birds chirped in the trees, and the air smelled crisp and clean. Saturated by rain the night before, the ground was soft and spongy under her feet as she and Jupiter walked to the woods at the edge of the property. Tom and Batiste were busy at the sugar house, so she went alone to gather greens to decorate the ballroom.

When her big basket was filled with feathery branches, Simone walked back toward the house. As she reached the edge of the lawn, it began to rain, gently at first. Then thunder rumbled overhead, and it began to pour. Slogging across the lawn in front of her, Jupiter wisely made for the nearest building, the carriage house.

Simone followed, surprised to find the door open. Dripping, she ducked inside just as Jupiter gave a surprised *woof*. Happy, snuffling sounds followed . . . and a low, male voice responding.

In the dim interior Simone spotted Alain, who sensing her dismay, quickly advised, "Don't go. You will get soaked."

Simone was not sure that being wet was not preferable to being alone with him. She wavered at the door, prepared to flee.

"Why are you afraid, Simone?" Alain asked quietly. He was kneeling between two rigs, scratching the dog's stomach. Jupiter sprawled on the dirt floor, his hind foot pumping blissfully.

"I'm not afraid." She hoped she sounded more confident than she felt.

"Then stay." With a final, friendly thump on Jupiter's belly, he rose. "Don't you think you should come away from the door before you get wetter than you already are?"

She did not reply, but she walked a few steps into the carriage house and set her basket heavily on the ground. Then she turned to look out again at the rain.

She heard Alain stir and knew he was standing behind her. He was right, she realized. She was afraid to be alone with him.

"You're shivering," he murmured, placing his jacket over her shoulders.

Glancing back, she found he stood much too close for comfort. "*Merci*," she said, sidling away, "I am cold."

After a long, uncomfortable moment, she asked, "What are you doing here, Alain?"

"Seeking shelter from the storm, like you. I was out walking."

The silence returned, and Simone stared out at the wet landscape while Alain stared at her.

Even with her hair hanging in sodden ropes, she was beautiful. Droplets of rain beaded on her eyebrows and lashes as she looked down at Jupiter, who had returned to her side. Framed by the doorway, she made a pretty picture as she stroked the big dog's muddy coat.

As he looked at her, Alain despaired. He never should have come to LaVictoire. He had believed himself strong enough to control his emotions, to forget he had ever wanted Simone. But he was not so strong, after all. He had thought, when he came, that he would prove something to himself. Now he realized he was proving only his weakness for her.

He hated this weakness that made him desire her. He did not want to want her. She belonged to another man, a man he had come to like. Where was his highly valued honor, Alain asked himself savagely, when he would take her if she offered herself?

"I must go," he said abruptly.

"But it's still raining." She turned, surprised by the harsh note in his voice, and found herself gazing into his tortured face. Struck by the hostility in his dark eyes, she stared up at him. "You really do hate me," she whispered.

"*Non.*" Seizing her arms, he drew her to him. His mouth came down on hers, briefly but fiercely, and just as fiercely, he pushed her away from him. "I hate what you do to me."

With that pronouncement, he was gone.

Shaken, Simone watched him stride across the rain-washed lawn. His wet hair was plastered against his head, and the sleeves of his white shirt clung to his muscular arms.

When the rain let up, she folded his jacket with trembling hands and laid it neatly on the seat of one of the carriages. Then she picked up her basket and trudged sadly toward the house.

Simone set a circlet of white roses intertwined with dainty sprigs of ivy upon her head. The garland matched the ivy motif embroidered along the hem of her white satin gown, and her emerald necklace was the perfect complement. But her mind was not on her appearance. It was on the house party. She was glad it was nearly over. This morning, Alain had gotten the bean in his plum cake, and thus, for today, he had been the king. He had entered into the spirit of things, amiably ordering Lisette to be his partner at lunch while the Martin females sulked. Throughout the day, he had taken pains to avoid Simone as she did him.

"You look beautiful, darlin'." Tom came to stand behind her, elegant in his evening clothes.

"And you look very handsome, my love," she answered, kissing his cheek. Then they went to the ballroom.

The guests were assembled when Alain arrived and was shown to his place on the dais. Taking a place in the middle of the room, Tom said so everyone could hear, "You haven't been with us before on Twelfth Night, 'Lain, but what these folks are waiting for is your word as king to begin the festivities."

Affecting a deadpan, haughty mien, Alain looked out over the revelers and announced, "As king of Twelfth

Night, it is our pleasure that our subjects celebrate. And we claim as our royal right the first dance with our hostess."

A murmur ran through the room but subsided when the others realized the newcomer did not know that Tom and Simone always danced the first dance of the evening on their wedding anniversary.

Caught up in the spirit of Twelfth Night, Tom seemed unperturbed by the change in routine. Attentive to the playacting, no one but Lisette noticed how pale Simone's face was behind her mask. Her cheeks burned with two bright spots of color when Alain took her hand and led her out onto the floor.

Graceful and elegant, the couple made one circuit of the room before the other dancers joined them.

"Do not hold me so tightly, Alain," Simone bade through stiff lips. "Everyone is watching."

"Let them watch." He smiled down at her.

Simone gazed up at him in wary confusion. Yesterday he had thrust her away from him. Now, through the slits in his black half mask, his dark eyes were warm with passion, and he held her near.

"You look as lovely tonight as you did the last time we danced at a masque," he murmured. "Do you remember?"

"I remember," she answered, trying to remain unaffected by the memory.

"You wore roses in your hair that night, too." He breathed in the scent deeply.

"Alain, what happened seven years ago is past," she began desperately. "You must forget what was once between us."

"What was once between us is still between us," he said flatly. "You can't deny it."

"*Non*!" Simone protested. "I'm a happily married woman. I have given you no reason to think otherwise."

"Then these were not a signal to me?" He indicated

the jewels that sparkled around her neck.

Her hand going to her throat, Simone remembered she was wearing the emeralds he had given her so long ago. Inwardly, she cursed her preoccupation when she had dressed; she had not thought of the beautiful necklace's potential effect on Alain.

"I'm sorry, 'Lain," she said gently, "I didn't intend them to be any kind of sign."

"I see." His manner abruptly changed, and he held her in rigid arms until the end of their waltz. Releasing her, he sniped, "You urge me to forget while you flaunt what I gave you to remember me by. It seems, madame, you got considerably more from our liaison than I did."

Behind her half mask, Simone's green eyes glittered in fury, but she did not betray her anger when she left the dance floor.

Fulfilling his obligation as king, Alain danced with every woman present. Then he returned to his "throne," where he watched Tom and Simone waltz together. Tom held his wife as if she were a treasure, gazing down at her lovingly. Petite and exquisite, Simone seemed to float across the floor in his arms, her lips curved in a smile for him alone.

As he observed the spellbound couple, Alain forced himself to examine his emotions honestly. It was true he felt a stab of pain at the love shining on both their faces. He even admitted to a stir of envy for Tom. But he could feel no malice toward the man, and no real hatred for Simone. Weary and disgusted by the constant battle raging inside him, he excused himself as soon as it was seemly and returned to the garçonnière.

He was packing the next morning when he heard a stealthy tread on the stairs outside his room. Holding the leather case that contained his shaving gear, he moved to stand behind the door.

Slowly it swung open, and through the crack Alain saw a trim, familiar figure hover hesitantly in the doorway. He waited until she was inside, then he closed the door.

Simone whirled. "I thought you were playing cards with the men in the library," she gasped.

"I am preparing to leave." Alain walked to his bag, open on the bed, and tossed the leather case he carried inside. "What do you want?"

"I . . . I came to bring these back." She handed him a velvet box, its edges now worn. "I hadn't thought of it until last night, but it's not right that I should keep them."

He opened the box and admired the beautiful necklace and earrings. "Your father used to say that emeralds meant lucky in love," he mused. "Perhaps he was right. I have not been as lucky in love as you."

Turning his back on her pained expression, he snapped closed the box and tossed it into his bag as well. "You'd better go now," he said coldly. "Tom might be upset to discover his wife in another man's room."

Simone fled, leaving him to curse the yearning that gnawed at him still.

21

"There y'all are," Tom said, finding his wife and daughter sitting on the floor before the fire. "What are you doing?"

"Drawing pictures, *Papa*," Rory answered for both, holding out a wrinkled paper. "Do you want to see you?"

Tom examined the drawing approvingly. "Very nice, Rory. What are these dots beside me?"

"Pralines coming out of your pocket."

"Is that all you think I'm good for, bringing you sweets?"

"No, sometimes you bring presents for *maman*, too," she answered gravely, settling in Simone's lap.

"It's nice to know where I stand in this house," Tom grumbled good-naturedly. Indicating a letter he took from his pocket, he said to his wife, "Alain sends his best. He'll be here next week to discuss the partnership. I'm beginning to think this can work."

Simone stared into the fire. She had known that Alain would be returning, but she was not ready to face him. He and Tom had kept up a steady correspondence since Tom had convinced him that the screw-propeller oceangoing steamships being tested in England were the future of the shipping industry.

The captain had investigated the cost of commissioning a screw-propeller ship, and he had more than half the money to construct the boat he was already calling *Queen New Orleans*. He was determined to build it and hoped Alain would put up the remainder. If not, he would even deal with bankers, if he had to.

Fortunately, Alain was interested. Unfortunately, he was coming to LaVictoire to discuss the final details for what would become Queen Enterprises.

Tom glanced up from the letter, his distracted expression clearing as he smiled at his wife and daughter. "The two of you look so pretty there. Your eyes are like emeralds.

"Speaking of emeralds, Simone," he said slowly, "I haven't seen you wear yours for a while."

"I—I broke the clasp," she answered quickly. "I must have them repaired the next time I go to New Orleans."

She was glad Tom's attention was already back on the letter, for she imagined her guilt must be visible on her face. She had never lied to him before. There were things she had not told him, such as her relationship with Alain, but she had never lied to him. She discovered she did not like it.

"So we'll need an extra guest room prepared," Tom was saying. He stopped when she looked at him blankly.

"I'm sorry, *cher*, I am afraid I wasn't listening," she confessed, shifting Rory so the sleepy child leaned against her chest. "Why do we need another guest room?"

"One for Hiram, one for Alain, and one for Dominique Cuvillion."

"Dominique?"

"He's still Alain's attorney."

"I know," she answered, sighing. "It's just . . ."

"You may have hurt him when you wouldn't marry him," Tom murmured, "but that was a long time ago. Dominique is an old married man now with a passel of children. Everything will be fine, you'll see."

When he left, Simone sat with her drowsy daughter in her lap. Her chin resting lightly on top of Rory's head, she breathed in the warm, milky smell of the child, but it did not comfort her or chase away the sense of foreboding she felt.

Alain and Dominique were coming to LaVictoire. For a moment, Simone wished she could run away. But it seemed she had been running all her life. Rising awkwardly under the weight of her sleeping child, she resolved she could face anything—even two former suitors—as long as Tom was by her side.

When their guests arrived on the *Bayou Queen*, the entire Franklin family went to the landing to greet them. Rory met Alain with an exuberant cry which ended in a squeal of delight as she was swept up in strong arms. Hiram hugged Simone and Dominique bowed courteously and kissed her hand.

The lawyer was little changed, except that he had lost most of his hair, retaining only a fringe around the sides. And the glass of his spectacles was perhaps a bit thicker.

After the travelers had had time to refresh themselves, Tom showed them to the study. "Aren't you coming?" he asked Simone when she lingered in the hall.

"Are you sure you want me to?" she whispered so the men in the room would not hear.

"Of course. You're my partner, aren't you?"

Hiram was shuffling through his papers when the couple entered, but the Creoles' brows rose in astonishment.

"First of all, gentlemen," Hiram began, his eyes on his papers, "we'll need five directors."

"Surely three will do," Dominique interjected.

"That would hardly be fair to Mr. de Vallière."

Hiram looked up in surprise. "Captain and Mrs. Franklin could outvote him at any time."

"Mrs. Franklin?" Alain and Dominique questioned in unison.

"Simone is to be a partner," Tom stated unequivocally.

"A partner?" Dominique looked as if he could not believe his ears.

"She's been my partner in every business venture I've undertaken for the last seven years," Tom said firmly. "I see no reason she should not be this time as well."

"I do," Alain objected. "A woman doesn't belong in business. She belongs at home, caring for her husband and family."

"I have no complaints, and I don't think Rory does either," Tom drawled.

"*Pardon*, Capitaine Franklin," Dominique said smoothly, "but we are speaking of the establishment of a trans-Atlantic network, worth tens—no, hundreds of thousands of dollars. No offense is intended to your wife, but what does a woman know of these things?"

Aware his wife's temper was about to flare, Tom laid a warning hand on her arm and declared quietly, "Without Simone, there would have been no Franklin Steamboat Company. Without Simone, there will be no Queen Enterprises."

The lawyers held their breath at Tom's uncompromising statement, but Alain ruminated, "Whether one or both of you is responsible for the operation of your businesses, you have made them great successes. *Très bien*, I accept Simone as a partner and a director."

After staring at his client in amazement, Dominique forced his attention back to the remainder of the negotiations.

* * *

"Will you be coming to town before *la saison* is over, Tom?" Alain asked over dinner that evening.

"Probably," the Virginian allowed. "Can't keep Simone in the country all the time. I don't want her to get bored."

"There's no time at LaVictoire to be bored. Still, I know how Tom misses the opera," Simone teased with a theatrical sigh. "And the gossip from the custom-house."

"Speaking of gossip," Alain said suddenly, "have you heard the latest rumor, Simone? Marcel Baudin is dead."

Her face blanched. "But . . . how? When?"

"It's said he drowned trying to escape the asylum. I am not sure I will believe it, however, until his body is recovered," he said pointedly.

"So he wasn't invincible, after all," Tom muttered, recalling his encounter with the madman.

"Poor, unhappy Marcel . . ." Simone murmured, lost in thought on this last chapter of so long and sad a story.

"How can you say that," Alain lashed out, "after all he put you through?"

"I still feel sorry for him." Her green eyes flashed. "Think how troubled, how tormented, he must have been to behave the way he did."

"Already I'm beginning to question the wisdom of taking a soft-hearted female as a business partner," Alain muttered.

"This conversation is becoming entirely too serious," Tom insisted, rising. "Shall we have coffee in the parlor, gentlemen?"

While Tom, Hiram, and Alain talked with enthusiasm about horses, Dominique joined Simone on the settee.

"More *café*, M'sieur Cuvillion?" she asked brightly.

"Can't you call me Dominique?" he requested. "You did at one time."

"*Oui.*" Simone shifted uncomfortably.

"I've been wanting to talk to you all day."

"Oh?" She stared hard at Tom across the room, hoping to catch his eye.

"I want to thank you for being so wise those many years ago."

"Wise?" She looked at the bookish man.

"You knew a marriage between us would not work if you didn't return my feelings. I married Bernadette, and now even I see the wisdom of letting love grow over time. She is a wonderful woman."

"She was a wonderful girl," Simone said sincerely, even as she remembered the terrible night Dominique had proposed. "I would love to see her again. Perhaps you can bring her for a visit."

"I'm sure she would like that, when she feels she can leave our youngest child. We have five now, you know."

They sat in silence for a moment, pondering the vagaries of fate. At last Dominique said with a reminiscent smile, "I remember the first time Alain came to see me about you, before I ever met you."

"Alain went to see you about me?"

"To arrange the 'inheritance' for his ward," he chuckled. "I could not understand why he would entrust so much money to a child. But you weren't a child at all."

"What do you mean, 'to arrange the inheritance'?"

Dominique's smile faded as Simone's eyes bored into him.

"My father didn't leave me anything, did he?" she asked in sudden comprehension.

"*Non,*" the lawyer admitted, clearly embarrassed by the revelation. He watched Simone anxiously, certain her temper was about to explode. "Alain . . . Alain wanted to be sure you were cared for, in case anything happened to him. He said you were too proud to accept money from him, so we set up the trust for you."

"I see. . . ." Then she shrugged, as if the subject were unimportant. "Well, what's past is past. More *café*, anyone?" she asked.

Simone's smile felt painted on her face as her thoughts roiled. The money she had invested in the *Emerald Queen* had not been her own, after all. And Alain, the arrogant cad, had known it even as he had accepted her as a partner that very afternoon.

She hated the idea that the money—that her new life!—had come from him. Somehow she would have to repay him. She could not bear to remain in his debt now that she knew.

The next day, while the men took a respite from work to go hunting, Simone rode over to Hideaway.

"Oh, *ma petite*, you didn't!" Lisette protested, laughing. "You sent the amount of your 'inheritance' to a home for unwed mothers—as a contribution from Alain de Vallière?"

"*Oui*," Simone acknowledged with a saucy nod. "He has always had a soft spot in his heart for girls in trouble, *non*?" she said mischievously.

"I wish I could be there when he receives the thank-you note from the good sisters," Lisette said, her gray eyes sparkling.

"So do I," Simone answered with a grin. "So do I."

Neither woman would have wished to be present if they could have anticipated the thunderous expression on Alain's face when he opened his mail the next week. When he first read the effusive letter of appreciation, he was baffled. Then he became angry. A donation to a home for unwed mothers! Whose idea of a joke was this? When he got his hands on the prankster, he would throttle him.

By week's end, he would have throttled almost anyone. Not only did the sisters speak widely of him in the most glowing terms imaginable, they also announced their intention to hold a party in his honor.

When that information reached him, Alain went in

person to straighten out the misunderstanding. Unfortunately, the mother superior merely admonished him that false modesty was a sin. Besides, the invitations had already been sent.

By afternoon, the news was all over the Vieux Carré and spreading like wildfire toward the American Section. A few brave souls teased the man about his choice of charities, but seeing his grim expression, they swiftly apologized. No one wanted to find himself under the Oaks with Alain de Vallière.

Alain was still in a foul temper when Tom and Simone arrived a few days later for the first board of directors meeting for Queen Enterprises. He kept his promise to meet them at the wharf, but, his mood was not improved by the rain, the *Bayou Queen*'s tardiness, or the mountain of luggage they brought for their stay. When Jupiter bounded off the boat, it was the last straw.

"I am not taking him in my new coach," Alain announced brusquely. "I don't want muddy paw prints all over the upholstery."

"I want to stay with Jupiter," Rory said at once, her lower lip trembling at the thought of leaving the big dog.

"Jupiter will follow in the coach with the luggage," Simone soothed her daughter.

"I thought you'd want to ride with Uncle Alain," Tom cajoled. "Didn't you say you loved him almost as much as me?"

"*Oui*." Rory sniffled and slipped her small hand into Alain's.

When Simone joined the others in the carriage, she looked back regretfully at the *Bayou Queen*. As they had drifted along on the current this afternoon while the engineer tried to repair the engine, Tom had told her that this would be the faithful old packet's last trip. She knew it was silly, but her throat burned with unshed tears at the thought of retiring Tom's first boat.

"You're telling me that someone made a contribution in your name to this home for unwed mothers, and you don't know who it was?" Tom guffawed, suddenly drawing her attention to the conversation.

"If I knew, I would have met him under the Oaks by now," Alain growled. "As I was saying, there is a reception tonight in my honor, and I would like you to go with me."

"What do you think, Simone? Do you need time to rest?"

"We should go. Charity functions attract businessmen, and we could always use new contacts," she improvised. Not for the world would she miss this event!

"That's my girl." Tom grinned. "All right, 'Lain, we'll be happy to join you."

In fact, Simone thought smugly, we can hardly wait.

When Alain's carriage pulled under the porte cochere at the house on St. Charles Avenue, Wakefield hurried out to meet them. "Welcome home, Mrs. Franklin, Captain."

"What about me, Wakefield?" Rory tugged on his coattail.

The old man's lined face arranged itself into a fond smile. "Welcome home, Miss Rory. And good afternoon to you, Mr. de Vallière. Come in. There's a fire in the library to take away the chill of the rain."

As they trooped into the elegant house, Tom stopped and inspected a shiny object hanging on the doorjamb. "Wakefield," he asked casually, "why is there a sifter hanging on the door?"

The butler looked embarrassed. "Well, sir, the slaves consider that it was put there to keep away the *loup-garou*. You know, the werewolf. I consider it was put there to appease the slaves. They've been talking among themselves about, er, 'ha'nts.' They're quite upset over the reports in the newspapers of sightings of the beast and of nocturnal attacks near the back of town."

"How long has this been going on?" Simone asked.

"For several weeks, madame. Just two nights ago, one of the maids swore she saw a face in the window. But when we investigated, there was no sign of anyone."

Her eyes round, Rory said in a hushed voice, "I'm glad Jupiter is coming. He will protect us."

That night, the ferocious watchdog was sound asleep beside Rory's bed when Tom and Simone left with Alain for the party. Neither he nor the little girl awoke as the carriage rolled away down the drive.

The rain had stopped, and the night was cool. The breeze carried Simone's rose scent to Alain, reminding him disturbingly of other nights. He was glad when they reached the old mansion that served as the charity home. Every window was lit with a candle and the building seemed an earthly extension of the starlit sky.

Alain was met by the mother superior and whisked away at once. After several rhapsodic introductions, he asked to speak to her privately.

"Madame, you must temper your praise," he requested. "What I told you before was not false modesty. I'm here tonight because you named me your guest of honor, but I did not send you any money."

"But you are the only person I know to thank," the woman said, confounded. "Someone certainly made a generous contribution, and your name, Monsieur de Vallière, was on the envelope."

"The envelope?" He seized on the tidbit. "Do you still have it?"

"I am sure I do." Leading him to her spare, tiny office, she dug in a drawer and withdrew a small square envelope. The handwriting on its face was feminine, and the scent wafting from the paper was the fragrance of roses. Simone's scent.

"May I have this?" Alain asked, gripping it tightly.

"If—if you wish," the nun stammered, taken aback by the ominous glint in his eyes.

The furious man went in search of his tormentor. He

found her in the dining room, standing alone near the door to the courtyard. Going directly to her, he took her elbow and guided her outside, unmindful of whether anyone watched.

"What are you doing?" Simone demanded, wrenching from his grip in the dark courtyard.

"The question, madame, is what have *you* done?" He waved the envelope accusingly under her nose.

Seeing it would do no good to deny it, she lifted a defiant gaze to his. "Just as you knew I would not take my 'inheritance' from you, I knew you would not accept repayment from me. You made your arrangements," she said with a shrug, "and I made mine."

"You made me a laughingstock," he growled.

"I made you a benefactor to the needy," she retorted, sweeping past him toward the house.

His face dark with anger, he whirled her to face him. "I ought to wring your pretty neck."

"I am surprised you don't try. You always were a bully."

They scowled at each other, almost nose to nose.

"Damn it, Simone." Alain's voice was strangled. Suddenly he was holding her in his arms, and his mouth was upon hers. His lips were at first hard and demanding, but they softened to a kiss of aching tenderness.

Different than the brutal kisses he had stolen in his hotel room or in the carriage house, this one shook Simone far more. Involuntarily, she found herself beginning to respond. Summoning all her will, she pulled away and glared at him accusingly. "How could you?"

"The same way you could . . . quite by accident," he answered hoarsely. "I beg your pardon, madame, and I assure you, it will not happen again. You go in. I will follow in a moment. We don't want to give the gossip mill any more fodder."

Inwardly trembling but with her head held high, Simone hurried through the French doors into the house. Alain remained in the courtyard, smoking moodily for a time until he collected himself sufficiently to return to the damnable party given in his honor.

Growling, Jupiter rose from his spot beside the bed and padded in front of the windows.

"What's the matter, Jupe?" Tom whispered sleepily. Rising, he went to look out. The moon was behind the clouds, and the lawn below was dark.

With a glance at his sleeping wife, Tom opened the bedroom door for the dog and followed him downstairs.

"What is it, boy?" Tom asked as Jupiter scratched at the French doors in the dining room. The dog pranced in excitement, hackles raised and still growling. Tom let him out, and the animal charged into the night, his bark bugling.

Tom followed, looking around as the damp earth squished beneath his bare toes. In the darkness, he could hear Jupiter, but the dog was nowhere in sight. Behind him, in the house, Simone opened a window and leaned out.

"What is it, Tom?"

"Jupiter heard something. Sounds like he's got it treed. We'll be in as soon as I round him up."

Jupiter finally returned to Tom's side, now silent, his tail wagging. The moon broke through the clouds as they started back to the house, and in the mud near the door, the man saw footprints. Someone in boots. The prints were not his, and they certainly were not Jupiter's. He scanned the area, but whoever had been there was clearly long gone.

Deciding to say nothing to worry Simone or disturb the household, he headed back to bed, having secured the doors behind him.

Rising early the next morning, he strolled around the perimeter of the property. Discovering a gate swinging open, he ordered Rufus, a young black slave, to have the locks replaced with sturdier ones. Then he returned to the house where Simone waited for him in the foyer.

"There you are, Tom. Are you ready?"

"Don't you look pretty in your Sunday-go-to-meeting clothes," he teased. "Is this to impress our new partner?"

"No." She made a face at him. "It's to impress my old one. Come on, we're going to be late."

When their carriage reached Canal Street, the broad avenue was nearly devoid of its usual drays and cabs. In its center, a crowd was massing for the St. Patrick's Day Parade, an event that was becoming a tradition among the Irish immigrants in New Orleans.

As the documents formalizing Queen Enterprises were signed and witnessed in Hiram Anderson's spacious new office, the sounds of revelry could be heard from outside. Their business completed, Hiram called for champagne.

"I thought you might like to toast this auspicious occasion," he suggested.

Everyone lifted a glass and looked to Tom. Smiling broadly, the captain said, "To Queen Enterprises, may we all—"

"Make a fortune," they all chimed in, laughing.

Grimacing good-naturedly at their teasing, he added, "And to Simone, the loveliest member of the board."

"And the bravest," Alain murmured behind her. Lifting his glass, he said so only she could hear, "You always did flirt with danger, *ma chère.*"

That evening, Simone thought it was Alain who flirted with danger. She and Tom were invited, along with the Andersons, to his home for a celebration. Besides Dominique and Bernadette, he had invited Emilie Thibault, Bernadette's cousin, as his dinner partner.

Emilie was a pale, fragile-looking woman in her midtwenties, past the usual marriageable age for a Creole woman. Though she was not a great beauty, she was not unattractive. In her youth she had turned down several offers of marriage, waiting for the one that had not come. Now there was a quiet desperation about her, for it would not be long before she would be expected to put away her maidenly attire and don the lace spinster's cap.

Through dinner she flirted with Alain, and, prompted by the sight of Tom and Simone together, he responded. Fleetingly he wondered if he could ever have the same closeness with Emilie, who so clearly wished it.

He noticed the married couple's every exchange. When the women adjourned to the parlor after dinner, Tom winked at his wife, as if they had a private secret between them. When the men joined the ladies, he stood behind her chair, one hand on her shoulder. Without even realizing it, she laid her hand on his as she talked.

Suddenly feeling he must get away for a moment, Alain rose to his feet and requested, "Bernadette, will you pour the *café*?"

Emilie looked chagrinned, for she had expected to serve as Alain's hostess, but her face brightened when he asked, "Emilie, would you join me in the courtyard for a breath of fresh air?"

With a hopeful gleam in her eyes, Bernadette watched the couple step outside. When the coffee had been served, she confided to Simone and Dulcie, "Surely Alain will speak for *ma cousine* soon, perhaps even tonight."

Ever romantic, Dulcie brightened at the prospect of a wedding, but Simone felt oddly relieved when Emilie returned a little later, sullen and obviously without a fiancé.

Later, when the others were engaged in conversations, Emilie asked Simone quietly, "You have known Alain for years, have you not, Madame Franklin?"

"Since I was a child," Simone answered cautiously.

"Then perhaps you can tell me," Emilie appealed miserably, "whom did he love so much that he cannot love another?"

"I . . . I cannot say," Simone responded.

"He is still in love with someone, I know it," the other woman lamented. "She seems always to be between us. He may carry with him the memory of a living, breathing woman, but I feel as if I fight a ghost."

"Perhaps 'Lain just needs time," Simone said, sorry for the woman. "No man can love a memory—or a ghost—forever."

"I fear Alain will," Emilie replied sadly.

A shaggy, unkempt figure, unrecognizable as the elegant Creole he had once been, Marcel Baudin lingered in the shadows beside the levee. Across the street, he could see the comings and goings from the offices of Franklin Steamboats. He saw the glow of a lamp. Simone worked inside. He knew it.

He had been frustrated by the new locks on the gates at her home, and he had wondered how he would ever reach her. Then she began going to the office every day. He had been watching her, following her, and now he had begun a new game.

Since everyone thought him dead, it seemed he was not only invincible, but invisible. Sometimes he had been so close to Simone he might have touched her, but the time had not been right. Other times, he had ducked from sight just when she looked in his direction. She must have felt his presence. Her perplexed expression when she saw no one there greatly pleased Marcel.

Soon he would replace that perplexity with fear. He had decided, at last, that he would have Simone Devereaux—and then he must kill her. But first she must tremble before her murderer, she must hear the reason for her destruction. She must suffer, as she had made him suffer. If he could not have her, then no one could, not even her American husband. Only when she was dead, Marcel had concluded, would he lose this craving that brought him such pain. The very thought of her caused his blood to rush, pounding, to his head. Moaning, Marcel rubbed his temples and waited. He would be patient, but he must be rid of her.

In the office, Simone frowned down at a bill of lading. Obadiah's handwriting was still deplorable. The two of them had been managing the office since Jim Reynolds returned to North Carolina. Tom was busy with Queen Enterprises, and Ethan, who would take over this office, had not yet arrived.

During the past month, Simone had enjoyed working with Obie, now the warehouse manager, and he wholeheartedly welcomed her direction. But not everyone was so willing to accept a woman here. In moments of discouragement, she sometimes wondered if she could function in business at all without her husband's supporting presence.

Taking the bill, she stepped out of the office and walked toward the row of warehouses. The evening was cool for late July, and fog rolled in from the river, swirling around the pylons on the piers across the way, turning them into rows of ghostly sentinels.

Thinking she saw a form in the darkness as she approached the warehouses, she called out "Obie?" But there was no response.

Suddenly apprehensive, she glanced over her shoulder. The lit office windows seemed far away, and her sense of foreboding was nearly overpowering.

At the first warehouse, she slid the door back and called again, her voice sounding high and unnatural in the fog. When there was no answer, she bit her lower lip to keep from shouting Obadiah's name until he came.

How foolish to let darkness and a little fog frighten

her. Still, she could not shake the feeling that someone was watching her.

Then she heard it. A sound like a low laugh. She halted, listening, but there was no other sound. Wavering irresolutely, she told herself she was being ridiculous, but she could not bring herself to pass the dark passageway between the buildings. She would wait for Obadiah in the office.

Forcing herself to stay calm, she retraced her steps. She had almost reached the office when a hand touched her shoulder. Gasping, she whirled. "Obadiah!"

"Miss Simone, where you been?" he asked reproachfully.

"Looking for you." She could have wept with relief, but she did not voice her feelings. They seemed silly as they walked toward the office.

"This very mornin' when I picked you up, I heard Cap'n Tom say he don't want you workin' alone in the office at night," Obadiah scolded. "What you think he'd say if he knew you was out wanderin' alone in the yard?"

"I'm not alone. You're here," she pointed out.

"And he'll probably skin me alive for lettin' you stay so late. Get your things, and lemme drive you home now."

In the dark passage, Marcel laughed again. Simone did not know how close to death she had come tonight.

When Simone arrived at home that night, Jupiter padded out to meet her, sitting beside her while she sorted through the mail, his tail thumping on the foyer floor. The dog's ears pricked up and the thumping increased when Tom arrived moments later.

"Caught in the act," her husband greeted her, kissing her cheek. "I see you've been keeping long hours again."

"Not as long as yours." She brushed the curl back from his forehead. "You look so tired."

"I think I'm getting my second wind." Smiling, he pulled her to him and kissed her in earnest.

"I've missed you, *mon amour*," Simone breathed. "I feel I haven't seen you for a month."

"I know, but things'll settle down with the new business, and Ethan will be here soon. Then we can go home to LaVictoire, just you and me and—"

"Papa, Maman!" An elated cry cut through their quiet moment.

"And Rory," they said in unison, laughing as they looked up at their nightgown-clad daughter, who stood on the landing, clapping gleefully. Hand in hand, her parents mounted the stairs toward her.

"Why aren't you in bed, young lady?" Tom's smile destroyed the stern effect he sought to create.

"I can't sleep until I have a story. *Maman* told me one last night. I want you to tell me one tonight."

"It'll cost you a kiss," her father laughed, scooping her up. Throwing her arms around his neck, Rory kissed him soundly.

"Mmm, that was good enough for two stories. Now kiss *Maman* good night," he said, holding her toward Simone so she could do so.

"Now *I'll* kiss *Maman* good night." He brushed his wife's lips with his and carried the squirming child toward the nursery.

Wearing a cool, feminine nightgown, Simone was brushing her hair when Tom joined her in the bedroom.

Bending, he pressed a kiss on her bare shoulder. "I didn't get a chance to tell you I've missed you, too."

They slipped into bed and into each other's arms. Cuddled together, they talked in the quiet, comfortable, and comforting manner of couples long and happily married.

"Tom," Simone said softly, "I am not sure yet, so I probably shouldn't even tell you, but I think I'm going to have another baby."

She did not have to see his face to know he was beaming as he rose on his elbow above her, straining to see through the darkness. "That's wonderful, darlin'."

"I think so." She snuggled happily against him.

Lying down, he put his arm around her and tucked her even closer. "I hope it's a boy this time." His whisper drifted on the night breeze. "We'll name him John Paul Jones Franklin."

"Jean-Paul is a nice name," she said, giving it the French pronunciation.

"Figured you'd like it." He chuckled. "Named after a naval hero—and his mother. What a scrapper the boy will be!"

22

Ethan and Gisèle returned to New Orleans during one of the hottest Augusts in memory and moved into the house on St. Charles Avenue with Tom and Simone until they could buy their own. Gisèle was expecting their fourth child shortly, and she was glad to be with her dear friends.

With Ethan managing the office, Simone no longer spent her days there. She enjoyed being at home, and, with five extra guests and their servants in the house, she was so busy, she scarcely heeded the troubling feeling that someone was watching her.

One sultry afternoon, she and Gisèle sat sipping lemonade, beneath an oak tree in the backyard, watching Gisèle's youngest, Paul Revere, try to ride the patient Jupiter.

"Oh! The baby is kicking again." Gisèle placed a hand on her side. "I think this one will be an acrobat. Not very proper pastime for a girl, *oui*?"

"How do you know it will be a girl?"

"I don't, but I hope. I would like a little girl." Gisèle smiled as she watched Simone's rambunctious daughter. "Do you ever wish for another child?"

"I don't think I will have to wish much longer," Simone confided with a smile.

"That is wonderful!" The pregnant woman sat up awkwardly. "Tom must be thrilled."

"Yes, he'd like to have a whole houseful of children."

"I hope more of them are girls," Gisèle teased. "Think how hard he would have to work to find names for so many boys."

"*Oui*, we don't want a Benjamin Franklin Franklin," Simone chuckled.

"Excuse me, madame." Wakefield approached with a small envelope in hand. "A boy just delivered this."

"*Merci*." Opening it, Simone read it and groaned aloud.

"Is something wrong?" Gisèle asked worriedly.

"We're all invited to a party at the Andersons."

"A party? What is that to groan about?"

"It is to be a house party, and the 'entertainment' is to be fortune-telling. It seems Dulcie has hired Marie LeVeau for the evening," Simone answered with a shudder.

"Why are Dulcie and Barbara so fascinated by voodoo?" Gisèle asked in bafflement. "It is slave magic."

Dulcie's invitation left Simone feeling uneasy throughout the day and into the evening. After dinner the entire Franklin family sat on the dark veranda; they had not lit a lamp for fear a cloud of gnats would engulf them.

Beside his mistress, Jupiter suddenly got to his feet, growling, his hackles rising. As everyone tried to see what had affected the dog, Simone thought she glimpsed a shadowy figure near the front gate. But when a lamplighter appeared around the corner, no one was there.

"You must go," Gisèle argued. "This is your last party before harvest begins."

"I don't like leaving you like this," Simone muttered, gazing down at her friend's mounded figure outstretched on the bed.

Gisèle rolled her eyes. "I only have a backache. Ethan will be here, and he's been through this more than once. If you don't go, who will report to me what happens?"

"Très bien." Simone smiled at her. "I'll tell you every detail when I come home."

Stripped to her petticoat against the heat, Simone bustled about their room at the Andersons' plantation.

"Come over here, darlin'." Her husband patted the mattress beside him. "It's too hot to be moving around so much."

"I know that gleam in your eyes, Thomas Jefferson Franklin," she chided in mock exasperation. "You'll make us late for dinner."

"There's plenty of time," he drawled. With a playful wag of his eyebrows, he patted the mattress again.

"I thought you said it was too hot to be moving around," Simone protested with a grin. Perching on the edge of the bed, she rained kisses all over the face smiling at her from the pillow.

Laughing, Tom captured her in his arms and rolled until she was beside him on the bed. "It's never too hot for what I've got in mind. Just get rid of a few more clothes."

They shed their few garments rapidly, reveling in their joyful merging. Their skin sheened with perspiration, the lovers sought—and found—sweet release in each other. Then, their limbs still intertwined, they lay quietly, in the dusk, murmuring intimate words of love.

Tom and Simone joined the others downstairs just in time for dinner. The women were dressed in their finest gowns and glittered with jewelry. The men in their evening clothes were elegant and courtly. And the mood was festive.

After the meal, Dulcie announced, "Marie LeVeau will see each guest separately in the second parlor, beginning with the ladies. I'm afraid you gentlemen will have to wait. Please enjoy your brandy and cigars."

"I don't want to do this," Simone muttered to her husband as she rose, "but I don't want to hurt Dulcie's feelings."

"Where's your sense of adventure?" he teased softly. "Even Alain is going to have his fortune read."

"He said he didn't believe in fortune-telling," she contended with a sour expression.

"Maybe he wants to know if Emilie's going to win in the end," Tom whispered merrily. "That gal's almost as stubborn as you."

Simone waited tensely while the other women went in to see Marie LeVeau, one after another. Most were thrilled by their fortunes, but when Emilie returned to the first parlor, her face was grim. Evidently Marie LeVeau saw no wedding for her.

At last the moment Simone had dreaded arrived. Stepping through the doorway, she hesitated a moment. The second parlor was stifling and almost unrecognizable. Catholic icons, primitive pictures, and dozens of candles surrounded the voodooienne in the darkened room.

"If you wish to know the secret of the obeah, madame, come and I will tell you what I see," Marie LeVeau intoned in the imperious voice reserved for her white patrons.

"I don't want my fortune told," Simone answered softly.

"Let us speak of the past then, madame," the woman proposed indifferently. Before Simone could answer, Marie had closed her eyes. "Everything about you is unclear," she muttered. "You are not always what you seem."

"Who of us is?" Simone refused to be swayed.

"You have longed for revenge, but it eludes you. You have blood on your hands, and still revenge will not be yours." Opening her eyes, she looked at Simone intently. "You!" she whispered. "I should have known. You will not let me tell your future, because you fear it."

"That's enough," Simone commanded shakily, preparing to leave.

"Wait!" Marie insisted. "You have changed from the last time we met, *ma petite*, but I don't forget the obeah once it has spoken. Hear me well, you bring danger to those you love."

"*Non*," Simone whispered, her green eyes wide with horror.

"Can you deny it?"

Simone was silent, thinking of Alain's misfortunes.

"I have told you before, the obeah never lies," the voodoo queen said. Then, as at their last meeting, she closed her eyes and leaned back in her chair wearily.

With trembling fingers, Simone placed a coin on the table and stepped silently into the hall.

As she paused to collect herself, Simone heard Tom's voice, and she spotted him through the open front door on the veranda with their slave, Rufus.

"Go to the stable and tell them to get our carriage ready," he instructed. "Then ride back and tell Ethan we're coming."

"What is it, Tom?" Simone asked when he came inside.

"Gisèle has gone into labor early. The doctor is with her, but we need to get home."

"At once," she agreed. "We can send the servants for our things tomorrow."

They offered hurried apologies to their host and hostess, then hastened out to the deserted *allée*.

The night was dark, and, after the extreme heat of the day, the evening had grown cool. A breeze came from the river, bearing wisps of fog to play among the trees.

"What's taking those grooms so long?" Tom fretted. "I could've hitched the team myself by now."

They began to walk through the shadows at the side of the house toward the stables. Suddenly a menacing, shaggy form loomed in their path, brandishing a sword. Even in the darkness, Simone could identify the scarred face. . . . Marcel Baudin!

"I have waited a long time to meet you again, Simone Devereaux," he snarled.

"What the hell?" Tom exploded, shoving his wife safely behind him. "What are you supposed to be?" He scowled at the tattered madman without recognizing him. "Go on! Get out of here!"

"It's Marcel Baudin." Simone tried to step around Tom to face the Creole, but he blocked her way with a shielding arm.

"You are Simone's husband?" Marcel eyed him arrogantly.

"I am."

"Your wife owes me a debt of blood for the scar you see, and I will make her pay. But I think I will kill you first. I demand satisfaction, m'sieur," he pronounced haughtily.

"I never cared much for the idea of dueling, but I reckon satisfaction can be arranged," the Virginian drawled. His fist lashed out and rammed Marcel squarely in the face, sending him sprawling in the dust, his sword landing a few feet away.

"Damn, that was satisfying." As he nursed his fist, Tom grinned over his shoulder at his wife. "So much for the polecat who's been bothering you all these years. I thought he was dead."

"Tom, watch out!" Simone cried as Marcel struggled to his feet and fumbled inside his jacket.

The captain turned just as the other man drew a pistol. Before he could defend himself, the gun fired with a sharp report and a small flare at its muzzle. Tom crumpled to the ground at Simone's feet.

"Tom!" she screamed, dropping to her knees beside her fallen husband.

"Now for you, *ma chère*," Marcel sneered. Stepping closer, he pointed the gun at her head, oblivious to the sounds coming from the house behind them. "I believe I will kill you with the weapon the crude Kaintocks favor. You might even say you chose your fate when you married an American. *L'américan*," he repeated bitterly. "How could you do such a thing?"

"What does my marriage . . . What do *I* have to do with you?" she cried looking around desperately for a weapon.

"You have everything to do with me. Because of you, they say I am mad. I am not mad. My logic is quite unflawed," he assured her, chillingly rational in his derangement. "If I cannot have you, you must die. When you are dead, I shall be free of you."

"Simone, Tom!" Alain's voice rang out from the front of the house. With a feral snarl, Marcel whirled and pointed the gun in his direction instead.

When her assailant's back was turned, Simone leapt to her feet and scooped his sword from the ground. Lunging toward him, she brought the dull weapon down on his arm, managing to cut him slightly and knock the gun from his hand. Marcel howled in enraged pain and, seeing himself soon to be outnumbered, fled into the darkness.

Alain was beside her at once as she dropped to kneel again by Tom's side. Weeping and conscious only of her injured husband, she pressed a lacy handkerchief against his chest in an effort to stem the blood pumping from his wound. Nearby, Hiram bellowed for a slave to ride for a doctor.

Tom's eyelids fluttered open, and he grinned weakly at his distraught wife. "What's all the commotion, sugar?"

"Be still, my love," she whispered. "We've sent for a doctor."

"Too . . . late for that," he said hoarsely. "Tell me, darlin', do you love me?"

"With all my heart. Be still now," she ordered tenderly, tears streaming down her face.

"I love you, too, Simone." He moved his hand heavily to cover hers. "What . . . are you going to do without me? You need . . . someone to keep you in line."

"Don't talk like that, Tom. You are not going to die. I won't let you," she vowed.

"You are the stubbornest woman . . ." He panted from the effort. He rolled his head, and his glazed eyes found Alain. "Will you . . . take care of Simone and my children for me, 'Lain?"

"*Oui, mon ami*," Alain choked.

"That's . . . fine." Tom drew a deep, rattling breath. "Think I'll just . . . lie here now and enjoy all the attention."

His blue eyes closed, and he looked as if he were peacefully sleeping. But beneath the blood-soaked handkerchief, Simone no longer felt the labored rise and fall of his chest, and his hand, covering hers, became limp.

"*Non!*" Simone whispered in disbelief. "*Non*, Tom!"

Slowly, Alain rose to his feet, pulling her up with him. Briefly, he sheltered her against his chest. Then, gripping her arms, he forced her to turn her blank eyes toward his. "I could not see clearly in the darkness, Simone. Was it Marcel?"

At her mute nod, he grimly beckoned Dulcie to take her inside.

Marie LeVeau stood on the veranda, watching as the men organized a search party. "The obeah never lies," she muttered.

* * *

Dry-eyed and withdrawn, Simone sat beside Tom's body in one of the bedrooms while the men searched through the night and slaves were dispatched to fetch the sheriff and Ethan. A candle was lit on the bedside table, and drink and fresh clothing were brought, but she sat, still wearing her blood-stained gown, and stared into a dark corner of the room.

Indifferent to what was happening around her, she roused herself from her abstraction only long enough to answer the sheriff's questions. When he left, Dulcie tried to convince her to rest, but Simone would not move from her husband's side.

She could hear the murmur of conversation from downstairs and the sound of the clock striking. Gisèle's baby must have been born by now, she realized. It had probably come into the world as Tom was leaving it. She smiled sadly; the idea would have appealed to him.

Near dawn, Alain returned. "We didn't find him," he said wearily when he entered the room. The search party had followed a trail of blood to the edge of the swamp, but they never found Marcel. Most believed he perished there, but Alain was unconvinced. He said none of this to Simone as they sat together silently, grieving. Finally he, too, went downstairs, giving her time alone to deal with her shock and sorrow.

As soon as he was sure Gisèle and the baby were all right, Ethan arrived at the Anderson plantation at a gallop and raced to his cousin's side. The candle on the bedside table had guttered, and Simone sat, silent, in the gloom. Then she asked, "Is it a boy or a girl?"

"Another boy," Ethan answered, going to his cousin's widow.

Her green eyes shadowed by weariness and pain, she smiled up at him. "Are mother and baby well?"

"They are fine," he replied, his heart aching for her. "Simone, Gisèle and I would like to name him Thomas Jefferson, if you don't mind."

There was a hint of her dazzling smile when she

agreed. "I don't mind at all, Ethan, and I know Tom would like it."

"I've come to take you home," he said awkwardly, "and to help you make arrangements."

"*Merci. Mais, encore un moment* . . . just a little longer . . ." Her voice trailed off and she turned dull eyes to the shadows. Sorrowfully, Ethan went to join the others downstairs.

The sun was up when Simone appeared in the doorway to the dining room. Still dressed in their rumpled finery from the evening before, the house party had just finished breakfast. They fell silent and regarded the petite woman with concern. She had finally changed from her ruined evening gown. Wearing a day dress, she looked calm and efficient, but her eyes were flat and lifeless, without a trace of their usual emerald brilliance.

"*Bonjour.*" Her gaze swept all assembled around the table.

"Simone," Dulcie cajoled, "come and have something to eat."

"*Non, merci,*" she answered politely. "Hiram, Alain, Ethan, I'm sorry to disturb your breakfast, but I would like to speak to all three of you before I leave."

"You're not disturbing us, Simone," Hiram assured her. "Shall we step into my study, gentlemen?"

Simone sat in a chair near the window, her hands clasped in her lap. The men listened silently as she spoke to each in turn.

"Hiram, I know, as Tom's attorney, you have many duties, but I would trouble you to send for the undertaker so his body can be prepared for return to LaVictoire.

"Ethan, I'm sorry, but the entire operation of Franklin Steamboats rests with you for the time being.

"A heavy burden falls on you, as well, Alain. I must ask you to look after Queen Enterprises without Tom or me. I know you and Hiram and Dominique will man-

age quite well while I am at LaVictoire. I cannot think
of such things now."

"Nor do you have to, my dear, as long as you have
us," Hiram said staunchly.

"Is there anything else we can do?" Alain asked quietly as Simone rose and walked toward the door.

"There is one thing," she requested, pausing. "Post a
reward of ten thousand dollars for Marcel's capture."
Then, squaring her slender shoulders, she departed.

The hot, humid breeze rippling the limp flag on the
stern provided the only relief from the stifling heat as
the *Bayou Queen* made its way upriver on its final trip
to LaVictoire. On the levee, those who watched the
black-draped steamboat's progress removed their hats
in honor of the man whose body it bore home.

Captain Franklin's black-clad widow could sometimes be seen at the railing, staring out at the graceful
homes and the white carpets of cotton they passed. At
times, her little daughter, subdued and bewildered,
stood beside her.

At LaVictoire, a mournful procession waited: Batiste
and Rosette; Lisette and Monsieur Guilbeau; the
Haleys, father and son; Ardoin Naquin; Mr. Martin;
several other of the neighbors and the slaves. Tom's
body was interred in a crypt beside the chapel. Before
the day was out, Batiste had taken the bell from the
Bayou Queen and affixed it outside the tomb at
Simone's request.

That evening, Hiram called Simone, Alain,
Ethan, and Batiste into the study for the reading of
Tom's will. To Batiste, he had left a generous
bequest. His will instructed that his Franklin Steamboats shares be divided between Simone and Ethan,
giving his cousin one quarter ownership of the company. His Queen Enterprises shares were to be split
between Simone and Alain, making them equal

partners. All else, he left to his widow.

Simone sat quietly through the reading. Studying her, Alain was not sure she heard, for she had no reaction. When the attorney finished, she murmured, "*Merci*, Hiram," and departed wearily.

Boarding a steamboat in the sweltering sun, Alain was troubled as he and Simone's other guests set out for New Orleans. Last night, unable to sleep, he had walked the grounds of LaVictoire and discovered her sitting beside Tom's grave, staring at the moon reflected on the bayou nearby.

Reluctant to disturb her, he had kept his distance at first, watching over her silently. At last he stepped forward. "Don't you think you should come back to the house now, Simone?"

"*Non.*" She did not even look at him.

"If you won't think of yourself, at least think of the baby.

"Tom did ask me to care for his children, didn't he?" he asked when she turned to glare at him through the darkness.

"I will come soon," she answered with a sigh. "Please, Alain, I need to be alone."

He had gone back to his room, but he had waited beside the window until he saw Simone return near dawn.

Now, as the current carried the boat southward and LaVictoire disappeared from view, the big Creole sighed heavily. Four terrible days had passed since Tom's death, and the numbness was wearing off. But if he felt profound sorrow and weariness, what must Simone be feeling? He wished he had been able to convince her to let him stay for a while.

For days after the funeral, Simone wandered through empty rooms of the house she had shared with Tom. She spent hours in his study, sitting in his old chair, holding the questioning Rory on her lap and staring off into space.

She was in the study when the cramps seized her, doubling her over, holding her in a painful grip until her body rejected the fatherless child she was carrying.

One crisp fall morning, Alain paced in the parlor, pondering the wisdom of arriving at LaVictoire uninvited. But he had heard nothing from Simone for six weeks, and he had to know if she was well. Only when Viviane returned to the room did he cease his restless movement.

"I've looked everywhere," she said, shaking her head, "but my niece is not here."

"Where can she be?" he asked with a perplexed frown.

"If I know Simone, she is riding that uncontrollable animal of Tom's," the woman said with a shudder.

"She rides Hocus Pocus?" Alain asked, incredulous.

"*Oui*, since she recovered from her, er, illness. She is still not well, yet every day she gallops over the fields as if pursued. When she returns, her spirit leaves her again. I don't know what to do." The usually unruffled Viviane Chauvin was near tears.

"How is Rory?"

Viviane smiled at the thought of the bright little girl. "Sometimes she cries for her *papa*, but she is well. She is out checking crab pots with Batiste this morning. Aurora is the only thing in which Simone shows any interest. I've even begun to wish she would take notice of the sugar cane, or her businesses—anything."

"Ethan says Simone hasn't answered his letters."

"She sees almost no one, communicates with almost no one."

"Why is she cutting herself off this way?"

"Perhaps she is simply not ready to deal with people yet," Simone's aunt reflected. "We should try not to worry too much, Alain. With the help of *le bon Dieu*, Simone will be herself again in time, but now . . ." She shrugged expressively.

When the man left the house, he turned his horse up the River Road toward Hideaway. Urging the animal to the top of the levee, he rode along moodily.

Alain worried for Simone, perceiving now, without jealousy, how much she had loved Tom. He felt the loss of his friend heavily and tried to imagine her feelings at losing a mate. He realized she was a strong woman indeed to have coped with a lifetime of losses: Nicholas . . . himself, when she had believed him dead . . . and now Tom. But he did not want her to face this loss alone. He wanted, with all his heart, to support and strengthen her.

Suddenly, over the lap of the river, the Creole heard distant hoofbeats. Reining his own horse to a stop, he surveyed the field across the road. Simone sat astride Tom's bay gelding, her unbound hair flowing behind her, glistening in the midday sun, as she galloped recklessly, Jupiter at the big horse's heels.

"Simone!" Alain shouted, standing in his stirrups. He could have sworn she glanced toward the levee, but she leaned low over her mount, urging it on, and disappeared into the woods.

He rode slowly toward Lisette's house. Behind him, he heard the gong at LaVictoire, calling the men in from the fields, and the homey sound only deepened his discontent.

On the morning of All Saints Day, Rosette watched an odd parade set out. At its head, two adolescent slave boys hauled ladders and buckets of whitewash. Simone followed with a broom and a basket. Rory trailed behind, picking flowers from the beds without a word of reprimand from her mother.

"You think the mistress is better?" Celestina asked

her sister as they watched the group disappear down the path toward the cemetery.

"Day by day," Rosette answered with a sigh, "but it will take time. She loved Cap'n Tom very much."

In the tiny graveyard, Simone cleaned and weeded while the boys whitewashed the tombs. After a time, she sat on the bench with Jupiter at her feet and watched until they were done.

It was a warm November day, and Simone felt a certain tranquility despite her somber errand. She did not even mind that, in her efforts to "assist" with the whitewashing, Rory had streaks of white all over her dress and in her thick black hair.

When the boys finished their task, they took the ladders back to the shed. Alone with her daughter, Simone polished the bell on Tom's tomb until it gleamed dully. Taking the vases from their holders, she filled them with bayou water and arranged flowers in them. Rory rubbed the brass nameplate, chattering about her father as though he had gone for a trip and would soon return.

Her heart aching, Simone wondered what to say to the child. Then she heard her cry, "Look, *Maman*, Oncle Alain is here!"

Rory launched herself gladly toward the man as he approached, carrying a bouquet. Jupiter, too, rose, stretched, and lumbered toward Alain, his tail wagging in welcome.

"*Bonjour, ma petite.*" Alain swooped Rory into a one-armed hug as he regarded her mother anxiously. Though Simone was thin and pale, she looked beautiful and sadly serene in the wintry sunlight.

"I hope I'm not intruding," he said uncertainly, "but since I was at Lisette's, I wanted to bring these over."

"That was very kind of you." Simone took the bouquet and laid it at the doorstep of the crypt.

"I brought something for Rory, too." He smiled and

stood the little girl on the bench as he fished in his pocket.

"Pralines! Look, *Maman*." Rory waved the bag in the air.

"I . . . I was with Tom once when he stopped to buy a treat for her," he explained.

"That was kind of you, too," Simone said quietly.

While the little girl busied herself with her candies, the couple stood silently before the tomb.

"How are you, Simone?" Alain asked after a moment.

"Well enough."

"Lisette told me about the baby. I'm sorry."

"I suppose it was not meant to be." She stared at the placid bayou.

Alain watched her from beneath the broad brim of his hat. "I know it is not customary during mourning to receive a male visitor who is not a relative," he said awkwardly, "but . . ."

"A guardian is almost a relative." A slow smile crept over Simone's face. "I'm glad you came, 'Lain."

His face brightening, he took her hand and squeezed it affectionately. But before either could speak, Rory jumped down from the bench and began to tug on his other hand.

"Come to the house," she entreated. "Savannah makes the best cocoa in the world, and she'll make some for us."

Alain turned questioning eyes to Simone.

"Yes, come up to the house," she invited, gathering her basket and broom.

Clasping Rory's little hand in his, Alain walked mother and daughter toward the gracious house at the end of the path.

After lunch, the adults retreated to the fire in the study. Simone sat in Tom's big old chair, her feet tucked beside her, as they sipped their coffee.

"I'm glad to see you, *chère*," Alain said. "I've been very worried about you."

"I know," she acknowledged softly, "but you mustn't concern yourself. I have good days and bad days. On bad days it seems that nothing will ever be right again. On good days, I know it just takes time."

"But you must take care of yourself," he chided. "You're so thin and pale."

"I know how I look. We do not turn our mirrors to the wall in mourning here. Tom thought that a stupid custom." For an instant Simone showed a spark of her old spirit, then she sat back and heaved a sigh. "I'm sorry, Alain. I shouldn't have snapped. You, Lisette, Batiste, Rosette, Tante Viviane—everyone worries. I can take care of myself, you know. I've done it before."

"I recall a belligerent green-eyed boy telling me that," Alain remarked lightly, "then setting out to prove it."

"That seems a lifetime ago." She smiled crookedly. "I have not even picked up a sword since last summer."

"Shall we see if you still have the knack?" he challenged.

Sitting forward in her chair again, Simone showed more verve than she had since Tom's death. "Can you wait while I change?"

Alain nodded. "I'll find Batiste and borrow his fencing gear. Meet you in the ballroom in ten minutes?"

"I'll be there," she called over her shoulder, already headed for her room.

That afternoon, steel rang against steel at LaVictoire again. Batiste watched approvingly while the pair fenced. Alain paced himself, for Simone was indeed out of practice, but he was surprised at just how good she was. Rosette, Celestina, and Rory sat in chairs out of the way, and slave children lined the gallery, pampering Jupiter, who whined to be let inside.

When the fencing was finished and the others had departed, Simone and Alain lingered in the gathering dusk.

"I've had so many good times in this ballroom," she murmured, looking around.

"I enjoyed Twelfth Night here, though you might have warned me about the Martin females," Alain said with a wry smile.

"Sorry." Simone flashed an unrepentant smile toward him, looking more like her old self.

"You should be," he grumbled good-naturedly. "I did everything but barricade myself inside the *garçonnière*. Madame Martin is a determined woman."

"But she did not catch the elusive Alain de Vallière for her Nell," Simone joshed gently.

"*Non*," he murmured, his dark eyes pensive. "May I come again tomorrow?" he asked as they walked to the *allée*.

"I don't think that is a good idea."

"I shouldn't have asked. I would do nothing to damage your reputation, to hurt you."

"No, not anymore," she said simply.

"I know I was a cad when I returned to New Orleans, and I have behaved badly," he admitted. "I hurt inside, and I wanted you to feel the same pain. But now I would do anything to take your hurt away, Simone."

"You've become a good friend, 'Lain." Tiptoeing, she kissed his cheek, then stepped back and offered her hand formally. "I enjoyed your visit, but I should not see you again for a while."

"I understand. *Au revoir*," he murmured regretfully, kissing her hand in farewell.

As he rode away, Simone returned to the house, feeling her loneliness acutely. Yet she knew she had done the right thing in telling Alain to stay away. Though he had behaved well, had even apologized, and had offered genuine friendship, she had seen something unsettled—and unsettling— in his eyes. It would be better if he stayed away.

"She tries," Batiste told Lisette as he paced before her fireplace at Hideaway. "When the slaves gathered

for their gifts at Christmas, she was almost the old
Simone."

"I had hoped she was getting better," Lisette said
with a sigh. "For nearly two months she threw herself
into harvest, riding at your side as Tom would have,
but now I see, she fills her days with work so she
doesn't have to think."

"I don't think she has ever cried, ever gotten her
sadness out," the big man said. "And now Twelfth
Night is coming."

"I agree she should not be alone," Lisette mused,
"but I don't think she will welcome a houseguest, even
me. Still, I plan to visit LaVictoire on New Year's with
a gift for Rory. Maybe . . ."

"Simone, come quickly!" Batiste bellowed as he
bore Lisette in his brawny arms toward the house.

Her heart in her throat, Simone flew to meet them
on the gallery. "What happened?"

"How stupid! I turned my ankle getting out of my
carriage," Lisette answered through clenched teeth.
"It's nothing really."

"Napoleon," Batiste summoned the gawking boy,
"bring ice from the icehouse. *Petite amie*, could you
fetch some bandages?"

"*Oui*." Simone raced to do his bidding. When she
returned, Lisette groaned, "I do not know what has
come over me, *chère*, but I feel so faint."

"I'll get you a cordial." Shoving the bandages toward
Batiste, Simone hurried into the library.

By the time she came back, he had wrapped the
injured foot and was telling Lisette, "It's a bad sprain,
and you're going to have to stay off of it. You should
not travel, not even to Hideaway."

"Oh, dear." Lisette gazed at Simone helplessly.

"Don't worry," her hostess soothed. "We'll send
word to Monsieur Guilbeau that you won't be home

for a few days and ask your servants to send some clothes for you."

"*Oui*, I'm ill-prepared for a long stay," Lisette agreed. "I hope you don't mind having a guest for a few days, *ma petite*."

"Of course not." Already searching for paper and pen in order to write a note to Monsieur Guilbeau, Simone did not see the satisfied look that passed between her two old friends.

After a couple of days Batiste declared Lisette fit enough to hobble around the house with the aid of a cane. Simone was glad to have her friend staying with her, and she did not seem to notice how everyone watched her or that no one left her alone.

The day of Twelfth Night passed without comment from Simone, and, though she seemed preoccupied, she behaved as if it were a day like any other. As Lisette watched her trudge away early to bed, she wondered if perhaps they had worried for no reason.

But during the night she was awakened by light footsteps on the stairs. Rising, she went to the balustrade and peered down into the foyer. Simone's nightgown-clad figure was unmistakable in the darkness as she crossed to the ballroom.

Stealing downstairs, Lisette opened the huge sliding doors a crack to see Simone standing in the middle of the ballroom, bathed in moonlight. Her heart ached when she heard her friend's words.

"Tom," Simone whispered into the darkness, "are you here? It is Twelfth Night, when we always celebrated our anniversary. You wouldn't leave me alone tonight of all nights, would you?"

The only sound was the wind in the trees.

"Alone," she muttered dismally, sinking to sit on the floor. "All alone." Suddenly she buried her face in her hands, and her body shook with sobs. "I need you so, Tom. How could you leave me?"

Lisette stayed where she was for a moment, letting

her friend weep cleansing tears. Then she went to kneel beside her huddled figure. "You are not alone, Simone," she said quietly.

The grieving woman raised her tear-stained face, and an anguished cry rose from deep inside her. "But I have never felt so alone."

"I know, dear one." Lisette sat down beside her and placed her arm around her quaking shoulders. "Cry and get it over. Scream and wail, if you must, but let your sorrow out. Tom would not want you to live in this lonely, silent mourning forever."

"No, he believed in living life to the fullest," Simone sobbed. "That makes it even worse. I should have been the one Marcel killed. How I wish I were. I was the one he hated. I was the one he wanted to destroy. Tom had done nothing to him. Don't you see? It's all my fault. Marie LeVeau was right—I bring danger to those I love."

"Hush, you are not to blame." Lisette rocked her gently. "Marcel Baudin was a madman."

"But if it were not for his hatred of me, Tom would still be alive," Simone wept.

"And if it were not for you, Tom would have missed out on the happiest years of his life," the other woman argued kindly. "Tom loved you, and he would want you to go on living . . . to the fullest."

"I know what you say is true," Simone sniffled, "but it is so hard without him."

"But you will go on living. It will take time, and there will be pain, but you will do it." Lisette rose and offered a hand. "After all, you are the stubbornest woman . . ."

Simone smiled through her tears and allowed her friend to hoist her to her feet. "I know, I'm the stubbornest woman you've ever met. *Merci*, Lise." She kissed her cheek.

"Tell me," she said as, arm in arm, they went upstairs, "how is it you are no longer limping?"

"Oh, my ankle is much better, *chère*," Lisette answered with a rich laugh. "In fact, I think everything will be better now."

23

It was nearly midnight when Alain and Lisette lingered over coffee. The windows and doors of Hideaway were open, and a small slave operated the punkah over the table, but nothing relieved the discomfort of the muggy summer night.

"Will you see Simone while you're here, Alain?" Lisette asked. "It's been more than six months since you saw her last, after all."

"I plan to try," he answered, sipping his coffee. "The worst she can do is to say no again. Sooner or later, she must say yes."

They were silent for a moment, then he asked, "Simone takes an interest in LaVictoire now?"

"*Oui*," she affirmed. "Since January, she's been keeping the books, much to Batiste's relief. He'd rather be outdoors, especially now. Harvest is coming, and he is trying to finish the installation of that centrifugal machine Tom wanted."

"I'm glad Batiste stayed with Simone," Alain said sincerely. "She needed him."

"He's been invaluable," she agreed. "He makes a lot of the decisions at LaVictoire, though most factors think they're dealing with his mistress through an agent."

"She is well?" His voice was low but urgent.

"She works too hard, and she tries to be both mother and father to Rory, but she seems fit enough."

"And how is Aurora?" He smiled indulgently.

"The most perfect child who ever lived," her godmother answered promptly, her gray eyes twinkling. "You'll see. Celestina will bring her over later this week.

"I'm glad you're here, 'Lain," Lisette added candidly. "Much has happened in the past year, but I feel I have my old friend back."

"I'm glad to be back," he responded with a smile. But Lisette saw the glimmer of pain that lingered in his deep brown eyes.

In a bedroom at LaVictoire, Jupiter was instantly awake when his mistress sat up in bed.

It was no use, Simone brooded, she could not sleep in this heat. Clawing at the *baire*, she climbed out of bed, her nightgown clinging to her sweat-dampened body. Tugging the fabric away from her skin, she padded barefoot across the room to shove the window open farther and await the breeze that did not come.

Opening the French doors, she stepped out onto the moonlit gallery. Jupiter yawned loudly behind her, and his nails clicked on the floor as he followed her outside.

In the flowerboxes, red geraniums drooped pitifully. Not a breath of air stirred as Simone's eyes alit on the summerhouse near the shadowy woods. Its white latticework seemed to shimmer, beckoning in the moonlight.

"Come, Jupiter," she murmured and set out for the coolest place at LaVictoire.

Stripped down to his shirtsleeves, Alain wandered along the bayou that bordered Lisette's property, listening to the croaking of frogs and a plop in the water as a snake slid down the bank. Finding the path from the water, he made his way past LaVictoire's chapel and the crypts gleaming and ghostly in the moonlight. At the edge of the lawn he stopped beneath a tree and stared at the dark house. He didn't know why he had been drawn here at this hour of the night, but he had felt compelled to come.

When a spectral figure flitted across the lawn, his eyes narrowed. Simone's nightgown took on an unearthly glow in the moonlight. Behind her, Jupiter seemed to weave in and out of the dappled shadows.

Purposefully, Alain followed when they disappeared into the summerhouse. As he approached, he heard the dog growl.

"Who is it?" Simone asked without fear.

"Alain."

"Friend, Jupiter," she said. Immediately the big dog bounded down the steps, tail wagging, to meet the man.

"*Bonsoir*," Simone said simply when Alain joined her. She sat on one of the cushioned benches that bordered the interior of the summerhouse. Her face was obscured by shadow, but her hair, hanging almost to her waist, seemed to reflect the silvery moonlight pouring through an open window behind her.

"What are you doing out here, Simone?" he asked in greeting.

"I might ask you the same thing."

Suddenly, Alain felt ill at ease and acutely aware that neither of them was fully dressed. "I . . . I'm staying at Hideaway. I couldn't sleep, so I took a walk. Somehow I ended up here."

"I couldn't sleep either," she said quietly.

"It's not good for you to be out alone . . . unprotected."

"I have . . ." Her voice trailing off, she looked around. "I *had* Jupiter with me. He's probably off chasing rabbits now."

"Why don't I walk you back to the house?"

Safe in the shadows, Simone was unwilling to move, afraid to be near Alain, chagrinned at being caught in nothing more than her batiste nightgown. "*Non, merci*," she demurred. "Jupiter will return soon."

"I'll wait with you," the man insisted, sitting down across from her on the bench beside the door. For his own sanity, he could not go too close to her. At their last farewell, it had taken all his control not to hold her and kiss her and comfort her. He could not sit beside her in the summer night without taking her in his arms, and he would not risk scaring her away.

"You don't have to wait." Simone's nervousness was apparent in her protest.

"I want to."

She said nothing, but she leaned farther into the shadows. Uncomfortably aware of each other, they sat in silence, the cries of the night birds the only sounds.

What was wrong with her? Simone asked herself. She was a grown woman, widowed, with a child, and still Alain made her nervous and uncertain. Her heart pounded at the memory of the love they had once shared. He had still wanted her when he reappeared in her life. Perhaps he did yet. But desire alone would never be enough. Why, then, did her body yearn for his touch?

"Perhaps I should go in, after all," she blurted out, rising.

Alain's breath caught as the moonlight washed over her, illuminating her delicate features and outlining the curves under her sheer nightgown.

"I'll be fine." She hastened toward the door. "You needn't bother to walk me."

"No bother," he forced himself to reply calmly. He stood, but he could not, would not, take her arm or touch her at all. After all, he was only flesh and blood.

Wordlessly, they crossed the lawn. At the foot of the stairs, Simone stopped to bid him good night, but Alain began to climb to the lower gallery.

She stared after him. "Where are you going?"

"To see the lady to her door. Yours is the one that is open upstairs, isn't it?"

"*Oui.*" She passed him, unaware that he watched the sway of her full nightgown as she preceded him along the dark gallery.

When they reached the stairs that led to the upper floor, Simone stopped again and turned to say good night. Unprepared for the rapid halt, Alain collided with her, his arms reflexively catching her, steadying her against his chest.

She gasped, feeling the heat of his hands and his bare forearms encircling her waist, searing her body through her thin gown. One of his long, lean legs was pressed insistently between hers.

With Simone's sudden intake of breath, Alain felt her breasts, soft yet firm, crushed against his chest, and suddenly, he was in no hurry to let her go. When she had feared she was falling, her hands had gripped his broad shoulders, and there they rested as she looked up at him in dismay, her green eyes jewel-like in the moonlight.

"Alain, don't—"

"I haven't yet." His husky voice floated over her like a caress as he lowered his mouth to hers.

She became very still in his arms. But her heart pumped blood, like liquid fire, to the very core of her being. His kiss did nothing to lessen the burning within her, but she craved it all the more. Her arms stole around his neck, and her fingers laced through his hair.

Then his hands were on her everywhere, kindling flames of desire. His mouth blazed a scorching trail downward to the breasts straining against the gauzy fabric of her nightgown. Her pulse pounded beneath his lips as they grazed the soft flesh of her neck.

Alain stared down at her as if looking for a sign. Simone's unguarded face was luminous with desire, inviting his caresses. Her head was thrown back, her throat offered for kissing. Her eyes closed, she stirred in his embrace, her lips seeking his.

Having found his answer, he scooped her into his arms and bore her up the stairs. In her moonlit room, he stood her beside the bed and untied the ribbons at her shoulders. Her nightgown slipped down, sliding over her hips to the floor.

"You're even more beautiful than I remembered," he murmured when she stood naked before him. His hungry gaze fed upon her small, slender frame with its high, firm breasts and flat stomach, and he starved for more. His eyes roamed over her, pausing at the scar marking her side, showing silver in the dimness, before they drifted down, lingering at her most secret place.

Simone felt no embarrassment at his admiring gaze, only a smoldering passion stunning in its intensity. She watched with a hunger to match his as he swiftly shed his clothing and came to stand beside her. She found his powerful body beautiful and could not resist tracing the cleft in his muscled chest with her fingers. The muscles twitched at her light touch, and Alain drew a ragged breath. Crushing her in his arms, he kissed her.

Laying her gently on the bed, he joined her, caressing her, exciting her, inciting her to fiery response. They came together urgently, rapturously, as on the night they had first made love. Scaling the heights of passion with dizzying speed, they reached the peak together, then slowly, languorously, they descended to luxuriate in the tenderness of each other's touch. At last they slept.

Simone awakened near dawn. Hearing the rustle of fabric, she opened her eyes and saw Alain dressing as if he could not wait to leave.

Appalled by her actions last night, she sat up, shamefaced, and propped herself against the headboard. Pulling the sheet up over her breasts, she tucked it under her arms.

When he saw that she was awake, Alain came to sit beside her on the bed, but she would not meet his eyes. Placing his hands on her shoulders, he kissed the top of her bowed head and whispered, "I must go before anyone knows I was here."

"Of course," she agreed harshly, shrugging from his grip.

Crooking a finger, he lifted her chin so she looked into his eyes. "What is wrong, Simone?"

Though he held her chin, she shifted her gaze away from him and muttered, "I wish last night had never happened."

Alain's eyes clouded and he relinquished his hold.

Simone looked at him, her green eyes brimming with tears. "Tom was my husband," she blurted out. "He was your friend."

"So that's what this is about? You think we betrayed Tom last night?"

"Don't you?" she accused.

"*Non, ma chère*, I do not. Our feelings now have nothing to do with Tom. I've always wanted you, Simone. You know that. After I knew Tom, I did not begrudge him his wife, but I never stopped wanting you. You were a good and faithful mate while he lived, *ma petite*, but he is dead now, and you're a living, breathing woman with needs and desires. And last night you wanted me just as much as I wanted you."

She did not answer, but Alain saw the spasm of pain cross her face.

In her heart, Simone knew it was true that her life must go on. But what had she done, taking a man to her bed who spoke only of wants and needs and not of love?

"This cannot happen again, Alain," she said unsteadily. "We must have this clear between us, for I'll be returning to New Orleans soon."

"What will you do there?" he asked.

"Manage the Franklin Steamboats office."

"Manage the office?" he repeated, aghast. "What about Ethan?"

"He's in St. Louis, rebuilding. You know about the waterfront fire there?"

"*Oui*, I was sorry to hear of it. But you can't mean you plan to operate the office yourself."

"Why not?" she demanded.

"Because you're a woman," he said simply, rising. "It's not right. I cannot allow you to run a business."

"You cannot *allow* . . ." Simone's eyes blazed and she sat bolt upright. "What makes you think you can tell me what to do?"

"I'm concerned about your reputation," he answered illogically.

"Not so concerned that you did not spend the night with me," she snapped.

Alain blinked in surprise. "That's different. I plan to marry you. You shouldn't have to worry about business anymore."

"They are *my* businesses to worry about," she countered tersely.

Alain's jaw worked as he struggled to hold on to his patience. "Haven't you learned yet that a woman has no place in commerce? Why can't you marry me and spend your time taking care of me and Rory?"

"I take care of Rory. I take very good care of Rory," Simone informed him hotly. "Further, you have not *asked* to marry me, and I have certainly not accepted. I have no desire to be a proper Creole wife, and I don't want a proper Creole husband."

Alain's face darkened, and he said, "Whether you marry me or not, I promised Tom I would look after you, and I will."

"So that's it!" She jumped from the bed to face him, dragging the sheet with her as she rose. "You would marry me because of the promise you made to Tom? No, thank you again!" she shouted without giving him a chance to respond. "I will not be an obligation fulfilled. Unlike my father, my husband did not charge you to marry me off—to yourself or anyone else."

Alain glared at her, out of patience at last. "This is where I came in!" he roared. "And, I find, after all these years, you're just as stubborn and prickly as you ever were!"

The woman followed as he stormed out onto the gallery. Wrapped in the sheet, she stood at the railing, uncaring that someone might see. "Just a minute, Alain de Vallière!" she yelled after him. "I haven't finished!"

"Oh, yes, madame, you have." He strode furiously down the *allée* toward the front gate. The last Simone saw of him, he was marching up the River Road toward Hideaway.

Simone sat for a moment in her carriage, taken aback by the changes in Franklin Steamboats' yard in just one year. On the adjacent lot she and Tom had bought just before his death, the Queen Enterprises office was already finished.

"Miss Simone, welcome home." Obadiah escorted her to the office.

"*Merci*, Obie." Standing in the doorway, she surveyed the big, drafty room with its marred, ink-stained wooden counter and rickety chairs.

Some things never changed, she thought gratefully. The anniversary of Tom's death had just passed, and it was difficult to return to the business they had built together. Comforted somehow by the grimy, familiar office, she asked, "How are things here?"

"Been hard the last few weeks without Ethan. I'm glad you're here, but *you* ain't gonna be when you see the mountain of paperwork waitin' upstairs," Obadiah answered with a chuckle. "Have you heard how things are goin' in St. Louis?"

"Ethan's last letter said we must rebuild from the ground up. It's good that he took Gisèle and the boys with him, for it's likely to take awhile," she called, heading up the stairs to the manager's office.

Simone did not descend again until dark. Serenaded by the songs of the screwmen working at the dock across the road, she read the journal Ethan had kept for the past year, carefully recording new developments at Franklin Steamboats. When she had reacquainted herself with her business, she sorted through the paperwork, which was, as Obie had said, mountainous.

She settled quickly into a routine, spending each day at the office, leaving Jupiter at home with Rory. She was cautious at the freight yard, seldom staying late. She had made the mistake of believing Marcel dead once before. The sheriff might assume he had perished in the swamp, but she assumed nothing.

The evenings Simone spent with her daughter. Gradually, with effort, she became accustomed to living in the house on St. Charles Avenue without Tom.

Simone sat on the terrace of Barbara and Jeremy Nash's new home, sipping sherry and listening to the conversation around her. The female guests were seated at a small table, a citronella candle in its center the only light. The men clustered in the darkness at the top of the steps leading to the garden.

The rather pregnant Barbara leaned toward her and said quietly, "Father told me our dinner party was your first outing, Simone. We're honored to have you here."

"I am pleased to be here," she answered with a smile. "Your new home is lovely."

"Doesn't Simone look exquisite in lavender?" Dulcie asked the others. "I'm so glad your year of mourning is over, my dear, so you don't have to wear black all the time."

"She looks very pretty," answered Bernadette Cuvillion.

"*Très jolie*," Emilie Thibault agreed dutifully.

"*Merci.*" Simone was uncomfortable with their well-intentioned compliments. She had not wanted to come to the soiree, but she could not afford to miss a dinner party held for William Clive Leighton, a representative of the company building Queen Enterprises' screw propeller ship.

When she had joined the women at the table, her spirits had sunk to see Emilie among them. Alain had been out of town for the past few days, and Simone had hoped he was still away. But if Emilie was present, he must be here, as well.

She sensed his presence the moment he arrived. He stood in the doorway to the house, his back to the light, but she did not need to see his face to know he watched her.

"*Bonsoir*, ladies," he greeted them evenly.

Suddenly Simone wished in earnest that she had not come. Though she worked next door to Alain's office, she seldom saw him, and he had not entered the Franklin building since her return to New Orleans. She would have to face him sooner or later, but she was not sure she was ready to spend an evening in his company just yet. Though absorbed in her thoughts, she noticed the pain on Emilie's face when he passed them without stopping.

Alain stood at the edge of the terrace with William Leighton and Hiram, his mind half on their discussion. He was grateful for the concealment of the darkness as his gaze rested on Simone. He had known she would be present this evening, but he was unprepared for the rush of emotion he had felt at seeing her.

Acutely aware of his eyes upon her, Simone was also having difficulty following the conversation around her. She was caught off guard when the other women stood to take a quick look at the nursery Barbara was preparing. She rose, too, somewhat belatedly.

"*Pardon*, but you ladies will not mind if I borrow my business partner for a few moments," Alain requested, appearing beside them. "We have not had a chance to talk since her return."

"Can't this wait?" Simone objected at once.

"I don't think so," he answered pleasantly, capturing her arm.

The women faltered as the partners glared at each other, and Barbara said swiftly, "We'll be on the third floor, Simone. Why don't you join us after you've spoken with Alain?"

Her face rigid, Simone sat down and watched the others troop inside. Alain slouched in a chair beside her, his long legs stretched out in front of him, and regarded her closely.

"I heard you were back," he said after a time. "How are you?"

"Very well, very busy."

"I'm sorry I haven't had a chance to stop by the house."

"You needn't trouble yourself." Simone said coolly. "My office is a short walk across the yard from yours."

Alain snorted, but did not take the bait. Instead he said, "I would have come for you at LaVictoire. Why didn't you let me know you were returning?"

"Because I did not want a scene like this one," she snapped.

"This is not a scene," he contradicted mildly.

"What do you call it?"

"Either a business meeting or the surest way I've found to have the pleasure of your company. I want to talk to you, Simone," he began tentatively. "About the night at LaVictoire . . . ."

She felt nearly weak with relief when the butler appeared in the doorway to announce dinner."

She fled to William Leighton, her dinner partner for the evening. She had met the fatuous middle-aged man when he arrived at the Vieux Carré wharf. Recognizing her as the widow of one of Queen Enterprises' owners, he had greeted her patronizingly, unwilling to discuss any subject weightier than his voyage.

Over dinner, she set out to learn as much about screw propellers as she could, and she did so, so innocently that, utterly charmed, the Englishman told her far more about his business than he realized.

Across the table, Alain, moody and withdrawn, watched her. When her eyes happened to meet his, the storminess in their dark depths snatched her breath away.

After dinner, Simone sat with Bernadette and Dominique for a time. Bernadette's expression as she watched her cousin with Alain was troubled, and, sighing, she asked, "Aren't Emilie and Alain a handsome couple?"

"*Oui*," Simone replied without a glance in their direction.

"I cannot understand why Alain waits. I thought surely he would propose to her by now."

"You've been saying that for two years," Dominique chided.

"Perhaps he is just not the marrying kind. He is sometimes so cool and aloof, I think he doesn't know how to love," Bernadette mused.

"I think he does," Dominique murmured, watching Simone. "I think he loves very deeply."

Alain stood at the window of the Queen Enterprises office, frowning as he looked out. In the yard below, Simone, dressed in a simple gray gown, moved between bales of cotton and barrels of molasses with Obadiah at her side. Then, climbing the steps of the building across the way, she disappeared inside.

Damn it, he needed to talk to her, he brooded. When he had stomped away from LaVictoire the morning after their lovemaking, Alain had been determined she would have her wish: He had even told himself that what had occurred between them would never happen again. He had tried to believe it, but he could not. He wanted her, and, despite her protests to the contrary, Simone wanted him. She had met his passion with a fiery intensity he could not forget.

Since his return from the West Indies, he had striven

to banish his desire for her. He had tried to hate her. He had become the family friend. He had even toyed with the idea of marrying Emilie Thibault and getting on with his life. But none of those ideas had worked, and they never would. Even though he and Simone were constantly at odds, he loved her. And he had to make her believe it.

With a smothered curse, Alain pulled on his jacket and strode out of his office. No one was in Franklin Steamboat's outer office when he marched through, headed upstairs to find Simone.

Sitting in front of the huge rolltop desk, she looked up from a column of figures when he halted in her doorway. "Alain," she breathed in surprise.

"*Bonjour*." He nodded. "As you pointed out last night, we are neighbors. I thought I would come over and say hello."

She smiled at his conciliatory manner. "Won't you come in and sit down?"

"*Merci*." Stepping into the office, he looked around. How could someone as lovely as Simone belong here? Ill at ease, he sat down across from her and said, "It was good to see you last night."

"Was it?" Her eyebrows rose skeptically.

He decided to ignore her incredulity. "Simone, I want you to know I'm sorry about . . ." He trailed off, uncertain where to begin.

"The night at LaVictoire?" Her smile suddenly lost its good humor, and her expression became tight.

"*Non*, the morning after. I said some things I didn't mean."

"So did I," she surprised him by saying. She heaved a gusty sigh. "I shouldn't have lost my temper, Alain. You were only saying what everyone thinks about my managing Franklin Steamboats. But, try to understand, Tom and I built this company from three little bayou packets. With Ethan in St. Louis, someone has to run it."

"But you are a well-born lady," he tried reasonably.

"Breeding does not change because a person owns a business."

"But a lady doesn't belong in business. You should not be exposed to the rough types who work on the docks."

"Like the roué from next door?" she teased unexpectedly, widening her green eyes innocently.

"The very one." He laughed, pleased that the ice was broken.

"Will you have some *café*?" she invited. "Obie brews the best on the waterfront. He always makes sure I have a pot of my own in the mornings."

"*Oui, merci.*" Sipping the bitter black brew, Alain revised her boast with a grimace, "Obie makes the *strongest café* on the waterfront."

"It does well enough for us," Simone said. "It's like our office here—not fancy, but it serves our purpose."

"Why don't you move into the new offices? There's room."

Simone suspected he would like her to be where he could keep an eye on her, but she declined tactfully. "This is a shipping office. We don't need the elegance of Queen Enterprises to impress clients. We don't even sell tickets here. All we do is work."

"That's something else I wanted to talk to you about."

"The office?"

"No, work. Too much work," he amended hastily, seeing her draw herself up defensively. "You need some time for pleasure."

To his amazement, she blushed.

"I—I mean . . ." he stammered. "Damn it, Simone, you make me feel like a tongue-tied schoolboy. What I am trying to say is that I'd like to take you to dinner tomorrow evening. Strictly as friends . . . no business, no pressure . . . of any kind."

Simone stared at him in surprise before replying, "I would be delighted, if we can go late. I'd like to put Rory to bed first."

Before Alain could respond, a voice interrupted, "*Pardon*, since no one was downstairs, I took the liberty of coming up."

The couple turned to see a handsome young man in the doorway, his hat in his hands.

"*Bonjour*, Claude," Simone greeted the interloper graciously. "Do you know Monsieur de Vallière?" she asked innocently.

"Alain de Vallière," Claude Galvez greeted the other man with surprised affability. "I didn't know you knew Simone."

Nonplussed, Alain rose and shook the younger man's hand. "Nor did I know you did." He glanced at the woman, who smiled smugly.

"We are old acquaintances," Claude assured him. His eyes on Simone, he missed Alain's look of shock. "I met her when she managed the company before," he continued. "She was most gracious in assisting me, and we've been friends ever since, *n'est-ce pas*, Simone?"

Alain watched tensely as the young man kissed the hand she offered. His face was alight with pleasure, but on it was no glimmer of recognition for his one-time protégé, Jean-Paul Sonnier.

"I trust I am not interrupting anything?" Claude asked politely.

"M'sieur de Vallière and I were just talking business."

"*Mais oui*," Claude exclaimed, addressing Alain. "You two are now business partners. Have I interrupted an important meeting then?"

Seeing Alain's ominous glower, Simone said smoothly, "Nothing that will not wait. Won't you sit down, M'sieur Galvez?"

"*Non, merci*. I just stopped by to see if you have heard anything further about the construction of a railroad."

"Only that there will be another meeting here in New Orleans before the end of the year."

"Do you truly think Louisiana needs another railroad?" Claude's brow was furrowed in thought.

"Goods may be shipped upriver," Simone responded, "but they must be hauled west. Why not an interstate railroad?"

"You realize someday it could put your steamboat company out of business?"

"Someday," she acknowledged, "but if we work hard now, we can make a name for Queen Enterprises in international shipping."

"Ever ambitious, eh, *chère*?" Alain jibed.

"You are fortunate to have such a partner—a beautiful woman with the business sense of a man," Claude said in her defense.

"A man has never had such a partner," Alain muttered.

"I have taken enough of your time today, Simone." Claude seemed ill at ease. "Good to see you, de Vallière. *Au revoir.*"

"*Au revoir,*" Simone echoed as the young Creole departed. She turned to Alain, anticipating disapproval.

His face looked as if it were chiseled from stone as he rose. "I will pick you up at eight tomorrow evening, Madame Partner," he informed her coolly. Then he pivoted and was gone.

24

At the top of stairs, Simone stopped and smoothed the skirt of her forest-green gown. There was no reason to be nervous, she chided herself. She was only going to dinner with a man she had known most of her life. Hearing Rory's voice coming from the second parlor, her brows knit in a frown.

"Aurora Marthe Marie-Louise," she scolded as she entered.

"Oh, no." Rory rolled her green eyes at Alain. "I'm in trouble when she uses all my names."

"I put you to bed half an hour ago," her mother admonished her.

"It was too early, *Maman,* and I heard Nonc' Alain coming—"

"And we had a good visit," the man defended Rory staunchly.

"Did you know he forgot my birthday?" the little girl asked in amazement.

"He has had a great deal on his mind."

"That's what he said, but he remembers now."

"I'd bet the farm he does," Simone muttered, borrowing one of Tom's old phrases.

"He's going to buy me a fishing pole. That's what I want, so when we all go home to LaVictoire, we can go on picnics."

"I told Rory we could go fishing here in New Orleans," Alain interjected smoothly. "I know a good spot out at the lake. Perhaps we can go next week."

"Can we, *Maman*?" Rory asked eagerly.

"We *could* discuss it in the morning before I go to work . . . but you'll probably be asleep, since you did not stay in bed tonight," Simone answered with a dubious sigh.

"I'll go to bed right now. *Bonne nuit*." Rory blew a kiss from the doorway as she scampered out.

Alain watched her departure with a fond smile. "She is a wonderful little girl."

"And always in trouble for something," Simone chuckled.

"Just like another little girl I once knew," he reminded her with a grin. "Shall we go?"

Simone's heart was unaccountably light as Alain walked her to the carriage, but she was disturbed by the effect his nearness had on her as they drove through the American Section to the Vieux Carré. Seated beside her, he smiled down at her companionably. She returned the smile, then looked away, strangely flustered.

"Emeraude, me lovely," a voice called as the couple alit on the *banquette* outside the restaurant. They turned to see Devlin Hennessey sauntering toward them.

"Thought 'twas you," the Irishman said with a charming smile.

"Dev Hennessey, may I present my old friend, Alain de Vallière." Simone introduced the men who regarded each other through narrowed eyes. "Alain, Dev was a friend of Tom's and mine aboard the *Emerald Queen*."

"A pleasure to meet ye, sir." The gambler bowed politely before turning back to the woman. "I was sorry to hear of Tom's death, Simone. Is there anything I can do for ye?"

"Non, merci," she murmured.

"I can see I'm delaying yer dinner," he said with a glance at Alain's glowering face. "May I call on ye soon? We've a great deal of visiting to do."

"Stop by the house one evening, or come to the yard during the day," Simone replied. "You remember where my office is?"

"I do. I'll see ye soon." Dev kissed her hand, then nodded amiably to Alain. "Good evening to ye, sir."

"*Bonsoir*, m'sieur," the Creole answered in clipped tones as he led Simone into the restaurant.

"Who was that?" he growled when they were seated at the table.

"Devlin Hennessey—"

"I got his name. He looks like a lace curtain Irishman to me. And I've seen you with him before."

Simone frowned. "He's an old friend. You saw us together some time ago at a *banquette* café. I know what you thought."

"I'm sure it doesn't matter what I thought." Alain scanned the menu, refusing to meet her eyes.

"Alain de Vallière, you are behaving like a jealous man," she accused incredulously.

"Why should I be jealous?" he snapped.

"Why indeed?" Her retort was just as nasty. "When you have Emilie Thibault to keep you busy."

"At least Emilie is a lady," he rejoined, sorry the moment the words were out.

Simone's mouth tightened. "I will not argue about this again, Alain. I have made my position clear. I am what I am, and I am in business to stay."

"Stay at Franklin Steamboats, if you must," he warned her, "but don't interfere in Queen Enterprises."

"I am your equal partner, until death do us part or you sell out. But I thought we agreed not to talk about business tonight. Shall we order?" Simone smiled with sticky sweetness.

Through dinner, Alain's mind roiled with the things he wanted to say to her, but it was not until he drove her home that he brought up the topic that weighed most heavily on his mind. "Simone, we still need to talk about the night at LaVictoire."

"I would rather not." She stared at the night sky with seeming fascination.

"Then listen instead," he persisted.

"I said—" she began.

"I know what you said, but there was nothing wrong with what happened between us."

Simone remembered another time he had offered the same reassurance. So many years, so many changes, but he was still explaining that what had happened was natural between a man and a woman. She didn't know whether to laugh or cry.

"It doesn't matter whether it was right or wrong," she told him sadly. "It must never happen again."

"But why? I want to marry you—and not because of any promises I made to Tom."

"It would never work, Alain. You find me stubborn and independent and prickly—those are your own words—because I insist on being my own person. I don't want to be protected from living my own life. I think Emilie is much more the kind of woman you need as a wife," Simone concluded, trying to ignore the despair she felt at the thought.

"Thank you for your kind advice," he said sarcastically, stopping at her door. "But how do you know what I need or want?"

"You've told me often enough what you *don't* want," she answered, her temper flaring. "And you don't want me."

Illuminated by the light from the house, his gaze conveyed utter exasperation. "I've told you repeatedly that I do want you."

"But not as I am," she insisted.

"Simone—"

"Please, Alain," she said, preparing to go inside, "think on what I have said, and you will see that I am right."

Before she could step down, he caught her. His dark eyes held hers when she turned in surprise. Without warning, he drew her against him and kissed her. Just as abruptly, he released her and commanded, "Think on *that*, and you will see that I love you."

"You can't love me," she whispered, staring at him as if stricken.

"I can, and I do."

"You can't," she repeated shakily. Then, stepping down from the carriage, she fled into the house.

Alain swore under his breath. Nothing this evening had gone as he planned. Of course, when Simone was involved, nothing ever did. In a dark mood, he turned his team down the drive. Simone watched from a window until Alain's carriage was out of sight. Then, slowly, she trudged up to her room, her emotions in turmoil. Alain loved her! her heart sang. But her mind told her she dare not love him in return . . . or she would bring danger to him.

The next morning, Simone awoke when Rory crawled into bed with her.

"See, *Maman*, I didn't oversleep," the child announced the moment her mother opened her eyes. "Now can we talk about going fishing with Oncle 'Lain?"

"What time is it?" Simone asked with a yawn.

"Early," Rory answered, snuggling beside her. "Not even Tina is awake yet."

"That is early." Simone was still tired, for she had not slept until near dawn. As she tossed and turned, her mind had been full of Alain. Now, her arms around her daughter's solid little body, she drowsed.

Rory sat up suddenly. "Oh, *Maman*, do you know what today is? It's Yvette Cuvillion's birthday."

"That's right," Simone recollected with a sleepy smile. "You and Celestina are going on a picnic with the whole Cuvillion clan."

"I have to wake Tina so we don't miss all the fun." Rory squirmed from her mother's grasp and let herself down from the bed, her original objective forgotten in the excitement of the moment.

"You have plenty of time," Simone told her with affectionate exasperation.

"I don't want to be late," Rory contended.

Moments after the child had padded out of the room, Jupiter came to the other side of the bed, whining to be let out. She might as well forget sleep, Simone decided without rancor. Rising, she dressed and went down to breakfast with her excited daughter.

Obadiah had arrived to take Simone to the office by the time Bernadette's family arrived. They waved from the drive as the wagon, laden with children, lumbered forth to the Lake. When Simone climbed into Obie's small open rig, Jupiter paced on the shell-covered drive and whined pitifully.

"He don't wanna be left alone all day," Obadiah said, bending to scratch behind the dog's ears.

Simone laughed when both he and Jupiter gazed at her entreatingly. "Oh, all right, he can come, but he'll have to stay with you while I see Monsieur Leighton off."

Obie was already loading Jupiter into the space behind the seat. The big dog's head jutted out one side, and his tail stuck out the other as the carriage rolled along.

At her office, Simone found Devlin Hennessey waiting for her. "*Bonjour*, Dev. What are you doing here, so early?"

"I have such fond remembrances of Obadiah's coffee, I couldn't wait for a cup," Dev answered, his hazel eyes twinkling. "And I thought we might have that visit you promised last night."

They were chatting in Simone's office when Alain appeared in the doorway.

"*Bonjour*," he said with the barest of nods for Devlin

Hennessey. "Simone, I just came to remind you we must pick up Monsieur Leighton at four o'clock to take him to the boat."

"I'll be ready."

"*Très bien.*"

He pivoted and stalked away, leaving Simone bemused. Alain had pointedly refused to visit her in her office before, and now he had come here twice in two days.

Simone and Alain waved from the dock as the *Queen of Hearts* backed out of her mooring and straightened, her bow pointed north. As the big boat steamed upriver toward the wilds of St. Louis, William Clive Leighton waved excitedly from the stern.

With a chuckle, Alain helped Simone into the carriage and turned it in the opposite direction from the office.

"Where are we going?" she asked at once.

"To my house."

"Why?" She glared at him suspiciously.

"So we can talk privatcly."

"We can talk at the office."

"Not privately enough," he countered in a tone that would brook no argument. "I told Obadiah you wouldn't be back this afternoon."

She knew she should not go to a man's home unchaperoned, but if she and Alain were to have another of their battles, perhaps it would be better if no one was around to witness it. Simone shot him an uneasy glance but said nothing as the carriage rolled along Esplanade.

Certain the Vieux Carré's gossip mill was already at work, she sat rigidly erect while Alain opened the carriage gate. When they alit on the drive, a young groom appeared to take the carriage to the stables.

Turning to Simone, Alain offered his arm. "Come with me."

He led her through the sun-dappled courtyard to a small table near the fountain, set with crystal and linen and silver. Across one of the two plates lay a single red rose. Pleased with his morning's preparations, Alain pulled out the chair for her.

"What is all this?" Simone asked, perching on the edge of her seat.

"An early supper," he replied. "And the rose is a token of my affections for you." His dark eyes seemed to caress her.

She looked away, her face hidden by the brim of her bonnet, and said almost accusingly, "I thought you wanted to talk to me."

"I do," he answered quietly.

Though she did not look at him, Simone felt his gaze upon her as he stood beside her. "Did you want to talk about business?"

"Not about business."

"I should not have come." She rose suddenly, then wished she had not. He stood too near.

"You're not leaving until you've heard what I have to say," he said gently. Untying the ribbons of her bonnet, he lifted it from her head. "You might as well be comfortable."

Simone knew she should protest. She should leave. But her legs . . . and her heart . . . would not cooperate. Her willpower deserted her when she needed it most. She raised her green eyes to meet Alain's beseechingly. "Please, this is not a good idea."

"Why not?" His hands ran over her arms, his touch, even through the sleeves of her dress, making her shiver.

She forced herself to concentrate, to remember her objections. "I don't think it is a good idea for me to be here alone with you."

"I think it's a good idea." His grip on her arms tightened, and he drew her against him. "A very good idea," he said softly as his lips met hers.

For a moment, Simone neither responded nor resisted as Alain's arms slipped around her. His lips on hers were tender and warm, heating hers with slowly smoldering passion. Yielding finally to the hot wave of desire that engulfed her, she hungrily molded her mouth to his.

Alain fought the urge to crush her against him. Her willingness had come too hard; he did not want to rush her. Instead, he kissed her, leisurely, savoring the taste, the scent, the feel of her.

Withdrawing with effort, he said hoarsely, "I have something for you."

Simone's fingers trembled as she accepted the familiar box, containing the brilliant emerald necklace.

"Will you put it on?"

Nodding mutely, she tried to comply, but she could not manage the clasp.

"Allow me." Alain's voice was low, his manner intimate as he stepped behind her to fasten it. When it was done, he pressed a kiss to her temple and murmured, "Emeralds mean lucky in love, you know." Turning her to face him, he was staggered by the glow in her eyes. "*Je t'aime*, Simone."

"'Lain," she whispered tenderly. Though she offered no words of love as her lips sought his, she could no longer fight it. Perhaps sanity would return later, and she would be sorry she gave herself to him, knowing it wrong . . . but so very right. It did not matter. At this moment, Simone wanted nothing more than their joining, body and soul.

"I want you, Simone," he said, his voice thick with passion.

"I am shameless," she answered with a sigh. "I want you, too."

"There is no shame in that, my only love." Smiling down on her, Alain led her to his bedchamber.

In the waning afternoon, the lovers came together, uniting joyfully, all doubts and questions set aside. The world faded away, and they knew only each other and the fulfillment to be found in their joining.

Afterward, they lay together in the dusk, Simone's head resting on Alain's shoulder, and his arms wrapped around her.

"I would like to spend every afternoon this way," he murmured.

"It is lovely," she agreed lazily.

"We could make love every afternoon if you would marry me."

Raising herself on one elbow, she looked him in the eye. "I've told you, Alain," she said evenly, "I cannot marry you."

He pushed her back on the bed, rolling so he lay partly upon her, pinning her beneath him. "Listen to me, Simone. I love you. I love everything about you—your humor, your spirit, and, yes, damn it, even your independence. I find you infuriating and irresistible, and I wouldn't want you any other way. And you love me. I know you do. Why do you fight it?" His dark eyes sought to hold hers, but she would not meet his gaze.

Simone struggled to hide the battle raging within her. She ached to give in, but she could not. It was too dangerous. Drawing a shuddering breath, she forced herself to say, "I do not love you."

Alain's expression darkened. "Look at me and tell me that."

"Don't you understand?" she asked, meeting his eyes hopelessly. "I don't love you."

"Don't . . . or won't?" His voice was harsh.

"I cannot love you." Unexpectedly, she broke from his grasp and rolled from the bed, quickly gathering her garments.

He got to his feet and stood beside her, watching as she hastily donned her clothes and raked her fingers through her tousled hair. "I would understand if you truly *did* not love me, but that you *cannot* is the most ridiculous thing I've ever heard."

"I bring danger to those I love, and I will not bring it

to you again," she tossed over her shoulder, hurrying toward the door.

"If you're talking about my kidnapping," he contended, catching her arm, "that had nothing to do with you."

"You were on your way to fight Marcel for me when you were taken. I will not allow you to put yourself in jeopardy again." She jerked free of his grasp and fled.

Pulling on a robe, he followed her down to the courtyard. "Don't you think I should have something to say about this?" he demanded.

So intent were they on their argument that neither heard footsteps approaching until Emilie Thibault emerged from the passageway to the street. The woman's face paled as she took in the couple's dishabille.

"Simone," she whispered in shock. "What are you doing here?"

"Leaving," Simone answered tersely, about to brush past her.

"No, you are not." Alain stopped her. Turning to Emilie, he asked mildly, "What are *you* doing here? How did you get in?"

Her colorless face suffused with red as she admitted, "I took Dom's key. I . . . I swallowed my pride and came here to do what it seems Simone has already done. I have enough pride left, however, to know when to give up a losing battle.

"Just tell me one thing, Madame Franklin," she requested, turning to Simone. "I asked you once whom Alain loved. Do you remember?"

"I remember," the other woman answered wearily.

"Why did you lie to me?"

"I didn't lie."

"If you did not realize he loved you, you are a bigger fool than I am," Emilie muttered. "I thought to make him mine, but he was yours. Always yours."

"I don't want him."

"Don't you?" Emilie smiled cynically, the expression

out of place on her thin face. Placing the key on the table, she departed.

Simone tore herself free of Alain's grip and turned a withering stare on him. "You could have stopped her. You could have explained."

"Explained what? That I love you, not her? That I want to marry you, not her?"

"You've ruined your chances with her. For nothing."

"For you," he countered.

"For nothing," Simone repeated adamantly. Then she wheeled and stormed out the passageway.

"Wait!" Behind her, Alain winced as the shells on the drive cut his bare feet. He had forgotten he was wearing nothing more than a robe. Cursing eloquently, he went to dress.

On the street, Simone hailed a cab, debating for a moment whether to go to the office or home. It was late, and Obie would have left the office by now, taking Jupiter with him. In a black mood, she instructed the driver to take her home.

Wakefield met her at the door, his gaunt face distraught. A weeping Celestina followed on his heels. "Mrs. Franklin," he greeted her, "I was about to send Rufus for you."

"What's wrong?" Simone asked, filled with dread.

"We cain't find Rory nowhere,"Celestina wailed before the butler could answer. "Somebody done took her and lef' this."

Numbly Simone accepted the soiled sheet of paper the slave handed her.

Simone, mon amour,

Love and hate have kept me alive. Now I would settle the score between us.

I have your child. She will not be harmed if you meet me alone tonight at the edge of the swamp beyond Faubourg Marigny, in the clearing where the three large cypresses stand. At last we will meet—on the field of honor.

If you notify the police or bring help with you, be assured I will kill your little green-eyed daughter.

Until tonight, I remain

Your adoring Marcel

Her face pale and set, she looked up and ordered, "Wakefield, tell Rufus to saddle a horse for me quickly."

"What we gonna do, Miss Simone?" Celestina wept. "That man took my baby, and I didn't see nothin', not even what he looks like."

"I know," her mistress said grimly. "And I will find him."

"Shouldn't we report this crime to the constabulary, madame?" Wakefield fretted.

"No," she answered vehemently, already on her way upstairs. "I will get Rory back."

That lunatic had her daughter, Simone agonized while she changed into her fencing costume. She could hardly bear the thought of Rory's fright. She should have left Jupiter to protect her, but she had thought her safe with the servants. Marcel must have been watching.

Once again, she had brought danger to one she loved, she thought sadly, one who could not protect herself. If Marcel harmed one hair on Rory's head, she would kill him, she vowed. Picking up her father's sword, Simone set out to rescue her child.

She had galloped away only moments before Alain arrived at the house, determined to make her listen to him. The big Creole listened in stony silence as Wakefield anxiously related what had happened. Then, without a word, he wheeled his horse and raced through the night after Simone.

A full moon had risen above the dark outline of lush growth when he reached the swamp's edge. The ring of steel and the flicker of a torch drew him to a clearing, where he saw Marcel, with Aurora tied on the ground behind him. The little girl's eyes were wide, but she made no sound as her mother faced the madman, meeting his advances, speaking quietly, urgently, as she retired.

As Alain dismounted in the shadows, he could hear her words. "Give her back, Marcel. She is only a child. She's done nothing to harm you."

"Indeed. She has helped me by bringing her mother to me," he acknowledged. "Very useful, this little green-eyed one." Simone forgot herself for a furious instant and advanced savagely. Then, aware of the danger to Rory if she were to be killed through carelessness, she slowed her attack.

"This is a side of you I've never seen, *chère*, the part of you that loves," Marcel reflected bitterly. "I always wanted to feel it, but you never let me. I could change my mind about killing you, you know. I could keep you with me."

His fond smile was chased away by rage when he caught sight of Alain approaching behind Simone. "I told you to come alone!" he roared at her.

"I did come alone," she answered frantically. Following his furious gaze, she glanced over her shoulder. "You shouldn't have come, Alain. Please go!" she shouted.

But in that instant of distractions Marcel scooped up Rory and raced with her into the swamp.

"Marcel, wait!" Simone cried in horror, plunging into the tangled undergrowth behind them. "Go back, Alain!"

He charged in after her. "Not until we get Rory back."

Marcel splashed through the murky waters, heedless of their dangers, jeering at his pursuers. They followed, beating back vines and hanging moss with their swords, sinking past their knees in dank, slimy mud.

At last they overtook him on a small island surrounded by looming cypress trees. In moonlight nearly as bright as day, the madman whirled to face them, his sword pressed to Aurora's throat. Alain captured Simone's wrist and held her beside him when she would have pressed forward.

"There is no need to harm the child, Marcel," he said quietly. "Simone did not betray your meeting. She didn't know I was coming."

"I do as I please." Marcel's voice was petulant, and he watched the pair cagily as he dangled a frightened Rory in front of him. "If I want to kill her, I will."

Alain felt Simone tense, but he held her still. Keeping his eyes on Marcel, he insisted, "You do not want to harm a little girl, any more than you want to kill Simone."

The madman shrugged carelessly. "We have some longstanding matters to be settled between us, she and I."

Alain glanced at the woman who watched helplessly as her innocent daughter was threatened. Then pushing her behind him, he turned to challenge Marcel. "You and I have matters to be settled as well, Baudin. Perhaps you do not remember the outcome of our last meeting under the Oaks? And have you forgotten it was I who stole Simone from you? I took her to my bed when you wanted her," he deliberately goaded.

With an inarticulate roar, Marcel dumped Rory on the ground and faced Alain, careful to position himself between the child and her would-be rescuers. Then, without warning, he launched himself at his opponent.

Always a good swordsman, Marcel now fought with the strength and fury of the unprincipled madman he had become. Alain met his deadly thrusts, parrying tirelessly. Dripping sweat, they fought as the still night rang with the clash of their blades. Steel skittered against steel down the length of their swords, and they met nearly eye to eye. Swiftly, Marcel jumped back, but not so quickly that Alain did not draw first blood.

"Have done with it, Marcel," he panted. "I don't want to kill you."

"I will never yield to you, de Vallière," Marcel snarled, attacking vigorously.

Her eyes on the combatants, Simone edged toward Rory each time the action shifted, but Marcel managed to keep himself between mother and daughter. Before she could reach Rory, Alain stumbled over a root and fell heavily on one knee. Marcel lunged forward and brought the hilt of his sword down on his head. Alain groaned and collapsed facedown. Laughing menacingly, Marcel stood over the stunned man, prepared to finish him.

"*Non!*" Simone screamed. She flung herself at the madman, determined to keep him from killing either of the people she loved.

Marcel darted back and snatched up Rory, again placing his sword at her throat. "Drop your sword, Simone," he ordered.

"Drop it or I will kill her!" he bellowed when she faltered.

Reluctantly, she obeyed.

"That's better," he muttered, holding Rory out tantalizingly. "Come and get her."

Her green eyes locked on his pale blue ones, Simone approached distrustfully, giving a cry of pure relief when Marcel thrust her daughter into her arms.

Sinking to the ground, Simone buried her face in Rory's hair for a long, sweet moment. Then she hurried to loosen the child's bonds.

A few feet away, Alain lifted himself painfully on all fours and shook his head to clear it. A trickle of blood from a cut in his scalp flowed unheeded down his forehead. Through a red haze, he saw the madman place the point of his sword against Simone's neck.

"I've won, de Vallière," Marcel taunted the addled man. "Now I have both of your green-eyed beauties. I am the better fighter, the better man. I will be the better lover, too," he boasted.

Simone stared up at him in horror as he bent over her, laughing softly, maniacally.

"Releasing her, Baudin!" Alain shouted, struggling to his feet on the boggy ground. He hesitated, off-balance and swaying as he sank almost to his knees in the mud.

"Shall I kill you or keep you?" Marcel crooned to Simone, twining his fingers through her hair, yanking her head back suddenly, he kissed her.

"No!" Alain tried to lurch toward them. but his knees gave way under him and he collapsed again.

Giving an enraged cry, Marcel nursed the lip Simone had bitten. "Don't anger me, *chère*," he advised her hotly, "or I could forget my tender feelings for you." To stress his words, he jabbed lightly, and a bead of blood appeared on her neck, rolling down to well in the hollow at the base of her throat.

"Your 'tender feelings' were what started this madness," she spat, glaring up at him.

"Madness? Don't use that word with me," he warned ominously.

"What do you call it, if not madness? You have killed my father, chased me from my home, killed my husband, kidnapped my child. Who but a madman would do such things?"

Marcel blinked, trying to clear his vision of the red mist suddenly obscuring it. Though he continued to hold his sword to Simone's throat, it now wobbled, and one of his hands rose to massage his throbbing temples.

Alain stirred again and called out, "Leave Simone, Marcel. You want to fight me."

"I would like to kill you, de Vallière," the lunatic growled, "but better you live your wretched life while Simone sees I am the better man. I will give her the world. I'll make her happy. We'll even take the child with us when we go away."

"Where could you go where I would not find you?" Alain asked with a dangerous note in his voice as he managed to rise and plow through the mire toward them. "Where could you hide from me, Baudin?"

"You'll never find them in the swamp." Marcel yanked Simone to her feet beside him, Rory still cradled in her arms, and dragged her toward the undergrowth. But his sneer gave way to astonishment when the earth beneath his feet gave way and he began to sink. "Quicksand!" he gasped. A frantic light in his pale eyes, he clutched Simone's waist tightly. "I won't let de Vallière have you."

"'Lain, take Rory," Simone screamed, struggling futilely against captor and consuming bog. with strength born of fear for her daughter, she nearly threw the little girl into Alain's outstretched arms

The heavier Marcel sank faster than Simone, but still he held her. The muck bound her heavy clothing around her legs, lapped against her ribs, and sucked her steadily downward. She clawed at her captor's hand, attempting to pry the fingers open before they were both swallowed up. Desperately, she strained, arching her body toward solid ground, gasping with the effort as her fingers left furrows on its soft surface.

When Aurora was safe, Alain returned for Simone, reaching out desperately over the mire for her hand. He almost touched her, but she sank deeper, held in the madman's grasp. Flinging himself on his stomach, Alain inched forward, farther, farther . . . until his fingers curled around her wrist.

But the pull of the quicksand on its captives slowly dragged Alain toward the quagmire. Trembling with strain, he threw his free arm around a slippery clump of reeds and stubbornly hung onto Simone.

Suddenly Marcel gasped, "You never understood, Simone. I loved you." Then he sank beneath the slimy surface, releasing his deadly grip.

Mere moments from suffocation, Simone struggled to free herself from the mire. Panting, every muscle quivering, Alain held fast to her and the reeds and began to pull back, his boot toes making deep furrows in the soft ground behind him.

As he slid laboriously backward, muttering incoherent encouragement, his stubborn, prickly darling managed a mighty heave toward him. Inch by inch, sheened by muck and sweat and tears, they fought the lethal quicksand and at last lay side by side on solid ground, gulping for air.

When their breath had returned, they crawled, wet

and exhausted, to the sobbing Rory.

Simone gathered the weeping child in her arms and Alain knelt beside them. "It's all right now," he whispered, wiping mother's and daughter's tears.

One arm around her mother's neck, the sobbing child wrapped the other around Alain's and pulled them close. "Is . . . is he gone?" she whimpered.

"He's gone, *ma petite*. And the danger is over," he told Simone with grim but tender certainty. "Do you know how close I came to losing you—again?"

"You will never lose me, Alain," Simone answered, lifting a muddy hand to caress his cheek. "I love you."

"I love you, too, Nonc' 'Lain," Rory piped.

"And I love you—both of you," he said, hugging them tightly.

"It seems Rory and I have chosen the man we love," Simone said with a wry smile. "But remember what I told you long ago—you must love us forever."

"Forever," Alain agreed tenderly just before his smiling lips claimed Simone's.